# FINAL PROOF

*or*
*The Value of Evidence*

# RODRIGUES OTTOLENGUI

Edited, with an introduction and notes,
by Leslie S. Klinger

**LIBRARY** LIBRARY OF CONGRESS

*Poisoned Pen*
PRESS

Published by Poisoned Pen Press, an imprint of Sourcebooks,
in association with the Library of Congress
P.O. Box 4410, Naperville, Illinois 60567-4410
(630) 961-3900
sourcebooks.com

This edition of *Final Proof* is based on the first edition in the Library of Congress's collection,
originally published by G. P. Putnam's Sons/The Knickerbocker Press in 1898.

Library of Congress Cataloging-in-Publication Data

Names: Ottolengui, Rodrigues, author. | Klinger, Leslie S.,
    editor.
Title: Final proof : or, The value of evidence / R. Ottolengui ; edited,
    with an introduction and notes, by Leslie S. Klinger.
Other titles: Value of evidence
Description: Naperville, Illinois : Library of Congress ; Poisoned Pen
    Press, [2020] | "This edition of Final Proof is based on the first
    edition in the Library of Congress's collection, originally published by
    Sons/The Knickerbocker Press in 1898"--Title page verso.
Identifiers: LCCN 2020018068 (trade paperback)
Classification: LCC PS2509.O46 A6 2020 (print) |
    DDC 813/.4--dc23
LC record available at https://lccn.loc.gov/2020018068

Printed and bound in the United States of America.
SB 10 9 8 7 6 5 4 3 2 1

# CONTENTS

# FOREWORD

Crime writing as we know it first appeared in 1841, with the publication of *The Murders in the Rue Morgue*. Written by American author Edgar Allan Poe, the short story introduced C. Auguste Dupin, the world's first wholly fictional detective. Other American and British authors had begun working in the genre by the 1860s, and by the 1920s, we had officially entered the golden age of detective fiction.

Throughout this short history, many authors who paved the way have been lost or forgotten. Library of Congress Crime Classics bring back into print some of the finest American crime writing from the 1860s to the 1960s, showcasing rare and lesser known titles that represent a range of genres, from cozies to police procedurals. With cover designs inspired by images from the Library's collections, each book in this series includes the original text, reproduced faithfully from an early edition in the Library's collections and complete with strange spellings and unorthodox punctuation. Also included are a contextual introduction, a brief biography of the author, notes, recommendations for further reading, and suggested discussion questions. Our hope is for these books to start conversations, inspire further research, and bring obscure works to a new generation of readers.

Early American crime fiction is not only entertaining to read, it also sheds light on the culture of its time. While many of the titles in this series include outmoded language and stereotypes now considered offensive, these books give readers the opportunity to reflect on how our society's perceptions of race, gender, ethnicity, and social standing have evolved over more than a century.

More dark secrets and bloody deeds lurk in the massive collections of the Library of Congress. I encourage you to explore these works for yourself, here in Washington, D.C., or online at www.loc.gov.

—Carla D. Hayden, Librarian of Congress

# INTRODUCTION

In December 1893, Sherlock Holmes's death (two years earlier) was announced to the reading public in "The Final Problem," the last of the adventures of Sherlock Holmes published in the *Strand Magazine* between 1891 and 1893. When Holmes vanished from the scene, a score of American and English writers rushed to fill the vacuum, with tales of official and amateur detectives of all types and kinds. Among them was a young American dentist with the unlikely name of Benjamin Adolph Rodrigues Ottolengui. Early in his career, he began to read detective fiction because, he said, it "sharpens my wits. It is like solving chess problems. The analytical powers of the brain are developed. Therefore, a properly constructed detective story, free from pruriency, is wholesome reading."* Perhaps, like Arthur Conan Doyle, he turned to writing while waiting for patients to engage his services.

Ottolengui's first try at crime fiction was a novel, *An Artist in Crime*, first published in 1892; this was swiftly followed by three other novels: *A Conflict of Evidence* (1893), *A Modern Wizard* (1894), and *The Crime of the Century* (1896). All featured a pair of sleuths: a professional, Jack Barnes, and an amateur, Robert

---

*"Writing Detective Stories," *Little Falls (MN) Weekly Transcript*, February 15, 1895.

Leroy Mitchel. Ottolengui wrote no further novels, however, and took up penning short stories about Barnes and Mitchel— following in the footsteps of Conan Doyle, who had also written two Holmes novels before turning to the shorter format. The first four of Ottolengui's short stories, included in this volume, were commissioned by Jerome K. Jerome, the publisher of the highly successful London-based magazine *The Idler*. The stories appeared in 1895. Another appeared in 1898, published in *The Black Cat*, an American magazine featuring short fiction; several more were written for the present volume, also first published in 1898. Ottolengui's success was not limited to the United States. Early on, his books were reprinted several times and translated into German, French, Danish, and Polish, among other languages.

Though for many years mystery scholars thought that Ottolengui had abandoned crime fiction after 1898—Anthony Boucher, the prominent mystery critic, wrote that he had "abandoned the sleuth for the tooth"—in fact, Ottolengui wrote six more stories published under the series title of *Before the Fact*. The series appeared in 1901 in *Ainslee's Magazine*. However, with that final burst of literary energy in 1901, Ottolengui returned to his scientific pursuits, including advances in dentistry, photography, and entomology. Ellery Queen called him "one of the most neglected authors in the entire history of the detective story," and perhaps without Queen's inclusion of the present volume in his highly influential *Queen's Quorum: A History of the Detective Crime Short Story as Revealed in the 106 Most Important Books Published in this Field Since 1845* (first published in 1948), Ottolengui's crime fiction would have vanished into the fog.

Later scholars, such as LeRoy Lad Panek, have seen Ottolengui's work for what it was: clear, compelling tales, based on reason and not the detective's personality, that introduced forensic tools and scientific reasoning that were ahead of their time. For example, in "The Phoenix of Crime," Ottolengui advances the theory of

forensic dentistry, complete with reproduction of a dental chart.*
In "A Shadow of Proof," his detective uses an X-ray to find a lost
item of jewelry. Yet his aim was not didactic. In his remarks at the
beginning of *The Crime of the Century*, Ottolengui wrote:

> After all, the major object of fiction is to entertain, and
> even though a little instructive lesson may be deftly
> interwoven with the plot, I fear that the modern novel is
> too highly spiced with philosophic dissertations. And in
> seeking to entertain is it not best to offer something out
> of the common? Something a little different from the
> dull routine of daily existence?†

As a result, the stories in this volume feature jewel robberies,
too many corpses, cowboys, Aztec idols, and talking monkeys
as well as serious suggestions for the budding science of foren-
sics. Ottolengui was evidently fascinated by the science of the
day and was apparently widely read in bacteriology, hypnotism
(both of which subjects have a prominent part in his novel
*A Modern Wizard*), archaeology, the history of the Aztecs,
Darwinism, and other scientific developments and discoveries.
His work also contains many shrewd observations on human
nature, especially with regard to the social customs of his own
patients, New Yorkers of the Gilded Age. Yet he also apparently
knew the underworld of New York, well described in his novel
*The Crime of the Century*.

Ottolengui certainly acknowledged his debt to Conan Doyle
and, at the same time, sought to capitalize on that author's
success. An advertisement for *An Artist in Crime* published
in an American newspaper in 1896 hailed Ottolengui as "the
American Conan Doyle, and his New York detective is quite

---

*Gardner P. H. Foley, in his column "A Treasury of Dentistry" in the *Journal of the American
College of Dentists* (vol. 51, no. 4 [Winter 1984]: 14), noted that interest in the tale was revived a
few years later when a young girl's body was found in Yonkers, NY. The local sheriff, familiar with
Ottolengui's story, asked a dentist to create a chart of her teeth, which led to her identification.

†Rodrigues Ottolengui, *The Crime of the Century* (New York; G. P. Putnam's Sons, 1896), iv.

as ingenious as the famous Sherlock Holmes."* In the first story in this volume, "The Phoenix of Crime," Ottolengui's wealthy amateur sleuth Robert Leroy Mitchel shows off to his sometimes-partner, professional investigator Jack Barnes:

"...but how do you know that I came off in a hurry and had no coffee at home? It seems to me that if you can tell that, you are becoming as clever as the famous Sherlock Holmes."

"Oh, no, indeed! You and I can hardly expect to be as shrewd as the detectives of romance. As to my guessing that you have had no coffee, that is not very troublesome. I notice three drops of milk on your coat, and one on your shoe, from which I deduce, first, that you have had no coffee, for a man who has his coffee in the morning is not apt to drink a glass of milk besides. Second, you must have left home in a hurry, or you would have had that coffee. Third, you took your glass of milk at the ferry-house of the Staten Island boat, probably finding that you had a minute to spare; this is evident because the milk spots on the tails of your frock-coat and on your shoe show that you were standing when you drank, and leaned over to avoid dripping the fluid on your clothes. Had you been seated, the coat tails would have been spread apart, and drippings would have fallen on your trousers. The fact that in spite of your precautions the accident did occur, and yet escaped your notice, is further proof, not only of your hurry, but also that your mind was abstracted,— absorbed no doubt with the difficult problem about which you have come to talk with me. How is my guess?"

"Correct in every detail. Sherlock Holmes could have done no better."†

---

*Oakes Weekly Republican* (Dakota Territory), January 10, 1896.

†See pages 1–2.

Despite his subsequent literary obscurity, Ottolengui's work is an important bridge between the dime-store novels and sensational detective fiction that prevailed in the mid-nineteenth century and the later stream of American crime writing that began in the 1920s. With the exceptions of Edgar Allan Poe, Mark Twain, and Thomas Bailey Aldrich—all of whom made their reputations with work other than detective fiction—Ottolengui is the first American writer featured in Ellery Queen's chronological history of detective short stories. Ottolengui's creations were a long step forward from the police detectives and wild amateur sleuths that were staples of the dime novels. Jack Barnes, for example, is a serious professional detective with his own agency. Robert Leroy Mitchel, though he is an amateur, is a gifted reasoner, usually "out-deducing" the professionals. Mitchel takes on the prevention of crime out of a sense of duty arising from his wealth, often at significant risk to his own person. Yet he is not above using this "duty" as a handy pretext for acquiring a collection of fabulous gemstones, to prevent the gems from tempting others to do evil.

Like Holmes and Watson, Mitchel and Barnes share a deep friendship, but unlike Conan Doyle's duo, they are also rivals. Mitchel loves to outdo Barnes, and in their first outing, *An Artist in Crime*, he wagers $1,000—more than $30,000 in 2020 dollars*—that he can outwit Barnes. Tellingly, at the end of "A Frosty Morning," Mitchel tells Barnes that he was luckier than Barnes in coming to the solution of the mystery—but that he doesn't believe in luck.

Ottolengui may have been inspired by the work of Arthur Conan Doyle, but he brought his own wide interests to bear on his crime fiction and introduced many original ideas. While his sleuths Barnes and Mitchel would never replace the immortal Watson and Holmes, their adventures deserve a broader audience than they have had to date.

—Leslie S. Klinger

*www.measuringwealth.com

# PREFATORY

The first meeting between Mr. Barnes, the detective, and Robert Leroy Mitchel, the gentleman who imagines himself to be able to outdo detectives in their own line of work, was fully set forth in the narrative entitled *An Artist in Crime*. Subsequently the two men occupied themselves with the solution of a startling murder mystery, the details of which were recorded in *The Crime of the Century*. The present volume contains the history of several cases which attracted their attention in the interval between those already given to the world, the first having occurred shortly after the termination of the events in *An Artist in Crime*, and the others in the order here given, so that in a sense these stories are continuous and interdependent.

—R. O.

# I

## THE PHOENIX OF CRIME*

### I

Mr. Mitchel was still at breakfast one morning, when the card of Mr. Barnes was brought to him by his man Williams.

"Show Mr. Barnes in here," said he. "I imagine that he must be in a hurry to see me, else he would not call so early."

A few minutes later the detective entered, saying:

"It is very kind of you to let me come in without waiting. I hope that I am not intruding."

"Not at all. As to being kind, why I am kind to myself. I knew you must have something interesting on hand to bring you around so early, and I am proportionately curious; at the same time I hate to go without my coffee, and I do not like to drink it too fast, especially good coffee, and this is good, I assure you. Draw up and have a cup, for I observe that you came off in such a hurry this morning that you did not get any."

"Why, thank you, I will take some, but how do you know that I came off in a hurry and had no coffee at home? It seems

*Final Proof, in which this story first appeared, was published in 1898.

to me that if you can tell that, you are becoming as clever as the famous Sherlock Holmes."

"Oh, no, indeed! You and I can hardly expect to be as shrewd as the detectives of romance. As to my guessing that you have had no coffee, that is not very troublesome. I notice three drops of milk on your coat, and one on your shoe, from which I deduce, first, that you have had no coffee, for a man who has his coffee in the morning is not apt to drink a glass of milk besides. Second, you must have left home in a hurry, or you would have had that coffee. Third, you took your glass of milk at the ferry-house of the Staten Island boat, probably finding that you had a minute to spare; this is evident because the milk spots on the tails of your frock-coat and on your shoe show that you were standing when you drank, and leaned over to avoid dripping the fluid on your clothes. Had you been seated, the coat tails would have been spread apart, and drippings would have fallen on your trousers. The fact that in spite of your precautions the accident did occur, and yet escaped your notice, is further proof, not only of your hurry, but also that your mind was abstracted,—absorbed no doubt with the difficult problem about which you have come to talk with me. How is my guess?"

"Correct in every detail. Sherlock Holmes could have done no better. But we will drop him and get down to my case, which, I assure you, is more astounding than any, either in fact or fiction, that has come to my knowledge."

"Go ahead! Your opening argument promises a good play. Proceed without further waste of words."

"First, then, let me ask you, have you read the morning's papers?"

"Just glanced through the death reports, but had gotten no further when you came in."

"There is one death report, then, that has escaped your attention, probably because the notice of it occupies three columns. It is another metropolitan mystery. Shall I read it to you?

I glanced through it in bed this morning and found it so absorbing; that, as you guessed, I hurried over here to discuss it with you, not stopping to get my breakfast."

"In that case you might better attack an egg or two, and let me read the article myself."

Mr. Mitchel took the paper from Mr. Barnes, who pointed out to him the article in question, which, under appropriate sensational headlines, read as follows:

"The account of a most astounding mystery is reported to-day for the first time, though the body of the deceased, now thought to have been murdered, was taken from the East River several days ago. The facts are as follows. On Tuesday last, at about six o'clock in the morning, several boys were enjoying an early swim in the river near Eighty-fifth Street, when one who had made a deep dive, on reaching the surface scrambled out of the water, evidently terrified. His companions crowded about him asking what he had seen, and to them he declared that there was a 'drownded man down there.' This caused the boys to lose all further desire to go into the water, and while they hastily scrambled into their clothes they discussed the situation, finally deciding that the proper course would be to notify the police, one boy, however, wiser than the others, declaring that he 'washed his hands of the affair' if they should do so, because he was not 'going to be held as no witness.' In true American fashion, nevertheless, the majority ruled, and in a body the boys marched to the station-house and reported their discovery. Detectives were sent to investigate, and after dragging the locality for half an hour the body of a man was drawn out of the water. The corpse was taken to the Morgue, and the customary red tape was slowly unwound. At first the police thought that it

was a case of accidental drowning, no marks of violence
having been found on the body, which had evidently been
in the water but a few hours. Thus no special report of
the case was made in the press. Circumstances have
developed at the autopsy, however, which make it probable that New Yorkers are to be treated to another of
the wonderful mysteries which occur all too frequently
in the metropolis. The first point of significance is the
fact, on which all the surgeons agree, that the man was
dead when placed in the water. Secondly, the doctors
claim that he died of disease, and not from any cause
which would point to a crime. This conclusion seems
highly improbable, for who would throw into the water
the body of one who had died naturally, and with what
object could such a singular course have been pursued?
Indeed this claim of the doctors is so preposterous that
a second examination of the body has been ordered, and
will occur to-day, when several of our most prominent
surgeons will be present. The third, and by far the most
extraordinary circumstance, is the alleged identification of the corpse. It seems that one of the surgeons
officiating at the first autopsy was attracted by a peculiar mark upon the face of the corpse. At first it was
thought that this was merely a bruise caused by some
thing striking the body while in the water, but a closer
examination proved it to be a skin disease known as
'lichen.' It appears that there are several varieties of
this disease, some of which are quite well known. That
found on the face of the corpse, however, is a very rare
form, only two other cases having been recorded in this
country. This is a fact of the highest importance in relation to the events which have followed. Not unnaturally,
the doctors became greatly interested. One of these, Dr.
Elliot, the young surgeon who first examined it closely,

having never seen any examples of lichen before, spoke of it that evening at a meeting of his medical society. Having looked up the literature relating to the disease in the interval, he was enabled to give the technical name of this very rare form of the disease. At this, another physician present arose, and declared that it seemed to him a most extraordinary coincidence that this case had been reported, for he himself had recently treated an exactly similar condition for a patient who had finally died, his death having occurred within a week. A lengthy and of course very technical discussion ensued, with the result that Mr. Mortimer, the physician who had treated the case of the patient who had so recently died, arranged with Dr. Elliot to go with him on the following day and examine the body at the Morgue. This he did, and, to the great amazement of his colleague, he then declared that the body before him was none other than that of his own patient, supposed to have been buried. When the authorities learned of this, they summoned the family of the deceased, two brothers and the widow. All of these persons viewed the corpse separately, and each declared most emphatically that it was the body of the man whose funeral they had followed. Under ordinary circumstances, so complete an identification of a body would leave no room for doubt, but what is to be thought when we are informed by the family and friends of the deceased that the corpse had been cremated? That the mourners had seen the coffin containing the body placed in the furnace, and had waited patiently during the incineration? And that later the ashes of the dear departed had been delivered to them, to be finally deposited in an urn in the family vault, where it still is with contents undisturbed? It does not lessen the mystery to know that the body in the Morgue (or the ashes at the cemetery) represents all that is left of one of our most esteemed citizens, Mr. Rufus Quadrant, a gentleman who in life enjoyed that share of wealth which made it possible for him to connect his name with so many charities; a gentleman whose family in the past and in the present has ever been and still is above the breath of suspicion. Evidently there is a mystery that will try the skill of our very best detectives."

"That last line reads like a challenge to the gentlemen of your profession," said Mr. Mitchel to Mr. Barnes as he put down the paper.

"I needed no such spur to urge me to undertake to unravel this case, which certainly has most astonishing features."

"Suppose we enumerate the important data and discover what reliable deduction may be made therefrom."

"That is what I have done a dozen times, with no very satisfactory result. First, we learn that a man is found in the river upon whose face there is a curious distinguishing mark in the form of one of the rarest of skin diseases. Second, a man has recently died who was similarly afflicted. The attending physician declares upon examination that the body taken from the river is the body of his patient. Third, the family agree that this identification is correct. Fourth, this second dead man was cremated. Query, how can a man's body be cremated, and then be found whole in the river subsequently? No such thing has been related in fact or fiction since the beginning of the world."

"Not so fast, Mr. Barnes. What of the Phoenix?"

"Why, the living young Phoenix arose from the ashes of his dead ancestor. But here we have seemingly a dead body reforming from its own ashes, the ashes meanwhile remaining intact and unaltered. A manifest impossibility."

"Ah; then we arrive at our first reliable deduction, Mr. Barnes."

"Which is?"

"Which is that, despite the doctors, we have two bodies to deal with. The ashes in the vault represent one, while the body at the Morgue is another."

"Of course. So much is apparent, but you say the body at the Morgue is another, and I ask you, which other?"

"That we must learn. As you appear to be seeking my views in this case I will give them to you, though of course I have nothing but this newspaper account, which may be inaccurate. Having concluded beyond all question that there are two bodies in this case, our first effort must be to determine which is which. That is to say, we must discover whether this man, Rufus Quadrant, was really cremated, which certainly ought to be the case, or whether, by some means, another body has been exchanged for his, by accident or by design, and if so, whose body that was."

"If it turns out that the body at the Morgue is really that of Mr. Quadrant, then, of course, as you say, some other man's body was cremated, and—"

"Why may it not have been a woman's?"

"You are right, and that only makes the point to which I was about to call your attention more forcible. If an unknown body has been incinerated, how can we ever identify it?"

"I do not know. But we have not arrived at that bridge yet. The first step is to reach a final conclusion in regard to the body at the Morgue. There are several things to be inquired into, there."

"I wish you would enumerate them."

"With pleasure. First, the autopsy is said to have shown that the man died a natural death, that is, that disease, and not one of his fellow-beings, killed him. What disease was this, and was it the same as that which caused the death of Mr. Quadrant? If the coroner's physicians declared what disease killed the man, and named the same as that which carried off Mr. Quadrant, remembering that the body before them was unknown, we would have a strong corroboration of the alleged identification."

"Very true. That will be easily learned."

"Next, as to this lichen. I should think it important to know more of that. Is it because the two cases are examples of the same rare variety of the disease, or was there something so distinct about the location and area or shape of the diseased surface, that the doctor could not possibly be mistaken?—for doctors do make mistakes, you know."

"Yes, just as detectives do," said Mr. Barnes, smiling, as he made notes of Mr. Mitchel's suggestions.

"If you learn that the cause of death was the same, and that the lichen was not merely similar but identical, I should think that there could be little reason for longer doubting the identification. But if not fully satisfied by your inquiries along these lines, then it might be well to see the family of Mr. Quadrant, and inquire whether they too depend upon this lichen as the only means of identification, or whether, entirely aside from that diseased spot, they would be able to swear that the body at the Morgue is their relative. You would have in connection with this inquiry an opportunity to ask many discreet questions which might be of assistance to you."

"All of this is in relation to establishing beyond a doubt the identity of the body at the Morgue, and of course the work to that end will practically be simple. In my own mind I have no doubt that the body of Mr. Quadrant is the one found in the water. Of course, as you suggest, it will be as well to know this rather than merely to think it. But once knowing it, what then of the body which is now ashes?"

"We must identify that also."

"Identify ashes!" exclaimed Mr. Barnes. "Not an easy task."

"If all tasks were easy, Mr. Barnes," said Mr. Mitchel, "we should have little need of talent such as yours. Suppose you follow my advice, provided you intend to accept it, as far as I have indicated, and then report to me the results."

"I will do so with pleasure. I do not think it will occupy much time. Perhaps by luncheon, I—"

"You could get back here and join me. Do so!"

"In the meanwhile shall you do any—any investigating?"

"I shall do considerable thinking. I will cogitate as to the possibility of a Phoenix arising from those ashes."

## II

Leaving Mr. Mitchel, Mr. Barnes went directly to the office of Dr. Mortimer, and after waiting nearly an hour was finally ushered into the consulting-room.

"Dr. Mortimer," said Mr. Barnes, "I have called in relation to this remarkable case of Mr. Quadrant. I am a detective, and the extraordinary nature of the facts thus far published attracts me powerfully, so that, though not connected with the regular police, I am most anxious to unravel this mystery if possible, though, of course, I should do nothing that would interfere with the regular officers of the law. I have called, hoping that you might be willing to answer a few questions."

"I think I have heard of you, Mr. Barnes, and if, as you say, you will do nothing to interfere with justice, I have no objection to telling you what I know, though I fear it is little enough."

"I thank you, Doctor, for your confidence, which, I assure you, you shall not regret. In the first place, then, I would like to ask you about this identification. The newspaper account states that you have depended upon some skin disease. Is that of such a nature that you can be absolutely certain in your opinion?"

"I think so," said the doctor. "But then, as you must have found in your long experience, all identifications of the dead should be accepted with a little doubt. Death alters the appearance of every part of the body, and especially the face. We think that we know a man by the contour of his face, whereas we often depend, during life, upon the habitual expressions which the face ever carries. For example, suppose that we know a young girl, full of life and happiness, with a sunny disposition undimmed by care or the world's worry. She is ever smiling, or ready to smile. Thus we know her. Let that girl suffer a sudden and perhaps painful death. In terror and agony as she dies, the features are distorted, and in death the resultant expression is somewhat stamped upon the features. Let that body lie in the water for a time, and when recovered it is doubtful whether all of her friends would identify her. Some would, but others would with equal positiveness declare that these were mistaken. Yet you observe the physical contours would still be present."

"I am pleased, Doctor, by what you say," said Mr. Barnes, "because with such appreciation of the changes caused by death and exposure in the water, I must lay greater reliance upon your identification. In this case, as I understand it, there is something peculiar about the body, a mark of disease called lichen, I believe?"

"Yes. But what I have said about the changes caused by death must have weight here also," said the doctor. "You see I am giving you all the points that may militate against my identification, that you may the better judge of its correctness. We must not forget that we are dealing with a disease of very great rarity; so rare, in fact, that this very case is the only one that I have ever seen. Consequently I cannot claim to be perfectly familiar with the appearance of surfaces attacked by this disease, after they have suffered the possible alterations of death."

"Then you mean that, after all, this spot upon which the identification rests does not now look as it did in life?"

"I might answer both yes and no to that. Changes have occurred, but they do not, in my opinion, prevent me from recognizing both the disease and the corpse. To fully explain this I must tell you something of the disease itself, if you will not be bored?"

"Not at all. Indeed, I prefer to know all that you can make intelligible to a layman."

"I will use simple language. Formerly a great number of skin diseases were grouped under the general term 'lichen,' which included all growths which might be considered fungoid. At the present time we are fairly well able to separate the animal from the vegetable parasitic diseases, and under the term 'lichen' we include very few forms. The most common is *lichen planus*, which unfortunately is not infrequently met, and is therefore very well understood by the specialists. *Lichen ruber*, however, is quite distinct. It was first described by the German, Hebra, and has been sufficiently common in Europe to enable the students to thoroughly well describe it. In this country, however, it seems to be one of the rarest of diseases. White of Boston reported a case, and Fox records another, accompanied by a colored photograph, which, of course, aids greatly in enabling any one to recognize a case should it occur.* There is one more fact to which I must allude as having an important bearing upon my identification. *Lichen ruber*, like other lichens, is not confined to any one part of the body; on the contrary, it would be remarkable, should the disease be uncontrolled for any length of time, not to see it in many places. This brings me to my point. The seat of the disease, in the case of Mr. Quadrant, was the left cheek, where a most disfiguring spot appeared. It happened that I was in constant attendance upon Mr. Quadrant for the trouble which finally caused his decease, and therefore I saw this lichen in its incipiency, and more fortunately I recognized its true nature. Now whether due to my treatment or not, it is a fact that the disease did not spread; that is to say, it did not appear elsewhere upon the body."

"I see! I see!" said Mr. Barnes, much pleased. "This is an important point. For if the body at the Morgue exhibits a spot in that exact locality and nowhere else, and if it is positively this

---

*Ottolengui's information is quite accurate. Ferdinand Ritter von Hebra's work is described by Dr. Tilbury Fox in the *British Medical Journal* of April 15, 1871. The origin of the disease remains unknown; originally thought to be fungoid in origin (hence the name), it is now considered a possible autoimmune response. The variety of the disease that Ottolengui refers to as *lichen ruber* is referred to in the 2020 *Merck Manual* as *Pityriasis rubra pilaris*.

same skin disease, it is past belief that it should be any other than the body of your patient."

"So I argue. That two such unique examples of so rare a disease should occur at the same time seems incredible, though remotely possible. Thus, as you have indicated, we have but to show that the mark on the body at the Morgue is truly caused by this disease, and not by some abrasion while in the water, in order to make our opinion fairly tenable. Both Dr. Elliot and myself have closely examined the spot, and we have agreed that it is not an abrasion. Had the face been thus marked in the water, we should find the cuticle rubbed off, which is not the case. Contrarily, in the disease under consideration, the cuticle, though involved in the disease, and even missing in minute spots, is practically present. No, I am convinced that the mark on the body at the Morgue existed in life as the result of this lichen, though the alteration of color since death gives us a much changed appearance."

"Then I may consider that you are confident that this mark on the body is of the same shape, in the same position, and caused by the same disease as that which you observed upon Mr. Quadrant?"

"Yes. I do not hesitate to assert that. To this you may add that I identify the body in a general way also."

"By which you mean?"

"That without this mark, basing my opinion merely upon my long acquaintance with the man, I would be ready to declare that Mr. Quadrant's body is the one which was taken from the water."

"What, then, is your opinion as to how this strange occurrence has come about? If Mr. Quadrant was cremated, how could—"

"It could not, of course. This is not the age of miracles. Mr. Quadrant was not cremated. Of that we may be certain."

"But the family claim that they saw his body consigned to the furnace."

"The family believe this, I have no doubt. But how could they be sure? Let us be accurate in considering what we call facts. What did the family see at the crematory? They saw a closed coffin placed into the furnace."

"A coffin, though, which contained the body of their relative."

Mr. Barnes did not of course himself believe this, but made the remark merely to lead the doctor on.

"Again you are inaccurate. Let us rather say a coffin which once contained the body of their relative."

"Ah; then you think that it was taken from the coffin and another substituted for it?"

"No. I do not go so far. I think, nay, I am sure, that Mr. Quadrant's body was taken from the coffin, but whether another was substituted for it, is a question. The coffin may have been empty when burned."

"Could we settle that point by an examination of the ashes?"

The doctor started as though surprised at the question. After a little thought he replied hesitatingly:

"Perhaps. It seems doubtful. Ashes from bone and animal matter would, I suppose, bring us chemical results different from those of burned wood. Whether our analytical chemists could solve such a problem remains to be seen. Ordinarily one would think that ashes would resist all efforts at identification." The doctor seemed lost in thoughtful consideration of this scientific problem.

"The trimmings of the coffin might contain animal matter if made of wool," suggested Mr. Barnes.

"True; that would certainly complicate the work of the chemist, and throw doubt upon his reported results."

"You admitted, Doctor, that the body was placed in the coffin. Do you know that positively?"

"Yes. I called on the widow on the night previous to the funeral, and the body was then in the coffin. I saw it in company with the widow and the two brothers. It was then that it was decided that the coffin should be closed and not opened again."

"Whose wish was this?"

"The widow's. You may well understand that this lichen greatly disfigured Mr. Quadrant, and that he was extremely sensitive about it. So much so that he had not allowed any one to see him for many weeks prior to his death. It was in deference to this that the widow expressed the wish that no one but the immediate family should see him in his coffin. For this reason also she stipulated that the coffin should be burned with the body."

"You say this was decided on the night before the funeral?"

"Yes. To be accurate, about five o'clock in the afternoon, though at this season and in the closed rooms the lamps were already lighted."

"Was this known to many persons? That is, that the coffin was not again to be opened?"

"It was known of course to the two brothers, and also to the undertaker and two of his assistants who were present."

"The undertaker himself closed the casket, I presume?"

"Yes. He was closing it as I escorted the widow back to her own room."

"Did the brothers leave the room with you?"

"I think so. Yes, I am sure of it."

"So that the body was left with the undertaker and his men, after they knew that it was not to be opened again?"

"Yes."

"Did these men leave before you did?"

"No. I left almost immediately after taking the widow to her own room and seeing her comfortably lying down, apparently recovered from the hysterical spell which I had been summoned to check. You know, of course, that the Quadrant residence is but a block from here."

"There is one more point, Doctor. Of what disease did Mr. Quadrant die?"

"My diagnosis was what in common parlance I may call cancer of the stomach. This, of course, I only knew from the symptoms. That is to say, there had been no operation, as the patient was strenuously opposed to such a procedure. He repeatedly said to me, 'I would rather die than be cut up.' A strange prejudice in these days of successful surgery, when the knife in skilful hands promises so much more than medication."

"Still these symptoms were sufficient in your own mind to satisfy you that your diagnosis was accurate?"

"I can only say in reply that I have frequently in the presence of similar symptoms performed an operation, and always with the same result. The cancer was always present."

"Now the coroner's autopsy on the body at the Morgue is said to have shown that death was due to disease. Do you know what they discovered?"

"Dr. Elliot told me that it was cancer of the stomach."

"Why, then, the identification seems absolute?"

"So it seems. Yes."

## III

Mr. Barnes next called at the home of the Quadrants, and was informed that both of the gentlemen were out. With some hesitation he sent a brief note in to the widow, explaining his purpose and asking for an interview. To his gratification his request was granted, and he was shown up to that lady's reception-room.

"I fear, madame," said he, "that my visit may seem an intrusion, but I take the deepest sort of interest in this sad affair of your husband, and I would much appreciate having your permission and authority to investigate it, with the hope of discovering the wrong-doers."

"I see by your note," said Mrs. Quadrant in a low, sad voice, "that you are a detective, but not connected with the police. That is why I have decided to see you. I have declined to see the regular detective sent here by the police, though my husband's brothers, I believe, have answered all his questions. But as for myself, I felt that I could not place this matter in the hands of men whom my husband always distrusted. Perhaps his prejudice was due to his politics, but he frequently declared that our police force was corrupt. Thus you understand why I am really glad that you have called, for I am anxious, nay, determined, to discover if possible who it was who has done me this grievous wrong. To think that my poor husband was there in the river, when I thought that his body had been duly disposed of. It is horrible, horrible!"

"It is indeed horrible, madame," said Mr. Barnes sympathizingly. "But we must find the guilty person or persons and bring them to justice."

"Yes! That is what I wish. That is what I am ready to pay any sum to accomplish. You must not consider you are working, as you courteously offer, merely to satisfy your professional interest in a mysterious case. I wish you to undertake this as my special agent."

"As you please, madame, but in that case I must make one condition. I would ask that you tell this to no one unless I find it necessary. At present I think I can do better if I am merely regarded as a busybody detective attracted by an odd case."

"Why, certainly, no one need know. Now tell me what you think of this matter."

"Well, it is rather early to formulate an opinion. An opinion is dangerous. One is so apt to endeavor to prove himself right, whereas he ought merely to seek out the truth. But if you have any opinion, it is necessary for me to know it. Therefore I must answer you by asking the very question which you have asked me. What do you think?"

"I think that some one took the body of my husband from the coffin, and that we burned an empty casket. But to guess what motive there could be for such an act would be beyond my mental abilities. I have thought about it till my head has ached, but I can find no reason for such an unreasonable act."

"Let me then suggest one to you, and then perhaps your opinion may be more useful. Suppose that some person, some one who had the opportunity, had committed a murder. By removing the body of your husband, and replacing it with that of his victim, the evidences of his own crime would be concealed. The discovery of your husband's body, even if identified, as it has been, could lead to little else than mystification, for the criminal well knew that the autopsy would show natural causes of death."

"But what a terrible solution this is which you suggest! Why, no one had access to the coffin except the undertaker and his two men!"

"You naturally omit your two brothers, but a detective cannot make such discrimination."

"Why, of course I do not count them, for certainly neither of them could be guilty of such a crime as you suggest. It is true that Amos—but that is of no consequence."

"Who is Amos?" asked Mr. Barnes, aroused by the fact that Mrs. Quadrant had left her remark unfinished.

"Amos is one of my brothers—my husband's brothers, I mean. Amos Quadrant was next in age, and Mark the youngest of the three. But, Mr. Barnes, how could one of the undertakers have made this exchange which you suggest? Certainly they could not have brought the dead body here and my husband's body never left the house prior to the funeral."

"The corpse which was left in place of that of your husband must have been smuggled into this house by some one. Why not by one of these men? How, is a matter for explanation later. There is one other possibility about which you may be able to enlighten me. What opportunity, if any, was there that this substitution may have occurred at the crematory?"

"None at all. The coffin was taken from the hearse by our own pall-bearers, friends all of them, and carried directly to the room into which the furnace opened. Then, in accordance with my special request, the coffin, unopened, was placed in the furnace in full view of all present."

"Were you there yourself?"

"Oh! no, no! I could not have endured such a sight. The cremation was resorted to as a special request of my husband. But I am bitterly opposed to such a disposition of the dead, and therefore remained at home."

"Then how do you know what you have told me?—that there was no chance for substitution at the crematory?"

"Because my brothers and other friends have related all that occurred there in detail, and all tell the same story that I have told you."

"Dr. Mortimer tells me that you decided to have the coffin closed finally on the evening prior to the funeral. With the casket closed, I presume you did not consider it necessary to have the usual watchers?"

"Not exactly, though the two gentlemen, I believe, sat up through the night, and occasionally visited the room where the casket was."

"Ah! Then it would seem to have been impossible for any one to enter the house and accomplish the exchange, without being detected by one or both of these gentlemen?"

"Of course not," said Mrs. Quadrant, and then, realizing the necessary deduction, she hastened to add: "I do not know. After all, they may not have sat up through all the night."

"Did any one enter the house that night, so far as you know?"

"No one, except Dr. Mortimer, who stopped in about ten as he was returning from a late professional call. He asked how I was, and went on, I believe."

"But neither of the undertakers came back upon any excuse?"

"Not to my knowledge."

At this moment some one was heard walking in the hall below, and Mrs. Quadrant added:

"I think that may be one of my brothers now. Suppose you go down and speak to him. He would know whether any one came to the house during the night. You may tell him that you have seen me, if you wish, and that I have no objection to your endeavoring to discover the truth."

Mr. Barnes bade Mrs. Quadrant adieu and went down to the parlor floor. Not meeting any one, he touched a bell, and when the servant responded, asked for either of the gentlemen of the house who might have come in. He was informed that Mr. Mark Quadrant was in the library, and was invited to see him there.

Mr. Mark Quadrant was of medium height, body finely proportioned, erect figure, a well-poised head, keen, bright eyes, a decided blond, and wore a Vandyke beard, close trimmed. He looked at Mr. Barnes in such a manner that the detective knew that whatever he might learn from this man would be nothing that he would prefer to conceal, unless accidentally surprised from him. It was necessary therefore to approach the subject with considerable circumspection.

"I have called," said Mr. Barnes, "in relation to the mysterious circumstances surrounding the death of your brother."

"Are you connected with the police force?" asked Mr. Quadrant.

"No. I am a private detective."

"Then you will pardon my saying that you are an intruder—an unwelcome intruder."

"I think not," said Mr. Barnes, showing no irritation at his reception. "I have the permission of Mrs. Quadrant to investigate this affair."

"Oh! You have seen her, have you?"

"I have just had an interview with her."

"Then your intrusion is more than unwelcome; it is an impertinence."

"Why, pray?"

"You should have seen myself or my brother, before disturbing a woman in the midst of her grief."

"I asked for you or your brother, but you were both away. It was only then that I asked to see Mrs. Quadrant."

"You should not have done so. It was impertinent, I repeat. Why could you not have waited to see one of us?"

"Justice cannot wait. Delay is often dangerous."

"What have you to do with justice? This affair is none of your business."

"The State assumes that a crime is an outrage against all its citizens, and any man has the right to seek out and secure the punishment of the criminal."

"How do you know that any crime has been committed?"

"There can be no doubt about it. The removal of your brother's body from his coffin was a criminal act in itself, even if we do not take into account the object of the person who did this."

"And what, pray, was the object, since you are so wise?"

"Perhaps the substitution of the body of a victim of murder, in order that the person killed might be incinerated."

"That proposition is worthy of a detective. You first invent a crime, and then seek to gain employment in ferreting out what never occurred."

"That hardly holds with me, as I have offered my service without remuneration."

"Oh, I see. An enthusiast in your calling! A crank, in other words. Well, let me prick your little bubble. Suppose I can supply you with another motive, one not at all connected with murder?"

"I should be glad to hear you propound one."

"Suppose that I tell you that though my brother requested that his body should be cremated, both his widow and myself were opposed? Suppose that I further state that my brother Amos, being older than I, assumed the management of affairs, and insisted that the cremation should occur? And then suppose that I admit that to thwart that, I removed the body myself?"

"You ask me to suppose all this," said Mr. Barnes quietly. "In reply, I ask you, do you make such a statement?"

"Why, no. I do not intend to make any statement, because I do not consider that you have any right to mix yourself up in this affair. It is my wish that the matter should be allowed to rest. Nothing could be more repugnant to my feelings, or to my brother's, were he alive, poor fellow, than all this newspaper notoriety. I wish to see the body buried, and the mystery with it. I have no desire for any solution."

"But, despite your wishes, the affair will be, must be, investigated. Now, to discuss your imaginary proposition, I will say that it is so improbable that no one would believe it."

"Why not, pray?"

"First, because it was an unnatural procedure upon such an inadequate motive. A man might kill his brother, but he would hardly desecrate his brother's coffin merely to prevent a certain form of disposing of the dead."

"That is mere presumption. You cannot dogmatically state what may actuate a man."

"But in this case the means was inadequate to the end."

"How so?"

"If the combined wishes of yourself and the widow could not sway your brother Amos, who had taken charge of the funeral, how could you hope when the body should be removed from the river, that he would be more easily brought around to your wishes?"

"The effort to cremate the body having failed once, he would not resist my wishes in the second burial."

"That is doubtful. I should think he would be so incensed by your act, that he would be more than ever determined that you should have no say in the matter. But supposing that you believed otherwise, and that you wished to carry out this extraordinary scheme, you had no opportunity to do so."

"Why not?"

"I suppose, of course, that your brother sat up with the corpse through the night before the funeral."

"Exactly. You suppose a good deal more than you know. My brother did not sit up with the corpse. As the coffin had been closed, there was no need to follow that obsolete custom. My brother retired before ten o'clock. I myself remained up some hours longer."

Thus in the mental sparring Mr. Barnes had succeeded in learning one fact from this reluctant witness.

"But even so," persisted the detective, "you would have found difficulty in removing the body from this house to the river."

"Yet it was done, was it not?"

This was unanswerable. Mr. Barnes did not for a moment place any faith in what this brother had said. He argued that had he done anything like what he suggested, he would never have hinted at it as a possibility. Why he did so was a puzzle. Perhaps he merely wished to make the affair seem more intricate, in the hope of persuading him to drop the investigation, being, as he had stated, honestly anxious to have the matter removed from the public gaze, and caring nothing about any explanation of how his brother's body had been taken from the coffin. On the other hand, there was a possibility which could not be entirely overlooked. He might really have been guilty of acting as he had suggested, and perhaps now told of it as a cunning way of causing the detective to discredit such a solution of the mystery. Mr. Barnes thought it well to pursue the subject a little further.

"Suppose," said he, "that it could be shown that the ashes now in the urn at the cemetery are the ashes of a human being?"

"You will be smart if you can prove that," said Mr. Quadrant. "Ashes are ashes, I take it, and you will get little proof there. But since you discussed my proposition, I will argue with you about yours. You say, suppose the ashes are those of a human being. Very well, then, that would prove that my brother was cremated after all, and that I have been guying you, playing with you as a fisherman who fools a fish with feathers instead of real bait."

"But what of the identification of the body at the Morgue?"

"Was there ever a body at the Morgue that was not identified a dozen times? People are apt to be mistaken about their friends after death."

"But this identification was quite complete, being backed up by scientific reasons advanced by experts."

"Yes, but did you ever see a trial where expert witnesses were called, that equally expert witnesses did not testify to the exact contrary? Let me ask you a question. Have you seen this body at the Morgue?"

"Not yet."

"Go and see it. Examine the sole of the left foot. If you do not find a scar three or four inches long the body is not that of my brother. This scar was the result of a bad gash made by stepping on a shell when in bathing. He was a boy at the time, and I was with him."

"But, Mr. Quadrant," said Mr. Barnes, astonished by the new turn of the conversation, "I understood that you yourself admitted that the identification was correct."

"The body was identified by Dr. Mortimer first. My sister and my brother agreed with the doctor, and I agreed with them all, for reasons of my own."

"Would you mind stating those reasons?"

"You are not very shrewd if you cannot guess. I want this matter dropped. Had I denied the identity of the body it must have remained at the Morgue, entailing more newspaper sensationalism. By admitting the identity, I hoped that the body would be given to us for burial, and that the affair would then be allowed to die."

"Then if, as you now signify, this is not your brother's body, what shall I think of your suggestion that you yourself placed the body in the river?"

"What shall you think? Why, think what you like. That is your affair. The less you think about it, though, the better pleased I should be. And now really I cannot permit this conversation to be prolonged. You must go, and if you please I wish that you do not come here again."

"I am sorry that I cannot promise that. I shall come if I think it necessary. This is your sister's house, I believe, and she has expressed a wish that I pursue this case to the end."

"My sister is a fool. At any rate, I can assure you, you shall not get another chance at me, so make the most of what information I have given you. Good morning."

With these words Mr. Mark Quadrant walked out of the room, leaving Mr. Barnes alone.

## IV

Mr. Barnes stood for a moment in a quandary, and then decided upon a course of action. He touched the bell which he knew would call the butler, and then sat down by the grate fire to wait. Almost immediately his eye fell upon a bit of white paper protruding from beneath a small rug, and he picked it up. Examining it closely, he guessed that it had once contained some medicine in powder form, but nothing in the shape of a label, or traces of the powder itself, was there to tell what the drug had been.

"I wonder," thought he, "whether this bit of paper would furnish me with a clue? I must have it examined by a chemist. He may discern by his methods what I cannot detect with the naked eye."

With this thought in his mind, he carefully folded the paper in its original creases and deposited it in his wallet. At that moment the butler entered.

"What is your name?" asked Mr. Barnes.

"Thomas, sir," said the man, a fine specimen of the intelligent New York negro. "Thomas Jefferson."

"Well, Thomas, I am a detective, and your mistress wishes me to look into the peculiar circumstances which, as you know, have occurred. Are you willing to help me?"

"I'll do anything for the mistress, sir."

"Very good. That is quite proper. Now, then, do you remember your master's death?"

"Yes, sir."

"And his funeral?"

"Yes, sir."

"You know when the undertaker and his men came and went, and how often, I presume? You let them in and saw them?"

"I let them in, yes, sir. But once or twice they went out without my knowing."

"At five o'clock on the afternoon before the funeral, I am told that Mrs. Quadrant visited the room where the body was, and ordered that the coffin should be closed for the last time. Did you know this?"

"No, sir."

"I understand that at that time the undertaker and two of his men were in the room, as were also the two Mr. Quadrants, Mrs. Quadrant, and the doctor. Now, be as accurate as you can, and tell me in what order and when these persons left the house."

"Dr. Mortimer went away, I remember, just after Mrs. Quadrant went to her room to lie down. Then the gentlemen went in to dinner, and I served them. The undertaker and one of his men left together just as dinner was put on table. I remember that because the undertaker stood in the hall and spoke a word to Mr. Amos just as he was entering the dining-room. Mr. Amos then turned to me, and said for me to show them out. I went to the door with them, and then went back to the dining-room."

"Ah! Then one of the undertaker's men was left alone with the body?"

"I suppose so, unless he went away first. I did not see him go at all. But, come to think of it, he must have been there after the other two went away."

"Why?"

"Because, when I let out the undertaker and his man, their wagon was at the door, but they walked off and left it. After dinner it was gone, so the other man must have gone out and driven off in it."

"Very probably. Now, can you tell me this man's name? The last to leave the house, I mean?"

"I heard the undertaker call one 'Jack,' but I do not know which one."

"But you saw the two men—the assistants, I mean. Can you not describe the one that was here last?"

"Not very well. All I can say is that the one that went away with the undertaker was a youngish fellow without any mustache. The other was a short, thick-set man, with dark hair and a stubby mustache. That is all I noticed."

"That will be enough. I can probably find him at the undertaker's. Now, can you remember whether either of the gentlemen sat up with the corpse that night?"

"Both the gentlemen sat in here till ten o'clock. The body was across the hall in the little reception-room near the front door. About ten the door-bell rang, and I let in the doctor, who stopped to ask after Mrs. Quadrant. He and Mr. Amos went up to her room. The doctor came down in a few minutes, alone, and came into this room to talk with Mr. Mark."

"How long did he stay?"

"I don't know. Not long, I think, because he had on his overcoat. But Mr. Mark told me I could go to bed, and he would let the doctor out. So I just brought them a fresh pitcher of ice-water, and went to my own room."

"That is all, then, that you know of what occurred that night?"

"No, sir. There was another thing, that I have not mentioned to any one, though I don't think it amounts to anything."

"What was that?"

"Some time in the night I thought I heard a door slam, and the noise woke me up. I jumped out of bed and slipped on some clothes and came as far as the door here, but I did not come in."

"Why not?"

"Because I saw Mr. Amos in here, standing by the centre-table with a lamp in his hand. He was looking down at Mr. Mark, who was fast asleep alongside of the table, with his head resting on his arm on the table."

"Did you notice whether Mr. Amos was dressed or not?"

"Yes, sir. That's what surprised me. He had all his clothes on."

"Did he awaken his brother?"

"No. He just looked at him, and then tiptoed out and went upstairs. I slipped behind the hall door, so that he would not see me."

"Was the lamp in his hand one that he had brought down from his own room?"

"No, sir. It was one that I had been ordered to put in the room where the coffin was, as they did not want the electric light turned on in there all night. Mr. Amos went back into the front room, and left the lamp there before he went upstairs."

"Do you know when Mr. Mark went up to his room? Did he remain downstairs all night?"

"No, sir. He was in bed in his own room when I came around in the morning. About six o'clock, that was. But I don't know when he went to bed. He did not come down to breakfast, though, till nearly noon. The funeral was at two o'clock."

"That is all, I think," said Mr. Barnes. "But do not let any one know that I have talked with you."

"Just as you say, sir."

As it was now nearing noon, Mr. Barnes left the house and hastened up to Mr. Mitchel's residence to keep his engagement for luncheon. Arrived there, he was surprised to have Williams inform him that he had received a telephone message to the effect that Mr. Mitchel would not be at home for luncheon.

"But, Inspector," said Williams, "here's a note just left for you by a messenger."

Mr. Barnes took the envelope, which he found enclosed the following from Mr. Mitchel:

"FRIEND BARNES:—

"*Am sorry I cannot be home to luncheon. Williams will give you a bite. I have news for you. I have seen the ashes, and there is now no doubt that a body, a human body, was burned at the crematory that day. I do not despair that we may yet discover whose body it was. More when I know more.*"

## V

Mr. Barnes read this note over two or three times, and then folded it thoughtfully and put it in his pocket. He found it difficult to decide whether Mr. Mitchel had been really detained, or whether he had purposely broken his appointment. If the latter, then Mr. Barnes felt sure that already he had made some discovery which rendered this case doubly attractive to him, so much so that he had concluded to seek the solution himself.

"That man is a monomaniac," thought Mr. Barnes, somewhat nettled. "I come here and attract his attention to a case that I know will afford him an opportunity to follow a fad, and now he goes off and is working the case alone. It is not fair. But I suppose this is another challenge, and I must work rapidly to get at the truth ahead of him. Well, I will accept, and fight it out."

Thus musing, Mr. Barnes, who had declined Williams's offer to serve luncheon, left the house and proceeded to the shop of the undertaker. This man had a name the full significance of which had never come home to him until he began the business of caring for the dead. He spelled it Berial, and insisted that the pronunciation demanded a long sound to the "i," and a strong accent on the middle syllable. But he was constantly annoyed by the cheap wit of acquaintances, who with a significant titter would call him either Mr. "Burial," or Mr. "Bury all."

Mr. Barnes found Mr. Berial disengaged, undertakers, fortunately, not always being rushed with business, and encountered no difficulty in approaching his subject.

"I have called, Mr. Berial," said the detective, "to get a little information about your management of the funeral of Mr. Quadrant."

"Certainly," said Mr. Berial; "any information I can give, you are welcome to. Detective, I suppose?"

"Yes; in the interest of the family," replied Mr. Barnes. "There are some odd features of this case, Mr. Berial."

"Odd?" said the undertaker. "Odd don't half cover it. It's the most remarkable thing in the history of the world. Here I am, with an experience in funerals covering thirty years, and I go and have a man decently cremated, and, by hickory, if he ain't found floating in the river the next morning. Odd? Why, there ain't any word to describe a thing like that. It's devilish; that's the nearest I can come to it."

"Well, hardly that," said Mr. Barnes, with a smile. "Of course, since Mr. Quadrant's body has been found in the river, it never was cremated."

"Who says so?" asked the undertaker, sharply. "Not cremated? Want to bet on that? I suppose not. We can't make a bet about the dead. It wouldn't be professional. But Mr. Quadrant was cremated. There isn't any question about that point. Put that down as final."

"But it is impossible that he should have been cremated, and then reappear at the Morgue."

"Just what I say. The thing's devilish. There's a hitch, of

course. But why should it be at my end, eh? Tell me that, will you? There's just as much chance for a mistake at the Morgue as at the funeral, isn't there?" This was said in a tone that challenged dispute.

"What mistake could have occurred at the Morgue?" asked Mr. Barnes.

"Mistaken identification," replied the undertaker so quickly that he had evidently anticipated the question. "Mistaken identification. That's your cue, Mr. Barnes. It's happened often enough before," he added, with a chuckle.

"I scarcely think there can be a mistake of that character," said Mr. Barnes, thinking, nevertheless, of the scar on the foot. "This identification is not merely one of recognition; it is supported by scientific reason, advanced by the doctors."

"Oh! doctors make mistakes too, I guess," said Mr. Berial, testily. "Look here, you're a detective. You're accustomed to weigh evidence. Now tell me, will you, how could this man be cremated, as I tell you he was, and then turn up in the river? Answer that, and I'll argue with you."

"The question, of course, turns on the fact of the cremation. How do you know that the body was in the coffin when it was consigned to the furnace?"

"How do I know? Why, ain't that my business? Who should know if I don't? Didn't I put the body in the coffin myself?"

"Very true. But why could not some one have taken the body out after you closed the coffin finally, and before the hour of the funeral?"

Mr. Berial laughed softly to himself, as though enjoying a joke too good to be shared too soon with another. Presently he said:

"That's a proper question, of course; a very proper question, and I'll answer it. But I must tell you a secret, so you may understand it. You see in this business we depend a good deal on the recommendation of the attending physician. Some doctors are real professional, and recommend a man on his merits. Others are different. They expect a commission. Surprises you, don't it? But it's done every day in this town. The doctor can't save his patient, and the patient dies. Then he tells the sorrowing friends that such and such an undertaker is the proper party to hide away the result of his failure; failure to cure, of course. In due time he gets his little check, ten per cent, of the funeral bill. This seems like wandering away from the point, but I am coming back to it. This commission arrangement naturally keeps me on the books of certain doctors, and vicy versy it keeps them on mine. So, working for certain doctors, it follows that I work for a certain set of people. Now I've a Catholic doctor on my books, and it happens that the cemetery where that church buries is in a lonesome place; just the spot for a grave-robber to work undisturbed, especially if the watchman out there should happen to be fond of his tipple, which I tell you, again in confidence, that he is. Now, then, it has happened more than once, though it has been kept quiet, that a grave filled up one afternoon would be empty the next morning. At least the body would be gone. Of course they wouldn't take the coffin, as they'd be likely to be caught getting rid of it. You see, a coffin ain't exactly regular household furniture. If they have time they fill the grave again, but often enough they're too anxious to get away, because, of course, the watchman might not be drunk. Well, these things being kept secret, but still pretty well known in the congregation, told in whispers, I might say, a sort of demand sprung up for a style of coffin that a grave-robber couldn't open,—a sort of coffin with a combination lock, as it were."

"You don't mean to say—" began Mr. Barnes, greatly interested at last in the old man's rather lengthy speech. He was interrupted by the undertaker, who again chuckled as he exclaimed:

"Don't I? Well, I do, though. Of course I don't mean there's really a combination lock. That would never do. We often have to open the coffin for a friend who wants to see the dead face again, or for folks that come to the funeral late. It's funny, when you come to think of it, how folks will be late to funerals. As they only have this last visit to make, you'd think they'd make it a point to be on time and not delay the funeral. But about the way I fasten a coffin. If any grave-robber tackles one of my coffins without knowing the trick, he'd be astonished, I tell you. I often think of it and laugh. You see, there's a dozen screws and they look just like ordinary screws. But if you work them all out with a screw-driver, your coffin lid is just as tight as ever. You see, it's this way. The real screw works with a reverse thread, and is hollow on the top. Now I have a screw-driver that is really a screw. When the screw-threaded end of this is screwed into the hollow end of the coffin-bolt, as soon as it is in tight it begins to unscrew the bolt. To put the bolt in, in the first place, I first screw it tight on to my screw-driver, and then drive it in, turning backwards, and as soon as it is tight my screw-driver begins to unscrew and so comes out. Then I drop in my dummy screw, and just turn it down to fill the hole. Now the dummy screw and the reverse thread of the real bolt is a puzzle for a grave-robber, and anyway he couldn't solve it without one of my own tools."

Mr. Barnes reflected deeply upon this as a most important statement. If Mr. Quadrant's coffin was thus fastened, no one could have opened it without the necessary knowledge and the special screw-driver. He recalled that the butler had told him that one of Mr. Berial's men had been at the house after the departure of the others. This man was therefore in the position to have opened the coffin, supposing that he had had one of the screw-drivers. Of this it would be well to learn.

"I suppose," said Mr. Barnes, "that the coffin in which you placed Mr. Quadrant was fastened in this fashion?"

"Yes; and I put the lid on and fastened it myself."

"What, then, did you do with the screw-driver? You might have left it at the house."

"I might have, but I didn't. No; I'm not getting up a combination and then leaving the key around loose. No, sir; there's only one of those screw-drivers, and I take care of it myself. I'll show it to you."

The old man went to a drawer, which he unlocked, and brought back the tool.

"You see what it is," he continued—"double-ended. This end is just the common every-day screw-driver. That is for the dummies that fill up the hollow ends after the bolts are sent home. The other end, you see, looks just like an ordinary screw with straight sides. There's a shoulder to keep it from jamming. Now that's the only one of those, and I keep it locked in that drawer with a Yale lock, and the key is always in my pocket. No; I guess that coffin wasn't opened after I shut it."

Mr. Barnes examined the tool closely, and formed his own conclusions, which he thought best to keep to himself.

"Yes," said he aloud; "it does seem as though the mistake must be in the identification."

"What did I tell you?" exclaimed Mr. Berial, delighted at thinking that he had convinced the detective. "Oh, I guess I know my business."

"I was told at the house," said Mr. Barnes, "that when you left, after closing the coffin, one of your men stayed behind. Why was that?"

"Oh, I was hungry and anxious to get back for dinner. One of my men, Jack, I brought away with me, because I had to send him up to another place to get some final directions for another funeral. The other man stayed behind to straighten up the place and bring off our things in the wagon."

"Who was this man? What is his name?"

"Jerry, we called him. I don't know his last name."

"I would like to have a talk with him. Can I see him?"

"I am afraid not. He isn't working with me any more."

"How was that?"

"He left, that's all. Threw up his job."

"When was that?"

"This morning."

"This morning?"

"Yes; just as soon as I got here, about eight o'clock."

Mr. Barnes wondered whether there was any connection between this man's giving up his position, and the account of the discoveries in regard to Mr. Quadrant's body which the morning papers had published.

## VI

"Mr. Berial," said Mr. Barnes after a few moments' thought, "I wish you would let me have a little talk with your man—Jack, I think you called him. And I would like to speak to him alone if you don't mind. I feel that I must find this other fellow, Jerry, and perhaps Jack may be able to give me some information as to his home, unless you can yourself tell me where he lives."

"No; I know nothing about him," said Mr. Berial. "Of course you can speak to Jack. I'll call him in here and I'll be off to attend to some business. That will leave you alone with him."

Jack, when he came in, proved to be a character. Mr. Barnes soon discovered that he had little faith in the good intentions of any one in the world except himself. He evidently was one of those men who go through life with a grievance, feeling that all people have in some way contributed to their misfortune.

"Your name is Jack," said Mr. Barnes; "Jack what?"

"Jackass, you might say," answered the fellow, with a coarse attempt at wit.

"And why, pray?"

"Well, a jackass works like a slave, don't he? And what does he get out of it? Lots of blows, plenty of cuss words, and a little fodder. It's the same with yours truly."

"Very well, my man, have your joke. But now tell me your name. I am a detective."

"The devil a much I care for that. I ain't got nothin' to hide. My name's Randal, if you must have it. Jack Randal."

"Very good. Now I want to ask you a few questions about the funeral of Mr. Quadrant."

"Ask away. Nobody's stoppin' you."

"You assisted in preparing the body for the coffin, I think?"

"Yes, and helped to put him in it."

"Have you any idea how he got out of it again?" asked Mr. Barnes suddenly.

"Nit. Leastways, not any worth mentionin', since I can't prove what I might think."

"But I should like to know what you think, anyway," persisted the detective.

"Well, I think he was took out," said Randal with a hoarse laugh.

"Then you do not believe that he was cremated?"

"Cremated? Not on your life. If he was made into ashes, would he turn up again a floater and drift onto the marble at the Morgue? I don't think."

"But how could the body have gotten out of the coffin?"

"He couldn't. I never saw a stiff do that, except once, at an Irish wake, and that fellow wasn't dead. No, the dead don't walk. Not these days. I tell you, he was took out of the box. That's as plain as your nose, not meanin' to be personal."

"Come, come, you have said all that before. What I want to know is, how you think he could have been taken out of the coffin."

"Lifted out, I reckon."

Mr. Barnes saw that nothing would be gained by getting angry, though the fellow's persistent flippancy annoyed him extremely. He thought best to appear satisfied with his answers, and to endeavor to get his information by slow degrees, since he could not get it more directly.

"Were you present when the coffin lid was fastened?"

"Yes; the boss did that."

"How was it fastened? With the usual style of screws?"

"Oh, no! We used the boss's patent screw, warranted to keep the corpse securely in his grave. Once stowed away in the boss's patent screw-top casket, no ghost gets back to trouble the long-suffering family."

"You know all about these patent coffin-screws?"

"Why, sure. Ain't I been working with old Berial these three years?"

"Does Mr. Berial always screw on the coffin lids himself?"

"Yes; he's stuck on it."

"He keeps the screw-driver in his own possession?"

"So he thinks."

"What do you mean?" asked Mr. Barnes, immediately attentive.

"Just what I say. Old Berial thinks he's got the only screw-driver."

"But you know that there is another?"

"Who says so? I don't know anything of the sort."

"Why, then, do you cast a doubt upon the matter by saying that Mr. Berial thinks he has the only one?"

"Because I do doubt it, that's all."

"Why do you doubt it?"

"Oh, I don't know. A fellow can't always account for what he thinks, can he?"

"You must have some reason for thinking there may be a duplicate of that screw-driver."

"Well, what if I have?"

"I would like to know it."

"No doubt! But it ain't right to cast suspicions when you can't prove a thing, is it?"

"Perhaps others may find the proof."

"Just so. People in your trade are pretty good at that, I reckon."

"Good at what?"

"Proving things that don't exist."

"But if your suspicion is groundless, there can be no harm in telling it to me."

"Oh, there's grounds enough for what I think. Look here, suppose a case. Suppose a party, a young female party, dies. Suppose her folks think they'd like to have her hands crossed on her breast. Suppose a man, me, for instance, helps the boss fix up that young party with her hands crossed, and suppose there's a handsome shiner, a fust-water diamond, on one finger. Suppose we screw down that coffin lid tight at night, and the boss carts off his pet screw-driver. Then suppose next day, when he opens that coffin for the visitors to have a last look at the young person, that the other man, meanin' me, happens to notice that the shiner is missin'. If no other person notices it, that's because they're too busy grievin'. But that's the boss's luck, I say. The diamond's gone, just the same, ain't it? Now, you wouldn't want to claim that the young person come out of that patent box and give that diamond away in the night, would you? If she come out at all, I should say it was in the form of a ghost, and I never heard of ghosts wearin' diamonds, or givin' away finger rings. Did you?"

"Do you mean to say that such a thing as this has occurred?"

"Oh, I ain't sayin' a word. I don't make no accusations. You can draw your own conclusions. But in a case like that you would think there was more than one of them screw-drivers, now, wouldn't you?"

"I certainly should, unless we imagined that Mr. Berial himself returned to the house and stole the ring. But that, of course, is impossible."

"Is it?"

"Why, would you think that Mr. Berial would steal?"

"Who knows? We're all honest, till we're caught."

"Tell me this. If Mr. Berial keeps that screw-driver always in his own possession, how could any one have a duplicate of it made?"

"Dead easy. If you can't see that, you're as soft as the old man."

"Perhaps I am. But tell me how it could be done."

"Why, just see. That tool is double-ended. But one end is just a common, ordinary screw-driver. You don't need to imitate that. The other end is just a screw that fits into the thread at the end of the bolts. Now old Berial keeps his precious screw-driver locked up, but the bolts lay around by the gross. Any man about the place could take one and have a screw cut to fit it, and there you are."

This was an important point, and Mr. Barnes was glad to have drawn it out. It now became only too plain that the patented device was no hindrance to any one knowing of it, and especially to one who had access to the bolts. This made it the more necessary to find the man Jerry.

"There was another man besides yourself who assisted at the Quadrant funeral, was there not?" asked Mr. Barnes.

"There was another man, but he didn't assist much. He was no good."

"What was this man's name?"

"That's why I say he's no good. He called himself Jerry Morton, but it didn't take me long to find out that his name was really Jerry Morgan. Now a man with two names is usually a crook, to my way of thinkin.'"

"He gave up his job here this morning, did he not?"

"Did he?"

"Yes. Can you tell why he should have done so? Was he not well enough paid?"

"Too well, I take it. He got the same money I do, and I done twice as much work. So he's chucked it, has he? Well, I shouldn't wonder if there was good reason."

"What reason?"

"Oh, I don't know. That story about old Quadrant floatin' back was in the papers to-day, wasn't it?"

"Yes."

"Very well. There you are."

"You mean that this man Morgan might have had a hand in that?"

"Oh, he had a hand in it all right. So did I and the boss, for that matter. But the boss and me left him screwed tight in his box, and Jerry he was left behind to pick up, as it were. And he had the wagon too. Altogether, I should say he had the chance if anybody. But mind you, I ain't makin' no accusations."

"Then, if Jerry did this, he must have had a duplicate screw-driver?"

"You're improvin', you are. You begin to see things. But I never seen him with no screw-driver, remember that."

"Was he in Mr. Berial's employment at the time of the other affair?"

"What other affair?"

"The case of the young lady from whose finger the diamond ring was stolen."

"Oh, that. Why, he might have been, of course, but then, you know, we was only supposin' a case there. We didn't say that was a real affair." Randal laughed mockingly.

"Have you any idea as to where I could find this man Morgan?"

"I don't think you will find him."

"Why not?"

"Skipped, I guess. He wouldn't chuck this job just to take a holiday."

"Do you know where he lived?"

"Eleventh Avenue near Fifty-fourth Street. I don't know the number, but it was over the butcher shop."

"If this man Morgan did this thing, can you imagine why he did it?"

"For pay; you can bet on that. Morgan ain't the man as would take a risk like that for the fun of the thing."

"But how could he hope to be paid for such an act?"

"Oh, he wouldn't hope. You don't know Jerry. He'd be paid, part in advance anyway, and balance on demand."

"But who would pay him, and with what object?"

"Oh, I don't know. But let me tell you something. Them brothers weren't all so lovin' to one another as the outside world thinks. In the fust place, as I gathered by listenin' to the talk of the servants, the one they called Amos didn't waste no love on the dead one, though I guess the other one, Mark, liked him some. I think he liked the widow even better." Here he laughed. "Now the dead man wanted to be cremated—that is, he said so before he was dead. The widow didn't relish the idea, but she ain't strong-minded enough to push her views. Now we'll suppose a case again. I like that style, it don't commit you to anything. Well, suppose this fellow Mark thinks he'll get into the good graces of the widow by hindering the cremation. He stands out agin' it. Amos he says the old fellow wanted to be burned, and let him burn. 'He'll burn in hell, anyway.' That nice, sweet remark he did make, I'll tell you that much. Then the brothers they quarrel. And a right good row they did have, so I hear. Now we'll suppose again. Why couldn't our friend, Mr. Mark, have got up this scheme to stop the cremation?"

Mr. Barnes was startled to hear this man suggest exactly what Mark himself had hinted at. Could it be only a coincidence or was it really the solution of the mystery? But if so, what of the body that was really cremated? But then again the only evidence in his possession on that point was the bare statement in the note received from Mr. Mitchel. Two constructions could be placed upon that note. First, it might have been honestly written by Mr. Mitchel, who really believed what he wrote, though, smart as he was, he might have been mistaken. Secondly, the note might merely have been written to send Mr. Barnes off on a wrong clue, thus leaving Mr. Mitchel a chance to follow up the right one. Resuming his conversation with Randal, Mr. Barnes said:

"Then you imagine that Mr. Mark Quadrant hired this man Morgan to take away the body and hide it until after the funeral?"

"Oh, I don't know. All I'll say is, I don't think Jerry would be too good for a little job like that. Say, you're not a bad sort, as detectives go. I don't mind givin' you a tip."

"I am much obliged, I am sure," said Mr. Barnes, smiling at the fellow's presumption.

"Don't mention it. I make no charge. But see. Have you looked at the corpse at the Morgue?"

"No. Why?"

"Well, I stopped in this morning and had a peep at him. I guess it's Quadrant all right."

"Have you any special way of knowing that?"

"Well, when the boss was injectin' the embalmin' fluid, he stuck the needle in the wrong place first, and had to put it in again. That made two holes. They're both there. You might wonder why we embalmed a body that was to be cremated. You see, we didn't know the family wasn't going to let him be seen, and we was makin' him look natural."

"And you are sure there are two punctures in the body at the Morgue?"

"Dead sure. That's a joke. But that ain't the tip I want to give you. This is another case of diamond rings."

"You mean that there were diamond rings left on the hand when the body was placed in the coffin?"

"One solitaire; a jim dandy. And likewise a ruby, set deep like a carbuncle, I think they call them other red stones. Then on the little finger of the other hand there was a solid gold ring, with a flat top to it, and a letter 'Q' in it, made of little diamonds. Them rings never reached the Morgue."

"But even so, that does not prove that they were taken by the man who removed the corpse from the coffin. They might have been taken by those who found the body in the river."

"Nit. Haven't you read the papers? Boys found it, but they

called in the police to get it out of the water. Since then the police has been in charge. Now I ain't got none too good an opinion of the police myself, but they don't rob the dead. They squeeze the livin', all right, but not the dead. Put that down. You can believe, if you like, that Jerry carted that body off to the river and dumped it in, diamond rings and all. But as I said before, you don't know Jerry. No, sir, if I was you, I'd find them rings, and find out how they got there. And maybe I can help you there, too,—that is, if you'll make it worth my while."

Mr. Barnes understood the hint and responded promptly:

"Here is a five-dollar bill," said he. "And if you really tell me anything that aids me in finding the rings, I will give you ten more."

"That's the talk," said Randal, taking the money. "Well, it's this way. You'll find that crooks, like other fly birds, has regular haunts. Now I happen to know that Jerry spouted his watch, a silver affair, but a good timer, once, and I take it he'd carry the rings where he's known, 'specially as I'm pretty sure the pawnbroker ain't over inquisitive about where folks gets the things they borrow on. If I was you, I'd try the shop on Eleventh Avenue by Fiftieth Street. It don't look like a rich place, but that kind don't want to attract too much attention."

"I will go there. I have no doubt that if he took the rings we will find them at that place. One thing more. How was Mr. Quadrant dressed when you placed him in the coffin? The newspapers make no mention of the clothing found on him."

"Oh, we didn't dress him. You see, he was to be burned, so we just shrouded him. Nothin' but plain white cloth. No buttons or nothin' that wouldn't burn up. The body at the Morgue was found without no clothes of any kind. I'd recognize that shroud, though, if it turns up. So there's another point for you."

"One thing more. You are evidently sure that Mr. Quadrant's body was taken out of the coffin. Do you think, then, that the coffin was empty when they took it to the crematory?"

"Why, sure! What could there be in it?"

"Suppose I were to tell you that another detective has examined the ashes and declares that he can prove that a human body was burned with that coffin. What would you say?"

"I'd say he was a liar. I'd say he was riggin' you to get you off the scent. No, sir! Don't you follow no such blind trail as that."

## VII

As Mr. Barnes left the undertaker's shop he observed Mr. Burrows coming towards him. It will be recalled that this young detective, now connected with the regular police force of the metropolis, had earlier in life been a *protégé* of Mr. Barnes. It was not difficult to guess from his being in this neighborhood that to him had been entrusted an investigation of the Quadrant mystery.

"Why, hello, Mr. Barnes," Mr. Burrows exclaimed, as he recognized his old friend. "What are you doing about here? Nosing into this Quadrant matter, I'll be bound."

"It is an attractive case," replied Mr. Barnes, in non-committal language. "Are you taking care of it for the office?"

"Yes; and the more I look into it the more complicated I find it. If you are doing any work on it, I wouldn't mind comparing notes."

"Very well, my boy," said Mr. Barnes, after a moment's thought, "I will confess that I have gone a little way into this. What have you done?"

"Well, in the first place, there was another examination by the doctors this morning. There isn't a shadow of doubt that the man at the Morgue was dead when thrown into the water. What's more, he died in his bed."

"Of what disease?"

"Cancer of the stomach. Put that down as fact number one. Fact number two is that the mark on his face is exactly the same, and from the same skin disease that old Quadrant had. Seems he also had a cancer, so I take it the identification is complete; especially as the family say it is their relative."

"Do they all agree to that?"

"Why, yes—that is, all except the youngest brother. He says he guesses it's his brother. Something about that man struck me as peculiar."

"Ah! Then you have seen him?"

"Yes. Don't care to talk to detectives. Wants the case hushed up; says there's nothing in it. Now I know there is something in it, and I am not sure he tells all he knows."

"Have you formed any definite conclusion as to the motive in this case?"

"The motive for what?"

"Why, for removing the body from the coffin."

"Well, I think the motive of the man who did it was money. What the motive of the man who hired him was, I can't prove yet."

"Oh! Then you think there are two in it?"

"Yes; I'm pretty sure of that. And I think I can put my finger on the man that made the actual transfer."

The two men were walking as they talked, Mr. Burrows having turned and joined the older detective. Mr. Barnes was surprised to find his friend advancing much the same theory as that held by Randal. He was more astonished, however, at the next reply elicited. He asked:

"Do you mind naming this man?"

"Not to you, if you keep it quiet till I'm ready to strike. I'm pretty sure that the party who carried the body away and put it in the river was the undertaker's assistant, a fellow who calls himself Randal."

Mr. Barnes started, but quickly regained his self-control. Then he said:

"Randal? Why, how could he have managed it?"

"Easily enough. It seems that the coffin was closed at five on the afternoon before the funeral, and the undertaker was told, in the presence of this fellow Randal, that it would not be opened again. Then the family went in to dine, and Berial and the other man, a fellow with an alias, but whose true name is Morgan, left the house, the other one, Randal, remaining behind to clear up. The undertaker's wagon was also there, and Randal drove it to the stables half an hour or so later."

Mr. Barnes noted here that there was a discrepancy between the facts as related by Mr. Burrows and as he himself had heard them. He had been told by Berial himself that it was "Jack" who had left the house with him, while Burrows evidently believed that it was Jack Randal who had been left behind. It was important, therefore, to learn whether there existed any other reason for suspecting Randal rather than Morgan.

"But though he may have had this opportunity," said Mr. Barnes, "you would hardly connect him with this matter without corroborative evidence."

"Oh, the case is not complete yet," said Mr. Burrows; "but I have had this fellow Randal watched for three days. We at the office knew about this identification before the newspapers got hold of it, be sure of that. Now one curious thing that he has done was to attempt to destroy some pawn-tickets."

"Pawn-tickets?"

"Yes. I was shadowing him myself last night, when I saw him tear up some paper and drop the pieces in the gutter at the side of the pavement. I let my man go on, for the sake of recovering those bits of paper. It took some perseverance and no little time, but I found them, and when put together, as I have said, they proved to be pawn-tickets."

"Have you looked at the property represented yet?"

"No. Would you like to go with me? We'll go together. I was about to make my first open appearance at the undertaker's shop to face this fellow, when you met me. But there's time enough for that. We'll go and look at the rings if you say the word."

"Rings, are they?" said Mr. Barnes. "Why, I would like nothing better. They might have been taken from the corpse."

"Haven't a doubt of it," said Mr. Burrows.

"Here are the pawn-tickets. There are two of them. Both for rings." He handed the two pawn-tickets to Mr. Barnes. The pieces had been pasted on another bit of paper and the two were consequently now on a single sheet. Mr. Barnes looked at them closely and then said:

"Why, Burrows, these are made out in the name of Jerry Morgan. Are you sure you have made no mistake in this affair?"

"Mistake? Not a bit of it. That fellow thinks he is smart, but I don't agree with him. He imagines that we might guess that one of those who had the handling of the body did this job, and when he pawned the rings he just used the other fellow's name. It's an old trick, and not very good, either."

Mr. Barnes was not entirely convinced, though the theory was possible, nay, plausible. In which case, the tip which Randal had given to Mr. Barnes was merely a part of his rather commonplace scheme of self-protection at the expense of a fellow-workman. He was glad now that he had met Burrows, for his possession of the pawn-tickets made it easy to visit the pawnbroker and see the rings; while his connection with the regular force would enable him to seize them should they prove to have been stolen from the body of Mr. Quadrant. It was noteworthy that the pawn-tickets had been issued by the man to whose place Randal had directed him. Arrived there, Mr. Burrows demanded to see the rings, to which the pawnbroker at first demurred, arguing that the tickets had been torn, that they had not been issued to the one presenting them, and that unless they were to be redeemed he must charge a fee of twenty-five cents for showing the goods. To all of this Mr. Burrows listened patiently and then showing his shield said meaningly:

"Now, friend Isaac, you get those rings out, and it will be

better for you. The Chief has had an eye on this little shop of yours for some time."

"So help me Moses!" said the man, "he can keep both eyes on if he likes."

But his demeanor changed, and with considerable alacrity he brought out the rings. There were three, just as Randal had described to Mr. Barnes, including the one with the initial "Q" set in diamonds.

"Who left these with you?" asked Mr. Burrows.

"The name is on the ticket," answered the pawnbroker.

"You are inaccurate, my friend. A name is on the ticket, yes, but not the name. Now tell me the truth."

"It's all straight. I ain't hiding anything. Morgan brought the things here."

"Morgan, eh? You are sure his name is Morgan? Quite sure?"

"Why, that's the name I know him by. Sometimes he goes by the name of Morton, I've heard. But with me it's always been Morgan, Jerry Morgan, just as it reads on the ticket."

"Oh, then you know this man Morgan?"

"No; only that he borrows money on security once in a while."

"Well, now, if his name is Morgan, did you think this ring with a 'Q' on it was his? Does 'Q' stand for Morgan?"

"That's none of my affair. Heavens, I can't ask everybody where they get things. They'd be insulted."

"Insulted! That's a good one. Well, when I get my hands on this chap he'll be badly insulted, for I'll ask him a lot of questions. Now, Isaac, let me tell you what this 'Q' stands for. It stands for Quadrant, and that's the name of the man found in the river lately, and these three rings came off his fingers. After death, Isaac; after death! What do you think of that?"

"You don't say! I'm astonished!"

"Are you, now? Never thought your friend Morgan or Morton, who works out by the day,[*] and brought valuable dia-

---

[*]That is to say, Morgan is a part-time employee, paid by the day.

monds to pawn, would do such a thing, did you? Thought he bought these things out of his wages, eh?"

"I never knew he wasn't honest, so help me Moses! or I wouldn't have had a thing to do with him."

"Perhaps not. You're too honest yourself to take 'swag' from a 'crook,' even though you loan about one quarter of the value."

"I gave him all he asked for. He promised to take them out again."

"Well, he won't, Isaac. I'll take them out myself."

"You don't mean you're going to keep the rings? Where do I come in?"

"You're lucky you don't come into jail."

"May I ask this man a few questions, Burrows?" said Mr. Barnes.

"As many as you like, and see that you answer straight, Isaac. Don't forget what I hinted about the Chief having an eye on you."

"Why, of course, I'll answer anything."

"You say you have known this man Morgan for some time?" asked Mr. Barnes. "Can you give me an idea of how he looks?"

"Why, I ain't much on descriptions. Morgan is a short fellow, rather stocky, and he's got dark hair and a mustache that looks like a paintbrush."

Mr. Barnes recalled the description which the butler had given of the man who had remained at the house when the others went away, and this tallied very well with it. As Berial had declared that it was Morgan who had been left at the house, and as this description did not fit Randal at all, he being above medium height, with a beardless face which made him seem younger than he probably was, it began to look as though in some way Mr. Burrows had made a mistake, and that Randal was not criminally implicated, though perhaps he had stolen the pawn-tickets, and subsequently destroyed them when he found that a police investigation was inevitable.

There was no object in further questioning the pawnbroker, who pleaded that as the owners of the property were rich, and as he had "honestly" made the loan, they might be persuaded to return to him the amount of his advance, adding that he would willingly throw off his "interest."

Leaving the place, and walking together across town, Mr. Barnes said to Mr. Burrows:

"Tom, I am afraid you are on a wrong scent. That man Randal stole those pawn-tickets. He did not himself pawn the rings."

"Maybe," said the younger man, only half convinced. "But you mark my word. Randal is in this. Don't believe all that 'fence' says. He may be in with Randal. I fancy that Randal pawned the things, but made the Jew put Morgan's name on them. Now that we ask him questions, he declares that Morgan brought them to him, either to protect Randal, or most likely to protect himself. Since there is a real Morgan, and he knew the man, he had no right to write his name on those tickets for things brought to him by some one else."

"But why are you so sure that Morgan is innocent? How do you know that he was the one that went off with old Berial when they left the house?"

"Simply because the other man, Randal, took the wagon back to the stables."

"Are you certain of that?"

"Absolutely. I have been to the stables, and they all tell the same story. Randal took the wagon out, harnessing the horse himself, as he often did. And Randal brought it back again, after six o'clock; of that they are certain, because the place is merely a livery for express wagons, trucks, and the like. The regular stable-boys go off between six and seven, and there is no one in charge at night except the watchman. The drivers usually take care of their own horses. Now the watchman was already there when Randal came in with the wagon, and two of the stable-boys also saw him."

"Now, Tom, you said that in your belief there was another man in this case,—one who really was the principal. Have you any suspicion as to that man's identity?"

"Here's my idea," said Mr. Burrows. "This fellow Randal was sounded by the man who finally engaged him for the job, and, proving to be the right sort, was engaged. He was to take the body out of the coffin and carry it away. The man who hired Randal must have been one of the brothers."

"Why?"

"It must have been, else the opportunity could not have been made, for, mark me, it was made. See! The widow was taken to the room to see the corpse, and then it was arranged that the coffin should be closed and not opened again before the funeral. That was to make all sure. Then came the closing of the coffin and the departure of two of the undertakers. The third, Randal, remained behind, and while the family lingered at dinner the job was done. The body was carried out to the wagon and driven off. Now we come to the question, which of the brothers did this?"

"Which have you decided upon?"

"Why, the object of this devilish act was to please the widow by preventing this cremation to which she objected. The man who concocted that scheme thought that when the body should be found it would then be buried, which would gratify the widow. Now why did he wish to gratify her? Because he's in love with her. She's not old, you know, and she's still pretty."

"Then you think that Mark Quadrant concocted this scheme?"

"No! I think that Amos Quadrant is our man."

It seemed destined that Mr. Burrows should surprise Mr. Barnes. If the older detective was astonished when he had heard Burrows suggest that Randal had been the accomplice in this affair, he was more astounded now to hear him accuse the elder brother of being the principal. For, had not Mark Quadrant told him that it was Amos who had insisted upon the cremation? And that Amos, being the elder, had assumed the control of the funeral?

"Burrows," said Mr. Barnes, "I hope that you are not merely following your impulsive imagination?"

Mr. Burrows colored as he replied with some heat:

"You need not forever twit me with my stupidity in my first case. Of course I may be mistaken, but I am doing routine work on this affair. I have not any real proof yet to support my theories. If I had I should make an arrest. But I have evidence enough to make it my duty to go ahead on definite lines. When the mystery clears a little, I may see things differently."

"I should like to know why you think that Amos is in love with his sister-in-law."

"Perhaps it would be safer to claim that he was once in love with her. The past is a certainty, the present mere conjecture. I got the tip from a slip of the tongue made by Dr. Mortimer, and I have corroborated the facts since. I was speaking with Dr. Mortimer of the possibility of there being any ill-feeling between the members of this family, when he said: 'I believe there was some hard feeling between the deceased and his brother Amos arising from jealousy.' When he had let the word 'jealousy' pass his lips, he closed up like a clam, and when I pressed him, tried to pass it off by saying that Amos was jealous of his brother's business and social successes. But that did not go down with me, so I have had some guarded inquiries made, with the result that it is certain that Amos loved this woman before she accepted Rufus."

"What if I tell you that I have heard that the younger brother, Mark, is in love with the widow, and that it was he who opposed cremation, while it was Amos who insisted upon carrying out the wishes of his brother?"

"What should I say to that? Well, I should say that you probably got that yarn from Randal, and that he had been 'stuffing you,' as the vernacular has it, hoping you'll excuse the vulgar expression."

It nettled Mr. Barnes to have his younger *confrère*[*] guess so accurately the source of his information, and to hear him discredit it so satirically. He recognized, however, that upon the evidence offered Mr. Burrows had not yet made out his case, and that therefore the mystery was yet far from solved.

"Look here, Burrows," said Mr. Barnes. "Take an older man's advice. Don't go too fast in this case. Before you come to any conclusion, find this man Jerry Morgan."

"Why, there won't be any trouble about that."

"Oh, then you know where he is?"

"Why, he is still with Berial. At least he was up to last night."

"Ah, now we come to it!" Mr. Barnes was gratified to find that Burrows had not kept full control of his case. "Last night was many hours ago. Morgan threw up his job this morning, and left."

"The devil you say!"

"Oh, yes," said Mr. Barnes, determined now to make Mr. Burrows a little uncomfortable. "I have no doubt he intends to skip out, but, of course, he cannot get away. You have him shadowed?"

"Why, no, I have not," said Mr. Burrows, dejectedly. "You see, I did not connect him in my mind with—"

"Perhaps he is not connected with the case in your mind, Burrows, but he is connected with it in fact. He is unquestionably the key to the situation at present. With him in our hands we could decide whether it was he or Randal who pawned those rings. Without him we can prove nothing. In short, until you get at him the case is at a standstill."

"You are right, Mr. Barnes," said Mr. Burrows, manfully admitting his error. "I have been an ass. I was so sure about Randal that I did not use proper precautions, and Morgan has

---

[*]A colleague or associate (usually in the same profession).

slipped through my fingers. But I'll find his trail, and I'll track him. I'll follow him to the opposite ocean if necessary, but I'll bring him back."

"That is the right spirit, Tom. Find him and bring him back if you can. If you cannot, then get the truth out of him. Let me say one thing more. For the present at least, work upon the supposition that it was he who pawned those rings. In that case he has at least two hundred dollars for travelling expenses."

"You are right. I'll begin at once without losing another minute."

"Where will you start?"

"I'll start where he started—at his own house. He's left there by now, of course, but I'll have a look at the place and talk a bit with the neighbors. When you hear from me again, I'll have Morgan."

## VIII

Mr. Barnes returned to his home that night feeling well satisfied with his day's work. With little real knowledge he had started out in the morning, and within ten hours he had dipped deeply into the heart of the mystery. Yet he felt somewhat like a man who has succeeded in working his way into the thickest part of a forest, with no certainty as to where he might emerge again, or how. Moreover, though he had seemingly accomplished so much during the first day, he seemed destined to make little headway for many days thereafter. On the second day of his investigation he ascertained one fact which was more misleading than helpful. It will be recalled that Mark Quadrant had told him that his brother had a scar on the sole of his foot made by cutting himself whilst in swimming. Mr. Barnes went to the Morgue early, and examined both feet most carefully. There was no such scar, nor was it possible that there ever could have been. The feet were absolutely unmarred. Could it be possible that, in spite of the apparently convincing proof that this body had been correctly identified, nevertheless a mistake had been made?

This question puzzled the detective mightily, and he longed impatiently for an opportunity to talk with one of the family, especially with the elder brother, Amos. Delay, however, seemed unavoidable. The police authorities, having finally accepted the identification, delivered the body to the Quadrants, and a second funeral occurred. Thus two more days elapsed before Mr. Barnes felt at liberty to intrude, especially as it was not known that he had been regularly retained by Mrs. Quadrant.

Meanwhile nothing was heard from Burrows, who had left the city, and, as a further annoyance, Mr. Barnes was unable to catch Mr. Mitchel at home though he called three times. Failing to meet that gentleman, and chafing at his enforced inactivity, the detective finally concluded to visit the cemetery in the hope of learning what had occurred when Mr. Mitchel had inspected the ashes. Again, however, was he doomed to disappointment. His request to be allowed to examine the contents of the urn was refused, strict orders to that effect having been imposed by the Chief of the regular detective force.

"You see," explained the superintendent, "we could not even let you look into the urn upon the order of one of the family, because they have claimed the body at the Morgue, and so they have no claim on these ashes. If a body was burned that day, then there is a body yet to be accounted for, and the authorities must guard the ashes as their only chance to make out a case. Of course they can't identify ashes, but the expert chemists claim they can tell whether a human body or only an empty coffin was put into the furnace."

"And are the experts making such an analysis?" asked Mr. Barnes.

"Yes. The Chief himself came here with two of them, the day before yesterday. They emptied out the ashes onto a clean marble slab, and looked all through the pile. Then they put some in two bottles, and sealed the bottles, and then put the balance back in the urn and sealed that also. So, you see, there isn't any way for me to let you look into that urn."

"No, of course not," admitted the detective, reluctantly. "Tell me, was any one else present at this examination besides the Chief and the two experts?"

"Yes. A gentleman they called Mitchel, I believe."

Mr. Barnes had expected this answer, yet it irritated him to hear it. Mr. Mitchel had information which the detective would have given much to share.

During the succeeding days he made numerous ineffectual efforts to have an interview with Amos Quadrant, but repeatedly was told that he was "Not at home." Mrs. Quadrant, too, had left town for a rest at one of their suburban homes, and Mark Quadrant had gone with her. The city house, with its closed shutters, seemed as silent as the grave, and the secret of what had occurred within those walls seemed almost hopelessly buried.

"What a pity," thought the detective, "that walls do not have tongues as well as ears."

A week later Mr. Barnes was more fortunate. He called at the Quadrant mansion, expecting to once more hear the servant say coldly, "Not at home," in answer to his inquiry for Mr. Quadrant, when, to his surprise and pleasure, Mr. Quadrant himself stepped out of the house as he approached it. The detective went up to him boldly, and said:

"Mr. Quadrant, I must have a few words with you."

"Must?" said Mr. Quadrant with an angry inflection. "I think not. Move out of my way, and let me pass."

"Not until you have given me an interview," said Mr. Barnes firmly, without moving.

"You are impertinent, sir. If you interfere with me further, I will have you arrested," said Mr. Quadrant, now thoroughly aroused.

"If you call a policeman," said Mr. Barnes, calmly, "I will have you arrested."

"And upon what charge, pray?" said Mr. Quadrant, contemptuously.

"I will accuse you of instigating the removal of your brother's body from the coffin."

"You are mad."

"There are others who hold this view, so it would be wise for you to move carefully in this matter."

"Would you object to telling me what others share your extraordinary opinion?"

"I did not say that it is my opinion. More than that, I will say that it is not my opinion, not at present at all events. But it is the view which is receiving close attention at police headquarters."

"Are you one of the detectives?"

"I am a detective, but not connected with the city force."

"Then by what right do you intrude yourself into this affair?"

Mr. Barnes knew that he must play his best card now, to gain his point with this man. He watched him closely as he answered:

"I am employed by Mrs. Quadrant."

There was an unmistakable start. Amos Quadrant was much disturbed to hear that his sister-in-law had hired a detective, and curiously enough he made no effort to hide his feelings. With some show of emotion he said in a low voice:

"In that case, perhaps, we should better have a talk together. Come in."

With these words he led the way into the house, and invited the detective into the same room wherein he had talked with Mark Quadrant. When they had found seats, Mr. Quadrant opened the conversation immediately.

"What is your name?" he asked.

"John Barnes," was the reply.

"Barnes? I have heard of you. Well, Mr. Barnes, let me be very frank with you. Above all things it has been my wish that this supposed mystery should not be cleared up. To me it is a matter of no consequence who did this thing, or why it was done. Indeed, what suspicions have crossed my mind make me the more anxious not to know the truth. Feeling thus, I should have done all in my power to hinder the work of the regular police. When you tell me that my sister-in-law has engaged your services, you take me so by surprise that I am compelled to think a bit in order to determine what course to pursue. You can readily understand that my position is a delicate and embarrassing one."

"I understand that thoroughly, and you have my sympathy, Mr. Quadrant."

"You may mean that well, but I do not thank you," said Mr. Quadrant, coldly. "I want no man's sympathy. This is purely an impersonal interview, and I prefer to have that distinctly prominent in our minds throughout this conversation. Let there be no misunderstanding and no false pretenses. You are a detective bent upon discovering the author of certain singular occurrences. I am a man upon whom suspicion has alighted; and, moreover, guilty or innocent, I desire to prevent you from accomplishing your purpose. I do not wish the truth to be known. Do we understand one another?"

"Perfectly," said Mr. Barnes, astonished by the man's manner and admiring his perfect self-control and his bold conduct.

"Then we may proceed," said Mr. Quadrant.

"Do you wish to ask me questions, or will you reply to one or two from me?"

"I will answer yours first, if you will reply to mine afterwards."

"I make no bargains. I will answer, but I do not promise to tell you anything unless it pleases me to do so. You have the same privilege. First, then, tell me how it happened that Mrs. Quadrant engaged you in this case."

"I called here, attracted merely by the extraordinary features of this case, and Mrs. Quadrant granted me a short interview, at the end of which she offered to place the matter in my hands as her representative."

"Ah! Then she did not of her own thought send for you?"

"No."

"You told me that the regular detectives are considering the theory that I instigated this affair. As you used the word instigated, it should follow that some other person, an accomplice, is suspected likewise. Is that the idea?"

"That is one theory."

"And who, pray, is my alleged accomplice?"

"That I cannot tell you without betraying confidence."

"Very good. Next you declared that you yourself do not share this view. Will you tell me on what grounds you exculpate me?"

"With pleasure. The assumed reason for this act of removing your brother from his coffin was to prevent the cremation. Now it was yourself who wished to have the body incinerated."

"You are mistaken. I did not wish it. On the contrary, I most earnestly wished that there should be no cremation. You see I incriminate myself."

He smiled painfully, and a dejected expression crossed his face. For an instant he looked like a man long tired of carrying some burden, then quickly he recovered his composure.

"You astonish me," said Mr. Barnes. "I was told by Mr. Mark that you insisted upon carrying out your brother's wish in this matter of disposing of his body."

"My brother told you that? Well, it is true. He and I quarrelled about it. He wished to have a regular burial, contrary to our brother's oft-repeated injunction. I opposed him, and, being the elder, I assumed the responsibility, and gave the orders."

"But you have admitted that you did not wish this?"

"Do we always have our wishes gratified in this world?"

The detective, watching the man's face closely, again noted that expression of weariness cross his features, and an instinctive feeling of pity was aroused. Once more the skein became more entangled. His own suspicion against Mark Quadrant rested upon the supposition that the act was committed with the intent of making capital out of it with the widow, and was based upon the theory that Amos wished to have his brother incinerated. If now it should transpire that after all it was Amos who managed the affair, his motive was a higher one, for, while appearing to carry out the wishes of his deceased brother, he must have aimed to gratify the widow, without admitting her to the knowledge that his hand had gained her purpose. This was a higher, nobler love. Was Amos Quadrant of this noble mould? The question crossing the detective's mind met a startling answer which prompted Mr. Barnes to ask suddenly:

"Is it true that, speaking of this cremation, you said: 'Let him burn; he'll burn in hell anyway'?"

Amos Quadrant flushed deeply, and his face grew stern as he answered:

"I presume you have witnesses who heard the words, therefore it would be futile to deny it. It was a brutal remark, but I made it. I was exasperated by something which Mark had said, and replied in anger."

"It is a sound doctrine, Mr. Quadrant," said the detective, "that words spoken in anger often more truly represent the speaker's feelings than what he says when his tongue is bridled."

"Well?"

"If we take this view, then it is apparent that you did not hold a very high regard for your brother."

"That is quite true. Why should I?"

"He was your brother."

"And because of the accident of birth, I was bound to love him? A popular fallacy, Mr. Barnes. He was equally bound, then, to love me, but he did not. Indeed he wronged me most grievously."

"By marrying the woman you loved?"

Mr. Barnes felt ashamed of his question, as a surgeon often

must be sorry to insert the scalpel. To his surprise it elicited no retort. Mr. Quadrant's reply was calmly spoken. All he said was:

"Yes, he did that."

"Did she know?" ventured the detective hesitatingly.

"No, I think not—I hope not."

There was a painful pause. Mr. Quadrant looked down at the floor, while Mr. Barnes watched him, trying to decide whether the man were acting a part with intent to deceive, as he had announced that he would not hesitate to do; or whether he were telling the truth, in which case the nobility of his character was brought more into perspective.

"Are you sure," said Mr. Barnes after a pause, "that the body taken from the river was that of your brother Rufus?"

"Why do you ask that?" said Mr. Quadrant, on the defensive at once. "Can there be any doubt?"

"Before I reply, let me ask you another question. Did your brother Rufus have a scar on the sole of his foot?"

The other man started perceptibly, and paused some time before answering. Then he asked:

"What makes you think so?"

"Mr. Mark Quadrant told me that his brother had such a scar, caused by gashing his foot while in swimming."

"Ah, that is your source of information. Well, when Mark told you that his brother had met with such an accident, he told you the truth."

"But did the accident leave a scar?" Mr. Barnes thought he detected a carefully worded evasive answer.

"Yes, the cut left a bad scar; one easily noticed."

"In that case I can reply to your question. If, as you both say, your brother had a scar on the sole of his foot, then there exists considerable doubt as to the identification of the body which was at the Morgue, the body which you have both accepted and buried as being that of your relative. Mr. Quadrant, there was no scar on that body."

"Odd, isn't it?" said Mr. Quadrant, without any sign of surprise.

"I should say it is very odd. How do you suppose it can be explained?"

"I do not know, and, as I have told you before, I do not care. Quite the reverse; the less you comprehend this case the better pleased I shall be."

"Mr. Quadrant," said Mr. Barnes, a little nettled, "since you so frankly admit that you wish me to fail, why should I not believe that you are telling me a falsehood when you state that your brother told me the truth?"

"There is no reason that I care to advance," said Mr. Quadrant, "why you should believe me, but if you do not, you will go astray. I repeat, what my brother told you is true."

It seemed to the detective that in all his varied experience he had never met with circumstances so exasperatingly intricate. Here was an identification for many reasons the most reliable that he had known, and now there appeared to be a flaw of such a nature that it could not be set aside. If the body was that of Mr. Quadrant, then both these men had lied. If they told the truth, then, in spite of science, the doctors, and the family, the identification had been false. In that case Rufus Quadrant had been cremated after all, and this would account for the statement in Mr. Mitchel's note that a human body had been incinerated. Could it be that these two brothers were jointly implicated in a murder, and had pretended to recognize the body at the Morgue in order to have it buried and to cover up their crime? It seemed incredible. Besides, the coincidence of the external and internal diseases was too great.

"I would like to ask you a few questions in relation to the occurrences on the day and evening preceding the funeral," said Mr. Barnes, pursuing the conversation, hoping to catch from the answers some clue that might aid him.

"Which funeral?" said Mr. Quadrant.

"The first. I have been told that you and your brother were present when the widow last viewed the face of her husband, and that at that time, about five o'clock, you jointly agreed that the coffin should not be opened again. Is this true?"

"Accurate in every detail."

"Was the coffin closed at once? That is, before you left the room?"

"The lower part of the coffin-top was, of course, in place and screwed fast when we entered the room. The upper part, exposing the face, was open. It was this that was closed in my presence."

"I would like to get the facts here very accurately, if you are willing. You say, closed in your presence. Do you mean merely covered, or was the top screwed fast before you went out of the room, and, if so, by whom?"

"Mark took our sister away, but Dr. Mortimer and myself remained until the screws were put in. Mr. Berial himself did that."

"Did you observe that the screws were odd? Different from common screws?"

Mr. Barnes hoped that the other man would betray something at this point, but he answered quite composedly:

"I think I did at the time, but I could not describe them to you now. I half remember that Mr. Berial made some such comment as 'No one can get these out again without my permission.'"

"Ah! He said that, did he? Yet some one must have gotten those screws out, for, if your identification was correct, your brother's body was taken out of that casket after the undertaker had put in those screws, which he said could not be removed without his permission. How do you suppose that was accomplished?"

"How should I know, Mr. Barnes, unless, indeed, I did it myself, or instigated or connived at the doing? In either case, do you suppose I would give you any information on such a point?"

"Did your brother Rufus have any rings on his fingers when placed in the coffin?" asked Mr. Barnes, swiftly changing the subject.

"Yes—three: a diamond, a ruby, and a ring bearing his initial set in diamonds."

"These rings were not on the body at the Morgue."

"Neither was that scar," said Mr. Quadrant, with a suppressed laugh.

"But this is different," said Mr. Barnes. "I did not find the scar, but I have found the rings."

"Very clever of you, I am sure. But what does that prove?"

"It proves that your brother's body was taken from the coffin before the coffin was placed in the crematory furnace."

"Illogical and inaccurate," said Mr. Quadrant. "You prove by the recovery of the rings, merely that the rings were taken from the coffin."

"Or, from the body after it was taken out," interjected Mr. Barnes.

"In either case it is of no consequence. You have rooted up a theft, that is all. Catch the thief and jail him, if you like. I care nothing about that. It is the affair of my brother's death and burial that I wish to see dropped by the inquisitive public."

"Yes, but suppose I tell you that the theory is that the man who stole the rings was your accomplice in the main matter? Don't you see that when we catch him, he is apt to tell all that he knows?"

"When you catch him? Then you have not caught him yet. For so much I am grateful." He did not seem to care how incriminating his words might sound.

"One thing more, Mr. Quadrant. I understand that you retired at about ten o'clock on that night—the night prior to the first funeral, I mean. You left your brother Mark down here?"

"Yes."

"Later you came downstairs again."

"You seem to be well posted as to my movements."

"Not so well as I wish to be. Will you tell me why you came down?"

"I have not admitted that I came downstairs."

"You were seen in the hall very late at night, or early in the morning. You took the lamp out of the room where the casket was, and came in here and looked at your brother, who was asleep. Then you returned the lamp and went upstairs. Do you admit now that you had just come downstairs?"

"I admit nothing. But to show you how little you can prove, suppose I ask you how you know that I had just come downstairs? Why may it not be that I had been out of the house, and had just come in again when your informant saw me?"

"Quite true. You might have left the house. Perhaps it was then that the body was taken away?"

"If it was taken away, that was certainly as good a time as any."

"What time?"

"Oh, let us say between twelve and two. Very few people would be about the street at that hour, and a wagon stopping before a door would attract very little attention. Especially if it were an undertaker's wagon."

"An undertaker's wagon?" exclaimed Mr. Barnes, as this suggested a new possibility.

"Why, yes. If, as you say, there was an accomplice in this case, the fellow who stole the rings, you know, he must have been one of the undertaker's men. If so, he would use their wagon, would he not?"

"I think he would," said Mr. Barnes sharply. "I thank you for the point. And now I will leave you."

## IX

Mr. Barnes walked rapidly, revolving in his mind the new ideas which had entered it during the past few minutes. Before this morning he had imagined that the body of Rufus Quadrant had been taken away between five and six o'clock, in the undertaker's wagon. But it had never occurred to him that this same wagon could have been driven back to the house at any hour of the day or night, without causing the policeman on that beat to suspect any wrong. Thus, suddenly, an entirely new phase had been placed upon the situation. Before, he had been interested in knowing which man had been left behind; whether it had been Morgan or Randal. Now he was more anxious to know whether the wagon had been taken again from the stable on that night, and, if so, by whom. Consequently he went first to the undertaker's shop, intending to interview Mr. Berial, but that gentleman was out. Therefore he spoke again with Randal, who recognized him at once and greeted him cordially.

"Why, how do you do," said he. "Glad you're round again. Anything turned up in the Quadrant case?"

"We are getting at the truth slowly," said the detective, watching his man closely. "I would like to ask you to explain one or two things to me if you can."

"Maybe I will, and maybe not. It wouldn't do to promise to answer questions before I hear what they are. I ain't exactly what you would call a fool."

"Did you not tell me that it was Morgan who was left at the house after the coffin was closed, and that you came away with Mr. Berial?"

"Don't remember whether I told you or not. But you've got it straight."

"But they say at the stables that it was you who drove the wagon back there?"

"That's right, too. What of it?"

"But I understood that Morgan brought the wagon back?"

"So he did; back here to the shop. He had to leave all our tools and things here, you see. Then he went off to his dinner, and I took the horse and wagon round to the stables."

"Where do you stable?"

"Harrison's, Twenty-fourth Street, near Lex."

"Now, another matter. You told me about the loss of those rings?"

"Yes, and I gave you the tip where you might find them again. Did you go there?"

"Yes; you were right. The rings were pawned exactly where you sent me."

"Oh, I don't know," said the fellow, airishly. "I ought to be on the police force, I guess. I can find out a few things, I think."

"It isn't hard to guess what you know," said the detective, sharply.

"What do you mean?" Randal was on the defensive at once.

"I mean," said Mr. Barnes, "that it was you who pawned those rings."

"That's a lie, and you can't prove it."

"Don't be too sure of that. We have the pawn-tickets."

This shot went home. Randal looked frightened, and was evidently confused.

"That's another lie," said he, less vigorously. "You can't scare me. If you have got them, which you haven't, you won't find my name on them."

"No; you used your friend Morgan's name, which was a pretty low trick."

"Look here, you detective," said Randal blusteringly, "I don't allow no man to abuse me. You can't talk that way to me. All this talk of yours is rot. That's what it is, rot!"

"Look here, Randal. Try to be sensible if you can. I have not yet made up my mind whether you are a scoundrel or a fool. Suppose you tell me the truth about those tickets. It will be safest, I assure you."

Randal looked at the detective and hesitated. Mr. Barnes continued:

"There is no use to lie any longer. You were shadowed, and you were seen when you tore up the tickets. The pieces were picked up and put together, and they call for those rings. Don't you see we have you fast unless you can explain how you got the tickets?"

"I guess you're givin' it to me straight," said Randal after a long pause. "I guess I better take your advice and let you have it right. One afternoon I saw Morgan hide something in one of the coffins in the shop. He tucked it away under the satin linin'. I was curious, and I looked into it after he'd gone that night. I found the pawn-tickets. Of course I didn't know what they were for except that it was rings. But I guessed it was for some stuff he'd stolen from the corpse of somebody. For it was him took the other jewels I told you about, and I seen him with a screw-driver the match to the boss's. So I just slipped the tickets in my pocket thinkin' I'd have a hold on him. Next day I read about this man bein' found in the river, and I stopped to the Morgue, and, just as I thought, his rings was gone. I worried over that for an hour or two, and then I thought I better not keep the tickets, so I tore them up and threw them away."

"That, you say, was the night after this affair was published in the papers?"

"No; it was the same night."

"That is to say, the night of that day on which I came here and had a talk with you?"

"No, it was the night before. You're thinkin' about the mornin' papers, but I seen it first in the afternoon papers."

This statement dispelled a doubt which had entered the mind of the detective, who remembered that Mr. Burrows had told him that the pawn-ticket incident had occurred on the evening previous to their meeting. This explanation, however, tallied with that, and Mr. Barnes was now inclined to credit the man's story.

"Very good," said he. "You may be telling the truth. If you have nothing to do with this case, you ought to be willing to give me some assistance. Will you?"

Randal had been so thoroughly frightened that he now seemed only too glad of the chance to win favor in the eyes of Mr. Barnes.

"Just you tell me what you want, and I'm your man," said he.

"I want to find out something at the stable, and I think you can get the information for me better than I can myself."

"I'll go with you right away. The boy can mind the shop while we're gone. Charlie, you just keep an eye on things till I get back, will you? I won't be out more'n ten minutes. Come on, Mr. Barnes, I'm with you."

On the way to the stable Mr. Barnes directed Randal as to what he wished to learn, and then at his suggestion waited for him in a liquor saloon nearby, while he went alone to the stable. In less than ten minutes Randal hurried into the place, flushed with excitement and evidently bubbling over with importance. He drew the detective to one side and spoke in whispers.

"Say," said he, "you're on the right tack. The wagon was out again that night, and not on any proper errand, neither."

"Tell me what you have learned," said Mr. Barnes.

"Of course the night watchman ain't there now, but Jimmy, the day superintendent, is there, and I talked with him. He says there was some funny business that night. First I asked him about the wagon bein' out or not, and he slaps his hand on his leg, and he says: 'By George!' says he, 'that's the caper. Didn't you put that wagon in its right place when you brung it in that afternoon?' he says to me. 'Of course,' says I; 'where do you think I'd put it?' 'Well,' says he, 'next mornin' it was out in the middle of the floor, right in the way of everything. The boys was cussin' you for your carelessness. I wasn't sure in my own mind or I would have spoke; but I thought I seen you shove that wagon in its right place.' 'So I did,' says I, 'and if it was in the middle of the stable, you can bet it was moved after I left. Now who moved it?' 'I don't know,' says he, 'but I'll tell you another thing what struck me as odd. I didn't have nothin' particular to do that night, and I dropped in for an hour or so to be sociable like with Jack'—that's the night watchman. 'While I was there,' he goes on, 'while I was there, who should come in but Jerry Morgan! He didn't stop long, but he took us over to the saloon and balled us off'—that means he treated to drinks. 'Next day I come round about six o'clock as usual,' says Jimmy, goin' on, 'and there was Jack fast asleep. Now that's the fust time that man ever dropped off while on watch, and he's been here nigh on to five years. I shook him and tried every way to 'waken him, but it didn't seem to do no good. He'd kind of start up and look about dazed, and even talk a bit, but as soon as I'd let up, he'd drop off again. I was makin' me a cup of coffee, and, thinkin' it might rouse him, I made him drink some, and, do you know, he was all right in a few minutes. At the time I didn't think much about it, but since then I have thought it over a good deal, and, do you know what I think now?' 'No,' says I; 'what do you think?' 'I think,' says he, 'I think that Jimmy was drugged, and if he was, Jerry Morgan done the trick when he balled us off, and you can bet it was him took that wagon out that night.' That's the story Jimmy tells, Mr. Barnes, and it's a corker, ain't it?"

"It certainly is important," said Mr. Barnes.

Once more he had food for thought. This narrative was indeed important; the drowsiness of the watchman and his recovery after drinking coffee suggested morphine. The detective likewise recalled the story of the butler who claimed that he had seen Mark Quadrant asleep while he was supposed to be guarding the coffin. Then, too, there was the empty paper which had once held some powder, and which he had himself found in the room where Mark Quadrant had slept. Had he too been drugged? If so, the question arose, Did this man Morgan contrive to mix the morphine with something which he thought it probable that the one sitting up with the corpse would drink, or had Amos given his brother the sleeping-potion? In one case it would follow that Morgan was the principal in this affair, while in the other he was merely an accomplice. If his hand alone managed all, then it might be that he had a deeper and more potent motive than the mere removal of the body to avoid cremation, the latter being a motive which the detective had throughout hesitated to adopt because it seemed so weak. If Morgan substituted another body for the one taken from the coffin, then the statement of Mr. Mitchel that a body had been cremated was no longer a discrepancy. There was but one slightly disturbing thought. All the theorizing in which he now indulged was based on the assumption that Randal was not deceiving. Yet how could he be sure of that? Tom Burrows would have said to him: "Mr. Barnes, that fellow is lying to you. His story may be true in all except that it was himself and not Morgan who did these things." For while he had thought it best to let Randal go alone to the stable to make inquiries, this had placed him in the position of receiving the tale at secondhand, so that Randal might have colored it to suit himself. For the present, he put aside these doubts and decided to pursue this clue until he proved it a true or false scent. He dismissed Randal with an injunction to keep his tongue from wagging, and proceeded to the house of the man Morgan, regretting now that he had not done so before.

The tenement on Eleventh Avenue was one of those buildings occupying half a block, having stores on the street, with narrow, dark, dismal hallways, the staircases at the farther end being invisible from the street door, even on the sunniest days, without a match. Overhead, each hallway offered access to four flats, two front and two back, the doors being side by side. These apartments each included two or three rooms and what by courtesy might be called a bathroom, though few indeed of the tenants utilized the latter for the purpose for which it had been constructed, preferring to occupy this extra space with such of their impedimenta as might not be in constant use.

When one enters a place of this character asking questions, if he addresses any of the adults he is likely to receive scant information in reply. Either these people do not know even the names of their next-door neighbors, or else, knowing, they are unwilling to take the trouble to impart the knowledge. The children, however, and they are as numerous as grasshoppers in a hayfield, not only know everything, but tell what they know willingly. It is also a noteworthy fact that amidst such squalor and filth, with dirty face and bare legs, it is not uncommon to find a child, especially a girl, who will give answers, not only with extreme show of genuine intelligence, but, as well, with a deferential though dignified courtesy which would grace the reception-rooms of upper Fifth Avenue.

It was from such an urchin, a girl of about twelve, that Mr. Barnes learned that Jerry Morgan had lived on the fifth floor back.

"But he's gone away, I guess," she added.

"Why do you think so?" asked Mr. Barnes.

"Oh, 'cause he ain't been in the saloon 'cross the way for 'bout a week, and he didn't never miss havin' his pint of beer every night 's long 's he's been here."

"Do you think I could get into his room?" asked Mr. Barnes.

"I could get you our key, an' you could try," suggested the girl. "I reckon one key will open any door in this house. It's cheaper to get locks in a bunch that way, I guess, an' besides, poor folks don't get robbed much anyhow, an' so they ain't got no 'casion to lock up every time they go out. What little they've got don't tempt the robbers, I guess. Maybe the 'punushment fits the crime' too quick."

"'The punishment fits the crime,' you think," said Mr. Barnes with a smile. "Where did you get that from?"

"Oh, I seen the Mikado oncet," said the girl rather proudly. "But I didn't mean what you said; I said it fits 'too quick'; that's too snug, you know, though sometimes it's 'quick' too. You see, I guess they don't get enough out of flats like these to pay for the risk."

"You are quite a philosopher," said Mr. Barnes, approvingly. "Now run and get the key, and we will see whether it fits or not."

She hurried upstairs, and was awaiting Mr. Barnes, with the key in her hand, when he reached the third landing. This she gave to him, and then followed him up the remaining flights, where she pointed out the door which led into Morgan's flat. The key was not needed, as the door was not locked, and the detective pushed it open and entered. The room seemed bare enough, what little furniture there was being too evidently the product of a second-hand furniture store. There seemed little hope of finding anything helpful to his investigation in this room, yet the detective, with his usual thoroughness, examined every drawer, and every corner or crevice in which anything might have been hidden, or have been accidentally dropped, and at last he did discover something which more than repaid him.

In the darkest corner of the dark closet, where perhaps it had dropped unperceived, he found an old vest, of no value in itself. But a search of the pockets brought an exclamation of gratification to the detective's lips, as from one of them he drew forth a folded paper still containing a whitish powder. Mr. Barnes was certain that this powder was morphine, and at length he felt his feet on solid ground in trailing the criminal. No longer need he doubt Randal. His story of the probable drugging of the night watchman at the stable now became not only credible, but probable. Thinking that he might gain something by further questioning the girl, Mr. Barnes said:

"Why, here is some medicine! Perhaps he was sick and has gone away for his health."

With the keen intelligence of her class, the girl replied:

"Some folks go away for their health without bein' sick."

"How do you mean?"

"When it gets so it ain't healthy for them to stay in town, you know."

"You mean for fear of the police?"

"Sure! What else?"

"But do you think that this man Morgan would do anything that would make him afraid of meeting a policeman?"

"Oh, I don't know. But 'birds of a feather flock together,' you know. One of his pals was pinched, and he's workin' for the country now, on the Island."

"Who was that?" Mr. Barnes did not regret the time spent in talking with this observing youngster.

"I don't know his right name. They called him Billy the Red, over to the saloon."

Mr. Barnes started. This was a clue indeed. This was a well-known criminal whom she had named; one who had earned his sobriquet by killing two men in a barroom fight, when he had been one of the celebrated Whyo gang. If Morgan consorted with such as he, there could be little doubt as to his social status.

"You say Billy the Red was one of Morgan's pals. Did he have any others that you know of?" Mr. Barnes continued.

"Well, he used to be with him most till he went up, but lately he's been travellin' with Tommy White."

"Where can I find him; do you know?"

"Better look him up on the Island, too, I guess. He ain't been round here for quite some days."

"Perhaps he does not come because Morgan is away?"

"Oh, no, that can't be, 'cause he stopped showin' up before Morgan left. The neighbors was beginnin' to wonder and talk, just 'bout the time Morgan skipped. You see, Tommy White he lived right next door, in the next flat, him and Nellie."

"Ah, he had a wife?"

"I don't know about that. She was his girl anyway, though some thought Morgan was sweet on her too."

Mr. Barnes thought the fog was lifting.

"Where is this Nellie now?"

"You can search me! She's gone too. The hull three has skipped out."

"What, all three at the same time?"

"No, that's the funny part of it. That's what makes folks talk. You see, we didn't see nothin' of Tommy White for two or three days, but Nellie she was round all right. But when Morgan he cut it, Nellie she lit out too."

"Let me get this right, my girl. And mind you make no mistake, for this is important."

"I ain't makin' no mistakes, mister. I'm givin' it to you dead right, and that's more 'n you'd get out of anybody else in this castle. But I've got my reasons, and," this she added with a sly wink, "you ain't fooled me any, you know. You're a detective, that's what you are."

"What makes you think so?"

"Oh, there ain't much to guess. People dressed like you don't come to a place like this and nose into another man's rooms just for amusement. Not much they don't. It's business with you."

"Well, never mind that. Tell me, are you sure that White disappeared first, and that the girl was here afterwards, but that she has not been seen since Morgan went away?"

"That's right. You got it straight the first time. Now what do you make of it? I know my own opinion."

"Suppose you tell me your opinion first," said Mr. Barnes, anxious to hear her answer.

"Well," said the girl, "it's very simple, what I think. I think Tommy's been done for."

"Done for?" Mr. Barnes comprehended her meaning but preferred to have her speak more plainly.

"Yes, done for, that's what I said. They've put him out of the way, those two. And if that's right, it's a shame, 'cause Tommy was a good fellow. It was him took me to the theatre, that time when I seen the Mikado."

Evidently this one visit to a theatre had been an event in

her weary little life, and the man who had given her that bit of pleasure and had afforded her that one glimpse of what she would have described as the "dressed-up folks," had by that act endeared himself to her childish heart. If he had been injured, her little soul longed for vengeance, and she was ready to be the instrument which might lead Justice to her victim.

Mr. Barnes began to believe that the solution of this mystery was near at hand. He left the building, thanking the child for what she had told him, and promising to find out what had become of her friend Tommy White. Crossing the street he entered the saloon where the girl had told him that Morgan had been in the habit of buying his daily pint of beer. By talking with the bartender he hoped to elicit further information.

The gentlemanly dispenser of liquid refreshment, whose constant boast was that he knew how to manufacture over three hundred different mixed drinks without using any intoxicant, stood beside the mahogany counter, polishing up the glasses, which he piled in an imposing pyramid on the shelf at the back, where the display was made doubly attractive by the plate mirror behind. His hair was scrupulously brushed and his short white coat was immaculately clean. Fortunately there was no one else in the place, so that the detective was afforded a good opportunity for free conversation. He asked for a Manhattan cocktail, and admired the dexterity with which the man prepared the drink. Raising it to his lips and tasting it as a connoisseur might, Mr. Barnes said:

"Could not be better at the Waldorf."

"Oh, I don't know," said the fellow, deprecatingly, but pleased at the implied compliment.

"Your face is very familiar to me," said Mr. Barnes; "have you ever met me before?"

"Never in my life," said the bartender, without the slightest change of expression.

"That's odd," said Mr. Barnes, pursuing the point with a

purpose; "I am pretty good at faces. I seldom forget one, and just as seldom make a mistake. I would almost swear I have seen you before."

"I was tending bar at the Astor House for two years. Perhaps you saw me there," suggested the man.

"Ah, that is it," said Mr. Barnes, pretending to accept this explanation; "I often take my luncheon there. By the way, I suppose you are pretty well acquainted around the neighborhood?"

"Oh, I know a few people," said the man, cautiously.

"You know Tommy White, of course?"

"Do I?"

"Don't you?"

"I might, without knowing his name. Our customers don't all leave their cards when they buy a drink. I don't know your name, for instance."

"Yes, but I do not live in the neighborhood. White must come here often."

"Well, he hasn't been in lately," said the bartender, and then stopped short as he noted the slip that he had made. The detective did not choose to appear to notice it, but asked:

"That is the point. Isn't it odd that he should have disappeared?"

"Oh, I don't know. A man can go out of town if he wants to, I guess."

"Do you know that White went out of town?"

"No."

"Have you seen Tommy White since Jerry Morgan skipped?"

"See here! what the devil are you asking me all these questions for? Who are you, anyway, and what are you after?"

"I am Jack Barnes, detective, but I'm not after you, Joe Allen, alias Fred Martin, alias Jimmy Smith, alias Bowery Bill, alias the Plug."

This sally left the man stolidly unmoved, but it affected his attitude towards his questioner, nevertheless, as he sullenly answered:

"There's nothing you can get against me, so I don't scare even if you know me. If you don't want me, what do you want?"

"Look here, Joe," said Mr. Barnes, in friendly, confidential tones, "a bluff does not go with me, and you know it never did. Now why did you not acknowledge that you knew me when I first came in?"

"What's the use of courtin' trouble? I wasn't sure you'd remember my face. It's quite a time since we met."

"True. It is five years since that Bond Street affair, and you got three years for that, if I remember rightly."

"Well, I served my time, didn't I? So that's ended, ain't it?"

"Yes. But what about that little business of the postage-stamp robbery out in Trenton?"

"Why, I didn't have no hand in that."

"Well, two of your pals did, and when they were caught and sent up they were square enough not to peach on you. The Mulberry Street crowd did not know how thick you were with those boys, or you might have got into trouble. But I knew, and you know that I knew."

"Well, what if you did? I tell you I wasn't in that."

"You would not like to be obliged to prove where you were that night, would you?"

"Oh, I suppose it's always hard to prove I was one place, when fellows like you go on the stand and swear I was somewhere else. So, as I said before, what's the use of courtin' trouble?"

"Now you are sensible, and as I said, I am not after you. All I want is some information. Give me another cocktail, and have one yourself."

"Thanks, I will. Go ahead with your catechism; I'll answer so long as you don't try to make me squeal on any of my friends. I'd go up before I'd do that. And you know that."

"That's all right. I know you're square, and that is why I feel sure you would not be mixed up in a murder."

"Murder?"

This time the fellow was frightened. How could he be sure that this detective was not trying to entrap him? How could he know positively that he had not been accused by some pal who wished to shift responsibility from himself to another? This is the Damocles sword that ever hangs over the head of the wrong-doer. His most chosen companions may either tell of what he has done, or accuse him of crime which he has not committed.

"I am afraid so. But what are you worrying over? Did I not tell you that you are not in it? Listen to me, Joe. This Jerry Morgan has skipped out of town, and it looks as though he took Tommy White's girl Nellie with him. Now, where is Tommy White?"

"I don't know a thing. I swear I don't."

"Yes, you do. You do not know what has become of him, but you know something. Morgan isn't any pal of yours, is he?"

"No."

"Very well. Then why not tell me what you know? If he has done anything to White, he ought not to go free, ought he? You do not stand in with murder, do you?"

"No, I don't. But how do I know there's been any murder?"

"You don't know it, but since I suggested it to you, you think so. I see that in your face. Now, what do you know?"

"Well, I don't know much, but what I know I don't want used to make another fellow go to the chair."

"That is no affair of yours. You are not responsible for what the law does. Come, I have no more time to waste. Tell me what you know, or say right out that you will not. Then I will know what to do."

The implied threat decided the man, and without further attempt at evasion he said:

"Well, I suppose there ain't any use my runnin' any risk for a man that's nothin' to me. It's this way: Morgan's an old-time crook—I suppose you know that?" Mr. Barnes nodded, although this was news to him. Allen continued: "He's been at it since he was a kid. Was in the reformatory, and learned more there about crooked work in a year than he would have picked up in ten out-side. He's never done time, though, since he graduated from that institution. Learned enough, I guess, to keep out of sight of your crowd. Two years ago he moved into this neighborhood and since then I've seen him in here a good deal. He took up with Tommy White—a young fellow that would have lived straight only he was in bad company, and was railroaded with a gang for a job he really had no hand in. That settled him. When he came out of Sing Sing he wasn't likely to go for a straight job at a dollar a day, when he could lay around idle and pick up a good thing every now and then that would keep him going. I guess he and Morgan done a good many jobs together; anyway, they never was short of money. One thing was funny about those two—nobody ever seen them in the daytime. They used to say they was 'workin',' but that didn't go with the crowd that hangs out here. Neither Morgan nor White would work if they could help it. They was just like brothers, those two, till White took up with this girl Nellie. I think Morgan was jealous of his luck from the first, 'cause the girl is a peach. One of your real blondes, without no bleachin' stuff. She's got a skin like velvet, and hands and feet like a lady. White soon found out that his pal was sweet on the girl, and many a time they've rowed over her. Finally, about two weeks ago the two of them was in here, and they was drinkin' pretty hard and just ready for a scrap, when the girl comes in. Morgan goes up to her and puts his arm round her and kisses her plump. White was mad in a minute, but he turned on her instead of him and he says, says he: 'Nellie, I want you to hammer that duffer over the head for doin' that,' and he picks up a beer glass and hands it to her. Nellie she takes the glass, and she says: 'I've heard of a kiss for a blow,' she says, 'but a blow for a kiss is a new one on me. It ain't that way in the Bible, Tommy, so I guess if you want any hammerin' done, you'd better do it yourself. I'm thinkin' of joinin' the Salvation Army, you know.' This made Morgan and the crowd laugh, and White got fierce. He snatched the glass out of Nellie's hand and made for Morgan. But Morgan he ducks and lets White go by him, and he picks up a beer glass too; then when White came for him again he landed a terrible blow with the glass right back of White's ear. Tommy went down in a heap and lay on the ground quiverin'. The whole thing happened so quick nobody could interfere. Morgan got sober in a second, I tell you, and he was scared. Everybody crowded round, and the girl she was a wonder. You'd think bein' a woman she'd cry and make a fuss? Not a bit of it. She got some ice and put it on White's head, and threw water in his face, and she puts her ear down to his heart, and then she looks up after a bit, and she says, as cool as could be: 'Boys, he's only stunned. He'll come round all right. Some of you help get him home, and I'll look after him. He'll sleep off his liquor and he won't know what hurt him when he wakes in the mornin'.' Well, Morgan and the others they did what she said. They took White up and carted him over to his flat, and put him to bed. My! but he was limp, and his face was that blue it's been before me ever since."

"Did White get over that blow?"

"That's the point. Nellie and Morgan said he did; that he was a bit sore next day and had a headache. That was likely enough. But when you talked about murder a while ago, I admit I got scared, cause White's never been seen since that night."

"You are sure of that?"

"Dead sure. Nellie said he was gone out of town, and the boys swallowed the story. But when both Morgan and Nellie skipped it looked bad, and folks began to talk. As for me, I've been nervous for days. Why, when that body was picked out of the river I just couldn't keep away from the Morgue. I just had to have a peep at it. I was sure it would be White, and that Morgan had pitched him over. My, but wasn't I glad to see it was another man!"

Assuring Allen that his story would not be used in any way that would bring him into conflict with the authorities, Mr.

Barnes left the saloon and went to his office, feeling that at last this problem had been solved. Evidently White had died of his wound, and when Morgan learned that the coffin of Mr. Quadrant was not to be opened before it was consigned to the crematory, he had conceived one of the most ingenious schemes ever devised for disposing of a murdered body. By placing White in the coffin and allowing his body to be incinerated, all traces of his crime would seem to have been obliterated. To accomplish this it was necessary to have the use of the undertaker's wagon, and this he had managed by drugging the watchman, as well as Mark Quadrant. The transfer made, he was still left with the other body, and his disposition of that was the most ingenious part of the plan. By throwing the corpse of Rufus Quadrant into the water he apparently took little risk. It could not be recognized as White of course, and if correctly identified a mystery would be created that ought to baffle the detectives, however clever they might be. Mr. Barnes felt that he had been fortunate to learn so much from such unpromising clues.

At his office he found a telegram and a letter, both bearing on the case. The telegram was from Mr. Burrows, and informed him that Morgan had been captured in Chicago, and would be in New York on the following day. This was more than gratifying, and Mr. Barnes mentally praised the young detective. The letter was from Mr. Mitchel, and read:

"Friend Barnes:

"*At last I have fathomed the Quadrant mystery. Will drop in on you about noon to-morrow and tell you how the affair was managed. You will be surprised, I am sure.*

"Mitchel."

"Will I?" said Mr. Barnes to himself.

# X

Mr. Burrows arrived at the offices of Mr. Barnes about eleven o'clock on the following morning, which much pleased the older detective, who wished to have his case complete before the arrival of Mr. Mitchel.

"Well, Tom," said Mr. Barnes, cordially, "so you have caught your man and brought him back?"

"Did I not promise you that I would?" replied Mr. Burrows.

"Yes, but even a cleverer man than yourself cannot always hope to keep such a promise. Do you know that this fellow, Morgan, is a professional crook who has never been caught at his work before?"

"So he has told me," said Mr. Burrows, modestly refraining from any boastfulness.

"He told you the truth in that instance, and I trust you have also succeeded in getting a confession from him as to his connection with this Quadrant matter?"

"He has pretended to make a clean breast of it, but of course we must verify his story. One cannot place too much faith in the confessions of a crook."

"Does he admit that he took the rings?"

"Yes, it seems you were right there."

"Does he explain how and why he took the body from the coffin?"

"On the contrary, he denies having done so."

"Then he lies," said Mr. Barnes. "I have not been idle since you went away, but my tale will keep. Let me hear first what Morgan's alleged confession amounts to."

"He admits that he stole the rings. He has a duplicate of that screw-driver of which old Berial is so fond of bragging, and when he was left alone with the body, he opened the coffin and took the rings, and, in keeping with his limited standard of morals, he offers a rather ingenious excuse for his act."

"I should like to hear a good excuse for robbing the dead."

"That is his point exactly. He says that as the dead cannot own property, the dead cannot be robbed. As the family had declared that the coffin was not to be opened again, Morgan says he considered the rings as practically consigned to the furnace, and then he asks, 'What was the use of seeing stuff like that burned up, when it was good money to me?' It is a nice point, Mr. Barnes. If the owner elects to throw away or destroy his property, can we blame a man for appropriating the same?"

"We may not be able to blame him, but we certainly have the power to punish him. The law will not accept such sophistry as palliation for crime. What else does the fellow admit?"

"The rest of his tale is quite interesting, and I think would surprise you, unless, indeed, you have discovered the truth yourself."

"I think I could make a shrewd guess," said Mr. Barnes.

"Well, I wish you would tell me your story first. You see, after all, I am the legally employed investigator of this matter, and I should like to hear your story before telling mine, that I may be absolutely certain that your results have been arrived at by a different line of work, though of course you understand that I do not for a moment imagine that you would intentionally color your story after hearing mine."

"I understand you perfectly, Tom," said Mr. Barnes, kindly, "and I am not at all offended. You are right to wish to have the two stories independently brought before your reasoning faculties. Morgan tells you that he stole the rings in the afternoon. Perhaps he did, and perhaps he took them later. It does not now seem to be material. The subsequent facts, as I deduce them from the evidence, are as follows: Morgan had a pal, who was sweet on a girl called Nellie. By the way, did you get any trace of her?"

"She was with Morgan when I found him and she has come back with us."

"Good. Very good. It seems that Morgan also admired the girl, and that finally he and his pal had a saloon fight over her, during which Morgan struck the other man with a beer glass. This man fell to the floor unconscious, and was taken to his home in that condition. He has not been seen in the neighborhood since. Now we come to another series of events. Morgan admits taking the rings. Suppose we accept his story. He then left the house and drove the wagon back to the shop. Randal took it from there to the stables, but later in the evening Morgan visited the stables and induced the night watchman to take a drink. That drink was drugged, and the drug was morphine. The watchman slept soundly, and there is little doubt that while thus unconscious Morgan took the undertaker's wagon out of the stable on some errand. There is an interesting series of links in this chain which convicts Morgan of using morphine to accomplish his purpose. First, it is nearly certain that the watchman was drugged; second, a witness will testify that he found Mr. Mark Quadrant sound asleep, when he was supposed to be watching the coffin; third, I have taken from the pocket of a vest found in Morgan's rooms a powder which a chemist declares is morphine. Is not that fairly good evidence?"

"It is good evidence, Mr. Barnes, but it does not prove that Morgan took that body from the coffin."

"What, then, does it show?"

"It makes him an accomplice at least. He undoubtedly drugged the watchman and took the wagon out of the stables, but beyond that you can prove nothing. You have not offered any motive that would actuate him in stealing the body."

"The motive is quite sufficient, I assure you. His pal, whom he struck down with the beer glass, and who has not been seen by his neighbors since that night, must have died from the blow. It was his body that was cremated."

Mr. Burrows shook his head, and seemed sorry to upset the calculations of his old friend.

"I am afraid you cannot prove that," said he. "Tell me, what was the name of this pal? Have you learned that?"

"Yes; Tommy White."

"Do you know him by any other name?"

"No; but as he is unquestionably a crook he probably has a dozen aliases."

"One will suffice at present. Tommy White is none other than your disinterested informant, Jack Randal."

"What!" exclaimed Mr. Barnes, recognizing instantly that if this were true his whole edifice tumbled to the ground.

"Yes. I think that Morgan has told me a clean-cut story, though, as I said before, we must verify it. You see, he is a crook and ready to acquire other people's property, but I think he has a wholesome dread of the electric chair that will keep him out of murder. He was at one time a pal of Billy the Red, now in Sing Sing. After that fellow was put away he took up with Tommy White, alias Jack Randal. Randal, it seems, induced Morgan to join him in his nefarious schemes. The undertaker has told you, perhaps, as he has told me, that he invented his patent coffin because of numerous grave robberies that had occurred in one of the cemeteries. He little suspected that the robbers were his two assistants. These fellows would steal from the dead, while preparing the bodies for burial, if it seemed safe, as, for example, was the case with Mr. Quadrant, where it was known that the coffin was not again to be opened. In other cases they would visit the grave together. Sometimes they merely appropriated what jewelry there might be, but in not a few instances they stole the bodies as well, disposing of them to medical students."

"What a diabolical partnership!"

"Yes, indeed. Now, coming to the saloon fight, you are correct enough except as to the results. White, or Randal, was unconscious during the greater part of the night, and in the morning had but a dim recollection of what had occurred. He understood, however, that his injury had been the result of a fight with

Morgan, and also that the girl Nellie had 'thrown him over,' to adopt the vernacular. He therefore left the neighborhood, and though the two men continued to work for Berial, they did not resume their friendship. White evidently was nursing his grievances, and only awaited an opportunity to make trouble for his old pal Morgan. This he hoped to accomplish by the information which he gave to you."

"You will hardly expect me to believe that Morgan gave up his position and left town without some better reason than a mere quarrel with his pal, and a petty theft?"

"Morgan did not give up his position, nor did he leave town of his own volition. He was sent away."

"Sent away? By whom?"

"By the principal in this case. I told you from the first that there were two in it. He has admitted to me what I did not know, but what I believe now because you tell me the same story. He confesses that he drugged the watchman at the stables and then drove the wagon away. But he denies that he either took Quadrant's body from the coffin, or indeed that he drove the wagon to the Quadrant house. In fact, he says he was paid to get the wagon unknown to the watchman, and that he was furnished with the powders with which he was to drug the man."

"Am I to understand that one of the dead man's brothers hired Morgan to do this?"

Mr. Barnes was thinking of his conversation with Amos Quadrant, during which that gentleman had suggested that an undertaker's wagon might approach the house at any hour without attracting attention. He was consequently astonished by the younger detective's reply.

"No," said Mr. Burrows; "he does not implicate either of the Quadrants. He declares that it was old Berial who hired him to do his part of the job."

# XI

New possibilities crowded into the thoughts of Mr. Barnes as he heard this unexpected statement. Berial hired Morgan to procure the wagon! Did it follow, then, that Berial was the principal, or was he in turn but the tool of another? Amos Quadrant had confessed that secretly it had not been his wish to have his brother cremated. Yet his was the authority which had engaged the undertaker and directed the funeral. Had he chosen to avoid the cremation without permitting the widow to know that his will accomplished her wish, how easy for him to engage the undertaker to carry out his purpose, oddly planned as it was! How readily might the poor undertaker have been bribed by this wealthy man to take the risk! After all, if this were the explanation, wherein lay the crime? By what name would it be designated in the office of the district attorney? Yet, even now, when all seemed known, two unexplained facts stood out prominently. How was it that the foot of the deceased Quadrant showed no scar? And what of the assertion made by Mr. Mitchel that a human body had been cremated? Could it be that Berial, taking advantage of the opportunity offered by his employer, had secretly disposed of some other body, while merely supposed to have removed Rufus Quadrant from his coffin? If so, whose body was it that had been cremated, and how could identification be looked for among the ashes in the urn at the cemetery? Mr. Barnes was chagrined to find such questions in his mind with no answer, when Mr. Mitchel might arrive with his promised surprise at any moment. Perhaps Morgan was lying when he accused the undertaker.

"Have you been able yet," asked Mr. Barnes, "to verify any part of this man's story?"

"Well, we only arrived at six this morning, but I may say yes, I have found some corroborative evidence."

"What?"

"I have the shroud in which Rufus Quadrant was dressed in his coffin."

"That is important. Where did you find it?"

"In quite a suggestive place. It was locked up in old Berial's private closet at the shop, which we searched this morning."

"That certainly is significant. But even so, Tom, how do we know that this Morgan, who robs the dead and has duplicate screw-drivers for opening patented coffin fastenings, would hesitate to place a shroud where it would seem to substantiate his accusation of another?"

"We do not know positively, of course. We have not fully solved this mystery yet, Mr. Barnes."

"I fear not, Tom," said Mr. Barnes, glancing at the clock as he heard a voice asking for him in the adjoining office; "but here comes a man who claims that he has done so."

Mr. Mitchel entered and saluted the two men cordially, after receiving an introduction to the younger.

"Well, Mr. Barnes," said Mr. Mitchel, "shall I surprise you with my story, or have you two gentlemen worked it all out?"

"I do not know whether you will surprise us or not," said Mr. Barnes. "We do not claim to have fully solved this mystery; that much we will admit at once. But we have done a great deal of work, and have learned facts which must in the end lead to the truth."

"Ah, I see. You know some things, but not all. The most important fact, of course, would be the identity of the body which is the centre of this mystery. Do you know that much?"

"I have no doubt that it has been correctly identified," said Mr. Barnes, boldly, though not as confident as he pretended. "It was the corpse of Rufus Quadrant, of course."

"You are speaking of the body at the Morgue?"

"Certainly. What other?"

"I alluded to the body which was cremated," said Mr. Mitchel quietly.

"It has not been proven that any body was cremated," replied Mr. Barnes.

"Has it not? I think it has."

"Ah, you know that? Well, tell us. Who was the man?"

"The man in the coffin, do you mean?"

"Yes. The man who was cremated in place of Mr. Quadrant."

"Have you any suspicion?"

"I did have until an hour ago. I supposed that the criminal who managed this affair had thus disposed of the remains of a pal whom he had killed in a saloon row—a man called Tommy White."

"No, that is wrong. The body cremated was the corpse of a woman."

"Of a woman!" exclaimed both detectives in concert.

"Yes, gentlemen," said Mr. Mitchel, "it was a woman's body that was placed in the furnace. I think, Mr. Barnes, that I suggested such a possibility to you on the day when you first called my attention to this affair?"

"Yes. You said it might be a woman as well as a man. But that was merely a caution against hastily deciding as to the sex of the victim, supposing that a murder had been committed and the criminal had thus proceeded to hide his crime. But subsequent investigations have not brought to us even a suspicion that any woman has been foully dealt with, who could have been placed in the coffin by any who had the opportunity."

"Which only proves," said Mr. Mitchel, "that as usual you detectives have worked in routine fashion, and consequently, by beginning at the wrong end, you have not reached the goal. Now I have reached the goal, and I venture the belief that I have not done one half of the work that either of you have been compelled to bestow upon your investigations."

"We cannot all be as intellectually brilliant as yourself," said Mr. Barnes testily.

"Come, come, Mr. Barnes. No offense meant, I assure you. I

am only upholding the argument, which I have advanced previously, that the very routine which gentlemen of your calling feel bound to follow often hampers if it does not hinder your work. I am merely a tyro,* but not being professionally engaged on this case I was perhaps freer to see things with eyes unblinded by traditional methods of work. It is just as the onlooker often sees an opportunity to win, which the men playing a game of chess overlook. The player has his mind upon many combinations and sees much that the onlooker does not see. So here. You and Mr. Burrows have probably discovered many things that I do not even suspect, but it has been my luck to get at the truth. If you care to hear it, I will describe in detail how I worked out the problem."

"Of course we wish to hear the truth," said Mr. Barnes reluctantly; "that is, if indeed you have learned what it is."

"Very good. As I have said, hampered by the seeming necessity of following your investigations along customary lines, you probably began with the body at the Morgue. I pursued the opposite course. The case seemed so unique that I was convinced that the motive would prove to be equally uncommon. If the body at the Morgue were really that of Mr. Quadrant, as seemed probable from the identifications by the family and the doctor, I was sure that it had been taken from the coffin to make room for the corpse of another. No other motive occurred to my mind which appeared to be adequate. Consequently I thought that the first essential in unravelling the mystery would be the establishment of the fact that a human body had been cremated, and then, if possible, to discover the identity of that body."

"In other words, to identify the ashes of a cremated body," interjected Mr. Barnes, with a slight sneer.

"Just so. That in itself was a problem so novel that it attracted my interest. It is usually considered that cremation has the objectionable feature that it offers a means of hiding the crime

---

*A novice or beginner.

of murder. This idea has contributed not a little to thwart those who have endeavored to make this means of disposing of the dead popular. Would it not be an achievement to prove that incineration is not necessarily a barrier against identification?"

"I should say so," said Mr. Barnes.

"So thought I, and that was the task which I set myself. I visited the chief of the detective bureau, and soon interested him in my theories. He even permitted me to be present at the examination of the ashes, which was undertaken at my suggestion, an expert chemist and his assistant going with us. At the cemetery the urn was brought forth and its contents spread out on a clean marble slab. It was not difficult to discern that a human being had been cremated?"

"Why was it not difficult?"

"When one hears of the ashes of the dead, perhaps it is not unnatural to think of these human ashes as similar to cigar ashes, or the ashes of a wood fire. Where complete combustion occurs the residue is but an impalpable powder. But this is not commonly the result in the cremation of the dead, or at least it does not invariably occur. It did not in this instance, and that is the main point for us. On the contrary, some of the bones, and parts of others, sufficiently retained their form to be readily distinguishable as having come from the human skeleton."

"As I have never examined a cremated body," said Mr. Barnes, "I must admit that your statement surprises me. I had supposed that all parts of the body would be brought to a similar state. But even if what you say is true, and granting that from pieces of charred bone it could be demonstrated that a human being had been burned, still I would like you to explain how you could differentiate between man and woman."

"Perhaps it would be difficult, or even impossible, judging from the charred bits of skeleton alone. But if we remember that a woman's garb is different from the dress of a man, we might find a clue. For example, if you saw what could unmistakably be recognized as parts of corset steels, what would you think?"

"Of course the deduction would be that the body had been that of a woman, but I should think it an odd circumstance to find that a body prepared for burial had been corseted."

"The same thought occurred to me, and from it I drew an important deduction, since substantiated by facts. I concluded from the corset steels that the body had not been prepared for burial."

"I follow you," said Mr. Barnes, now thoroughly interested in Mr. Mitchel's analytical method. "You mean that this woman was placed in the coffin clothed as she had died?"

"Practically so, but I did not decide that she had necessarily died clothed as she was when placed in the coffin. My conclusion was that it must have been as essential to dispose of the clothing as of the body. Thus the clothing would have been placed in the coffin with her, even though perhaps not on her."

"A good point! A good point!" nodded the detective, approvingly.

"So, you see, the ashes of the dead had already revealed two clues. We knew that a human being had been cremated, and we could feel reasonably sure, though not absolutely positive, that it had been a woman. Next, the question arose as to the identity. If cremation would hide that, then the criminal might hope to escape justice by this means."

"It seems incredible that the ashes could be identified, unless indeed some object, provably connected with a certain person, and which would resist fire, had been placed in the coffin."

"No, that would not satisfy me. A false identification could thus be planned by your thoughtful murderer. What I sought was some means of identifying the actual remains of a cremated body. I have succeeded."

"You have succeeded?"

"Yes. I had a theory which has proven to be a good one. If some of the bones of the body resist cremation, or at least retain their form though calcined, it should follow that the teeth, being the most resistant bones, and, moreover, protected by being imbedded in other bones, might well be expected to remain intact. If not all, at least a sufficient number of them might be found to serve the ends of justice."

"Even if you could find the teeth with shape undisturbed, I fail to see how you could identify the remains by them."

"The method is as reliable as it is unique. In these days of advanced dentistry, the people of this country have been educated up to such an appreciation of their dental organs that, from the highest to the lowliest, we find the people habitually saving their teeth by having them filled. I knew by personal experience that it is a common practice among dentists to register in a book of record all work done for a patient. In these records they have blank charts of the teeth, and on the diagram of each tooth, as it is filled, they mark in ink the size and position of the filling inserted. Now while the teeth themselves might resist the heat of the furnace, retaining their shapes, we would not expect the fillings, whether of gold or other material, to do so. Thus, I expected to find the teeth with cavities in them. I did find fourteen of the teeth fairly whole, sufficiently so that we might identify them, and know what position in the mouth they had occupied. No less than ten of these teeth had cavities, which, from the regularity of their outline, it was fair to assume had been filled. These I took to my dentist for an opinion. He was at once interested, because it seems that members of the dental profession have long urged upon the police the reliance that may be placed upon the dentist in identifying living criminals or unknown dead bodies.* He examined the charred teeth, and taking a blank chart of the mouth, he plotted out the size and positions of the fillings which

---

*The first fictional use of dental identification was by Joseph Sheridan le Fanu in his short 1872 novel *The Room in the Dragon Volant*. There, the victim is identified by his teeth, peculiar in workmanship, the work having been done "by one of the ablest dentists in Paris." In May 1897, the catastrophic fire at the Bazar de la Charité in Paris claimed over 125 victims, leaving many unrecognizable. Perhaps in an instance of life imitating art, for the first time in the annals of forensic science, some of the victims were eventually identified by means of their dental records.

once had been present. Another very interesting point was that we found two teeth, known as the central incisor and the cuspid (the latter commonly called the eye-tooth), united together by a staple of platinum. This staple had of course resisted the heat because platinum melts at so high a temperature. My dentist pointed out to me that this staple had been a foundation for what he called a bridge. One end of the staple had been forced into the root of one tooth, the other end passing similarly into the other. Thus the space was spanned, and an artificial tooth had been attached to the bar, thus filling the space. He also pointed out that the bar was covered with a mass which was evidently the porcelain of the tooth which had melted in the furnace."

"This is very interesting," said Mr. Barnes, "but unless you could find the man who did that work, you still could not identify the person cremated."

"My dentist, as I have said, made out for me a chart of the person's mouth, which you may examine. You will see that it is quite specific. With that number of fillings, occupying definite positions in special teeth, and coupled with the presence of the tooth bridged in and the manner of making the bridge, it would be an unexampled coincidence to find that two persons had obtained exactly similar dental services. Would it not?"

## CHART FURNISHED BY MR. MITCHEL'S DENTIST

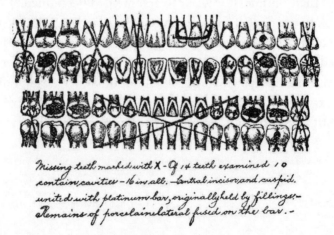

Missing teeth marked with X – Of 14 teeth examined 10 contain cavities – 16 in all. – Central incisor and cuspid. united with platinum bar, originally held by fillings – Remains of porcelain lateral fused on the bar. –

"That is sound reasoning," said Mr. Barnes.

"Very well. I had a statement published in the four leading dental magazines, accompanied by a facsimile of the chart made by my dentist, and I solicited correspondence with any dentist who could show a similar chart in his records."

"That was a good method, provided, of course, the dentist who did the work subscribed to one of these magazines."

"Of course the advertisement might not meet the eye of the dentist who treated the dead woman, but even though he were not a subscriber he might hear of this matter through some acquaintance, because, as I have said, this subject of identification through dental work is one that widely interests the dentists. However, success rewarded us. I received a letter from a dentist in one of the New Jersey towns, stating that he believed he could match my chart. I lost no time in visiting him, and, after examining his book, was satisfied that the person who had been cremated that day was an elderly, eccentric woman, named Miss Lederle, Miss Martha Lederle."

"Mr. Mitchel, you have done a remarkably clever bit of work, and though you have succeeded where I have failed, I must congratulate you. But tell me, after learning the name of the woman how did you trace her to this city?"

"I deserve no credit for that. It seems that Miss Lederle had long had a little fleshy tumor on the inside of her cheek, which had had an opportunity to grow because of the loss of a tooth. Her dentist often advised her to have it removed, lest it might become cancerous. She put it off from time to time, but recently it had grown more rapidly, and at last she called on the dentist and asked him to recommend a surgeon. He tells me that he gave her the names of three, one residing in Newark, and two in this city. Of the New York men, one was Dr. Mortimer."

"By Jove! Doctor Mortimer!" exclaimed Mr. Barnes. "I begin to see daylight. It was he who supplied the morphine powders, then?"

"Ah, then you know so much? Yes, Dr. Mortimer instigated the transfer of bodies. As soon as I charged him with murder, he thought it safest to tell me the truth and throw himself upon my mercy."

"Upon your mercy?" said Mr. Barnes, mystified.

"Yes; the man has not committed a crime, at least not the crime of murder. It seems that on the afternoon of the day before that fixed for the funeral of Mr. Quadrant, this Miss Lederle called at his office and requested him to remove the tumor from her cheek. He consented, and suggested the use of cocaine to deaden the parts. The woman insisted that she must have chloroform, and the doctor explained that in the absence of his assistant he would not care to undertake the administration of an anæsthetic. But the woman was persistent; she offered a liberal fee if the operation could be done immediately, since it had required so much time for her to bring her courage to the point of having the tumor removed; then the operation itself seemed so simple that at last the surgeon was overruled, and proceeded. He did cause the patient to remove her corset, and, her garments thoroughly loosened, she was placed on the operating-table. He says he administered very little chloroform, and had not yet attempted to operate when the patient exhibited dangerous symptoms. In spite of his most untiring efforts she succumbed, and he found himself in the dreadful position of having a patient die under an operation, with no witnesses present. He closed and locked his office and walked from the house in great mental agitation. He called at the Quadrants', and heard there that the coffin would not again be opened. Then a great temptation came to him. The woman had not given him her address, nor had she stated who had sent her to Dr. Mortimer, merely declaring that she knew him by reputation. There was no way to communicate with the woman's relatives except by making the affair public. He recalled that a similar accident to an old surgeon of long-established reputation, where several assistants had been present, had nevertheless ruined the man's practice. He himself was innocent of wrong-doing, except, perhaps, that the law forbade him to operate alone, and he saw ruin staring him in the face, just at a time, too, when great prosperity had appeared to be within his grasp. The undertaker, Berial, was an old acquaintance, indebted to him for many recommendations.

"The plan seemed more and more feasible as he thought of it, and finally he sought out Berial, and confided to him his secret. For a liberal fee the undertaker agreed to dispose of the body. Dr. Mortimer supplied him with a drug with which to overcome the watchman at the stables, so that the wagon could be taken out unknown. He himself visited the Quadrant house, and, under the plea of relieving Mark Quadrant of a headache, gave him also a dose of morphine. At the appointed time Berial arrived at the doctor's office and took away the woman's body, first replacing the corset, which, of course, they were bound to dispose of. Together they went to the Quadrants', and there exchanged the bodies. Subsequent events are known to you. Thus the truth has arisen, Phoenix-like, from the ashes of the dead. The question remaining is, what claim has Justice upon the doctor? Gentlemen, is it needful to disgrace that man, who really is a victim of circumstances rather than a wrong-doer? He tells me, Mr. Barnes, that he has not had a moment of mental rest since you asked him whether ashes could be proven to be the residue of a human body."

"I recall now that he started violently when I spoke to him. Perhaps, had I been more shrewd, I might have suspected the truth then. The difficulty of hushing this matter up, Mr. Mitchel, seems to be the friends and relatives of the dead woman. How can they be appeased?"

"I will undertake that. I think the real estate which she leaves behind will satisfy the one relative. I have already communicated with this man, a hard, money-grubbing old skinflint, and I think that with the assistance of Mr. Berial we can have one more funeral that will satisfy the curiosity of the few neighbors."

And thus the matter was permitted to rest. There was yet one point which puzzled Mr. Barnes, and which never was made clear to him.

"What of the scar that I could not find on Rufus Quadrant's foot?" he often asked himself. But as he could not ask either of the brothers, he never got a reply. Yet the explanation was simple. Mark Quadrant told Mr. Barnes that his brother had such a scar, his object being to baffle the detective by suggesting to him a flaw in the identification. The idea occurred to him because his brother Amos really had such a scarred foot, and he so worded his remark that he literally told the truth, though he deceived Mr. Barnes. When the detective repeated this statement to Amos, he noticed the care with which his brother had spoken, and, in turn, he truthfully said that his brother had spoken truthfully.

# II
## THE MISSING LINK*

"The object of my visit," began Mr. Barnes, "is of such grave importance that I approach it with hesitation, and I may even say reluctance. Will you give me your closest attention?"

"I understood from your note," replied Mr. Mitchel, "that you wished to consult me in regard to some case which you are investigating. As you are well aware, I take the keenest interest in the solving of criminal problems. Therefore proceed. But first let me light a Havana. A good cigar always aids my perception."

The two men were in the sumptuous library of Mr. Mitchel's new house, which he had bought for his wife shortly after their marriage. It was ten in the morning, and Mr. Mitchel, just from his breakfast-room, was comfortably attired in a smoking-jacket. After lighting his cigar, he threw himself into a large Turkish chair, rested his head upon the soft-cushioned back, and extended his slippered feet towards the grate fire, his legs crossed. As he blew little rings of smoke towards the detective, he seemed absolutely unsuspicious of the story about to be told.

Mr. Barnes, on the contrary, appeared ill at ease. He declined

*The story first appeared in the *Asheville Citizen-Times* (Asheville, NC) on March 15, 1897; it subsequently appeared in a number of newspapers in the ensuing months.

a cigar, and, without removing his overcoat, he leaned his left arm on the low marble mantel as he stood talking, his right being free for gestures when he wished to emphasize a point.

After a brief pause he began:

"Whilst I am not officially connected with the regular police, my young friend Burrows is, and is highly esteemed by the Chief. You will remember him in connection with the Quadrant case. He called upon me about noon on last Sunday. The story which he had to tell was the most remarkable in some respects that I have heard. Briefly, it is as follows: As you know, it is common practice among speculating builders to erect a row of houses, finishing them at one end first, so that, not infrequently, one or two of the row may be sold while the mechanics are still at work on the other end. In this manner ten houses have been built in this immediate vicinity."

"In the street just back of me," said Mr. Mitchel.

Mr. Barnes watched him closely at this moment, but he seemed entirely composed and merely attentive. The detective proceeded.

"It appears that two of these houses have been sold and are already occupied. The next four are completed, and the sign 'For Sale' appears in the windows. The others are still in the hands of the workmen. The four which are for sale are in the care of a watchman. They are open for inspection during the day, but he is supposed to lock all the doors before going to his home in the evening, and to open them to the public again on the following day. According to this man, he locked all the doors of these four houses on Saturday night at six o'clock, and opened them again at eight on Sunday morning. Between eight and nine he showed two parties through one of the houses and, after dismissing the last, was sitting on the stoop reading the morning paper, when he was startled by hearing a scream. A moment later he saw two women rush out of the house next to where he sat, and from their actions it was evident that they were terribly frightened. It was some time before he could get any lucid explanation from either, and when he did he understood them to intimate that some one had been murdered in the house. He asked them to show him to the spot, but they most positively declined. He therefore, with unusual display of common sense, summoned a policeman, and with him visited the room indicated by the frightened women, who made no attempt to run away, though they again refused to go into the house, even with the officer. What the two men found was horrible enough to account for the women's actions. In the bathtub lay the body of a woman, the head, hands, and feet having been cut off and removed."

"I should say that, under these circumstances, identification would be most difficult," said Mr. Mitchel, "unless, indeed, the clothing might afford some clue."

"The body was nude," said the detective.

"In that case, you have to deal with a man who has brains."

"Yes; the murderer has adopted just such methods as I imagine you would pursue, Mr. Mitchel, were you in his predicament."

Mr. Mitchel frowned very slightly, and said:

"You offer me a doubtful compliment, Mr. Barnes. Proceed with your case. It is interesting, to say the least."

"It grows more so as we proceed, for we have once more an evidence of the futility of planning a crime which shall leave no clue behind."

"Ah, then you have found a clue?" Mr. Mitchel removed his cigar to speak, and did not resume his smoking, but seemed more attentive.

"Listen," said the detective. "The policeman immediately notified his superiors, and by ten o'clock Burrows was at the house, having been detailed to make an examination. Having done so, and recognizing that he was face to face with a crime of unusual importance, he hastened to solicit my assistance, that I might be early upon the scene. I am satisfied that I reached the house before any material alteration had been made in any of those small and minute details which are overlooked by the careless eye, but which speak volumes to one with experience."

"I suppose, then, that you can describe what existed, from your personal investigation. That is more interesting than a report at second hand."

"I went over the ground thoroughly, as I think you will admit when I have told you all. Here was one of those wonderful cases where the criminal exercised extreme caution to obliterate all traces of the crime. His actions could only be surmised through analytical and deductive methods. There are some facts which cannot be hidden, and from these a keen mind may trace backwards. For example, the head and extremities had been removed, and a minute scrutiny of the remaining parts might disclose many things."

"Ah, here we note the triumph of mind over matter." There was just a slight sneer, which nettled the detective.

Mr. Barnes proceeded with some asperity. Indeed, he spoke more like himself; that is, with less hesitancy, as though heretofore he had found the story hard to tell, but that now his scruples had vanished.

"An examination of the stumps of the arms proved conclusively that a sharp knife had been used, for not only had the tendons and vessels been cleanly severed, but in two places the cartilage capping the ends of the bone had been shaved off smoothly."

"Come, Mr. Barnes," said Mr. Mitchel, "do not dwell so upon unimportant details."

"The weapon is always counted as a very important detail," said Mr. Barnes, sharply.

"Yes, yes, I know," said Mr. Mitchel. "But you are above the ordinary detective, and you surely perceive that it is a matter of no consequence whether the knife used was sharp or dull. In either case it could be hidden or destroyed, so that it could not be found to serve in evidence."

"Oh, very well," said Mr. Barnes, testily. "I will come to the deductions concerning the neck. Here there were several points of interest. Again it was evident that a sharp knife was used, and in this instance the condition of the edge of the knife becomes important."

"Indeed! How so?"

"The most minute scrutiny of the body disclosed no wound which could have been the cause of death. Unless poison had been administered, there are but three ways by which death could have been effected."

"And those are?"

"Suffocation, either by choking or otherwise; drowning, by holding the head under water in the bathtub; or by some mortal wound inflicted about the head, either by a blow, the use of a knife, or a pistol shot. I doubted the pistol, because so careful a man as the assassin evidently was, would have avoided the noise. A stab with a knife was possible, but unlikely because of the scream which would surely result. A blow was improbable, unless the man brought the weapon with him, as the house was empty, and nothing would accidentally be found at hand. To drown the woman, it would have been necessary to half fill the tub with water before thrusting the victim in it, and such an action would have aroused her suspicion. Besides, the clothes would have been wet, and this would have interfered with burning them. Thus by exclusion I arrived at the belief that the woman had been choked to death, a method offering the least risk, being noiseless and bloodless."

"What has the sharpness of the knife to do with this?"

"It was, in my mind, important to decide whether the head had been removed before or after death. A dull knife would not have aided me as a sharp one did. With a sharp knife a severing of the carotid artery before death would have resulted in a spurting of blood, which would have stained the walls or floor, so that it would have been difficult, or impossible, to wash away the telltale marks. But after death, or even while the victim was unconscious, a cool hand, with a sharp blade, could cut down upon the artery in such a way that the blood would flow regularly, and, the body being in the bathtub, and water flowing from the faucets, no stains would be left."

"Then you think that the woman was choked to death?"

"I have not a doubt of it. There was a terrible struggle, too, though in an empty house we could find no such signs as would inevitably have been made in a furnished apartment. But the woman fought for her life and died hard. This I know because, despite the precaution of the assassin in removing the head, there are two or three distinct marks on the neck, made by the ends of his fingers and nails."

"Well, having discovered so much, you are as far as ever from the identity of the criminal, or of the woman."

"Every point unravelled is so much gain," said Mr. Barnes, evasively. "My next deduction was more important. Let us picture the scene of the crime. For causes as yet unknown, this man wished to kill this woman. He lures her into this empty house, and, choosing a favorable moment, seizes her by the throat and strangles her to death. To prevent the identification of the corpse, he decides to remove the head, hands, and feet, parts which are characteristic. He takes off the clothes and burns them. We found the ashes in the kitchen stove. He takes the body to the bathroom, and, placing it in the porcelain tub, turns on the water, and then proceeds with his diabolical scheme. Even though we suppose that he first filled the tub with water, the better to avoid stains, when we remember that he took away the severed parts it is inconceivable that not a stain of blood, not a smudge of pinkish tint, would be left anywhere. Granting that he might have endeavored to wash away any such drippings, still it would be marvellous that not one stain should be left."

"Yet you found none?" Mr. Mitchel smiled, and resumed his smoking.

"Yet I found none," said Mr. Barnes. "But this was a most significant fact to me. It led me to a suspicion which I proceeded to verify. The plumbing in this house is of the most approved pattern. Under the porcelain bathtub there is a patent trap for the exclusion of sewer-gas. This is so fashioned that some water always remains. Supposing that bloody water had passed through it, I should find this trap partly filled with water tinted in color. I removed the screw, which enabled me to catch the water from the trap in a bowl. It was perfectly clear. Not a trace of color."

"From which you deduced?" asked Mr. Mitchel.

"From which I deduced," said the detective, "that the woman had not been killed, or dismembered, in the house where her body was found. By examining the other houses and emptying the traps, I found one which yielded water plainly colored with blood, and I also found a few smudges about the bathtub; places where blood had splashed and been washed off. The assassin thought that he had made all clean, but as so often happens with porcelain, when dried there still remained a slight stain, which even showed the direction in which it had been wiped."

"Very good! Very good indeed!" Mr. Mitchel yawned slightly. "Let me see. You have discovered—what? That the knife was sharp. And that the woman was killed in one house and carried to another. How does that help you?"

At this point Mr. Barnes gave Mr. Mitchel a distinct surprise. Instead of answering the question, he asked suddenly:

"Mr. Mitchel, will you permit me to examine that watch-chain which you are wearing?"

Mr. Mitchel sat straight up in his chair, and looked sharply at the detective, as though trying to read his innermost thoughts. The detective stared back at him, and both were silent a moment. Then without speaking, Mr. Mitchel removed the chain, and handed it to Mr. Barnes, who took it with him to the window, and there examined it closely through a lens. Mr.

Mitchel threw the remains of his cigar into the fire, and, placing both hands behind his head as he lay back in his chair, awaited developments. Presently Mr. Barnes returned to his place by the mantel, and in resuming his narrative it was noticeable from his tone of voice that he was more than ever troubled.

"You asked me," said he, "how my discoveries helped me. I say from the bottom of my soul that they have helped me only too well. That I proceed in this matter is due to the fact that I must follow the dictates of my conscience rather than my heart."

"Brutus yielded up his son," suggested Mr. Mitchel.*

"Yes. Well, to resume my story. The point of importance was this. Imagine the assassin with both hands at the woman's throat—two things were inevitable. The woman would surely struggle, with arms and legs, and the murderer would be unable to resist, his own hands being occupied. What more natural than that the arms of the dying woman should be wrapped about the body of her assailant? That the hands should grasp and rend the clothing? Might perhaps come into contact with a watch-chain and tear it off, or break it?"

"And you are intending to examine all the watch-chains in the neighborhood upon such a chance as that?" Mr. Mitchel laughed, but Mr. Barnes took no notice of the intended taunt.

"I have examined the only chain I wished to look at. Deducing the struggle, and the possible tearing off of some part of the assassin's attire, I was glad to know which house was the scene of the crime. Having satisfied myself in this direction, I proceeded to search for the missing link in the chain of evidence, though I must confess that I did not expect it to be truly a link, a part of a real chain. The idea that a watch-chain might have been broken in the struggle did not occur to me until I held the evidence in my hand."

"Oh; then you did find your missing link?"

---

*This is an historical reference to Lucius Junius Brutus (died 509 BCE), founder of the Roman Republic, whose sons were conspirators in a plot to reinstate the monarchy; Brutus suffered them to be executed.

"Yes. I personally swept every room, and the staircase, and at last I found the link. But it would be more correct to say your missing link, than mine, Mr. Mitchel, for it was from this chain that it was broken."

"Indeed!"

Mr. Barnes was amazed at the imperturbable manner in which this statement was received. Becoming slightly agitated himself, he continued:

"As soon as I picked up that link, I was shocked at my discovery, for, from its peculiar shape, I recognized it as similar to your chain, which I had often observed. Still, I hoped that there might be some mistake; that it might have fallen from some other man. But you permitted me to examine this chain, and the last doubt is swept away. I note that every alternate link is solid, the intermediate ones having a slit, by which the links are joined into a chain. The wrench given by the dying woman strained one of these links so that it opened, allowing the chain to part, and later this particular link dropped off. Either you did not observe it at once, or else, being small, you could not find it. If this occurred as I have described, what would be the result? Your chain, where parted, would terminate at each end with a solid link. Thus, to unite the chain again, my lens shows me that you have sawed through one link, and so rejoined your chain. And not only do I see the freshly sawed link, but, as must necessarily be the case, we have two links adjacent, each of which can be opened."

"And your next move will be?" asked Mr. Mitchel, still apparently undisturbed.

"I have no recourse open to me except to arrest you. That is why I have found this whole interview so painful."

"I understand your position, and sympathize with you thoroughly," said Mr. Mitchel. "And yet, see how easily you might dismiss this whole theory of yours. These houses are in my neighborhood, immediately back of me, in fact. I am a householder. What more natural than my taking an interest in property so near me? Why may I not have visited the houses to examine them? Then what more possible than the chance that in passing from one room to another, my chain should have caught on a door-knob, and have been broken, the link dropping as you have suggested? My repairing the damage would be but a natural sequence, and the subsequent murder and your train of reasoning is resolved into a mere coincidence."

"That is ingenious, Mr. Mitchel. But some instinct tells me that I am right, and that you did commit this crime."

"Intuition, which I suppose is what you mean by instinct, is not always reliable, but, oddly enough, in this instance you are correct. I did kill that creature. Moreover, the sequence of events was as you have deduced. I commend you for your skill, for, believe me, I used every precaution to prevent detection."

"Then you confess? My God! This is horrible!"

At the prospect of arresting Mr. Mitchel, a man who had won his most ardent admiration, Mr. Barnes was so overcome that he sank into a chair and stared blankly at his companion.

"Come! come!" said Mr. Mitchel. "Don't break down like that. The affair is bad enough, I admit, but it might be worse."

"Might be worse!" ejaculated Mr. Barnes, amazed at the words as well as the half-jocular tone.

"Why yes. Much worse. Why, Mr. Barnes, have you not had evidence of my ability to thwart detectives before to-day? Do you suppose that I shall permit myself to be detected, arrested, imprisoned in this affair? Nothing is further from my mind, I assure you. True, you have, with your uncommon skill, discovered a part of the truth. But that need not trouble me, for no other detective will be so shrewd."

"Do you mean to suggest that I should shield you in this matter?"

"Well, yes. That is about what I expect from your friendship."

"Impossible! Impossible! I wish that I could do what you ask! But no! It is impossible!"

"There. I have tried your patience long enough. Let me tell you the whole story, and then you may decide as you please. A few years ago, in Paris, a friend presented me with a poodle. French poodles, as you know, are considered the most intelligent of all dogs, and this one seemed to be the wisest of his species. My friend had already trained him to perform many tricks, and these were done at command, without special signals, so that I could but believe what my friend claimed, that the dog actually understood what was said to him. Thinking this matter over one day, it presented itself to me in a singular light.

"In the training of animals, man has always aimed to make the dumb brute understand, and carry out, the master's wishes. No one, so far as I then knew, had ever trained a dog to express his own wishes, in any way intelligible to the master. This I undertook to do, and was fairly successful. I printed words on cards, such as 'food,' 'drink,' 'yard,' etc., and, by means which I need not recapitulate, I taught my dog to bring me the special card which would represent his wishes. Thus, when he was thirsty, he could ask for 'water' or when he wished to leave the house, he brought the card marked 'yard.' Imagine my astonishment when one day a little sky-terrier, belonging to another lodger in the house, came to me with the 'food' card in his mouth. At first I supposed it to be merely an accident, but I soon discovered that the terrier understood the cards as well as did the poodle. How, unless the poodle had taught him? Do dogs, then, have a language by which they may communicate with each other?

"This was a new thought, which attracted me more and more as I revolved it in my mind. Then it occurred to me that if animals have a language, monkeys would offer the best field for study, and I began investigating. The discovery that the apes do have a language has been made by Mr. Garner,* and by him the fact has been published to the world. But I made the discovery several years ago, though I kept it to myself, for reasons which you shall hear.

"I practised upon the monkeys in the Zoological Gardens in Paris and London, until I was a veritable crank on the subject of monkey language. Nothing would satisfy me but a trip to Africa. Thither I went, and made great progress, so that by the time I captured a fine chimpanzee on the Congo, I was able to readily make him understand that I meant him no harm. At first he received my overtures with hesitation, his previous experience with my race rendering him skeptical as to my good qualities. But after a time, we became good friends; I might even say chums. After that I gave him his liberty, and we took strolls together. He was a very sociable fellow when one really got to know him well, but we found the resources of the monkey language inadequate to our needs. The experiment with my dog recurred to me, and I undertook to teach him a human tongue. I chose German as the best adapted to his limitations, and he made such progress that in a few months we could converse with tolerable ease.

"I decided to tell him something of the world of civilization, and one day it occurred to me to expound to him the Darwinian theory.† He listened with an expression of learned thought upon his face which would have well suited the countenance of a philosopher, but when I had finished, he astounded me by

---

*Richard Lynch Garner (1848–1920) was an amateur primatologist who recorded the sounds made by monkeys at zoos. In 1891, he published a paper, "The Simian Tongue," that asserted that these lower primates had a rudimentary language and that such language was the basis for human speech. The paper was expanded to a book, *The Speech of Monkeys*, in 1892. Garner was a careless researcher, however, and his work did not stand up to rigorous scrutiny. For a period of time, his conclusions were soundly rejected—only to be resurrected as other primatologists studied chimpanzees carefully. Nearly a century after Ottolengui invented Mitchel's pioneering work, scientists have actually managed to teach some primates a human vocabulary of several hundred words, though their responses are limited to lexigrams or sign language.

†"Darwinian theory" here means the idea that apes and humans shared a common ancestor, an idea put forth by Charles Darwin in his 1871 book, *The Descent of Man*. In the late-nineteenth century, scientists searched for a fossil specimen of such an ancestor. Between 1886 and 1895, for example, the Dutch paleontologist Eugene Dubois discovered a specimen that he termed "an intermediate species between humans and monkeys." At the time, the public hailed the find as "the missing link." For example, the *Philadelphia Inquirer* ran an article titled "The Missing Link: A Dutch Surgeon in Java Unearths the Needed Specimen" (February 3, 1895).

announcing that he thought he could show me that higher race of apes, which, being more humanly developed than any species now known, might well be designated 'the missing link' which connects the Simian race with man. I begged him to do so, and he undertook the task, though he said that it involved a long journey. I urged him to go, and he left me.

"A month had passed, and I had begun to think that my new-found friend had deserted me, when one day he walked into camp, accompanied by the most human-like ape I had ever seen. It was neither chimpanzee nor gorilla, but a combination of both in those characteristics which were most manlike. The most conspicuous advance beyond the anthropoid apes now known, was the hairless skin. The hands and feet, too, were more human in shape, though on the latter the hallux still retained its prehensile character, which perhaps is necessary to a tree dweller. The face was peculiarly human, though the jaws retained certain distinguishing attributes of the ape, as, for example, the space between the anterior and posterior teeth, and the fang-like canine teeth.

"As you must already suspect the sequel, I may hurry on to the end. The creature was a female, and in the trip to our camp my chimpanzee friend had become much attached to her; indeed, I may say he had fallen in love with her. He had also begun her higher education, so that when we met she was able to address a few words to me in German. As you may well imagine, I was greatly interested in this animal, and did all in my power to teach her. She made even more rapid progress than the chimpanzee had, and I was thinking of the sensation I could produce in Paris by sending cards of invitation to the nuptials of my monkey friends, which I determined should occur in the great metropolis.

"Imagine my horror one morning, upon finding the chimpanzee dead. I did not immediately comprehend the full significance of this, but upon questioning the ape a few days later, she candidly confessed to me that she had strangled the chimpanzee, her only reason being, that having decided for the future to live as a human being, she deemed it wise to destroy her companion, that he might not be able to divulge the secret of her origin.

"Instantly my mind was awakened to a danger which menaced myself. I too knew the secret of her savage ancestry, and the fact that she had not slain me also was probably due to her hope that I would fulfil my promise and take her with me to more civilized parts. Indeed, so certain was I of this, that I took the first opportunity to foster that ambition in her bosom. At the same time I carefully planned a secret departure, and a few nights later succeeded in getting away unobserved, while the ape slept. Throughout the journey to the coast I constantly feared pursuit, but was fortunate enough to get safely on shipboard without hearing more of the savage creature.

"At dusk on last Saturday, I was strolling through the next street, when, to my amazement, I saw coming towards me what appeared to be a woman, whose face however was so startlingly like the ape which I had left in Africa that for a moment I was dazed. In the next instant, realizing that if my suspicion was true, I might be in danger even after the lapse of time, and hoping that it was merely a chance resemblance, I quickly turned into one of the new houses still open for inspection. I did not dare to look behind me, and even thought it a trick of my excited imagination when I fancied that I heard steps following me as I ascended to the second floor. I turned upon reaching the floor above, and instantly with a savage cry the brute was upon me, her hands upon my throat, making a desperate effort to strangle me. I gripped her neck in a similar manner, scarcely hoping to save my life. Fortune favored me, however, and, after a lengthy struggle, the ape lay dead at my feet. I suppose that several years of life in civilization had sapped her savage strength.

"My subsequent proceedings were actuated by two motives.

In the first place any public connection of my name with such a horrible encounter would naturally have greatly annoyed my wife, and secondly I could not resist my innate fondness for contending with detectives. I removed the head, hands, and feet, to prevent identification, and also because with them I can convince you that the animal was an ape, and not a woman. As there is no law against the killing of an ape, you must see, Mr. Barnes, that it would be futile to arrest me."

"You are right," replied Mr. Barnes, "and I am truly glad that your explanation places you beyond the law. You must forgive me for my suspicion."

The two men joined hands in a firm clasp, which cemented their friendship, and guaranteed that the secret which they shared would never be divulged by either.

# III
## THE NAMELESS MAN*

Mr. Barnes was sitting in his private room, with nothing of special importance to occupy his thoughts, when his office boy announced a visitor.

"What name?" asked Mr. Barnes.

"None," was the reply.

"You mean," said the detective, "that the man did not give you his name. He must have one, of course. Show him in."

A minute later the stranger entered, and, bowing courteously, began the conversation at once.

"Mr. Barnes, the famous detective, I believe?" said he.

"My name is Barnes," replied the detective. "May I have the pleasure of knowing yours?"

"I sincerely hope so," continued the stranger. "The fact is, I suppose I have forgotten it."

"Forgotten your name?" Mr. Barnes scented an interesting case, and became doubly attentive.

"Yes," said the visitor; "that is precisely my singular predicament. I seem to have lost my identity. That is the object of my

*This story first appeared in *The Idler* in January 1895.

call. I wish you to discover who I am. As I am evidently a full-grown man, I can certainly claim that I have a past history, but to me that past is entirely blank. I awoke this morning in this condition, yet apparently in possession of all my faculties, so much so that I at once saw the advisability of consulting a first-class detective, and, upon inquiry, I was directed to you."

"Your case is most interesting—from my point of view, I mean. To you, of course, it must seem unfortunate. Yet it is not unparalleled. There have been many such cases recorded, and, for your temporary relief, I may say that, sooner or later, complete restoration of memory usually occurs. But now, let us try to unravel your mystery as soon as possible, that you may suffer as little inconvenience as there need be. I would like to ask you a few questions."

"As many as you like, and I will do my best to answer."

"Do you think that you are a New Yorker?"

"I have not the least idea whether I am or not."

"You say you were advised to consult me. By whom?"

"The clerk at the Waldorf Hotel, where I slept last night."

"Then, of course, he gave you my address. Did you find it necessary to ask him how to find my offices?"

"Well, no, I did not. That seems strange, does it not? I certainly had no difficulty in coming here. I suppose that must be a significant fact, Mr. Barnes?"

"It tends to show that you have been familiar with New York, but we must still find out whether you live here or not. How did you register at the hotel?"

"M. J. G. Remington, City."

"You are quite sure that Remington is not your name?"

"Quite sure. After breakfast this morning I was passing through the lobby when the clerk called me twice by that name. Finally, one of the hall-boys touched me on the shoulder and explained that I was wanted at the desk. I was very much confused to find myself called 'Mr. Remington,' a name which certainly is not my own. Before I fully realized my position, I said to the clerk, 'Why do you call me Remington?' and he replied, 'Because you registered under that name.' I tried to pass it off, but I am sure that the clerk looks upon me as a suspicious character."

"What baggage have you with you at the hotel?"

"None. Not even a satchel."

"May there not be something in your pockets that would help us; letters, for example?"

"I am sorry to say that I have made a search in that direction, but found nothing. Luckily I did have a pocketbook, though."

"Much money in it?"

"In the neighborhood of five hundred dollars."

Mr. Barnes turned to his table and made a few notes on a pad of paper. While so engaged his visitor took out a fine gold watch, and, after a glance at the face, was about to return it to his pocket, when Mr. Barnes wheeled around in his chair, and said:

"That is a handsome watch you have there. Of a curious pattern, too. I am rather interested in old watches."

The stranger seemed confused for an instant, and quickly put up his watch, saying:

"There is nothing remarkable about it. Merely an old family relic. I value it more for that than anything else. But about my case, Mr. Barnes; how long do you think it will take to restore my identity to me? It is rather awkward to go about under a false name."

"I should think so," said the detective. "I will do my best for you, but you have given me absolutely no clue to work upon, so that it is impossible to say what my success will be. Still I think forty-eight hours should suffice. At least in that time I ought to make some discoveries for you. Suppose you call again on the day after to-morrow, at noon precisely. Will that suit you?"

"Very well, indeed. If you can tell me who I am at that time I shall be more than convinced that you are a great detective, as I have been told."

He arose and prepared to go, and upon the instant Mr. Barnes touched a button under his table with his foot, which caused a bell to ring in a distant part of the building, no sound of which penetrated the private office. Thus any one could visit Mr. Barnes in his den, and might leave, unsuspicious of the fact that a spy would be awaiting him out in the street who would shadow him persistently day and night until recalled by his chief. After giving the signal, Mr. Barnes held his strange visitor in conversation a few moments longer to allow his spy opportunity to get to his post.

"How will you pass the time away, Mr. Remington?" said he. "We may as well call you by that name, until I find your true one."

"Yes, I suppose so. As to what I shall do during the next forty-eight hours, why, I think I may as well devote myself to seeing the sights. It is a remarkably pleasant day for a stroll, and I think I will visit your beautiful Central Park."

"A capital idea. By all means, I would advise occupation of that kind. It would be best not to do any business until your memory is restored to you."

"Business? Why, of course, I can do no business."

"No. If you were to order any goods, for example, under the name of Remington, later on when you resume your proper identity you might be arrested as an impostor."

"By George! I had not thought of that. My position is more serious than I had realized. I thank you for the warning. Sight-seeing will assuredly be my safest plan for the next two days."

"I think so. Call at the time agreed upon, and hope for the best. If I should need you before then, I will send to your hotel."

Then, saying "Good morning," Mr. Barnes turned to his desk again, and, as the stranger looked at him before stepping out of the room, the detective seemed engrossed with some papers before him. Yet scarcely had the door closed upon the retreating form of his recent visitor, when Mr. Barnes looked up, with an air of expectancy. A moment later a very tiny bell in a drawer of his desk rang, indicating that the man had left the building, the signal having been sent to him by one of his employees, whose business it was to watch all departures and notify his chief. A few moments later Mr. Barnes himself emerged, clad in an entirely different suit of clothing, and with such alteration in the color of his hair that more than a casual glance would have been required to recognize him.

When he reached the street the stranger was nowhere in sight, but Mr. Barnes went to a doorway opposite, and there he found, written in blue pencil, the word "up" whereupon he walked rapidly uptown as far as the next corner, where once more he examined a door-post, upon which he found the word "right" which indicated the way the men ahead of him had turned. Beyond this he could expect no signals, for the spy shadowing the stranger did not know positively that his chief would take part in the game. The two signals which he had written on the doors were merely a part of a routine, and intended to aid Mr. Barnes should he follow; but if he did so, he would be expected to be in sight of the spy by the time the second signal was reached. And so it proved in this instance, for as Mr. Barnes turned the corner to the right, he easily discerned his man about two blocks ahead, and presently was near enough to see "Remington" also.

The pursuit continued until Mr. Barnes was surprised to see him enter the Park, thus carrying out his intention as stated in his interview with the detective. Entering at the Fifth Avenue gate he made his way towards the menagerie, and here a curious incident occurred. The stranger had mingled with the crowd in the monkey-house, and was enjoying the antics of the mischievous little animals, when Mr. Barnes, getting close behind him, deftly removed a pocket-handkerchief from the tail of his coat and swiftly transferred it to his own.

On the day following, shortly before noon, Mr. Barnes walked quickly into the reading-room of the Fifth Avenue Hotel. In one corner there is a handsome mahogany cabinet, containing three compartments, each of which is entered through double doors, having glass panels in the upper half. About these panels are draped yellow silk curtains, and in the centre of each appears a white porcelain numeral. These compartments are used as public telephone stations, the applicant being shut in, so as to be free from the noise of the outer room.

Mr. Barnes spoke to the girl in charge, and then passed into the compartment numbered "2." Less than five minutes later Mr. Leroy Mitchel came into the reading-room. His keen eyes peered about him, scanning the countenances of those busy with the papers or writing, and then he gave the telephone girl a number, and went into the compartment numbered "1." About ten minutes elapsed before Mr. Mitchel came out again, and, having paid the toll, he left the hotel. When Mr. Barnes emerged, there was an expression of extreme satisfaction upon his face. Without lingering, he also went out. But instead of following Mr. Mitchel through the main lobby to Broadway, he crossed the reading-room and reached Twenty-third Street through the side door. Thence he proceeded to the station of the elevated railroad, and went uptown. Twenty minutes later he was ringing the bell of Mr. Mitchel's residence. The "buttons"* who answered his summons informed him that his master was not at home.

"He usually comes in to luncheon, however, does he not?" asked the detective.

"Yes, sir," responded the boy.

"Is Mrs. Mitchel at home?"

"No, sir."

"Miss Rose?"

---

*The "boy in buttons" or simply "buttons" was a liveried page boy, commonly employed in many upper-class households to answer the door and run errands. The phrase seems to have originated in England and migrated to Gilded Age New York, where servants teemed in the mansions of the wealthy.

"Yes, sir."

"Ah; then I'll wait. Take my card to her." Mr. Barnes passed into the luxurious drawing-room, and was soon joined by Rose, Mr. Mitchel's adopted daughter.

"I am sorry papa is not at home, Mr. Barnes," said the little lady, "but he will surely be in to luncheon, if you will wait."

"Yes, thank you, I think I will. It is quite a trip up, and, being here, I may as well wait a while and see your father, though the matter is not of any great importance."

"Some interesting case, Mr. Barnes? If so, do tell me about it. You know I am almost as interested in your cases as papa is."

"Yes, I know you are, and my vanity is flattered. But I am sorry to say that I have nothing on hand at present worth relating. My errand is a very simple one. Your father was saying, a few days ago, that he was thinking of buying a bicycle, and yesterday, by accident, I came across a machine of an entirely new make, which seems to me superior to anything yet produced. I thought he might be interested to see it, before deciding what kind to buy."

"I am afraid you are too late, Mr. Barnes. Papa has bought a bicycle already."

"Indeed! What style did he choose?"

"I really do not know, but it is down in the lower hall, if you care to look at it."

"It is hardly worth while, Miss Rose. After all, I have no interest in the new model, and if your father has found something that he likes, I won't even mention the other to him. It might only make him regret his bargain. Still, on second thoughts, I will go down with you, if you will take me into the dining-room and show me the head of that moose which your father has been bragging about killing. I believe it has come back from the taxidermist's?"

"Oh, yes. He is just a monster. Come on."

They went down to the dining-room, and Mr. Barnes

expressed great admiration for the moose's head, and praised Mr. Mitchel's skill as a marksman. But he had taken a moment to scrutinize the bicycle which stood in the hallway, while Rose was opening the blinds in the dining-room. Then they returned to the drawing-room, and after a little more conversation Mr. Barnes departed, saying that he could not wait any longer, but he charged Rose to tell her father that he particularly desired him to call at noon on the following day.

Promptly at the time appointed, "Remington" walked into the office of Mr. Barnes, and was announced. The detective was in his private room. Mr. Leroy Mitchel had been admitted but a few moment before.

"Ask Mr. Remington in," said Mr. Barnes to his boy, and when that gentleman entered, before he could show surprise at finding a third party present, the detective said:

"Mr. Mitchel, this is the gentleman whom I wish you to meet. Permit me to introduce to you Mr. Mortimer J. Goldie, better known to the sporting fraternity as G. J. Mortimer, the champion short-distance bicycle rider, who recently rode a mile in the phenomenal time of 1.36, on a three-lap track."*

As Mr. Barnes spoke, he gazed from one to the other of his companions, with a half-quizzical and wholly pleased expression on his face. Mr. Mitchel appeared much interested, but the newcomer was evidently greatly astonished. He looked blankly at Mr. Barnes a moment, then dropped into a chair with the query:

"How in the name of conscience did you find that out?"

"That much was not very difficult," replied the detective. "I can tell you much more; indeed, I can supply your whole past history, provided your memory has been sufficiently restored for you to recognize my facts as true."

---

*In 1899, "Mile-a-Minute" Murphy, whose real name was Charles Minthorn Murphy (1870–1950) rode his bicycle in the draft of a railroad train for one mile in 57.8 seconds. Mortimer's speed is theoretically possible but very unlikely—in 2020, the world record for a male cyclist for 1km from a standing start is 56 seconds, and theoretically, if that rider were able to sustain that speed for a mile, he would require 90 seconds.

Mr. Barnes looked at Mr. Mitchel, and winked one eye in a most suggestive manner, at which that gentleman burst out into hearty laughter, finally saying;

"We may as well admit that we are beaten, Goldie. Mr. Barnes has been too much for us."

"But I want to know how he has done it," persisted Mr. Goldie.

"I have no doubt that Mr. Barnes will gratify you. Indeed, I am as curious as you are to know by what means he has arrived at his quick solution of the problem which we set for him."

"I will enlighten you as to detective methods with pleasure," said Mr. Barnes. "Let me begin with the visit made to me by this gentleman two days ago. At the very outset his statement aroused my suspicion, though I did my best not to let him think so. He announced to me that he had lost his identity, and I promptly told him that his case was not uncommon. I said that in order that he might feel sure that I did not doubt his tale. But truly, his case, if he was telling the truth, was absolutely unique. Men have lost recollection of their past, and even have forgotten their names. But I have never before heard of a man who had forgotten his name, and at the same time knew that he had done so."

"A capital point, Mr. Barnes," said Mr. Mitchel. "You were certainly shrewd to suspect fraud so early."

"Well, I cannot say that I suspected fraud so soon, but the story was so improbable that I could not believe it immediately. I therefore was what I might call 'analytically attentive' during the rest of the interview. The next point worth noting which came out was that, although he had forgotten himself, he had not forgotten New York, for he admitted having come to me without special guidance."

"I remember that," interrupted Mr. Goldie, "and I think I even said to you at the time that it was significant."

"And I told you that it at least showed that you had been

familiar with New York. This was better proven when you said that you would spend the day at Central Park, and when, after leaving here, you had no difficulty in finding your way thither."

"Do you mean to say that you had me followed? I made sure that no one was after me."

"Well, yes, you were followed," said Mr. Barnes, with a smile. "I had a spy after you, and I followed you as far as the Park myself. But let me come to the other points in your interview and my deductions. You told me that you had registered as 'M. J. G. Remington.' This helped me considerably, as we shall see presently. A few minutes later you took out your watch, and in that little mirror over my desk, which I use occasionally when I turn my back upon a visitor, I noted that there was an inscription on the outside of the case. I turned and asked you something about the watch, when you hastily returned it to your pocket, with the remark that it was 'an old family relic.' Now can you explain how you could have known that, supposing that you had forgotten who you were?"

"Neatly caught, Goldie," laughed Mr. Mitchel. "You certainly made a mess of it there."

"It was an asinine slip," said Mr. Goldie, laughing also.

"Now, then," continued Mr. Barnes, "you readily see that I had good reason for believing that you had not forgotten your name. On the contrary, I was positive that your name was a part of the inscription on the watch. What, then, could be your purpose in pretending otherwise? I did not discover that for some time. However, I decided to go ahead, and find you out if I could. Next I noted two things. Your coat opened once, so that I saw, pinned to your vest, a bicycle badge, which I recognized as the emblem of the League of American Wheelmen."

"Oh! Oh!" cried Mr. Mitchel. "Shame on you, Goldie, for a blunderer."

"I had entirely forgotten the badge," said Mr. Goldie.

"I also observed," the detective went on, "little indentations on the sole of your shoe, as you had your legs crossed, which sat-isfied me that you were a rider even before I observed the badge. Now then, we come to the name, and the significance thereof. Had you really lost your memory, the choosing of a name when you registered at a hotel would have been a haphazard matter of no importance to me. But as soon as I decided that you were imposing upon me, I knew that your choice of a name had been a deliberate act of the mind; one from which deductions could be drawn."

"Ah; now we come to the interesting part," said Mr. Mitchel. "I love to follow a detective when he uses his brains."

"The name as registered, and I examined the registry to make sure, was odd. Three initials are unusual. A man without mem-ory, and therefore not quite sound mentally, would hardly have chosen so many. Then why had it been done in this instance? What more natural than that these initials represented the true name? In assuming an alias, it is the most common method to transpose the real name in some way. At least it was a work-ing hypothesis. Then the last name might be very significant. 'Remington.' The Remingtons make guns, sewing-machines, typewriters, and bicycles. Now, this man was a bicycle rider, I was sure. If he chose his own initials as a part of the alias, it was possible that he selected 'Remington' because it was familiar to him. I even imagined that he might be an agent for Remington bicycles, and I had arrived at that point during our interview, when I advised him not to buy anything until his identity was restored. But I was sure of my quarry when I stole a handker-chief from him at the Park, and found the initials 'M. J. G.' upon the same."

"Marked linen on your person!" exclaimed Mr. Mitchel. "Worse and worse! We'll never make a successful criminal of you, Goldie."

"Perhaps not. I shan't cry over it."

"I felt sure of my success by this time," continued Mr. Barnes, "yet at the very next step I was balked. I looked over a list of L. A. W. members and could not find a name to fit my initials, which shows, as you will see presently, that, as I may say, 'too many clues spoil the broth.' Without the handkerchief I would have done better. Next I secured a catalogue of the Remingtons, which gave a list of their authorized agents, and again I failed. Returning to my office I received information from my spy, sent in by messenger, which promised to open a way for me. He had followed you about, Mr. Goldie, and I must say you played your part very well, so far as avoiding acquaintances is concerned. But at last you went to a public telephone, and called up some one. My man saw the importance of discovering to whom you had spoken, and bribed the telephone attendant to give him the information. All that he learned, however, was that you had spoken to the public station at the Fifth Avenue Hotel. My spy thought that this was inconsequent, but it proved to me at once that there was collusion, and that your man must have been at the other station by previous appointment. As that was at noon, a few minutes before the same hour on the following day, that is to say, yesterday, I went to the Fifth Avenue Hotel telephone and secreted myself in the middle compartment, hoping to hear what your partner might say to you. I failed in this, as the boxes are too well made to permit sound to pass from one to the other; but imagine my gratification to see Mr. Mitchel himself go into the box."

"And why?" asked Mr. Mitchel.

"Why, as soon as I saw you, I comprehended the whole scheme. It was you who had concocted the little diversion to test my ability. Thus, at last, I understood the reason for the pretended loss of identity. With the knowledge that you were in it, I was more than ever determined to get at the facts. Knowing that you were out, I hastened to your house, hoping for a chat with little Miss Rose, as the most likely member of your family to get information from."

"Oh, fie! Mr. Barnes," said Mr. Mitchel; "to play upon the innocence of childhood! I am ashamed of you!"

"'All's fair,' etc. Well, I succeeded. I found Mr. Goldie's bicycle in your hallway, and, as I suspected, it was a Remington. I took the number and hurried down to the agency, where I readily discovered that wheel No. 5086 is ridden by G. J. Mortimer, one of their regular racing team. I also learned that Mortimer's private name is Mortimer J. Goldie. I was much pleased at this, because it showed how good my reasoning had been about the alias, for you observe that the racing name is merely a transposition of the family name. The watch, of course, is a prize, and the inscription would have proved that you were imposing upon me, Mr. Goldie, had you permitted me to see it."

"Of course; that was why I put it back in my pocket."

"I said just now," said Mr. Barnes, "that without the stolen handkerchief I would have done better. Having it, when I looked over the L. A. W. list I went through the 'G's' only. Without it, I should have looked through the 'G's,' 'J's,' and 'M's,' not knowing how the letters may have been transposed. In that case I should have found 'G. J. Mortimer,' and the initials would have proved that I was on the right track."

"You have done well, Mr. Barnes," said Mr. Mitchel. "I asked Goldie to play the part of a nameless man for a few days, to have some fun with you. But you have had fun with us, it seems. Though, I am conceited enough to say, that had it been possible for me to play the principal part, you would not have pierced my identity so soon."

"Oh, I don't know," said Mr. Barnes. "We are both of us a little egotistical, I fear."

"Undoubtedly. Still, if I ever set another trap for you, I will assign myself the chief *rôle*."

"Nothing would please me better," said Mr. Barnes. "But, gentlemen, as you have lost in this little game, it seems to me that some one owes me a dinner, at least."

"I'll stand the expense with pleasure," said Mr. Mitchel.

"Not at all," interrupted Mr. Goldie. "It was through my blundering that we lost, and I'll pay the piper."

"Settle it between you," cried Mr. Barnes. "But let us walk on. I am getting hungry."

Whereupon they adjourned to Delmonico's.

# IV

## THE MONTEZUMA EMERALD[*]

"Is the Inspector in?"

Mr. Barnes immediately recognized the voice, and turned to greet the speaker. The man was Mr. Leroy Mitchel's English valet. Contrary to all precedent and tradition, he did not speak in cockney dialect, not even stumbling over the proper distribution of the letter "h" throughout his vocabulary. That he was English, however, was apparent to the ear, because of a certain rather attractive accent, peculiar to his native island, and to the eye because of a deferential politeness of manner, too seldom observed in American servants. He also always called Mr. Barnes "Inspector," oblivious of the fact that he was not a member of the regular police, and mindful only of the English application of the word to detectives.

"Step right in, Williams," said Mr. Barnes. "What is the trouble?"

"I don't rightly know, Inspector," said Williams. "Won't you let me speak to you alone? It's about the master."

"Certainly. Come into my private room." He led the way and

---

*This story first appeared in *The Idler* in February 1895.

Williams followed, remaining standing, although Mr. Barnes waved his hand towards a chair as he seated himself in his usual place at his desk. "Now then," continued the detective, "what's wrong? Nothing serious I hope?"

"I hope not, sir, indeed. But the master's disappeared."

"Disappeared, has he." Mr. Barnes smiled slightly. "Now Williams, what do you mean by that? You did not see him vanish, eh?"

"No, sir, of course not. If you'll excuse my presumption, Inspector, I don't think this is a joke, sir, and you're laughing."

"All right, Williams," answered Mr. Barnes, assuming a more serious tone. "I will give your tale my sober consideration. Proceed."

"Well, I hardly know where to begin, Inspector. But I'll just give you the facts, without any unnecessary opinions of my own."

Williams rather prided himself upon his ability to tell what he called "a straight story." He placed his hat on a chair, and, standing behind it, with one foot resting on a rung, checked off the points of his narrative, as he made them, by tapping the palm of one hand with the index finger of the other.

"To begin then," said he. "Mrs. Mitchel and Miss Rose sailed for England, Wednesday morning of last week. That same night, quite unexpected, the master says to me, says he, 'Williams, I think you have a young woman you're sweet on down at Newport?' 'Well, sir,' says I, 'I do know a person as answers that description,' though I must say to you, Inspector, that how he ever came to know it beats me. But that's aside, and digression is not my habit. 'Well, Williams,' the master went on, 'I shan't need you for the rest of this week, and if you'd like to take a trip to the seashore, I shan't mind standing the expense, and letting you go.' Of course, I thanked him very much, and I went, promising to be back on Monday morning as directed. And I kept my word, Inspector; though it was a hard wrench to leave the young person last Sunday in time to catch the boat; the moon being bright and everything most propitious for a stroll, it being her Sunday off, and all that. But, as I said, I kept my word, and was up to the house Monday morning only a little after seven, the boat having got in at six. I was a little surprised to find that the master was not at home, but then it struck me as how he must have gone out of town over Sunday, and I looked for him to be in for dinner. But he did not come to dinner, nor at all that night. Still, I did not worry about it. It was the master's privilege, to stay away as long as he liked. Only I could not help thinking I might just as well have had that stroll in the moonlight, Sunday night. But when all Tuesday and Tuesday night went by, and no word from the master, I must confess that I got uneasy; and now here's Wednesday noon, and no news; so I just took the liberty to come down and ask your opinion in the matter, seeing as how you are a particular friend of the family, and an Inspector to boot."

"Really, Williams," said Mr. Barnes, "all I see in your story is that Mr. Mitchel, contemplating a little trip off somewhere with friends, let you go away. He expected to be back by Monday, but, enjoying himself, has remained longer."

"I hope that's all, sir, and I've tried to think so. But this morning I made a few investigations of my own, and I'm bound to say what I found don't fit that theory."

"Ah, you have some more facts. What are they?"

"One of them is this cablegram that I found only this morning under a book on the table in the library." He handed a blue paper to Mr. Barnes, who took it and read the following, on a cable blank:

"Emerald. Danger. Await letter."

For the first time during the interview Mr. Barnes's face assumed a really serious expression. He studied the despatch silently for a full minute, and then, without raising his eyes, said:

"What else?"

"Well, Inspector, I don't know that this has anything to do with the affair, but the master had a curious sort of jacket, made of steel links, so tight and so closely put together, that I've often wondered what it was for. Once I made so bold as to ask him, and he said, said he, 'Williams, if I had an enemy, it would be a good idea to wear that, because it would stop a bullet or a knife.' Then he laughed, and went on: 'Of course, I shan't need it for myself. I bought it when I was abroad once, merely as a curiosity.' Now, Inspector, that jacket's disappeared also."

"Are you quite sure?"

"I've looked from dining-room to garret for it. The master's derringer is missing, too. It's a mighty small affair. Could be held in the hand without being noticed, but it carries a nasty-looking ball."

"Very well, Williams, there may be something in your story. I'll look into the matter at once. Meanwhile, go home, and stay there so that I may find you if I want you."

"Yes, sir; I thank you for taking it up. It takes a load off my mind to know you're in charge, Inspector. If there's harm come to the master, I'm sure you'll track the party down. Good morning, sir."

"Good morning, Williams."

After the departure of Williams, the detective sat still for several minutes, lost in thought. He was weighing two ideas. He seemed still to hear the words which Mr. Mitchel had uttered after his success in unravelling the mystery of Mr. Goldie's lost identity. "Next time I will assign myself the chief *rôle*," or words to that effect, Mr. Mitchel had said. Was this disappearance a new riddle for Mr. Barnes to solve? If so, of course he would undertake it, as a sort of challenge which his professional pride could not reject. On the other hand, the cable despatch and the missing coat of mail might portend ominously. The detective felt that Mr. Mitchel was somewhat in the position of the fabled boy who cried "Wolf!" so often that, when at last the wolf really appeared, no assistance was sent to him. Only Mr. Barnes decided that he must chase the "wolf," whether it be real or imaginary. He wished, though, that he knew which.

Ten minutes later he decided upon a course of action, and proceeded to a telegraph office, where he found that, as he had supposed, the despatch had come from the Paris firm of jewellers from which Mr. Mitchel had frequently bought gems. He sent a lengthy message to them, asking for an immediate reply.

While waiting for the answer, the detective was not inactive. He went direct to Mr. Mitchel's house, and once more questioned the valet, from whom he obtained an accurate description of the clothes which his master must have worn, only one suit being absent. This fact alone, seemed significantly against the theory of a visit to friends out of town. Next, Mr. Barnes interviewed the neighbors, none of whom remembered to have seen Mr. Mitchel during the week. At the sixth house below, however, he learned something definite. Here he found Mr. Mordaunt, a personal acquaintance, and member of one of Mr. Mitchel's clubs. This gentleman stated that he had dined at the club with Mr. Mitchel on the previous Thursday, and had accompanied him home, in the neighborhood of eleven o'clock, parting with him at the door of his own residence. Since then he had neither seen nor heard from him. This proved that Mr. Mitchel was at home one day after Williams went to Newport.

Leaving the house, Mr. Barnes called at the nearest telegraph office and asked whether a messenger summons had reached them during the week, from Mr. Mitchel's house. The record slips showed that the last call had been received at 12.30 A.M., on Friday. A cab had been demanded, and was sent, reaching the house at one o'clock. At the stables, Mr. Barnes questioned the cab-driver, and learned that Mr. Mitchel had alighted at Madison Square.

"But he got right into another cab," added the driver. "It was just a chance I seen him, 'cause he made as if he was goin' into the Fifth Avenoo; but luck was agin' him, for I'd scarcely gone two blocks back, when I had to get down to fix my harness, and while I was doin' that, who should I see but my fare go by in another cab."

"You did not happen to know the driver of that vehicle?" suggested Mr. Barnes.

"That's just what I did happen to know. He's always by the Square, along the curb by the Park. His name's Jerry. You'll find him easy enough, and he'll tell you where he took that fly bird."

Mr. Barnes went downtown again, and did find Jerry, who remembered driving a man at the stated time, as far as the Imperial Hotel; but beyond that the detective learned nothing, for at the hotel no one knew Mr. Mitchel, and none recollected his arrival early Friday morning.

From the fact that Mr. Mitchel had changed cabs, and doubled on his track, Mr. Barnes concluded that he was after all merely hiding away for the pleasure of baffling him, and he felt much relieved to divest the case of its alarming aspect. However, he was not long permitted to hold this opinion. At the telegraph office he found a cable despatch awaiting him, which read as follows:

"Montezuma Emerald forwarded Mitchel tenth. Previous owner murdered London eleventh. Mexican suspected. Warned Mitchel."

This assuredly looked very serious. Casting aside all thought of a practical joke, Mr. Barnes now threw himself heart and soul into the task of finding Mitchel, dead or alive. From the telegraph office he hastened to the Custom-House, where he learned that an emerald, the invoiced value of which was no less than twenty thousand dollars, had been delivered to Mr. Mitchel in person, upon payment of the custom duties, at noon of the previous Thursday. Mr. Barnes, with this knowledge, thought he knew why Mr. Mitchel had been careful to have a friend accompany him to his home on that night. But why had he gone out again?

Perhaps he felt safer at a hotel than at home, and, having reached the Imperial, taking two cabs to mystify the villain who might be tracking him, he might have registered under an alias. What a fool he had been not to examine the registry, as he could certainly recognize Mr. Mitchel's handwriting, though the name signed would of course be a false one.

Back, therefore, he hastened to the Imperial, where, however, his search for familiar chirography was fruitless. Then an idea occurred to him. Mr. Mitchel was so shrewd that it would not be unlikely that, meditating a disappearance to baffle the men on his track, he had registered at the hotel several days prior to his permanently stopping there. Turning the page over, Mr. Barnes still failed to find what he sought, but a curious name caught his eye.

"Miguel Palma—City of Mexico."

Could this be the London murderer? Was this the suspected Mexican? If so, here was a bold and therefore dangerous criminal who openly put up at one of the most prominent hostelries. Mr. Barnes was turning this over in his mind, when a diminutive newsboy rushed into the corridor, shouting:

"Extra *Sun!* Extra *Sun!* All about the horrible murder. Extra!"

Mr. Barnes purchased a paper and was stupefied at the headlines:

ROBERT LEROY MITCHEL DROWNED!
*His Body Found Floating in the East River,*
A DAGGER IN HIS BACK.
*Indicates Murder.*

Mr. Barnes rushed out of the hotel, and, quickly finding a cab, instructed the man to drive rapidly to the Morgue. On the way, he read the details of the crime as recounted in the newspaper. From this he gathered that the body had been discovered early in the morning by two boatmen, who towed it to shore and handed it over to the police. An examination at the Morgue had established the identity by letters found on the corpse and the initials marked on the clothing. Mr. Barnes was sad at heart, and inwardly fretted because his friend had not asked his aid when in danger.

Jumping from the cab almost before it had fully stopped in front of the Morgue, he stumbled and nearly fell over a decrepit-looking beggar, upon whose breast was a printed card soliciting alms for the blind. Mr. Barnes dropped a coin, a silver quarter, into his outstretched palm, and hurried into the building. As he did so he was jostled by a tall man who was coming out, and who seemed to have lost his temper, as he muttered an imprecation under his breath in Spanish. As the detective's keen ear noted the foreign tongue an idea occurred to him which made him turn and follow the stranger. When he reached the street again he received a double surprise. The stranger had already sig-nalled the cab which Mr. Barnes had just left, and was entering it, so that he had only a moment in which to observe him. Then the door was slammed, and the driver whipped up his horses and drove rapidly away. At the same moment the blind beggar jumped up, and ran in the direction taken by the cab. Mr. Barnes watched them till both cab and beggar disappeared around the next corner, and then he went into the building again, deeply thinking over the episode.

He found the Morgue-keeper, and was taken to the corpse. He recognized the clothing at once, both from the description given by Williams, and because he now remembered to have seen Mr. Mitchel so dressed. It was evident that the body had been in the water for several days, and the marks of violence plainly pointed to murder. Still sticking in the back was a curious dagger of foreign make, the handle projecting between the shoulders. The blow must have been a powerful stroke, for the blade was so tightly wedged in the bones of the spine that it resisted ordi-nary efforts to withdraw it. Moreover, the condition of the head showed that a crime had been committed, for the skull and face had been beaten into a pulpy mass with some heavy instrument. Mr. Barnes turned away from the sickening sight to examine the letters found upon the corpse. One of these bore the Paris postmark, and he was allowed to read it. It was from the jewellers, and was the letter alluded to in the warning cable. Its contents were:

*"Dear Sir:—*

*"As we have previously advised you the Montezuma Emerald was shipped to you on the tenth instant. On the following day the man from whom we had bought it was found dead in Dover Street, London, killed by a dagger-thrust between the shoulders. The meagre accounts telegraphed to the papers here, state that there is no clue to the assassin. We were struck by the name, and remembered that the deceased had urged us to buy the emerald, because, as he declared, he feared that a man had followed him from Mexico, intending to murder him to get possession of it. Within an hour of reading the newspaper story, a gentlemanly looking man, giving the name of Miguel Palma, entered our store, and asked if we had purchased the Montezuma Emerald. We replied negatively, and he smiled and left. We notified the police, but they have not yet been able to find this man. We deemed it our duty to warn you, and did so by cable."*

The signature was that of the firm from which Mr. Barnes had received the cable in the morning. The plot seemed plain enough now. After the fruitless murder of the man in London, the Mexican had traced the emerald to Mr. Mitchel, and had followed it across the water. Had he succeeded in obtaining it? Among the things found on the corpse was an empty jewel-case, bearing the name of the Paris firm. It seemed from this that the gem had been stolen.

But, if so, this man, Miguel Palma, must be made to explain his knowledge of the affair.

Once more visiting the Imperial, Mr. Barnes made inquiry, and was told that Mr. Palma had left the hotel on the night of the previous Thursday, which was just a few hours before Mr. Mitchel had undoubtedly reached there alive. Could it be that the man at the Morgue had been he? If so, why was he visiting that place to view the body of his victim? This was a problem over which Mr. Barnes puzzled, as he was driven up to the residence of Mr. Mitchel. Here he found Williams, and imparted to that faithful servant the news of his master's death, and then inquired for the address of the family abroad, that he might notify them by cable, before they could read the bald statement in a newspaper.

"As they only sailed a week ago to-day," said Williams, "they're hardly more than due in London. I'll go up to the master's desk and get the address of his London bankers."

As Williams turned to leave the room, he started back amazed at the sound of a bell.

"That's the master's bell, Inspector! Some one is in his room! Come with me!"

The two men bounded upstairs, two steps at a time, and Williams threw open the door of Mr. Mitchel's boudoir, and then fell back against Mr. Barnes, crying:

"The master himself!"

Mr. Barnes looked over the man's shoulder, and could scarcely believe his eyes when he observed Mr. Mitchel, alive and well, brushing his hair before a mirror.

"I've rung for you twice, Williams," said Mr. Mitchel, and then, seeing Mr. Barnes, he added, "Ah, Mr. Barnes. You are very welcome. Come in. Why, what is the matter, man? You are as white as though you had seen a ghost."

"Thank God, you are safe!" fervently ejaculated the detective, going forward and grasping Mr. Mitchel's hand. "Here, read this, and you will understand." He drew out the afternoon paper and handed it to him.

"Oh, that," said Mr. Mitchel, carelessly. "I've read that. Merely a sensational lie, worked off upon a guileless public. Not a word of truth in it, I assure you."

"Of course not, since you are alive; but there is a mystery about this which is yet to be explained."

"What! A mystery, and the great Mr. Barnes has not solved it? I am surprised. I am, indeed. But then, you know, I told you after Goldie made a fizzle of our little joke that if I should choose to play the principal part you would not catch me. You see I have beaten you this time. Confess. You thought that was my corpse which you gazed upon at the Morgue?"

"Well," said Mr. Barnes, reluctantly, "the identification certainly seemed complete, in spite of the condition of the face, which made recognition impossible."

"Yes; I flatter myself the whole affair was artistic."

"Do you mean that this whole thing is nothing but a joke? That you went so far as to invent cables and letters from Paris just for the trifling amusement of making a fool of me?"

Mr. Barnes was evidently slightly angry, and Mr. Mitchel, noting this fact, hastened to mollify him.

"No, no; it is not quite so bad as that," he said. "I must tell you the whole story, for there is yet important work to do, and you must help me. No, Williams, you need not go out. Your anxiety over my absence entitles you to a knowledge of the truth. A short time ago I heard that a very rare gem was in the market, no less a stone than the original emerald which Cortez stole from the crown of Montezuma.* The emerald was offered in Paris,

---

*By the late nineteenth century, emeralds were already well connected to lore about South America. For example, an August 1861 article by "E. L. L." (possibly E. L. L. Blanchard) titled "Precious Stones" in the magazine *Temple Bar* (377–392, at 381) tells of "marvelous stories" of Aztec emperor Montezuma's clasp, consisting of an egg-shaped emerald surrounded by smaller emeralds. The article also states that Spanish explorer Hernan Cortez had stolen five emeralds, cut into the shapes of a cup, a rose, a toy, a fish, and a bell, from one of the temples of the region. Though clearly Montezuma had plentiful emeralds, if these tales are true, it is far from certain whether any crown worn by Montezuma actually contained emeralds.

and I was notified at once by the dealer, and authorized the purchase by cable. A few days later I received a despatch warning me that there was danger. I understood at once, for similar danger had lurked about other large stones which are now in my collection. The warning meant that I should not attempt to get the emerald from the Custom-House until further advices reached me, which would indicate the exact nature of the danger. Later, I received the letter which was found on the body now at the Morgue, and which I suppose you have read?"

Mr. Barnes nodded assent.

"I readily located the man Palma at the Imperial, and from his openly using his name I knew that I had a dangerous adversary. Criminals who disdain aliases have brains, and use them. I kept away from the Custom-House until I had satisfied myself that I was being dogged by a veritable cutthroat, who, of course, was the tool hired by Palma to rob, perhaps to kill me. Thus acquainted with my adversaries, I was ready for the enterprise."

"Why did you not solicit my assistance?" asked Mr. Barnes.

"Partly because I wanted all the glory, and partly because I saw a chance to make you admit that I am still the champion detective-baffler. I sent my wife and daughter to Europe that I might have time for my scheme. On the day after their departure I boldly went to the Custom-House and obtained the emerald. Of course I was dogged by the hireling, but I had arranged a plan which gave him no advantage over me. I had constructed a pair of goggles which looked like simple smoked glasses, but in one of these I had a little mirror so arranged that I could easily watch the man behind me, should he approach too near. However, I was sure that he would not attack me in a crowded thoroughfare, and I kept in crowds until time for dinner, when, by appointment, I met my neighbor Mordaunt, and remained in his company until I reached my own doorway late at night. Here he left me, and I stood on the stoop until he disappeared into his own house. Then I turned, and apparently had much trouble to place my latch-key in the lock. This offered the assassin the chance he had hoped for, and, gliding stealthily forward, he made a vicious stab at me. But, in the first place, I had put on a chain-armor vest, and, in the second, expecting the attack to occur just as it did, I turned swiftly and with one blow with a club I knocked the weapon from the fellow's hand, and with another I struck him over the head so that he fell senseless at my feet."

"Bravo!" cried Mr. Barnes. "You have a cool nerve."

"I don't know. I think I was very much excited at the crucial moment, but with my chain armor, a stout loaded club in one hand and a derringer in the other, I never was in any real danger. I took the man down to the wine-cellar and locked him in one of the vaults. Then I called a cab, and went down to the Imperial, in search of Palma; but I was too late. He had vanished."

"So I discovered," interjected Mr. Barnes.

"I could get nothing out of the fellow in the cellar. Either he cannot or he will not speak English. So I have merely kept him a prisoner, visiting him at midnight only, to avoid Williams, and giving him rations for another day. Meanwhile, I disguised myself and looked for Palma. I could not find him. I had another card, however, and the time came at last to play it. I deduced from Palma's leaving the hotel on the very day when I took the emerald from the Custom-House, that it was prearranged that his hireling should stick to me until he obtained the gem, and then meet him at some rendezvous, previously appointed. Hearing nothing during the past few days, he has perhaps thought that I had left the city, and that his man was still upon my track. Meanwhile I was perfecting my grand coup. With the aid of a physician, who is a confidential friend, I obtained a corpse from one of the hospitals, a man about my size, whose face we battered beyond description. We dressed him in my clothing, and fixed the dagger which I had taken from my would-be assassin so tightly in the backbone that it would not drop out. Then one night we took our dummy to the river and securely anchored it in the water. Last night I simply cut it loose and let it drift down the river."

"You knew of course that it would be taken to the Morgue," said Mr. Barnes.

"Precisely. Then I dressed myself as a blind beggar, posted myself in front of the Morgue, and waited."

"You were the beggar?" ejaculated the detective.

"Yes. I have your quarter, and shall prize it as a souvenir. Indeed, I made nearly four dollars during the day. Begging seems to be lucrative. After the newspapers got on the street with the account of my death, I looked for developments. Palma came in due time, and went in. I presume that he saw the dagger, which was placed there for his special benefit, as well as the empty jewel-case, and at once concluded that his man had stolen the gem and meant to keep it for himself. Under these circumstances he would naturally be angry, and therefore less cautious and more easily shadowed. Before he came out, you turned up and stupidly brought a cab, which allowed my man to get a start of me. However, I am a good runner, and as he only rode as far as Third Avenue, and then took the elevated railroad, I easily followed him to his lair. Now I will explain to you what I wish you to do, if I may count on you?"

"Assuredly."

"You must go into the street, and when I release the man in the cellar, you must track him. I will go to the other place, and we will see what happens when the men meet. We will both be there to see the fun."

An hour later, Mr. Barnes was skilfully dogging a sneaking Mexican*, who walked rapidly through one of the lowest streets

---

*Ottolengui was descended from Sephardic Jews (Jews from the Iberian Peninsula), and his birthplace, Charleston, South Carolina, was until after 1800 the center of North American Jewry (almost exclusively Sephardic). Both his mother's family (Rodrigues) and his father's family were of Hispanic origins. It is a little surprising, therefore, to find several slighting references to Mexicans in this and other stories. However, such slights were not only commonplace among educated classes of the late 1890s, they may also reflect class distinctions felt by those of Spanish descent—many "pureblood" Spaniards regarded themselves as distinctly superior to the "mixed" Hispanic races of South America, where Indian ancestry commingled with Spanish.

on the East Side, until finally he dodged into a blind alley, and before the detective could make sure which of the many doors had allowed him ingress he had disappeared. A moment later a low whistle attracted his attention, and across in a doorway he saw a figure which beckoned to him. He went over and found Mr. Mitchel.

"Palma is here. I have seen him. You see I was right. This is the place of appointment, and the cutthroat has come here straight. Hush! What was that?"

There was a shriek, followed by another, and then silence.

"Let us go up," said Mr. Barnes. "Do you know which door?"

"Yes; follow me."

Mr. Mitchel started across, but, just as they reached the door, footsteps were heard rapidly descending the stairs. Both men stood aside and waited. A minute later a cloaked figure bounded out, only to be gripped instantly by those in hiding. It was Palma, and he fought like a demon, but the long, powerful arms of Mr. Barnes encircled him, and, with a hug that would have made a bear envious, the scoundrel was soon subdued. Mr. Barnes then manacled him, while Mr. Mitchel ascended the stairs to see about the other man. He lay sprawling on the floor, face downward, stabbed in the heart.

# V

## A SINGULAR ABDUCTION*

Mr. Barnes was alone in his sanctum when an elderly gentleman of cultured manners was ushered in. The visitor sank into a seat and began his appeal at once.

"Oh, Mr. Barnes," said he, "I am in great distress. I hardly dared to hope that assistance was possible until I met my friend, Mr. Leroy Mitchel. You know him?" Mr. Barnes assented with a smile. "Well," continued the old gentleman, "Mr. Mitchel said that you could surely assist me."

"Certainly. I will do all that is in my power," said the detective.

"You are very kind. I hope you can aid me. But let me tell you the story. I am Richard Gedney, the broker. Perhaps you have heard the name?" Mr. Barnes nodded. "I thought so. 'Old Dick,' they call me on the street, and sometimes 'Old Nick,' but that is only their joke. I do not believe they really dislike me, though I have grown rich. I have never cheated any one, nor wronged a friend in my life. But that is immaterial, except that it makes it hard to understand how any one could have done me the great injury of stealing my daughter."

*This story first appeared in *The Idler* in March 1895.

"Stealing your daughter?" interrupted the detective. "Abduction?"

"Abduction I suppose is your technical term. I call it plain stealing. To take a girl of fourteen away from her father's home is stealing, plain and simple."

"When did this occur?"

"Two days ago. Tuesday morning we missed her, though she may have been taken in the night. She was slightly ill on Monday evening, and her maid sent for our doctor, who ordered her to be put to bed and kept there. Next morning, that is, Tuesday, he called early, as he was going out on his rounds. He was admitted by the butler and went straight up to her room. He came down a few minutes later, rang the door-bell to call a servant, and reported that the child was not in her room. He left word that she must be put back to bed and that he would return in an hour. The butler gave the message to her maid, who became alarmed, as she supposed her mistress to be in bed. A search was begun, but the child had vanished."

"How is it, Mr. Gedney, that the doctor did not speak to you personally instead of to the servant?"

"I cannot too much condemn myself. You see, I am an old whist player, and the temptation to play made me linger so late with some friends on Monday night that I preferred to remain in Newark where I was, and so did not reach home till ten o'clock Tuesday morning. By that time the misfortune had occurred."

"Have you made no discoveries as to what has become of her?"

"None. We have sent to all of our friends in the vain hope that she might have arisen early and gone out, but no one has seen her. She has disappeared as thoroughly as though she had been swallowed by an earthquake. Here, however, is a letter which reached me this morning. I cannot tell whether there is anything in it, or whether it is merely a cruel joke perpetrated by some crank who has heard of my loss." He handed the letter to the detective, who read as follows:

"Your daughter is safe if you are sensible. If you want her back all you have to do is to state your figures. Make them high enough, and she'll be with you. Put a 'Personal' in *Herald* for D. M., and I will answer."

"Mr. Gedney," said Mr. Barnes, "I am afraid this is a serious case. What has been done has been so thoroughly well accomplished that I believe we have no fool to deal with. His is a master hand. We must begin our work at once. I will take this up personally. Come, we must go out."

They proceeded first to the *Herald* uptown office, and Mr. Barnes inserted the following advertisement:

"D. M. Communicate at once, stating lowest terms. Gedney."

"Now we will go to your home, Mr. Gedney," said Mr. Barnes, and thither they went.

Seating himself in a comfortable leather chair in the library, Mr. Barnes asked that the butler should be called. The man entered the room, and it was apparent at once that here was a good servant of the English type.

"Moulton," began Mr. Barnes, "I am a detective. I am going to find out where your young mistress has been taken."

"I hope so, sir," said the butler.

"Very well," said the detective. "Now answer a few questions explicitly, and you may give me great assistance. On Tuesday morning you admitted the doctor. At what time was it?"

"It was about eight o'clock, sir. We had just taken our seats at breakfast in the servants' hall, when the bell rang. That is how I know the hour. We are regular about meals in this house. We eat at eight and the master at nine."

"What happened when you admitted the doctor?"

"He asked for Miss Nora, and I told him she was not down yet. He said he supposed he could go up, and I said I supposed so, and he went."

"What did you do next?"

"I went back to my breakfast."

"Did you tell the maid that the doctor had called?"

"Not just then, sir, for she had not come into the breakfast-room."

"When did you tell her?"

"After I saw the doctor the second time. I heard the door-bell again and went up, when, to my surprise, there was the doctor. He said he rang because he did not know how else to call me. Then he said that Miss Nora had left her room, which was against the orders he gave the night before, and that I was to tell the maid to have her back to bed, and he would call again. I went back to the breakfast-room. This time the maid was there, and frightened she was when I gave her the message."

"How long was it after you admitted the doctor the first time, when you answered his second ring?"

"I should think five minutes, sir; though it might have been ten."

"And during this five or ten minutes the maid was not in the breakfast-room?"

"No, sir."

"Send her to me." The butler left the room, and, whilst waiting for the maid, Mr. Barnes addressed Mr. Gedney.

"Mr. Gedney," said he, "you have not told me the name of the doctor."

"His name is Donaldson. Everybody knows Dr. Donaldson."

"Has he served you long?"

"Ever since I came to live in this neighborhood. About two years, I should say. He has seemed to be very fond of Elinora. Why, he has been here a half-dozen times asking for news of her since her disappearance. He has a curious theory which I can hardly credit. He thinks she may have wandered off in the night, asleep. But then he has not seen this letter from 'D. M.' yet."

"I would like to speak to him about his somnambulistic idea. Do you think he will drop in to-day?"

"He may be in at any moment, as he has not called yet this morning. Here is my daughter's maid."

This directed the attention of Mr. Barnes to a young woman who at that moment entered. She was evidently dreadfully alarmed at being summoned to meet a detective, and her eyes showed that she had been weeping.

"Come, my girl," said Mr. Barnes, reassuringly, "you need not be frightened. I am not an ogre. I only wish to ask you a few questions. You are willing to help me find your mistress, are you not?"

"Oh, indeed, indeed yes, sir!"

"Then begin by telling me how she was on Monday night when you sent for the doctor."

The girl composed herself with an effort, evidently satisfied that a detective was just like any ordinary man, and replied:

"Miss Nora acted rather odd all Monday, and was melancholy like. She would sit and stare out of the window and not answer when she was spoken to. I thought perhaps something had bothered her, and so I left her alone, meaning to speak to her father at dinner time. But he sent a telegram saying he had to go out of town. So when Miss Nora wouldn't come down to dinner, and wouldn't answer me, but just kept staring out of the window, I got scared a little, and thought it best to send for Dr. Donaldson."

"What did he say when he came?"

"He talked to her, but she wouldn't answer him either. He patted her on the head, and said she was sulky. Then he told me perhaps she was angry because her father hadn't come home, but that she must not be allowed to brood over trifles. He said I must put her to bed, and he gave her some medicine that he said would put her to sleep."

"Did you have any trouble to get her to bed?"

"No, sir, though that was strange. She just stood still and let me do everything. She did not help me or prevent me."

"When did you see her after that?"

"I never saw her after that," and she began to cry softly.

"Come, come, don't cry. Your mistress is all right. I will bring her back. Now tell me why you did not see her again. Is it not your business to attend her in the morning?"

"Yes, sir, but she only gets up about eight o'clock, and the doctor told me he would call the first thing in the morning, and that I must not disturb her till he came. He said he wanted to wake her himself and see how she acted."

"You were not in the breakfast-room at eight o'clock," said the detective, watching her closely; "where were you?"

The girl turned crimson, and stammered a few words inaudibly.

"Come, tell me where you were. You were somewhere, you know. Where were you?"

"I was in the downstairs hallway," she said, slowly.

"Doing what?"

"I was talking to the policeman," she replied, more reluctantly.

"Your beau?" asked Mr. Barnes, significantly.

"No, sir. He is my husband." She tossed her head defiantly, now that her secret was divulged.

"Your husband?" said Mr. Barnes, slightly surprised. "Why, then, did you hesitate to tell me of him?"

"Because — because," — she stammered, again much troubled, — "because, maybe, if I hadn't been talking to him, Miss Nora wouldn't have been carried off. He might have seen the thief."

"Just so," said Mr. Barnes. "Well, that will do." The girl retired only too gladly.

Mr. Barnes asked to be shown the room where the missing girl had slept, and made minute examinations of everything. Up in the room a thought occurred to him, and he once more asked for the maid.

"Can you tell me," he asked, "whether your mistress took any of her clothing with her?"

"Well, sir," she replied, "I miss the whole suit that she wore on Monday. It looks as though she must have dressed herself."

Mr. Barnes made a few notes in his memorandum-book, and then with Mr. Gedney returned to the library. Here they found Dr. Donaldson, who had arrived whilst they were upstairs. Mr. Gedney introduced the doctor, a genial, pleasant man, who shook Mr. Barnes cordially by the hand, saying:

"I am delighted, Mr. Barnes, that my old friend Gedney has been sensible enough to engage you to unravel this affair rather than call in the police. The police are bunglers anyway, and only make scandal and publicity. You have looked into the matter, eh? What do you think?"

"That is precisely the question, Doctor, which I wish to ask you. What do you think? Mr. Gedney says you suggest somnambulism."

"I only said it might be that. I would not like to be too positive. You know that I called to see the dear girl Monday night. Well, I found her in a strange mood. In fact, thinking it over, I have almost convinced myself that what we took for stubbornness— sulks, I think I called it—was somnambulism. That, in fact, she was asleep when I saw her. That would account for her not replying to questions, and offering no resistance when her maid removed her clothing to put her to bed. Still it is merely a guess. It is possible that she got up in the night and wandered out of the house. I only venture it as a possibility, a chance clue for you to work on."

"What do you think of this letter?" asked Mr. Barnes, handing the doctor the anonymous communication from "D. M."

The doctor read it over twice, and then said:

"Looks more like somnambulism than ever. Don't you see? She dressed herself in the night, and wandered off. Some scoundrel has found her and taken her to his home. Knowing that her father has money, he holds her for ransom."

"How do you know, Doctor," said Mr. Barnes, quietly, "that 'D. M.' is a he? The communication is in typewriting, so that nothing can be learned from the chirography."

"Of course I don't know it," said the doctor, testily. "Still I'll wager that no woman ever concocted this scheme."

"Again, how should her abductor know that her father is rich?"

"Why, I suppose her name may be on her clothing, and once he discovered her parentage, he would know that. However he found it out, it is plain that he does know, or how could they, or he, or she, if you wish me to be so particular, have written this letter?"

This was unanswerable, so Mr. Barnes remained silent.

"What move will you make first?" asked the doctor.

Mr. Barnes told him of the advertisement which he had inserted, and took his departure, requesting that if Mr. Gedney received any answer he should be notified at once.

About half-past ten the next morning, Mr. Gedney presented himself to the detective and handed him the following letter:

"I am glad you are sensible. Saw your advertisement, and I answer at once. I want twenty thousand dollars. That is my price. Now note what I have to say, and let me emphasize the fact that I mean every word. This is my first offer. Any dickering will make me increase my price, and I will never decrease it. To save time, let me tell you something else. I have no partner in this, so there is no one to squeal on me. No one on earth but myself knows where the girl is. Now for future arrangements. You will want to communicate with me. I don't mean you to have any chance to catch me with decoy letters or anything of that sort. I know already that you have that keen devil Barnes helping you. But he'll meet his match this time. Here is my plan. You, or your detective, I don't care which, must go to the public telephone station in the Hoffman House at two o'clock sharp. I will go to another, never mind where, and will ring you up. When you answer, I will simply say, 'D. M.' You will recognize the *signal and can do the talking. I will not answer except by letter, because I won't even run the risk of that detective's hearing my voice, and some time in the future recognizing it. You see, I may need Barnes myself some day and wouldn't like to be deprived of his valuable services. I enclose a piece of the girl's cloth dress and a lock of her hair to show that I am dealing square.*

*"D. M."*

"Mr. Gedney," said Mr. Barnes, "make your mind easy. Your daughter is safe, at all events. I suppose this bit of cloth and the hair satisfy you that the scoundrel really has her?"

"Yes, I am convinced of that. But how does that make the girl safe?"

"The fellow wants the money. It is to his interest to be able to restore your daughter. My business shall be to get her without payment of ransom, and to catch the abductor. I'll meet you at the Hoffman House at two o'clock."

As soon as Mr. Gedney had gone, Mr. Barnes wrote the following note:

"DR. DONALDSON:—

*"Dear Sir—I believe that I am on the right track, and all through the clue supplied by yourself. Please aid me a little further. I would like to know the exact size of the missing girl. As a physician, you will supply this even better than the father. Also inform me of any mark or peculiarity by which I might recognize her, alive or dead. Please answer at once.*

*"Yours truly,*
*"J. BARNES."*

This he sent by a messenger, and received the following in reply:

"MR. BARNES:—

"*Dear Sir—I hope you will succeed. Elinora is small and slim, being rather undersized for her age. I should say about four feet ten inches, or thereabout. I know of no distinctive mark whereby her body could be recognized, and hope that nothing of the sort seemingly suggested may be necessary.*

"*Yours truly,*
"ROBERT DONALDSON, M.D."

Mr. Barnes read this, and appeared more pleased than its contents seemed to authorize. At the appointed time he went to the Hoffman House. He found Mr. Gedney impatiently walking up and down the lobby.

"Mr. Gedney," said he, "at the beginning of this case you offered me my own price for recovering your daughter. Now, supposing that you pay this ransom, it would appear that you would have had little need of my services. If, however, I get your daughter, and save you the necessity of paying any ransom at all, I suppose you will admit that I have earned my reward?"

"Most assuredly."

After this, Mr. Gedney was rather startled when he heard what the detective said to "D. M." through the telephone. They shut themselves up in the little box, and very soon received the call and then the signal "D. M." as agreed. Mr. Barnes spoke to the abductor, who presumably was listening.

"We agree to your terms," said he. "That is, we will pay twenty thousand dollars for the return of the girl unharmed. You are so shrewd that we suppose you will invent some scheme for receiving the money which will protect you from arrest, but at the same time we must be assured that the girl will be returned to us unharmed. In fact, she must be given to us as soon as the money is paid. Notify us immediately, as the father is in a hurry."

Mr. Barnes put up the instrument and "rang off." Then he turned to Mr. Gedney and said:

"That may surprise you. But what may astonish you more is that you must obtain twenty thousand dollars in cash at once. We will need it. Ask no questions, but depend upon me and trust me."

On the next day Mr. Gedney received the following letter:

*"You have more sense than I gave you credit for. So has that Barnes fellow, for it was his voice I heard through the 'phone. You accept my terms. Very well. I'll deal square and not raise you, though I ought to have made it twenty-five thousand at least. Come to the 'phone to-day, same hour, and I'll ring you up, from a different station. Then you can tell me if you will be ready to-night, or to-morrow night. Either will suit me. Then here is the plan. You want to be sure the girl is all right. Then let the ambassador be your friend, Doctor Donaldson. He knows the girl and can tell that she is all right. Let him start from his house at midnight, and drive from his office up Madison Avenue rapidly till hailed by the signal D. M. He must go fast enough to prevent being followed on foot. If there is no detective with him or following him, he will be hailed. Otherwise he will be allowed to pass. I will be in hiding with the girl. Warn the doctor that I will be armed, and will have a bead on him all the time. Any treachery will mean death. I will take the cash, give up the girl, and the transaction will be ended."*

When this was shown to the detective, he proposed that he and Mr. Gedney should call upon the doctor. This they did, and, after some argument, persuaded him to undertake the recovery of the girl that same night.

"Mr. Gedney has decided to obtain his child at any sacrifice," said Mr. Barnes, "and this scoundrel is so shrewd that there seems to be no way to entrap him. No effort will be made to follow you, so you need have no fear of any trouble from the thief. Only be sure that you obtain the right girl. It would be just possible that a wrong one might be given to you, and a new ransom demanded."

"Oh, I shall know Elinora," said the doctor. "I will do this, but I think we ought to arrest the villain, if possible."

"I do not despair of doing so," said Mr. Barnes. "Get a glimpse of his face if you can, and be sure to note where you receive the girl. When we get her she may give me a clue upon which an arrest may be made. We will wait for you at Mr. Gedney's house."

After midnight that night, Mr. Gedney paced the floor anxiously, while Mr. Barnes sat at a desk looking over some memoranda. Presently he went into the hall and had a long talk with the butler. One o'clock passed, and still no news. At half-past, however, horses' hoofs sounded upon the asphalt pavement, and a few minutes later the door-bell jingled. The door was quickly opened, and the doctor entered, bearing little Elinora asleep in his arms.

"My daughter!" exclaimed the excited father. "Thank God, she is restored to me!"

"Yes," said the doctor, "here she is, safe and sound. I think, though, that she has been drugged, for she has slept ever since I received her."

"Did you have any trouble?" asked Mr. Barnes, entering at this moment. He had lingered outside in the hall long enough to exchange a word with the butler.

"None," said the doctor. "At One Hundred and Second Street I heard the signal and stopped. A man came out of the shadow of a building, looked into the carriage, said 'All right,' and asked if I had the cash. I replied affirmatively. He went back to the sidewalk and returned with the child in his arms, but with a pistol pointed at me. Then he said, 'Pass out the money.' I did so, and he seemed satisfied, for he gave me the child, took the package, and ran off. I saw his face, but I fear my description will not avail you, for I am sure he was disguised."

"Very possibly your description will be useless," said Mr. Barnes; "but I have discovered the identity of the abductor."

"Impossible!" cried the doctor, amazed.

"Let me prove that I am right," said Mr. Barnes. He went to the door and admitted the butler, accompanied by the policeman who had been off his beat talking with the maid. Before his companions understood what was about to happen, Mr. Barnes said:

"Officer, arrest that man!" Whereupon the policeman seized the doctor and held him as though in a vise.

"What does this outrage mean?" screamed the doctor, after ineffectually endeavoring to release himself.

"Put on the manacles, officer," said Mr. Barnes; "then we can talk. He is armed, and might become dangerous." With the assistance of the detective this was accomplished, and then Mr. Barnes addressed himself to Mr. Gedney.

"Mr. Gedney, I had some slight suspicion of the truth after questioning the butler and the maid, but the first real clue came with the answer to the 'Personal.' You brought that to me in the morning, and I noted that it was postmarked at the main office downtown at six A.M. Of course, it was possible that it might have been written after the appearance of the newspaper, but if so, the thief was up very early. The doctor, however, knew of the 'Personal' on the day previous, as I told him of it in your presence. That letter was written in typewriting, and I observed a curious error in the spelling of three words. I found the words 'emphasize,' 'recognize,' and 'recognizing.' In each, instead of the 'z' we have a repetition of the 'i,' that letter being doubled. I happen to know something about writing-machines. I felt certain that this letter had been written upon a Caligraph. In that machine the bar which carries the letter 'i' is next to that which carries the letter 'z.' It is not an uncommon thing when a typewriter is out of order for two bars to fail to pass one another. Thus, in writing 'emphasize' the rapid writer would strike the 'z' key before the 'i' had fully descended. The result would be that the 'z' rising, would strike the 'i' bar and carry it up again, thus doubling the 'i' instead of writing 'iz.' The repetition of the mistake was evidence that it was a faulty machine. I also noted that this anonymous letter was upon paper from which the top had been torn away. I wrote to the doctor here, asking about the 'size' of the girl, and for any marks whereby we might be able to 'recognize' the body. I used the words 'size' and 'recognize' hoping to tempt him to use them also in reply. In his answer I find the word 'recognized' and also a similar word, 'undersized.' In both we have a repetition of the double 'i' error. Moreover, the paper of this letter from the doctor matched that upon which the anonymous communication had been written, provided I tore off the top, which bore his letterhead. This satisfied me that the doctor was our man. When the last letter came, proposing that he should be the ambassador, the trick was doubly sure. It was ingenious, for the abductor of course assured himself that he was not followed, and simply brought the girl home. But I set another trap. I secretly placed a cyclometer upon the doctor's carriage. He says that to-night he drove to One Hundred and Second Street, and back here, a total of ten miles. The cyclometer, which the butler obtained for me when the doctor arrived a while ago, shows that he drove less than a mile. He simply waited at his house until the proper time to come, and then drove here, bringing the girl with him."

The doctor remained silent, but glared venomously at the man who had outwitted him.

"But how did he get Elinora?" asked Mr. Gedney.

"That queer yarn which he told us about somnambulism first suggested to me that he was possibly less ignorant than he pretended to be. I fear, Mr. Gedney, that your daughter is ill. I judge from the description of her condition, given by her maid, and admitted by this man, that she was suffering from an attack of catalepsy* when he was summoned. When he called the next day, finding the girl still in a trance, he quickly dressed her and took her out to his carriage. Then he coolly returned, announced that she was not in her room, and drove away with her."

"It seems incredible!" exclaimed Mr. Gedney. "I have known the doctor so long that it is hard to believe that he is a criminal."

"Criminals," said Mr. Barnes, "are often created by opportunity. That was probably the case here. The case is most peculiar. It is a crime which none but a physician could have conceived, and that one fact makes possible what to a casual observer might seem most improbable. An abduction is rarely successful, because of the difficulties which attend the crime, not the least of which are the struggles of the victim, and the story which will be told after the return of the child. Here all this was obviated. The doctor recognized catalepsy at the first visit. Perhaps during the night the possibility of readily compelling you to pay him a large sum of money grew into a tremendous temptation. With the project half formed, he called the next morning. Circumstances favored the design. He found the girl unattended, and unresistant because of her condition. He likewise knew that when he should have returned her, she could tell nothing of where she had been, because of her trance. He started downstairs with her. There was no risk. If he had met any one, any excuse for bringing her from her room would have been accepted, because uttered by the family physician. He placed her in the carriage unobserved, and the most difficult

---

*A medical condition exhibiting a trance or seizure, including loss of motor control or rigidity. Historically, this was a diagnosis; today, catalepsy is viewed as a symptom of a nervous disorder such as Parkinson's disease or epilepsy.

part of the affair was accomplished. Many men of high degree are at heart rascals; but through fear, either of law or loss of position, they lead fairly virtuous lives. Temptation, accompanied by opportunity, coming to one of these, compasses his downfall, as has occurred in this instance. Criminals are recruited from all classes."

The ransom money was recovered by searching the apartments of the doctor, and his guilt was thus indubitably proven. Mr. Mitchel, commenting upon the affair, simply said:

"I sent you to him, Mr. Gedney, because Mr. Barnes is above his kind. He is no ordinary detective."

# VI
## THE AZTEC OPAL*

"Mr. Mitchel," began Mr. Barnes, after exchanging greetings, "I have called to see you upon a subject which I am sure will enlist your keenest interest, for several reasons. It relates to a magnificent jewel; it concerns your intimate friends; and it is a problem requiring the most analytical qualities of the mind in its solution."

"Ah, then you have solved it?" asked Mr. Mitchel.

"I think so. You shall judge. I have to-day been called in to investigate one of the most singular cases that has fallen in my way. It is one in which the usual detective methods would be utterly valueless. The facts were presented to me, and the solution of the mystery could only be reached by analytical deductions."

"That is to say, by using your brains?"

"Precisely. Now, as you have admitted that you consider yourself more expert in this direction than the ordinary detective, I wish to place you for once in the position of a detective, and then see you prove your ability.

*This story first appeared in *The Idler* in April 1895.

"Early this morning I was summoned, by a messenger, to go aboard of the steam yacht *Idler* which lay at anchor in the lower bay."

"Why, the *Idler* belongs to my friend, Mortimer Gray!" exclaimed Mr. Mitchel.

"Yes," replied Mr. Barnes; "I told you that your friends are interested. I went immediately with the man who had come to my office, and in due season I was aboard of the yacht. Mr. Gray received me very politely, and took me to his private room adjoining the cabin. Here he explained to me that he had been off on a cruise for a few weeks, and was approaching the harbor last night, when, in accordance with his plans, a sumptuous dinner was served, as a sort of farewell feast, the party expecting to separate to-day."

"What guests were on the yacht?"

"I will tell you everything in order, as the facts were presented to me. Mr. Gray enumerated the party as follows: besides himself and his wife, there were his wife's sister, Mrs. Eugene Cortlandt, and her husband, a Wall Street broker; also, Mr. Arthur Livingstone and his sister, and a Mr. Dennett Moore, a young man supposed to be devoting himself to Miss Livingstone."

"That makes seven persons, three of whom are women. I ought to say, Mr. Barnes, that, though Mr. Gray is a club friend, I am not personally acquainted with his wife, nor with the others. So I have no advantage over you."

"I will come at once to the curious incident which made my presence desirable. According to Mr. Gray's story, the dinner had proceeded as far as the roast, when suddenly there was a slight shock as the yacht touched a bar, and at the same time the lamps spluttered and then went out, leaving the room totally dark. A second later the vessel righted herself and sped on, so that, before any panic ensued, it was evident to all that the danger had passed. The gentlemen begged the ladies to resume their seats, and remain quiet till the lamps were lighted; this, however, the attendants were unable to do, and they were ordered to bring fresh lamps. Thus there was almost total darkness for several minutes."

"During which, I presume, the person who planned the affair readily consummated his design?"

"So you think that the whole series of events was prearranged? Be that as it may, something did happen in that dark room. The women had started from their seats when the yacht touched, and when they groped their way back in the darkness some of them found the wrong places, as was seen when the fresh lamps were brought. This was considered a good joke, and there was some laughter, which was suddenly checked by an exclamation from Mr. Gray, who quickly asked his wife, 'Where is your opal?'"

"Her opal?" asked Mr. Mitchel, in tones which showed that his greatest interest was now aroused. "Do you mean, Mr. Barnes, that she was wearing the Aztec Opal?"

"Oh, you know the gem?"

"I know nearly all gems of great value; but what of this one?"

"Mrs. Gray and her sister, Mrs. Cortlandt, had both donned *décolleté* costumes for this occasion, and Mrs. Gray had worn this opal as a pendant to a thin gold chain which hung around her neck. At Mr. Gray's question, all looked towards his wife, and it was noted that the clasp was open, and the opal missing. Of course it was supposed that it had merely fallen to the floor, and a search was immediately instituted. But the opal could not be found."

"That is certainly a very significant fact," said Mr. Mitchel. "But was the search thorough?"

"I should say extremely thorough, when we consider it was not conducted by a detective, who is supposed to be an expert in such matters. Mr. Gray described to me what was done, and he seems to have taken every precaution. He sent the attendants out of the *salon,* and he and his guests systematically examined every part of the room."

"Except the place where the opal really was concealed, you mean."

"With that exception, of course, since they did not find the jewel. Not satisfied with this search by lamplight, Mr. Gray locked the *salon,* so that no one could enter it during the night, and another investigation was made in the morning."

"The pockets of the seven persons present were not examined, I presume?"

"No. I asked Mr. Gray why this had been omitted, and he said it was an indignity which he could not possibly show to a guest. As you have asked this question, Mr. Mitchel, it is only fair for me to tell you that when I spoke to Mr. Gray on the subject he seemed very much confused. Nevertheless, however unwilling he may have been to search those of his guests who are innocent, he emphatically told me that if I had reasonable proof that any one present had purloined the opal, he wished that individual to be treated as any other thief, without regard to sex or social position."

"One can scarcely blame him, because that opal is worth a fabulous sum. I have myself offered Gray twenty thousand dollars for it, which was refused. This opal is one of the eyes of an Aztec idol, and if the other could be found, the two would be as interesting as any jewels in the world."

"That is the story which I was asked to unravel," continued Mr. Barnes, "and I must now relate to you what steps I have taken towards that end. It appears that, because of the loss of the jewel, no person has left the yacht, although no restraint was placed upon anyone by Mr. Gray. All knew, however, that he had sent for a detective, and it was natural that no one should offer to go until formally dismissed by the host. My plan, then, was to have a private interview with each of the seven persons who had been present at the dinner."

"Then you exempted the attendants from your suspicions?"

"I did. There was but one way by which one of the servants could have stolen the opal, and this was prevented by Mr. Gray. It was possible that the opal had fallen on the floor, and, though not found at night, a servant might have discovered and have appropriated it on the following morning, had he been able to enter the *salon*. But Mr. Gray had locked the doors. No servant, however bold, would have been able to take the opal from the lady's neck."

"I think your reasoning is good, and we will confine ourselves to the original seven."

"After my interview with Mr. Gray, I asked to have Mrs. Gray sent in to me. She came in, and at once I noted that she placed herself on the defensive. Women frequently adopt that manner with a detective. Her story was very brief. The main point was that she was aware of the theft before the lamps were relighted. In fact, she felt some one's arms steal around her neck, and knew when the opal was taken. I asked why she had made no outcry, and whether she suspected any special person. To these questions she replied that she supposed it was merely a joke perpetrated in the darkness, and therefore had made no resistance. She would not name anyone as suspected by her, but she was willing to tell me that the arms were bare, as she detected when they touched her neck. I must say here, that although Miss Livingstone's dress was not cut low in the neck, it was, practically, sleeveless; and Mrs. Cortlandt's dress had no sleeves at all. One other significant statement made by this lady was that her husband had mentioned to her your offer of twenty thousand dollars for the opal, and had urged her to permit him to sell it, but she had refused."

"So it was madame who would not sell? The plot thickens."

"You will observe, of course, the point about the naked arms of the thief. I therefore sent for Mrs. Cortlandt next. She had a curious story to tell. Unlike her sister, she was quite willing to express her suspicions. Indeed, she plainly intimated that she supposed that Mr. Gray himself had taken the jewel. I will endeavor to repeat her words.

"'Mr. Barnes,' said she, 'the affair is very simple. Gray is a miserable old skinflint. A Mr. Mitchel, a crank who collects gems, offered to buy that opal, and he has been bothering my sister for it ever since. When the lamps went out, he took the opportunity to steal it. I do not think this—I know it. How? Well, on account of the confusion and darkness, I sat in my sister's seat when I returned to the table; this explains his mistake. He put his arms around my neck, and deliberately felt for the opal. I did not understand his purpose at the time, but now it is very evident.'

"'Yes, madame,' said I, 'but how do you know it was Mr. Gray?'

"'Why, I grabbed his hand, and before he could pull it away I felt the large cameo ring on his little finger. Oh, there is no doubt whatever.'

"I asked her whether Mr. Gray had his sleeves rolled up, and, though she could not understand the purport of the question, she said 'No.' Next I had Miss Livingstone come in. She is a slight, tremulous young lady, who cries at the slightest provocation. During the interview, brief as it was, it was only by the greatest diplomacy that I avoided a scene of hysterics. She tried very hard to convince me that she knew absolutely nothing. She had not left her seat during the disturbance; of that she was sure. So how could she know anything about it? I asked her to name the one who she thought might have taken the opal, and at this her agitation reached such a climax that I was obliged to let her go."

"You gained very little from her, I should say."

"In a case of this kind, Mr. Mitchel, where the criminal is surely one of a very few persons, we cannot fail to gain something from each person's story. A significant feature here was that though Miss Livingstone assures us that she did not leave her seat, she was sitting in a different place when the lamps were lighted again."

"That might mean anything or nothing."

"Exactly. But we are not deducing values yet. Mr. Dennett Moore came to me next, and he is a straightforward, honest man if I ever saw one. He declared that the whole affair was a great mystery to him, and that, while ordinarily he would not care anything about it, he could not but be somewhat interested, because he thought that one of the ladies, he would not say which one, suspected him. Mr. Livingstone also impressed me favorably, in spite of the fact that he did not remove his cigarette from his mouth throughout the whole of my interview with him. He declined to name the person suspected by him, though he admitted that he could do so. He made this significant remark:

"'You are a detective of experience, Mr. Barnes, and ought to be able to decide which man amongst us could place his arms around Mrs. Gray's neck without causing her to cry out. But if your imagination fails you, suppose you inquire into the financial standing of all of us, and see which one would be most likely to profit by thieving? Ask Mr. Cortlandt.'"

"Evidently Mr. Livingstone knows more than he tells."

"Yet he told enough for one to guess his suspicions, and to understand the delicacy which prompted him to say no more. He, however, gave me a good point upon which to question Mr. Cortlandt. When I asked that gentleman if any of the men happened to be in pecuniary difficulties, he became grave at once. I will give you his answer.

"'Mr. Livingstone and Mr. Moore are both exceedingly wealthy men, and I am a millionaire, in very satisfactory business circumstances at present. But I am very sorry to say that though our host, Mr. Gray, is also a distinctly rich man, he has met with some reverses recently, and I can conceive that ready money would be useful to him. But for all that, it is preposterous to believe what your question evidently indicates. None of the persons in this party is a thief, and least of all could we suspect Mr. Gray. I am sure that if he wished his wife's opal, she would give it to him cheerfully. No, Mr. Barnes, the opal is in some crack or crevice which we have overlooked. It is lost, not stolen.'

"That ended the interview with the several persons present, but I made one or two other inquiries, from which I elicited at least two significant facts. First, it was Mr. Gray himself who had indicated the course by which the yacht was steered last night, and which ran her over a sand-bar. Second, some one had nearly emptied the oil from the lamps, so that they would have burned out in a short time, even though the yacht had not touched."

"These, then, are your facts. And from these you have solved the problem. Well, Mr. Barnes, who stole the opal?"

"Mr. Mitchel, I have told you all I know, but I wish you to work out a solution before I reveal my own opinion."

"I have already done so, Mr. Barnes. Here; I will write my suspicion on a bit of paper. So. Now tell me yours, and you shall know mine afterwards."

"Why, to my mind it is very simple. Mr. Gray, failing to obtain the opal from his wife by fair means, resorted to a trick. He removed the oil from the lamps, and charted out a course for his yacht which would take her over a sand-bar, and when the opportune moment came he stole the jewel. His actions since then have been merely to cover his crime by shrouding the affair with mystery. By insisting upon a thorough search, and even sending for a detective, he makes it impossible for those who were present to accuse him hereafter. Undoubtedly Mr. Cortlandt's opinion will be the one generally adopted. Now what do you think?"

"I think I will go with you at once, and board the yacht *Idler*."

"But you have not told me whom you suspect," said Mr. Barnes, somewhat irritated.

"Oh, that is immaterial," said Mr. Mitchel, calmly preparing for the street. "I do not suspect Mr. Gray, so if you are correct you will have shown better ability than I. Come, let us hurry."

On their way to the dock from which they were to take the little steam launch which was waiting to carry the detective back to the yacht, Mr. Barnes asked Mr. Mitchel the following question:

"Mr. Mitchel," said he, "you will note that Mrs. Cortlandt alluded to you as a 'crank who collects gems.' I must admit that I have myself harbored a great curiosity as to your reasons for purchasing jewels which are valued beyond a mere conservative commercial price. Would you mind explaining why you began your collection?"

"I seldom explain my motives to others, especially when they relate to my more important pursuits in life. But in view of all that has passed between us, I think your curiosity justifiable, and I will gratify it. To begin with, I am a very wealthy man. I inherited great riches, and I have made a fortune myself. Have you any conception of the difficulties which harass a man of means?"

"Perhaps not in minute detail, though I can guess that the lot of the rich is not as free from care as the pauper thinks it is."

"The point is this: the difficulty with a poor man is to get rich, while with the rich man the greatest trouble is to prevent the increase of his wealth. Some men, of course, make no effort in that direction, and those men are a menace to society. My own idea of the proper use of a fortune is to manage it for the benefit of others, as well as one's self, and especially to prevent its increase."

"And is it so difficult to do this? Cannot money be spent without limit?"

"Yes; but unlimited evil follows such a course. This is sufficient to indicate to you that I am ever in search of a legitimate means of spending my income, provided that I may do good thereby. If I can do this, and at the same time afford myself pleasure, I claim that I am making the best use of my money. Now, I happen to be so constituted that the most interesting studies to me are social problems, and of these I am most entertained with the causes and environments of crime. Such a problem as the one you have brought to me to-day is of immense attractiveness to me, because the environment is one which is commonly supposed to preclude rather than to invite crime. Yet we have seen that despite the wealth of all concerned, some one has stooped to the commonest of crimes,—theft."

"But what has this to do with your collection of jewels?"

"Everything. Jewels—especially those of great magnitude— seem to be a special cause of crime. A hundred-carat diamond will tempt a man to theft as surely as the false beacon on a rocky shore entices the mariner to wreck and ruin. All the great jewels of the world have murder and other crimes woven in their histories.* My attention was first called to this by accidentally hearing a plot at a ball to rob the lady of the house of a large ruby which she wore on her breast. I went to her, and told her enough to persuade her to sell the stone to me. I fastened it into my scarf, where the plotters might see it if they remained at the ball. By my act I prevented a crime that night."

"Then am I to understand that you buy jewels with that end in view?"

"After that night I conceived this idea. If all the great jewels in the world could be collected together, and put in a place of safety, hundreds of crimes would be prevented, even before they had been conceived. Moreover, the search for, and acquirement of, these jewels would necessarily afford me abundant opportunity for studying the crimes which are perpetrated in order

---

*Mitchel here espouses the views of Sherlock Holmes, who, in "The Adventure of the Blue Carbuncle," said of the stolen gem: "Of course it is a nucleus and focus of crime. Every good stone is. They are the devil's pet baits. In the larger and older jewels every facet may stand for a bloody deed. This stone is not yet twenty years old.... In spite of its youth, it has already a sinister history. There have been two murders, a vitriol-throwing, a suicide, and several robberies brought about for the sake of this forty-grain weight of crystallized charcoal. Who would think that so pretty a toy would be a purveyor to the gallows and the prison?" Arthur Conan Doyle, *The Adventures of Sherlock Holmes* (London: George Newnes, 1892), 165.

to gain possession of them. Thus you understand more thoroughly why I am anxious to pursue this problem of the Aztec Opal."

Several hours later Mr. Mitchel and Mr. Barnes were sitting at a quiet table in the corner of the dining-room at Mr. Mitchel's club. On board the yacht Mr. Mitchel had acted rather mysteriously. He had been closeted a while with Mr. Gray, after which he had had an interview with two or three of the others. Then, when Mr. Barnes had begun to feel neglected, and tired of waiting alone on the deck, Mr. Mitchel had come towards him, arm in arm with Mr. Gray, and the latter had said:

"I am very much obliged to you, Mr. Barnes, for your services in this affair, and I trust the enclosed check will remunerate you for your trouble."

Mr. Barnes, not quite comprehending it all, had attempted to protest, but Mr. Mitchel had taken him by the arm, and hurried him off. In the cab which bore them to the club the detective asked for an explanation, but Mr. Mitchel only replied:

"I am too hungry to talk now. We will have dinner first."

The dinner was over at last, and nuts and coffee were before them, when Mr. Mitchel took a small parcel from his pocket, and handed it to Mr. Barnes, saying:

"It is a beauty, is it not?"

Mr. Barnes removed the tissue paper, and a large opal fell on the table-cloth, where it sparkled with a thousand colors under the electric lamps.

"Do you mean that this is—" cried the detective.

"The Aztec Opal, and the finest harlequin* I ever saw," interrupted Mr. Mitchel. "But you wish to know how it came into my possession? Principally so that it may join the collection and cease to be a temptation in this world of wickedness."

"Then Mr. Gray did not steal it?" asked Mr. Barnes, with a touch of chagrin in his voice.

*A harlequin is a stone in which the interior play of light or color (known as "fire") forms diamond- or rectangular-shaped patches. The more extensive the pattern, the more valuable.

"No, Mr. Barnes. Mr. Gray did not steal it. But you are not to consider yourself very much at fault. Mr. Gray tried to steal it, only he failed. That was not your fault, of course. You read his actions aright, but you did not give enough weight to the stories of the others."

"What important point did I omit from my calculations?"

"I might mention the bare arms which Mrs. Gray said she felt around her neck. It was evidently Mr. Gray who looked for the opal on the neck of his sister-in-law, but as he did not bare his arms before approaching her, he would not have done so later."

"Do you mean that Miss Livingstone was the thief?"

"No. Being hysterical, Miss Livingstone changed her seat without realizing it, but that does not make her a thief. Her excitement when with you was due to her suspicions, which, by the way, were correct. But let us return for a moment to the bare arms. That was the clue from which I worked. It was evident to me that the thief was a man, and it was equally plain that, in the hurry of the few moments of darkness, no man would have rolled up his sleeves, risking the return of the attendants with lamps, and the consequent discovery of himself in such a singular disarrangement of costume."

"How do you account for the bare arms?"

"The lady did not tell the truth, that is all. The arms which encircled her neck were not bare. Neither were they unknown to her. She told you that lie to shield the thief. She also told you that her husband wished to sell the Aztec Opal to me, but that she had refused. Thus she deftly led you to suspect him. Now, if she wished to shield the thief, yet was willing to accuse her husband, it followed that the husband was not the thief."

"Very well reasoned, Mr. Mitchel. I see now where you are tending, but I shall not get ahead of your story."

"So much I had deduced before we went on board the yacht. When I found myself alone with Gray I candidly told him of your suspicions, and your reasons for harboring them. He was very much disturbed, and pleadingly asked me what I thought. As frankly, I told him that I believed that he had tried to take the opal from his wife,—we can scarcely call it stealing since the law does not,—but that I believed he had failed. He then confessed; admitted emptying the lamps, though he denied running the boat on the sand-bar. But he assured me that he had not reached his wife's chair when the lamps were brought in. He was, therefore, much astonished at missing the gem. I promised him to find the jewel upon condition that he would sell it to me. To this he most willingly acceded."

"But how could you be sure that you would recover the opal?"

"Partly by my knowledge of human nature, and partly because of my inherent faith in my own abilities. I sent for Mrs. Gray, and noted her attitude of defense, which, however, only satisfied me the more that I was right in my suspicions. I began by asking her if she knew the origin of the superstition that an opal brings bad luck to its owner. She did not, of course, comprehend my tactics, but she added that she 'had heard the stupid superstition, but took no interest in such nonsense.' I then gravely explained to her that the opal is the engagement stone of the Orient. The lover gives it to his sweetheart, and the belief is, that should she deceive him even in the most trifling manner, the opal will lose its brilliancy and become cloudy. I then suddenly asked her if she had ever noted a change in her opal. 'What do you mean to insinuate?' she cried out angrily. 'I mean,' said I, sternly, 'that if any opal has ever changed color in accordance with the superstition, this one should have done so. I mean that though your husband greatly needs the money which I have offered him, you have refused to allow him to sell it, and yet you permitted another to take it from you last night. By this act you might have seriously injured if not ruined Mr. Gray. Why have you done it?'"

"How did she receive it?" asked Mr. Barnes, admiring the ingenuity of Mr. Mitchel.

"She began to sob, and between her tears she admitted that the opal had been taken by the man whom I suspected, but she earnestly declared that she had harbored no idea of injuring her husband. Indeed, she was so agitated in speaking upon this point, that I believe that Gray never thoroughly explained to her why he wished to sell the gem. She urged me to recover the opal if possible, and purchase it, so that her husband might be relieved from his pecuniary embarrassment. I then sent for the thief, Mrs. Gray having told me his name; but would you not like to hear how I had picked him out before he went aboard? I still have that bit of paper upon which I wrote his name, in confirmation of what I say."

"Of course I know that you mean Mr. Livingstone, but I would like to hear your reasons for suspecting him."

"From your account Miss Livingstone suspected some one, and this caused her to be so agitated that she was unaware of the fact that she had changed her seat. Women are shrewd in these affairs, and I was confident that the girl had good reasons for her conduct. It was evident that the person in her mind was either her brother or her sweetheart. I decided between these two men from your account of your interviews with them. Moore impressed you as being honest, and he told you that one of the ladies suspected him. In this he was mistaken, but his speaking to you of it was not the act of a thief. Mr. Livingstone, on the other hand, tried to throw suspicion upon Mr. Gray."

"Of course that was sound reasoning after you had concluded that Mrs. Gray was lying. Now tell me how you recovered the jewel."

"That was easier than I expected. When I got him alone, I simply told Mr. Livingstone what I knew, and asked him to hand me the opal. With a perfectly imperturbable manner, understanding that I promised secrecy, he quietly took it from his pocket and gave it to me, saying:

"Women are very poor conspirators. They are too weak."

"What story did you tell Mr. Gray?"

"Oh, he would not be likely to inquire too closely into what I should tell him. My check was what he most cared for. I told him nothing definitely, but I hinted that his wife had secreted the gem during the darkness, that he might not ask her for it again; and that she had intended to find it again at a future time, just as he had meant to pawn it and then pretend to recover it from the thief by offering a reward."

"One more question. Why did Mr. Livingstone steal it?"

"Ah; the truth about that is another mystery worth probing, and one which I shall make it my business to unravel. I will venture a prophecy. Mr. Livingstone did not steal it at all. Mrs. Gray simply handed it to him in the darkness. There must have been some powerful motive to lead her to such an act; something which she was weighing, and decided impulsively. This brings me to a second point. Livingstone used the word conspirators; that is a clue. You will recall that I told you that this gem is one of a pair of opals, and that with the other, the two would be as interesting as any jewels in the world. If anyone ever owns both it shall be your humble servant, Leroy Mitchel, Jewel Collector."

# VII
## THE DUPLICATE HARLEQUIN

One day about two weeks after the unravelling of the mystery of the opal lost on board the yacht *Idler*, Mr. Barnes called upon Mr. Mitchel and was cordially received.

"Glad to see you, Mr. Barnes. Anything stirring in the realm of crime?"

"'Stirring' would be a fitting adjective, I think, Mr. Mitchel. Ever since the *Idler* affair I have occupied myself with a study of the problem, which I am convinced we have but partially solved. You may recall that you gave me a clue."

"You mean that Livingstone, when he gave me the opal, remarked, 'Women are poor conspirators.' Yes, I remember calling your attention to that. Has your clue led to any solution?"

"Oh, I am not out of the maze yet; more likely just entering the most intricate depths. Still, I flatter myself that I have accomplished something; enough to satisfy me that 'mischief is brewing,' and that the conspirators are still conspiring. Moreover, there is little doubt that you are deeply concerned in the new plot."

"What! You insinuate that I am in this conspiracy?"

"Only as a possible victim. You are the object of the plot."

"Perhaps you think that I am in danger?" Mr. Mitchel smiled as though the idea of danger were a pleasurable one.

"Were you any other man than yourself, I should say most decidedly that you are in danger."

"But, being myself, you fancy that the danger will pass from me?"

"Being yourself, I anticipate that you will compel the danger to pass from you."

"Mr. Barnes, you flatter me. Perhaps I may be able to thwart the conspirators, now that you warn me; if I do, however, I must admit my great indebtedness to you. To be forewarned is to have the fight half won, and I candidly say that I was entirely unsuspicious of any lurking danger."

"Exactly. With all your acumen, I was sure that your suspicions had not been aroused. The conspirators are wary, and, I assure you, unusually skilful. So, under all the circumstances, I felt it my duty to be on the alert."

"Ah, I see," said Mr. Mitchel, in that tone peculiar to him, which made it doubtful whether he spoke in earnest, or whether his words hid keen satire. "The old cat being asleep, the kitten watches. That is very nice of you. Really, it is quite a comforting thought that so skilful a detective is ever guarding my person. Especially as I am the owner of so many gems to which the covetous must ever look longingly."

"That is just how I reasoned it," said Mr. Barnes, eagerly, wishing to justify his actions, which he began to suspect Mr. Mitchel might resent. "You explained to me your reasons why you have purchased so many valuable jewels. You claimed that almost every large gem has been the cause, or rather the object, of crime. The Aztec Opal came into your possession under most peculiar circumstances. In fact, you thwarted a criminal just as he had come into possession of it. But this criminal is a wealthy man. Not perhaps as rich as yourself, but rich enough to be above stealing even such a valuable bauble. It could not have been the intrinsic value of the opal which tempted him; it must have been that some special reason existed; some reason,

I mean, for his acquiring possession of this particular opal. All this being true, it would be a natural sequence that his efforts to get the opal would not cease merely because it had changed hands."

"Your argument is most interesting, Mr. Barnes, especially as it is without a flaw. As you say, from all this reasoning it was a natural sequence that Mr. Livingstone would continue his quest for the opal. This being so obvious, did you imagine that it had escaped me?"

Mr. Barnes was confused by the question. He really admired Mr. Mitchel very much, and though he considered him quite conceited, he also admitted that he had great analytical powers and remarkable acumen. He also, more than anything else, desired a perpetuation of his friendship; indeed, it had been with an idea of increasing the bond between them that he had called. He had spent much of his time, time which could have been occupied with other matters to better financial advantage, and all with the purpose of warding off from his friend a danger which he had at first considered as a distant possibility, but which later he looked upon as certain, if nothing intervened to hinder the plot, which he knew was rapidly approaching the moment of execution. He therefore hastened to make further explanation:

"Not at all—not at all. I am merely indicating the steps by which I reached my conclusions. I am giving you my reasons for what I fear you now may consider my interference in your affairs. Yet I assure you I meant it all—"

"For the best. Why, of course, my friend; did you suppose that I doubted your good intent, merely because I spoke brusquely?" Mr. Mitchel held out his hand cordially, and Mr. Barnes grasped it, glad to note the altered demeanor of his companion. Mr. Mitchel continued: "Will you never learn that my weakness is for antagonizing detectives? When you come here to tell me that you have been 'investigating' my private affairs, how could I resist telling you that I knew all about it, or that I could take care of myself? I would not be Leroy Mitchel were it otherwise."

"How do you mean that you know all about it?"

"Well, perhaps not all. I am not exactly omniscient. Still, I know something. Let me see, now. How much do I know? First, then, you have had this Livingstone watched. Second, you have introduced one of your spies, a young woman, into the home of Mrs. Gray. In spite of your alleged faith in Dennett Moore, you had him watched also, though for only two or three days. Lastly, you have discovered Pedro Domingo, and—"

"In Heaven's name, Mr. Mitchel, how do you know all this?" Mr. Barnes was utterly dumbfounded by what he had heard.

"All this?" said Mr. Mitchel, with a suave smile; "why, I have mentioned only four small facts."

"Small facts?"

"Yes, quite small. Let us run them over again. First, I stated that you had Mr. Livingstone watched. That was not hard to know, because I also had a spy upon his track."

"You?"

"Yes, I. Why not? Did you not just now agree that it was obvious that he would continue his efforts to get the opal? Being determined that I should never part with it whilst alive, it likewise followed that he must kill me, or have me killed, in order to obtain it. Under these circumstances it was only common caution to have the man watched. Indeed, the method was altogether too common. It was bizarre. Still, my spy was no common spy.

"In that, at least, my method was unique. Secondly, I claimed that you had introduced a woman spy into the home of Mrs. Gray. To learn this was even easier. I deduced it from what I know of your methods. You played the same trick on my wife once, I think you will recall. Supposing Mrs. Gray to be a conspirator (that was your clue, I think), you would hardly watch

Livingstone and neglect the woman. Yet the actual knowledge came to me in a very simple manner."

"How was that?"

"Why, Mr. Gray told me."

"Mr. Gray told you?"

"Mr. Gray himself. You see, your assistants are not all so clever as yourself, though I doubt not this girl may think that she is a genius. You told her to seek a position in the house, and what does she do? She goes straight to Mr. Gray and tells him her purpose; hints that it might be well for him to know just what really actuated Mrs. Gray in the curious affair on the yacht, and agrees to 'discover everything'—those were her words—if he would give her the opportunity. Poor man, she filled his mind with dire suspicions and he managed it so that she was taken into service. Up to the present time she has discovered nothing. At least, so she tells him."

"The little she-devil! You said that she explained her whole purpose. Do you mean—"

"Oh, no. She did not implicate you, nor divulge her true mission. The fun of the thing is that she claimed to be a 'private detective' and that this venture was entirely her own idea. In fact, she is working for Mr. Gray. Is not that droll?" Mr. Mitchel threw back his head and laughed heartily. Mr. Barnes did not quite see the fun, and looked grim. All he said was:

"She acted beyond her instructions, yet it seems that she has not done any harm; and though she is like an untamed colt, apt to take the bit between her teeth, still she is shrewd. But I'll curb her yet. Now as to your third fact. How did you know that I had Mr. Moore watched, and only for two or three days?"

"Why, I recognized one of your spies following him one day down Broadway, and as Moore sailed for Europe two days after, I made the deduction that you had withdrawn your watch-dog."

"Well, then," said Mr. Barnes, testily, "how did you know that I had, as you declare, 'discovered Pedro Domingo'?"

"How did I know that? Why—but that can wait. You certainly did not call this morning to ask me all these questions. You came, as I presume, to convey information."

"Oh, you know so much, it is evidently unnecessary for me to tell you of my trifling discoveries." Mr. Barnes was suffering from wounded pride.

"Come, come," exclaimed Mr. Mitchel, cheerily, "be a man; don't be downcast and fall into the dumps merely because I surprised a few trifling facts in your game, and could not resist the fun of guying you a little. You see, I still admit that what I know are but trifling facts; what you know, on the contrary, is perhaps of great importance. Indeed, I am assured that without your information, without a full knowledge of all that you have discovered, my own plans may go awry, and then the danger at which you hint might be all too real. Do you not see that, knowing that you are interested in this case, I have been only too willing to let half the burden of the investigation fall upon you? That to your skill I have entrusted all of that work which I knew you could do so well? That in the most literal sense we have been silent partners, and that I depended upon your friendship to bring you to me with your news, just as it has brought you?"

This speech entirely mollified Mr. Barnes, and, with a brightening countenance, he exclaimed:

"Mr. Mitchel, I'm an ass. You are right to laugh at me."

"Nonsense! I defy all other detectives, because Mr. Barnes works with me."

"Bosh!" said the detective, deprecatingly, but pleased nevertheless by the words of flattery. "Well, then, suppose I tell you my story from the beginning?"

"From the beginning, by all means."

"In speaking of the woman whom I set to spy upon Mrs. Gray, you just now mentioned that I had once played the same trick upon your wife. Very true, and not only is this the same trick, but it is the same girl."

"What! Lucette?"

"The same. This is not the first time that she has chosen to resort to her own devices rather than to follow strictly the orders given to her. In this case, however, as I said before, she has done no harm, and on the contrary, I think you would find her report, which I received an hour ago, quite interesting."

"Ah, you have brought it with you?"

"Yes. I will read it to you. Of course it is not addressed to me, neither is there any signature. No names are mentioned except by initial. All this is the girl's own devising, so you see she is not entirely stupid. She writes:

"'At last I have discovered everything.' You observe that she is not unappreciative of her own ability. 'Mr. L. was right. Women are bad conspirators. At least he is right as to Mrs. G. She has dropped the conspiracy entirely, if she ever was a real conspirator, which I doubt, for, though you may not suspect it, she loves her husband. How do I know? Well, a woman has instincts about love. A man may swear eternal devotion to a woman eight hours a day for a year, without convincing her, when she would detect the true lover by the way he ties her shoe-string, unasked. So here. I have not heard madame talking in her sleep, neither has she taken her maid for a confidante, though I think she might find a worse adviser. Still I say she loves her husband. How do I know? When a woman is constantly doing things which add to the comfort of a man, and for which she never receives thanks, because they are such trifles, you may be sure the woman loves the man, and by hundreds of such tokens I know that Mrs. G. is in love with her husband. To reach the next point I must give you an axiom. A woman never loves more than one man at a time. She may have many lovers in the course of a lifetime, but in each instance she imagines that all previous affairs were delusions, and that at last the divine fire consumes her. To this last love she is constant until he proves unworthy, and ofttimes even after. No, a man may be able to love two persons, but a woman's affections are ever centred in a single idol. From which it is a logical deduction that Mrs. G. does not and did not love Mr. L. Then why did she give him the opal? A question which will puzzle you, and for which you are at a loss for an answer.'"

"She is not complimentary," interrupted Mr. Mitchel.

"Not very," said Mr. Barnes, and then he continued reading:

"'This is a question at which I arrived, as you see, by logical mental stages. This is the question to which I have found the reply. This is what I mean when I say I have discovered all. Yesterday afternoon Mr. L. called. Madame hesitated, but finally decided to see him. From her glances in my direction, I was sure she feared I might accidentally find it convenient to be near enough to a keyhole to overhear the conversation which was about to ensue, and, as I did not wish her to make such an "accident" impossible, I innocently suggested that if she intended to receive a visitor, I should be glad to have permission to leave the house for an hour. The trick worked to a charm. Madame seemed only too glad to get rid of me. I hurried down stairs into the back parlor, where, by secreting myself between the heavy portieres and the closed folding-doors, my sharp ears readily followed the conversation, except such few passages as were spoken in very low tones, but which I am sure were unimportant. The details I will give you when I see you. Suffice it to say that I discovered that madame's reason for refusing to let her husband sell the jewel to that crank Mr. M.—'"

"Ah; I see she remembers me," said Mr. Mitchel, with a smile.

"How could she forget your locking her in a room when she was most anxious to be elsewhere? But let me finish this:

"'—to that crank Mr. M. was because Mr. L. was telling her how to make a deal more money out of the jewel. It seems that he has the mate to it, and that the two were stolen from an idol somewhere in Mexico, and that a fabulous sum could be obtained by returning the two gems to the native priests. Just how, I do not know.'"

"So she did not discover everything, after all," said Mr. Mitchel.

"No; but she is right in the main. Her report continues:

"'Madame, however, hesitated to go into the venture, partly because Mr. L. insisted that the matter be kept secret from her husband, and more particularly because the money in exchange was not to be forthcoming immediately. On the yacht she changed her mind impulsively. The result of that you know.'

"That is all," said Mr. Barnes, folding the paper and returning it to his pocket.

"That is all you know?" asked Mr. Mitchel.

"No; that is all that Lucette knows. I know how the fabulous sum of money was to be had in exchange for the two opals."

"Ah; that is more to our immediate purpose. How have you made this discovery?"

"My spies learned practically nothing by shadowing Livingstone, except that he has had several meetings with a half-breed Mexican who calls himself Pedro Domingo. I decided that it would be best for me to interview Señor Domingo myself, rather than to entrust him to a second man."

"What a compliment to our friend Livingstone!" said Mr. Mitchel, with a laugh.

"I found the Mexican suspicious and difficult to approach at first. So I quickly decided that only a bold play would be successful. I told him that I was a detective, and related the incident of the stealing of the opal. At this his eyes glistened, but when I told him that the gem had been sold to a man of enormous wealth who would never again part with it, his eyes glared."

"Yes, Domingo's eyes are glary at times. Go on."

"I explained to him that by this I meant that it would now be impossible for Mr. Livingstone to get the opal, and then I boldly asked him what reward I might expect if I could get it."

"How much did he offer?"

"At first he merely laughed at me, but then I explained that you are my friend, and that you merely buy such things to satisfy a hobby, and that, having no especial desire for this particular jewel, I had little doubt that I could obtain it, provided it would be of great financial advantage to myself. In short, that you would sell to a friend what none other could buy."

"Not bad, Mr. Barnes. What did Domingo say to that?"

"He asked for a day to think it over."

"Which, of course, you granted. What, then, is his final answer?"

"He told me to get the opal first, and then he would talk business."

"Bravo! Domingo is becoming quite a Yankee."

"Of course I watched the man during the interval, in order to learn whether or not he would consult with Mr. L., or any other adviser."

"What did this lead to?"

"It led to Pasquale Sanchez."

"What! More Mexicans?"

"One more only. Sanchez lives in a house near where Domingo has his room. He tells me that he comes from the same district as Domingo. Although Domingo did not make a confidant of him, or even ask his advice, his visit to his friend cleared up some things for me, for by following Domingo I came upon Sanchez."

"What could he know, if, as you say, he was not in the confidence of Domingo?"

"He knew some things which seem to be common knowledge in his native land. He is even more Americanized than his friend, for he fully appreciates a glass of whiskey, though I doubt not the habit was first acquired at home. I should think it would take many years to acquire such a—let me call it—capacity. I never saw a man who could swallow such powerful doses without a change of expression. The only effect seemed to be to loosen his tongue. It is needless to repeat all the stages by which

I approached my subject. He knew all about the Aztec opals,—
for really there are two of them,—except of course their present
whereabouts. I asked him if they would be valuable, supposing
that I could get possession of them. He was interested at once.
'You get them, and I show you million dollars.' I explained to
him that I might see a million dollars any day by visiting the
United States Treasury, upon which, with many imprecations
and useless interpolations of bad Spanish, he finally made it
clear to me that the priests who have the idol from which the
opals were obtained, have practically little power over their
tribe while the 'god is in heaven,' as has been explained to the
faithful, the priests not caring to exhibit the image without its
glowing eyes. These priests, it seems, know where the mine is
from which these opals were taken, and they would reveal this
secret in exchange for the lost opals, because, though this mine
is said to be very rich, they have been unable themselves to find
any pieces sufficiently large and brilliant from which to duplicate the lost gems."

"Then you think it was to obtain possession of this opal mine
that Mr. Livingstone sought to obtain Mrs. Gray's opal?"

"Undoubtedly. So certain am I of this that I would wager that
he will endeavor to get the opal from you."

"Let me read a letter to you, Mr. Barnes." Mr. Mitchel took
out a letter and read as follows:

"'LEROY MITCHEL, Esq.:—

"'Dear Sir—In my letter of recent date I offered to you the
duplicate of the Aztec Opal which you recently purchased
from Mr. Gray. You paid Gray twenty thousand dollars, and
I expressed my willingness to sell you mine for five thousand
dollars in advance of this sum. In your letter just received,
you agree to pay this amount, naming two conditions. First,
you ask why I consider my opal worth more than the other,

*if it is an exact duplicate. Secondly, you wish me to explain what I meant by saying on the yacht that "women are poor conspirators."*

"'In reply to your first question, my answer is, that however wealthy I may be I usually do business strictly on business principles. These opals separately are worth in the open market twenty thousand dollars each, which sum you paid to Gray. But considering the history of the gems, and the fact that they are absolute duplicates the one of the other, it is not too much to declare that as soon as one person owns both gems, the value is enhanced twofold. That is to say, that the pair of opals together would be worth seventy or eighty thousand dollars. This being true, I consider it fair to argue that whilst I should not expect more than twenty thousand dollars from any other person in the world, twenty-five thousand is a low sum for me to ask of the man who has the duplicate of this magnificent harlequin opal.*

"'In regard to my remark about the 'conspirators,' the conspiracy in which I had induced Mrs. Gray to take part was entirely honorable, I assure you. I knew of Gray's financial embarrassments and wished to aid him, without, however, permitting him to suspect my hand in the affair. He is so sensitive, you know. I therefore suggested to Mrs. Gray that she entrust her jewel to me, and promised to dispose of the two jewels together, thus realizing the enhanced value. I pointed out that in this manner she would be able to give her husband much more than he could possibly secure by the sale of the one stone.*

"'Trusting that I have fully complied with your conditions, I will call upon you at noon to-day, and will bring the opal with me. We can then complete the transaction, unless you change your mind in the interval. Cordially yours, etc.'*

"So you see," said Mr. Mitchel, "he offers to sell me his opal, rather than to purchase mine."

"It is strange," said Mr. Barnes, musingly. "Why should he relinquish his hope of getting possession of that mine? I do not believe it. There is some devilish trickery at work. But let me tell you the rest of my story."

"Oh, is there more?"

"Why, certainly. I have not yet explained my reason for thinking you might be in danger."

"Ah, to be sure. My danger. I had forgotten all about it. Pardon my stupidity."

"In further conversation with this Sanchez I put this proposition to him. 'Suppose,' said I, 'that your friend Domingo had one of these opals, and knew the man who had the other. What would he do?' His answer was short, but to the point. 'He get it, even if he kill.'"

"So you think that Domingo might try murder?"

"It is not impossible."

"But, Mr. Barnes, he does not want my life. He wants the opal, and as that is, or rather has been until to-day, in the safety-vaults, how could he get it, even by killing me?"

"You have just admitted that it is not in the vaults at present."

"But it is quite as much out of his reach in my safe here in this room."

"But you might take it out of the safe. You might, in some manner, be persuaded to do so, to show it to some one."

"Very true. In fact, that is why it is here. I must compare my opal with the one which Mr. Livingstone offers for sale, before I part with twenty-five thousand dollars. For you must remember that such a sum is a fabulous price for an opal, even though, as you know, these are the largest in the world."

"From a money standpoint, of course, your precaution is proper. But do you not see that you are really making possible the very danger of which I came to warn you?"

"You mean—"

"Murder in order to get possession of that accursed ill-luck stone. But I fear my warning is not appreciated."

"Indeed, my friend, it is, and I am glad that you have come in person to acquaint me with your anxiety in my behalf. This I will more thoroughly explain to you later. For the present, I may say that I am glad to have you here as a possible witness, in case murder, or any other crime, should be attempted."

"What other crime do you anticipate as possible? Surely not theft?"

"Why not?"

"What! Steal that opal from you, while you are present to see the deed committed? That is a joke." Mr. Barnes laughed heartily.

"Your laugh is a compliment," said Mr. Mitchel. "Yet that is exactly what I most anticipate—theft. I am not sure that it may not be undertaken before my very eyes. Especially as the thief did not hesitate at a table filled with men and women. Sh! He is here."

The electric street-door bell had sounded. Mr. Mitchel arose, and spoke hurriedly in a low tone.

"That is probably Mr. Livingstone come to sell his opal, or to steal mine. We shall see. Especially I desire that you should see. Consequently I have arranged matters in advance. Slip behind this bookcase, which I have placed across the corner that you may have room to breathe. The books on the top shelf have been removed, and the tinted glass of the doors will not obstruct your view. From behind you will be able to see through quite readily."

"Why, you seem to have expected me," said Mr. Barnes, getting into the hiding-place.

"Yes, I expected you," said Mr. Mitchel, vouchsafing no further explanation. "Remember now, Mr. Barnes, you are not to interfere, whatever happens, unless I call you. All I ask is that you use your eyes, and that good eyes will be required be sure, or I never should have arranged to have an extra pair to aid me on this occasion."

A moment later Williams announced Mr. Livingstone.

"Ask Mr. Livingstone to come up here to the library," said Mr. Mitchel, and a little later he greeted his guest.

"Ah, glad to see you, Mr. Livingstone. Take a seat here by my desk, and we can get right to business. First, though, let me offer you a cigar."

Mr. Livingstone chose one from the box which Mr. Mitchel offered to him, and lighted it as he sat down.

"What a companionable feeling steals over one as he puffs a fine cigar, Mr. Mitchel! Who would accept such an offering as this and betray the confidence of his host?"

"Who, indeed?" said Mr. Mitchel. "But why do you say that?"

"Why, I am not entirely a fool. You do not trust me. You are not sure in your own mind whether or not I committed a theft on board of the yacht."

"Am I not?" Mr. Mitchel asked this in a tone that made Mr. Livingstone look upon it in the light of a question, whereas Mr. Barnes, behind the bookcase, considered it as an answer.

"Why, no," said Mr. Livingstone, replying. "Had you believed that the opal changed hands honorably, even though secretly, under cover of the darkness, you would not have asked me to explain my allusion to 'conspirators.' I trust, however, that my letter made it all clear to you."

"Quite clear."

"Then you are still willing to make the purchase?"

"If you still desire to sell. A certified check for the amount is ready for you. Have you brought the opal?"

"Yes. Have you the duplicate? It would be well to compare them before you purchase."

"If you do not mind, I will do so."

Mr. Mitchel turned to his safe and brought out a box which Mr. Barnes thought he recognized. Opening it he drew out a marvellous string of pearls, which he laid aside, while he took from beneath, a velvet case which contained the opal. Returning the pearls to the box he restored that to the safe, which he locked.

"Now, if you will let me see your opal," said Mr. Mitchel, "I will compare the gems."

"Here it is," said Mr. Livingstone, handing Mr. Mitchel his opal.

Mr. Mitchel took the two opals in his hand, and, as they lay side by side, he examined them closely, observing the play of light as he turned them in various positions. To his critical eye they were marvellously beautiful; matchless, though matched. None could see these two and wonder that the old priests in Mexico had searched in vain for a second pair like them.

"Do you know why these opals are so exactly alike?" asked Mr. Livingstone.

"I am not sure," said Mr. Mitchel, apparently absorbed in his scrutiny of the opals. "I have heard many reasons suggested. If you know the true explanation, suppose you tell me."

"Willingly. You will observe that in each opal red lights seem to predominate on one side, while the blue and green are reflected from the other. Originally, this was one great egg-shaped opal, and it was cut in that shape, and then poised in the forehead of a single-eyed idol by the priests of a thousand years ago. By an ingenious mechanism the eye could be made to revolve in its socket, so that either the red or the blue-green side would be visible, as it suited the purpose of the priests, when overawing the tribesmen by pretended prophecies and other miraculous performances. In more recent times, since the advent of the Christians, one-eyed idols are not so plausible, and the priests cut the opal in half, thus making it serve in what may be termed a modernized idol."

"Yes, I have heard that tale before. In fact, I have a metal ring which I was told would exactly encircle the two opals, if placed together to form an egg."

"How could you have such a thing?" asked Mr. Livingstone, with genuine surprise.

"The man who stole the jewels, so the story goes, wishing to enhance their value as much as possible, arranged this as a scheme by which the genuineness of the opals could be tested. He placed the opals together, as before they were cut, and had a silver band made which would exactly clasp them in that position. This band opens and shuts with a spring catch, like a bracelet, and as, when closed, it exactly fits the opals, holding the two firmly together, the owner of the band could easily tell whether the true opals were before him, or not. In some way the opals were next stolen without the band, and their whereabouts was unknown when a dealer in Naples told me the story of the silver band, which he offered to sell me. I scarcely credited his tale, but as all large jewels might in time be offered to me, I thought it well to purchase the band."

"Why, then, if you still have it, it would be interesting to make the test, would it not?"

"Yes, I think so, I will get the band." Mr. Mitchel placed the two opals on the desk before him and went over to the safe, where he was occupied some time opening the combination lock. While he was thus busy a strange thing seemed to occur. At least it seemed strange to Mr. Barnes. He had marvelled to see Mr. Mitchel place the two opals within easy reach of Mr. Livingstone, and then deliberately turn his back while he opened the safe. But what seemed more mysterious was Mr. Livingstone's action. Mr. Mitchel had scarcely stooped before the safe when his guest leaned forward, with both arms outstretched simultaneously; his two hands grasped the opals, the hands then swiftly sought his vest pockets, after which he calmly puffed his cigar. Thus he seemed to have taken the opals from the table and to have placed them in his pockets. Yet how could he hope to explain their absence to Mr. Mitchel? This thought flashed through Mr. Barnes's mind as his eyes instinctively turned again to the desk, when, to his utter astonishment, he saw the opals exactly where Mr. Mitchel had placed them. Had the thought that he could not explain away the disappearance caused the man to change his mind at the very moment when he had impulsively clutched the treasures? Mr. Barnes was puzzled, and somewhat worried too, for he began to fear that more had happened, or was happening, than he comprehended.

"Here is the band," said Mr. Mitchel, returning to the desk, and resuming his seat. "Let us see how it fits the opals. First, let me ask you, are you confident that you are selling me one of the genuine Aztec opals?"

"I am. I have a history which makes its authenticity indubitable."

"Then we will try our little test. There; the band clamps the two perfectly. Look for yourself."

"Certainly; the test is complete. These are undoubtedly the Aztec opals. Mr. Mitchel, you are to be congratulated upon gaining possession of such unique gems."

Mr. Livingstone arose as though about to leave.

"One moment, Mr. Livingstone; the jewels are not mine, yet. I have not paid you for yours."

"Oh, between gentlemen there is no hurry about such matters."

"Between gentlemen it may be as you say. But you said this was to be strictly in accordance with business methods. I prefer to pay at once. Here is my certified check. I will also ask you to sign this receipt."

Mr. Livingstone seemed to hesitate for a moment. Mr. Barnes wondered why? He sat at the desk, however, and, after reading the receipt, he signed it, and took the check, which he placed in his pocketbook, saying:

"Of course we will be businesslike, if you insist, though I did not anticipate that you would take me so literally. That being over, Mr. Mitchel, I will bid you good morning."

"You may go, Mr. Livingstone, when the transaction is over, but not before."

"What do you mean?" demanded Mr. Livingstone aggressively, as he turned and faced Mr. Mitchel, who now stood close beside him.

"I mean that you have accepted my money. Now I wish you to give me the opal."

"I do not understand. There are your opals, just where you placed them on the table."

"We will have no quibbling, Mr. Livingstone. You have taken twenty-five thousand dollars of my money, and you have given me in exchange a worthless imitation. Not satisfied with that, you have stolen my genuine opal."

"Damn you—"

Mr. Livingstone made a movement as though to strike, but Mr. Mitchel stepped quickly back, and, quietly bringing forward his right arm, which had been held behind his back, it became evident that he held in his hand a revolver of large calibre. He did not raise the weapon, however, but merely remarked:

"I am armed. Think before you act."

"Your infernal accusation astounds me," growled Mr. Livingstone. "I hardly know what to say to you."

"There is nothing to say, sir. You have no alternative but to give me my property. Yes, you have an alternative,—you may go to prison."

"To prison!" The man laughed, but it was not a hearty laugh.

"Yes, to prison. I believe that is the proper lodging-place for a thief."

"Take care!" cried Mr. Livingstone, advancing upon Mr. Mitchel.

"Mr. Barnes," said Mr. Mitchel, still without raising his weapon. At this the man stopped as quickly as he had when the weapon was first shown. He seemed confounded when the detective stepped into view.

"Ah," he sneered; "so you have spies upon your guests?"

"Always, when my guests are thieves."

Again the words enraged him, and, starting forward, Mr. Livingstone exclaimed:

"If you repeat those words, I'll strangle you in spite of your weapon and your spy."

"I have no wish to use harsh language, Mr. Livingstone. All I want is my property. Give me the two opals."

"Again I tell you they are on your desk."

"Where are the genuine opals, Mr. Barnes? Of course you saw him commit the—that is, you saw the act."

"They are in his vest pocket, one in each," said the detective.

"Since you will not give them to me, I must take them," said Mr. Mitchel, advancing towards Mr. Livingstone. That gentleman stood transfixed, livid with rage. As his antagonist was about to touch his vest pocket, his hand arose swiftly and he aimed a deadly blow at Mr. Mitchel, but not only did Mr. Mitchel as swiftly lower his head, thus avoiding the blow, but before another could be struck, Mr. Barnes had jumped forward and grasped Mr. Livingstone from behind, pinioning his arms and holding him fast by placing his own knee in his adversary's back. Mr. Livingstone struggled fiercely, but almost instantly Mr. Mitchel took the opals from his pockets, and then quietly remarked:

"Release him, Mr. Barnes. I have my property."

Mr. Barnes obeyed, and for an instant Mr. Livingstone seemed weighing his chances, but evidently deciding that the odds were in all ways against him, he rushed from the apartment and out of the house.

"Well, Mr. Mitchel," said Mr. Barnes, "now that the danger has passed, an explanation seems to be in order. You seem to have four opals."

"Yes; but that is merely seeming. You will readily understand why I wished your eyes, for without them I could not have taken my own off of the opals even for an instant."

"Then you purposely turned your back when you went to get the silver band?"

"Assuredly. Why could I not have taken out the band in the first instance, and why did I lock the safe, making it necessary for me to take time with the combination? Simply to give my man the opportunity to do his trick. You see, I knew before he came here exactly what he would do."

"How did you know?"

"You will recall that in his letter he offers to sell me the duplicate opal. That made me smile when I read it, for I already had been notified that he had had duplicates of his opal made."

"You had been notified?"

"Yes. This whole affair flatters my vanity, for I anticipated the event in its minutest detail, and all by analytical deduction. You quite correctly argued that Livingston would not abandon his quest of the opal. I also reached that point, and then I asked myself, 'How will he get it, knowing that I would not sell?' I could find but one way. He would offer to sell his, and during the transaction try to steal mine. As he would need both opals in his Mexican mining venture, his only chance of carrying both away with him would be to have two others to leave in their stead. Thus I argued that he would endeavor to have two duplicates of his opal made. Ordinarily, opals are not sufficiently expensive to make it pay to produce spurious specimens. Consequently, it has been little done; indeed, I doubt that the members of the trade in this city have any idea that doublet opals have been made and sold in this city. But I know it, and I know the man who made the doublets. These were common opals, faced with thin layers of a fine quality of 'harlequin' which often comes in such thin layers that it is practically useless for cutting into stones, though it has been utilized for cameos and intaglios. This lapidary does his work admirably, and his cement is practically invisible. I went to this man and warned him that he might be called upon to duplicate a large and valuable opal, and I arranged that he should fill the order, but that he should notify me of the fact."

"Ah, now I understand. The genuine opals lay on the desk, and when you turned to the safe Livingstone merely exchanged them for the spurious doublets. But tell me why did he risk bringing the real opal here at all? Why not offer you one of the doublets, and then merely have one exchange to make?"

"He was too shrewd to risk that. In the first place, he knows I am an expert, and that I would compare the two jewels before making the purchase; he feared that under such close scrutiny I would discover the deception. Secondly, the two genuine opals absolutely match each other. So also the two doublets are actual mates. But the doublets only approximately resemble the real opals."

"Mr. Mitchel, you have managed Livingstone admirably, but there still remains the man Domingo. Until he is disposed of I still think there is danger. Pardon my pertinacity."

"I told you at the beginning of this incident that I had a spy upon Livingstone, but that though the method was commonplace, my choice of a spy was unique. My spy was Livingstone's partner, Domingo."

"What! You were on intimate terms with Domingo?"

"Was not that my best course? I found the man, and at once explained to him that as Livingstone never could get my opal, it would be best to shift the partnership and aid me to get Livingstone's. Thus you see, having, as it were, conceived the logical course for Livingstone to pursue, I had his partner Domingo suggest it to him."

"Even the idea of the doublets?"

"Certainly. I gave Domingo the address of the lapidary, and Domingo supplied it to Livingstone."

"Mr. Mitchel, you are a wonder as a schemer. But now you have Domingo on your hands?"

"Only for a short time. Domingo is not such a bloodthirsty

cutthroat as your friend Sanchez made you believe. He readily admitted that the game was up when I explained to him that I had one of the opals, a fact which Livingstone had not communicated to him. I had little difficulty in persuading him to become my assistant; money liberally applied often proving a salve for blasted hopes. Besides, I have raised his hopes again, and in a way by which he may yet become possessed of that opal mine, and without a partner."

"Why, how do you mean?"

"I shall give him the doublets, and I have no doubt he can palm them off on the old priests, who will not examine too closely, so anxious are they to see the eyes of the idol restored."

"There is yet one thing that I do not fully understand. Sanchez told me—"

"Sanchez told you nothing, except what he was instructed to tell you."

"Do you mean to say—"

"I mean that Sanchez's story of my danger was told to you so that you would come here this morning. You noted yourself that I must have expected you, when you found the bookcase arranged for you. I had an idea that I might need a strong and faithful arm, and I had both. Mr. Barnes, without your assistance, I must have failed."

# VIII

## THE PEARLS OF ISIS

Mr. Barnes sat for a while in silence, gazing at Mr. Mitchel. The masterly manner in which that gentleman had managed the affair throughout won his admiration and elevated him more than ever in his esteem. The denouement was admirable. Before handing over the check Mr. Mitchel had led Mr. Livingstone to state in the presence of a concealed witness that the opal about to be sold was genuine, whereas, as a matter of fact, the one on the desk at that moment was spurious. Then the payment with a check and the exacting of a receipt furnished tangible proofs of the nature of the transaction. Thus, even eliminating the theft of the other opal, Mr. Mitchel was in the position to prove that the man had obtained a large sum of money by false pretenses. The recovery of the stolen opal practically convicted Mr. Livingstone of a still greater crime, and with a witness to the various details of the occurrence Mr. Mitchel had so great a hold upon him that it would be most improbable that Mr. Livingstone would pursue his scheme further. The second conspirator, Domingo, was equally well disposed of, for if he returned to Mexico with the imitation opals, either the priests would discover the fraud and deal with the man themselves, or, by their failing to do so, he would gain possession of the opal mine.

In either event there would be no reason for him to return to trouble Mr. Mitchel.

"I see the whole scheme," said Mr. Barnes at length, "and I must congratulate you upon the conception and conduct of the affair. You have courteously said that I have been of some assistance, and though I doubt it, I would like to exact a price for my services."

"Certainly," said Mr. Mitchel. "Every man is worthy of his hire, even when he is not aware of the fact that he has been hired, I presume. Name your reward. What shall it be?"

"From my place of concealment, a while ago, I observed that before you took out the opal, you removed from the box a magnificent string of pearls. As you have claimed that all valuable jewels have some story of crime, or attempted crime, attached to them, I fancy you could tell an interesting tale about those pearls."

"Ah; and you would like to hear the story?"

"Yes; very much!"

"Well, it is a pretty old one now, and no harm can come, especially if you receive the tale in confidence."

"Assuredly."

"They are beautiful, are they not?" said Mr. Mitchel, taking them up almost affectionately, and handing them to Mr. Barnes. "I call them the Pearls of Isis."

"The Pearls of Isis?" said Mr. Barnes, taking them. "An odd name, considering that the goddess is a myth. How could she wear jewelry?"

"Oh, the name originated with myself. I will explain that in a moment. First let me say a few words in a general way. You ask me for the story of that string of pearls. If what is told of them in Mexico is true, there is a pathetic tale for each particular pearl, aside from the many legends that are related of the entire string."

"And do you know all of these histories?"

"No, indeed. I wish that I did. But I can tell you some of the legendry. In Humboldt's *American Researches* you will find an illustration showing the figure of what he calls 'The Statue of an Aztec Priestess.' The original had been discovered by M. Dupé.[†] The statue was cut from basalt, and the point of chief interest in it is the head-dress, which resembles the calantica, or veil of Isis, the Sphinxes, and other Egyptian statues. On the forehead of this stone priestess was found a string of pearls, of which Humboldt says: 'The pearls have never been found on any Egyptian statue, and indicate a communication between the city of Tenochtitlan,[‡] ancient Mexico, and the coast of California, where pearls are found in great numbers.' Humboldt himself found a similar statue decorated with pearls in the ruins of Tezcuco,[§] and this is still in the museum at Berlin, where I have seen it. Humboldt doubted that these statues represented priestesses, but thought rather that they were merely figures of ordinary women, and he bases this view on the fact that the statues have long hair, whereas it was the custom of the tepan-teohuatzin, a dignitary controlling the priestesses, to cut off the tresses of these virgins when they devoted themselves to the services of the temple.[¶] M. Dupé thought that this statue represented one of the temple virgins, while, as I have said, Humboldt concluded that they had no religious connection. My own view is that both of these gentlemen were wrong, and that these and similar statues were images of the goddess Isis."

"But I thought that Isis was an Old World goddess?"

*The Prussian baron Alexander von Humboldt (1769–1859) traveled extensively in the Americas between 1799 and 1804 and published a massive set of his journals over more than twenty years. *Vues des Cordillères et monumens des peuples indigènes de l'Amérique* (1810) was translated into English as *Researches, concerning the institutions & monuments of the ancient inhabitants of America* (1814). An image of the statue appears on page 42 of volume I.

†"Discovered" is a euphemism for "stolen"—Dupé (Captain Guillermo Dupaix of the Mexican Army) took it for his personal collection.

‡The capital city of the Aztec empire, sited on an island near the western shore of Lake Texcoco (Tezcuco) in present-day Mexico City. The city was destroyed in 1521 by the army of Cortez and subsequently built over.

§Tezcuco was the second-largest city of the Aztec era, with more than 140,000 houses, many built on the shores of Lake Texcoco, northeast of Tenochtitlan.

¶Humboldt makes this assertion about hair-cutting on page 46 of volume I. However, he also bases his conclusion on "the ornament of the neck and the natural form of the head."

"So she was, and the oldest world is this continent. We need not now enter upon a discussion of the reasons upon which I base my belief. Suffice it to say that I think I can prove to the satisfaction of any good archaeologist that both Isis and Osiris belong to Central America.* And as those pearls in your hand once adorned an Aztec basaltic statue similar to those of Dupé and Humboldt, I have chosen to call them the 'Pearls of Isis.'"

"Ah; then it is from their origin that you imagine that so many stories are connected with them. I have always heard that the priests of ancient Mexico were a bloodthirsty lot, and as pearls are supposed by the superstitious to symbolize tears, I can imagine the romances that might be built around these, especially if they were guarded by virgin priestesses."

"Now you are utilizing your detective instinct to guess my tale before it is told. You are partly right. Many curious legends are to be heard from the natives in Mexico, explanatory of these pearl-bedecked idols. Two are particularly interesting, though you are not bound to accept them as strictly true. The first was related to me personally by an old man, who claimed a connection with the priesthood through a lineage of priestly ancestors covering two thousand generations. This you will admit is a long service for a single family in worshipful care of a lot of idols, and it would at least be discourteous to doubt the word of such a truly holy man."

"Oh, I shall not attempt to discredit or disprove the old fellow's story, whatever it may be."

"That is very generous of you, considering your profession, and I am sure the old Aztec would feel duly honored. However, here is his story. According to him, there were many beautiful women among the Aztecs, but only the most beautiful of these were acceptable to the gods as priestesses. Their entrance into the service of the temple, I imagine, must have been most trying,

---

*Such a theory was espoused by Augustus Le Plongeon (1826–1908), a French American archaeologist and photographer who documented the Maya civilization on the northern Yucatán Peninsula. His peers largely discounted his theories.

for he stated that it was only when the women came before the priests with their chosen lovers to be married that the priests were permitted to examine their faces in order to determine whether they were beautiful enough to become temple virgins.* If, on such an occasion, the bride seemed sufficiently beautiful, the priest, instead of uniting her to her lover, declared that the gods demanded her as their own, and she was forthwith consecrated to the service of the temple. They were then compelled to forswear the world, and, under threats of mysterious and direful punishments, they promised to guard their chastity, and devote their virgin lives to the gods. The mysterious punishment meted out to transgressors the old priest explained to me. Usually in such instances the girl would elope, most often with the lover of whom she had been deprived at the altar. No effort was made to recapture her. Such was the power of the priests, and such the superstitious dread of the anger of the gods, that none would hold communication of any kind with the erring couple. Thus isolated and compelled to hide away in the forests, the unfortunate lovers would eventually live in hourly dread of disaster, until either the girl would voluntarily return to the priests to save her lover from the imagined fury of the gods, or else to save himself he would take the girl back. In either case the result would be the same. None ever saw her again. But, shortly after, a new pearl would appear upon the forehead of the idol."

"A new pearl? How?"

"The old priest, whose word you have promised not to doubt, claimed that beneath the temple there was a dark, bottomless pool of water in which abounded the shell-fish from which pearls were taken. These molluscs were sacred, and to them were fed the bodies of all the human beings sacrificed on their altars. Whenever one of the temple virgins broke her oath of fidelity to the gods, upon her return she was dropped alive into this pool, and, curious to relate, at the appearance of the

---

*Where Ottolengui got this idea is unknown. Many Aztec women were dedicated to the service of the temple in childhood, when their beauty was indeterminate.

next new moon the tepanteohuatzin would invariably discover a pearl of marvellous size."

"Why, then, each pearl would represent a temple virgin reincarnated, as it were?"

"Yes; one might almost imagine that in misery and grief over her unhappy love affair, she had wept until she had dissolved, and that then she had been precipitated, to use a chemical term, in the form of a pearl. Altogether the legend is not a bad one, and if we recall the connection between Isis and the crescent moon, you must admit my right to call these the Pearls of Isis."

"Oh, I promised to dispute nothing. But did you not say that there was another legend?"

"Yes, and I am glad to say it has a much more fortuitous finale and is altogether more believable, though this one was not told to me by a man of God, or perhaps to be more accurate I should say a 'man of the gods.' According to this rendition the temple virgins were chosen exactly as related in the other narrative, but before actually entering upon their duties there was a period of probation, a period of time covering 'one moon.' You see we cannot escape the moon in this connection. During this probationary period it was possible for the lover to regain his sweetheart by paying a ransom, and this ransom was invariably a pearl of a certain weight and quality. By placing these pearls on the forehead of the goddess she was supposed to be repaid for the loss of one of her virgin attendants. All of which shows that her ladyship, Isis, in her love for finery, was peculiarly human and not unlike her sisters of to-day."

"This second story is very easy to believe, if one could understand where the pearls were to be found."

"Oh, that is easily explained. Humboldt was right in supposing that there was a communication with the Californian coast. There was a regular yearly journey to and from that place for the purposes of trade, and many of the Aztecs travelled thither purposely to engage in fishing for pearls. Whenever one of these fishers was fortunate enough to find a pearl of the kind demanded by the priests, he would hoard it up, and keep his good luck a secret. For with such a pearl could he not woo and win one of the fairest daughters of his tribe? We can well imagine that without such a pearl the more cautious of the beauties would turn a deaf ear to lovers' pleadings, fearing to attract the eyes of the priests at the altar. Verily, in those days beauty was a doubtful advantage."

"Yes, indeed. Now I understand what you meant when you said that each of these pearls might have its own romance. For, according to the legends, they are either the penalty or the price of love. But you have not told me the particular story of these pearls."

"There may be as many as there are pearls, but I can tell you but one; though as that involves a story of crime, it will interest you I am sure. You will remember that when we were going to the yacht on that day when we solved the first opal mystery, I explained to you my reasons for buying up large gems. I think I told you of my first venture?"

"Yes; you overheard a plot to steal a ruby, and you went to the hostess and bought the jewel, which you then stuck in your scarf, where the plotters could see it and know that it had changed hands."

"That is the tale exactly. You will consider it a curious coincidence when I tell you that these pearls came into my possession in an almost similar manner."

"That is remarkable, I must say."

"And yet not so remarkable, either, all things considered. Crime, or rather the method of committing a crime, is often suggested by previous occurrences. A body is found in the river dismembered, and is a nine days' wonder. Yet, even though the mystery may be solved, and the murderer brought to justice, the police may scarcely have finished with the case before another dismembered body is discovered. Often, too, the second criminal goes unpunished; in imitating his predecessor he avoids, or attempts to avoid, his mistakes. I suppose that is easier than formulating an entirely new plan. So I imagine that the attempt to steal the ruby, which I frustrated, and the stealing of the pearls, which was successfully managed, may have some connection, more especially as both affairs occurred in the same house."

"In the same house?"

"Yes, and within a month, or, to follow the legend, I might say in the same 'moon.' I was in New Orleans at the time, and as it was in the Mardi Gras season, masked balls were common occurrences. One who was especially fond of this class of entertainment was Madame Damien. She was a widow, not yet thirty, and as her husband, Maurice Damien, had belonged to one of the wealthiest and most distinguished of the old Creole families, there was no apparently good reason for denying her the rightful privilege of mixing with and receiving the best people of the city. Nevertheless, there were a few who declined to associate with her, or to allow the younger members of their households to do so."

"What were their reasons?"

"Reasons there were, but of such an impalpable nature that even those who most rigorously shunned her, ventured not to speak openly against her. For reasons, it might have been said that she smoked cigarettes—but other good women did likewise; she entertained often, and served wine intemperately—others did the same; she permitted card-playing in her rooms, even for money stakes,—but the same thing occurred in other houses, though perhaps not so openly. Thus none of these reasons, you see, was sufficiently potent. But there were others, less easily discussed and more difficult to prove. It was whispered, very low and only in the ears of most trustworthy intimates, that Madame Damien permitted, nay, encouraged, young men to pay court to her. If true, she managed her courtiers most admirably, for openly she was most impartial in distributing her favors, while secretly—well, none penetrated the secrets of Madame Damien. One thing was certainly in her favor; there were no duels about her, and duelling was not uncommon in those days."

"I should say she was a clever woman."

"Just the word. Some, who could say nothing more, said she was altogether too clever. It was this woman who sold me the ruby."

"The first acquisition to your collection?"

"Yes. I may as well briefly give you the facts, for thus you may see the connection between the two affairs. Land is not so valuable in our southern country as it is here in New York, and the houses of the wealthy are often in the midst of extensive gardens. Some of these not only have beautiful flower-beds, but likewise palms, cacti, oleanders, azaleas, and other tropical plants. Madame Damien's residence was in a garden which might almost be called a miniature park. The paths were of snow-white oyster shells, rolled and beaten until they resembled smooth white marble. The hedges were of arbor vitæ cut with square top, except here and there where the trees were trained to form arched gateways through which the flower-beds could be reached. In places, often nearly concealed by flowering plants, were little houses,—lovers' nooks they are called,—made also of trained arbor vitæ. Of larger trees there were the palmetto, the orange, and the magnolia. On fête nights these beautiful grounds would be illuminated with Chinese lanterns, sufficiently numerous to make the scene a veritable fairy picture, but not shedding enough light to interfere with the walks of lovers who sought the garden paths between the dances."

"Your description reminds one of Eden."

"The similarity is greater than you imagine, for the serpent lurked in the rose bowers. At one of Madame Damien's masquerade fêtes I had left the warm rooms for a breath of the perfume-laden air without, and was walking along a path which led to the farthest end of the garden, when I was attracted by a stifled cry. I stopped and listened, and as it was not repeated I was just thinking that I had heard the mournful cry of a dove, when a tug at my sleeve caused me to turn quickly. At my side was a little creature in a green domino scarcely distinguishable from the shrubbery that lined the walk. The girl stood on her toes, drew my head down to hers, and in a frightened tone whispered:

"'The men. They mean mischief—to them—in there.'

"She pointed to one of the little arbor vitæ houses near us, and turning fled back along the path before I could restrain her.

"Much mystified, I stepped softly toward the little house, intending to discover if possible who might be within, when I seemed to hear voices behind me. Listening intently, I traced the sounds to the opposite side of the hedge, and therefore I crept cautiously in that direction, satisfied that here were the men to whom the girl had made allusion. Here is what I heard:

"'As they come out, we must follow them. When I whistle, you jump on madame; I will take care of him, I will undertake to hurt him enough to make him squeal. That will alarm madame, who will be so fearful lest her precious lover be hurt that you will have no difficulty in getting the ruby.'"

"Quite a neat little plot; only needs the detail of garroting to afford us a perfect picture of the Spanish brigand," said Mr. Barnes.

"The men were undoubtedly professional thieves who considered the masquerade a good opportunity. As soon as they mentioned the ruby, I knew that the woman was none other than Madame Damien, who possessed a stone of rare beauty which she frequently wore. The point of greatest interest was that madame seemed about to lose her usual good luck by having one of her love affairs discovered. How could I warn her without myself learning who was with her? Strange though it may seem, I had no wish to know the name of her companion, so I hit upon an expedient. Going to the door of the little house I called aloud:

"'Madame Damien! Will you allow me to speak to you a moment?' Of course she did not reply. From the deathlike stillness of the place one might have thought it empty. I was too sure, however, that she was there, so I spoke again.

"'Madame, your very life is in danger, if you do not come out and speak to me.' In an instant she was at my side, talking in a quick whisper.

"'Who are you? What do you mean?'

"'Pardon my intruding, but I was obliged to adopt this course, I assure you.'

"I was speaking loudly enough to be heard by the men on the other side of the hedge. 'I was passing here just now, with no suspicion that you were here, alone,'—I purposely used the word, so that she might feel easy about her companion,—'when I chanced to overhear the plotting of two ruffians who are even now hidden in the hedge. They are lying in wait for you, intending to rob you of your ruby.'

"'Steal my ruby? I don't understand.'

"'Had I not heard their plan, they would undoubtedly have partly strangled you while they stole the jewel. It was to save you from the danger of this encounter and the loss that I felt it my duty to call you out to speak with me.'

"'What shall I do?'

"'I advise you to sell the stone to me.'

"'Sell it to you? How would that help matters?'

"'I have my check-book with me. You know who I am,— Leroy Mitchel. There is light enough by this lantern to write, and I have a fountain-pen. If you sell me the ruby, and take the check, you may safely go to the house. The would-be thieves are listening and perhaps watching us. Consequently, they will know of this transaction and will have no reason to follow you.'

"'But yourself?'

"'I can take care of myself, especially as I am armed, I shall follow you in a few moments, and I am sure no attack will be made upon me.'

"She hesitated a moment. She did not really wish to sell the stone, yet her only other alternative was to inform me that as another man was present we might go to the house together without fear. But not wishing to disclose the presence of this other man, she decided to sell me the stone, or rather to appear to do so, for her plan was to return my check later and recover the ruby. This offer she made to me on the following day, but I declined because the idea of forming my collection of rare gems had entered my mind when I heard the plotters talking. Before finally yielding she made one effort, being a plucky woman.

"'I need not sell you the ruby, Mr. Mitchel, for if, as you say, you are armed, I have no fear of accepting your escort to the house.'

"This of course would have defeated my purpose, so I hastily explained to her that I wished to stay behind because I intended to attempt to capture one or both of the ruffians. Whether or not she might have found some other means of avoiding my offer, she did not think of one then, so she handed me the ruby and I gave her the check. After she had left me, I cautiously searched the hedges but met no one. I was satisfied, however, that the men had heard all that had passed, and I also believed that they might still imagine that there would be a chance to get the ruby, under the supposition that my purchase was but a pretense, and that as soon as I should return to the parlors I would restore the jewel. It was for this reason that I wore it conspicuously in my scarf."

"What of the little woman in the green domino? Did you see her again?"

"I caught a glimpse of her only, though I am sure she got a better view of me. It was in the house. Here, also, there was a profusion of green, the place being literally strewn with potted plants. I was standing near a group of palms when I caught sight of my lady of the green domino, gazing intently at me. As she saw that I had detected her presence, she swiftly glided away, and I lost her in the throng. I was certain, however, that she saw the ruby in my scarf, and so knew that I had prevented the mischief of which she had warned me."

"It would have been interesting to discover her identity."

"All in good time, Mr. Detective. We come now to the story of the string of pearls. It was just three weeks later. Madame was holding another fête. Once more I was destined to play eavesdropper, though this time with even still more startling results. I had been dancing a quadrille, my unknown partner being charmingly dressed in a costume which at the time I did not understand. I had noticed her several times during the evening, standing always alone, apparently neglected by the young men. So I asked her to be my partner, rather in the spirit of giving her some of the pleasures of the evening, though you must understand that I was at that time young myself and quite susceptible to the charms of the opposite sex. She had seemed reluctant at first to dance with me, and then, as though impulsively altering her mind, she had expressed her willingness more in act than by any word, for she had not spoken. Clutching my arm nervously, she had led me a little way across the floor, and stopped where a couple was needed to fill a quadrille. *En vis-à-vis** was a couple who attracted her attention to such an extent that I almost imagined that my partner had brought me into this set with the purpose of watching them. The man was unmistakably dressed as Romeo, while the costume of his partner was as mystifying to me as that of the girl beside me. I afterwards learned that she was assuming the guise of Helen of Troy."

"Your hostess, Madame Damien, I'll be bound."

"You make a good guesser, Mr. Barnes. Madame Damien it

---

*Literally, "face to face"—in this context, meaning "directly opposite" or "facing us."

was, though, truth to tell, I was so much interested in the silent, watchful girl beside me that I paid little attention to the others. The quadrille had just ended and I was wondering how best to make my little sphinx talk, when a strange thing happened. The couple opposite to us crossed toward us, and as they approached my partner swayed as though about to fall, and then suddenly toppled over against me, and in a whisper she said:

"'I am dizzy. Take me out in the air.'

"Just then, 'Helen of Troy,' hanging on the arm of her 'Romeo,' passed so close to us that the women's costumes touched. She looked scrutinizingly at the girl with me, and I heard her say to her companion,—

"'That girl is a sphinx.'

"'Then they passed on. Her words startled me, for I had just used the epithet in my own mind in connection with my partner. I thought of her as a sphinx because of her silence. But now that some one else called her a sphinx, I observed that she wore a curious head-dress which reminded one of the great monument of the Eastern desert. Perhaps, then, she was but playing the part which she had assumed with her costume. At all events there seemed to be a mystery worthy of the effort at penetration. So I hurried out into the air with my little sphinx, and soon we were walking up one of the snow-white walks. I tried to induce her to talk, but though she seemed willing to remain in my companionship, she trembled a good deal but kept as mum as the stone image to which I now likened her. I was wondering by what device I might make her talk, when she utterly startled me by crying out:

"'I wish I dared to tell you everything. Perhaps you might help me.'

"'Tell me what you will, little one,' said I, 'and I will help you if I can, and keep your secret besides.'

"'Oh, there is no secret,' she exclaimed; 'I am not so wicked as that. But we cannot talk here. Come, I know a place.'

"I followed her as she hurried me on, more mystified than before. She tells me 'there is no secret,' and that she is 'not as wicked as that.' Why need she be wicked, to have a secret? I could not fathom it, but as I was to know all, even though it were no secret, I was able to await the telling. Oddly enough, as it seemed to me then, she led me to the very lovers' nook in which I had found Madame Damien when I purchased the ruby. Before entering, my little sphinx took the precaution to extinguish the lanterns at the doorway, so that when we passed inside we were in gloom as impenetrable as that of one of the passageways in the pyramids. She seemed familiar with the place, for she took my hand and led me away to one side, where there was a rustic bench. Here we sat down, and after a few minutes she began.

"'You do not know me, of course,' said she.

"'Why, no,' I replied; 'how should I?'

"'I was afraid you might have recognized my voice. But then I haven't spoken much to you, have I?'

"'No; but now I do recognize your voice at least. It was you who warned me, here at this very spot, at the last fête. Was it not?'

"'Yes; I heard the men talking and I was afraid they might hurt—might hurt some one. Then you came along, and so I told you. I recognized you to-night because you have the same dress.'

"I began to suspect that the 'some one' whom she had shielded that night was not our fair hostess, but rather the man who had been with her. I was wondering whether it would be wise to ask her this question, or whether to wait for her to tell her story in her own way, when I was startled at feeling the softest of hands pressed tightly over my lips, and to hear a whisper close to my ear.

"'Don't speak,' she said; 'they are coming—they are coming here.'

"I strained my ears and at first heard nothing, but love sharpens the ears I suppose, for presently I did hear footsteps, and then low voices, growing louder as though approaching, and finally the persons, evidently a man and woman, actually entered our place of concealment. The situation was embarrassing, especially as that little hand still rested over my mouth as though warning me to do nothing. Luckily, the intruders did not come to our side of the place, but took seats apparently opposite. They were talking in earnest tones, the woman finishing a sentence as they came in.

"'—my mind, whether to release you or not. At all events, I must know more about this somewhat curious proposition of yours.'

"I recognized at once the voice of Madame Damien. It was evident, therefore, that the man was her partner of the dance, and that it was he who had been with her in this place on the other occasion seemed a probability. He answered her as follows:

"'I do not think the proposition is a curious one. I only do what women always do. Certainly my sex should have the same privileges in an affair of this character.'

"'That is a question that philosophers might discuss,' said Madame Damien, 'but we need not. Whether you have the right or not it is evident that you choose to exercise it. And what is this right?'

"'The right to tell you the truth. The right to tell you that I do not love you, that I have made a terrible blunder.'

"The little hand over my mouth trembled violently, and slipped away. I could hear the girl next to me breathing so distinctly that it seemed odd that the others did not hear also. Perhaps they were too much occupied with their own affair.

"'The right to tell me that you do not love me,' repeated madame; 'but you have so often told me that you do love me, and you have told me of your love so eloquently, that now when you come to me and say that you have made a blunder, naturally I have the right to question you. Here are two opposite statements. How am I to know which to believe?'

"'I am telling you the truth, now.'

"'Perhaps; you may be right. You may know your heart at last, and if what you say is really true, of course I have no desire to try to keep what you only supposed to be love, however eloquently you told about it, however well you played the part. The awkward thing is that to-morrow, next week, by the new moon perhaps, you may be at my feet again singing the same old songs, old love songs. You will tell me that what you say then is truth, but that what you are telling me now is false. How, then, shall I know what to think?'

"'What I tell you now is true. I shall not tell you otherwise at any time in the future.'

"'Of this you are quite sure?'

"'Quite sure!'

"Up to this point the woman had spoken softly, almost with love in her voice. It sounded like a mother talking with her son who was confessing a change of heart, or rather a change of sweethearts. Now, suddenly, all was changed. When she spoke again it was in the voice of rage, almost of hate. It was the woman spurned; more than that,—it was the woman jealous of the rival who had replaced her in her lover's heart.

"'So you are quite sure that you will not make love to me again!' she cried, with such ferocity that the girl beside me moved closer to me as though seeking protection; 'you are sure of that? Then you love another. There is no other test by which you could be so sure. Answer me, is it true? Is it true, I say? Answer me at once; I want no lies.'

"'Well, and what if it is true,' said the man, angered by her speech.

"'What if it is true? You ask me that? Well, I'll answer. If it is true, then the other girl is welcome to you. She may have you, with your secondhand love. May she be happy in the love that changes with the moon. So much for her. But with you. Ah, that must be different. You wish to be released? Well, you shall pay for your liberty, my fickle lover; you shall pay!'

"'I will pay you whatever you demand. What is it?'

"'So. You value your liberty so much that you promise before you know my terms! Very well, then. You will bring me to-night, before an hour has passed, the string of pearls that your mother wore on her wedding-day.'

"'My God, no! Not that! It is impossible!'

"'How quickly you make and break promises! Your ideas of honor are as slim as your notions of love. And why is it impossible to give me the pearls?'

"'They are not mine. Anything that is mine I will give. But the pearls are not mine.'

"'If not yours whose are they, pray?'

"'Let me explain. They have been in my family for generations. They were taken from an idol in Mexico by one of my ancestors who was with Cortez. He gave them to his bride, and declared that they should descend to the eldest sons for all time, to be given as a bridal present to their wives. Moreover he declared that so long as this behest was strictly followed, no dishonor should come to our house and name.'

"'What you tell me makes me only more determined to have the pearls. Your ancestor was a good prophet. You dishonor your house when you offer me your love and then withdraw from your contract. You asked me to be your wife, and according to your ancestor's will the pearls should be my bridal decoration. I could claim them in that manner, did I choose.'

"'What do you mean?'

"'I mean to have those pearls. No other woman shall wear them. If the loss brings dishonor to your house, yours is the fault. But I have talked long enough. I loathe myself for bartering with you. Now I give you my command. Bring me those pearls within an hour.'

"She rose and started to leave the place. The man jumped up and called after her:

"'What if I should refuse?'

"She paused for a moment to reply, and her words reminded me of the hiss of a serpent.

"'If you do not obey, when my guests unmask to-night I will announce my engagement, our engagement, and introduce you as my Romeo.'

"She laughed mockingly, and hurried away. The man did not wait, but went out immediately. I felt about for my companion, but she seemed not to be near me. I took out a match and struck it, only to find myself alone. Seated nearer to the door than I, she must have slipped out without my knowledge.'

"Then you did not learn the secret of your sphinx maiden after all," said Mr. Barnes.

"Not immediately. But hear the sequel. You may be sure I was near our hostess when midnight arrived and the moment came to unmask. Madame Damien herself gave the signal, and then, standing at the end of the room, she slowly unwound a thread-lace scarf which covered her head and face, serving in place of a mask, and draped about her shoulders. The shawl thrown aside revealed her bare neck, around which hung resplendent the pearls in your hand. Madame made a sensation with her pearls. Though she owned many jewels of rare price she often wore them, and her guests were quite familiar with her usual display; but pearls she had never worn before. And such pearls! What wonder there were whisperings and guessings! I looked around for the other two actors in the romantic drama, but neither Romeo nor my sphinx maiden was to be seen.

"Refreshments were served in several small rooms, and it was from one of these that presently a cry was heard that startled all of the guests, so that they rushed back into the main ballroom.

There we found Madame Damien, pale with rage, calling for her servants, who rushed from all directions.

"'I have been robbed,' she cried; 'robbed of my pearls! They have been taken from me within a minute! Let no one leave the house! Close and lock the doors! No one shall leave this house, until my pearls are restored!'

"Imagine the consternation and indignation which this aroused. Madame was so enraged at the loss, and so wildly determined to recover the jewels, her jealous fear lest her rival might obtain them so intense, that she had entirely forgotten all the courtesy and duties of a hostess to her guests. All that she knew, all that she cared for, was that the person who had robbed her was still in the house, and she wished to prevent escape.

"You may guess the hubbub that followed. Women and men congregated in groups asking each other what it all meant. Some demanded their wraps and the opportunity to leave instantly. Others declared that they were quite willing, nay, anxious, to await the denouement, which would certainly prove interesting. 'At least it was well to know who of their number might be a thief,' etc.

"In these circumstances, I undertook to relieve the tension and restore tranquillity. I went up to Madame Damien, and said to her in a low tone:

"'If you will let me speak to you alone for two minutes I will recover the lost pearls.'

"'What do you know? What can you do?' she asked eagerly. 'Come into this room; we will be alone.'

"I followed her into an anteroom, and we stood as we talked. She was laboring under such excitement that it was impossible for her to sit quietly.

"'Tell me first just how the pearls were taken, madame.'

"'That is the miserable part of it. To think that a thief could take them from my neck! It is mortifying. All I know is that I was in one of the refreshment-rooms, standing near the window that opens into the ballroom. I knew nothing, felt nothing, until like a flash they were twitched from my neck. I clutched at them, but too late. The thief had stood in the ballroom, and passed her arm through the window, till she reached and unlocked the clasp of the necklace. Then with one quick tug, she had the pearls. I cried out, and the stupid people crowded about me so that it was a whole minute, a precious minute, before I could get out into the ballroom. It was empty, of course. The woman had hurried into one of the small rooms. But she has not left the house and she shall not, until the pearls are in my possession again.'

"'You allude to the thief as a woman. How did you discover that, since from your account you could hardly have seen her?'

"'No; I saw no one. But I know it was a woman. Never mind how I know. What, though, if it were—no! no! Impossible. He is not here; besides, he would not dare.'

"Of course I understood that she referred to our friend Romeo, and I might also have thought of him, had I not made sure that he was not present after the unmasking.

"'If you did not see the thief, you cannot be sure it was a woman,' I continued. 'Now, madame, I have a proposal to make. I will purchase your pearls.'

"'You will do nothing of the sort, Mr. Mitchel. You got my ruby, but you will not get the pearls. Besides, I have not them to deliver, even if I were willing to sell them to you.'

"'That is the attractive feature of my proposition. I will pay for the pearls, their full value, and I will undertake to recover them.'

"'But I tell you I won't sell them. And besides, how could you recover them?'

"'I will tell you nothing in advance, except that I guarantee to recover them, and that, I imagine, is the main object with you.'

"'What do you mean? You talk in riddles.'

"'Listen. I will make my purpose clear to you. You obtained those pearls to-night, and—'

"'How do you know that?'

"'And you obtained them for a purpose,' I went on, ignoring her interruption. 'You made a man give them to you, because you were determined that another woman should not have them.'

"'You are a magician,' she cried in wonder.

"'You are angry at the loss of the pearls, not so much because of their value, as because you fear they may be restored to that other woman. You even think that she herself is the thief.'

"'You are right; I do think that. What other woman would do such a thing as to steal a string of pearls from a woman's very person?'

"'What if I tell you that she is not in the house?'

"'Ah, then you know her? Who is she? Tell me who she is and you may have the pearls.' Madame spoke eagerly.

"'I will only tell you enough to convince you that she is not the thief. You remember after one of the quadrilles passing a girl and saying, "That girl is a sphinx"?'

"'Yes; was she—'

"'Yes. Now if you search your rooms you will not find her. I know this because I have looked for her for half an hour.'

"'If not she, then the thief was some emissary of hers. Those pearls shall never reach her. Never! never! never! I'll search every person in this house first.'

"'And accomplish what? Nothing, except to ruin yourself before the world. Remember, your guests have rights. Already you have insulted them by having the doors locked. Come, we are wasting time. Sell me the pearls, and I will promise you two things. First, I will satisfy your guests and restore you to their good opinion. Secondly, I will recover and keep those pearls. Your rival shall never wear them.'

"'My rival?'

"'Your rival. Why mince matters? Is it not evident to you that I know all the details of this affair?'

"'You are a devil! Have your own way then. Take the pearls at your own price, and pay for them when you like. All I demand is that you fulfil your agreement. She must not have them. Good night. I cannot meet my guests again. Explain things for me, will you?'

"She was nothing but a woman again—a conquered woman, relying upon the chivalry of her conqueror.

"'Trust me,' I replied. 'Lean on me and I will escort you to the stairway.'

"All eyes followed us as we crossed the ballroom, and madame looked ill enough to evoke pity. At any rate, my explanation was accepted generously, and madame was forgiven."

"I am curious to know," said Mr. Barnes, "how you recovered or expected to recover those pearls?"

"It certainly was a unique bargain, to purchase stolen property while yet in the possession of the thief. I will tell you what I did. After leaving madame in the care of her maids at the foot of the stairway, I returned to the ballroom, and made a little speech. Addressing the throng that crowded about me, I said:

"'Friends, I beg that you will forgive Madame Damien's hasty words. She was overwrought, and spoke irresponsibly. She had just met with a serious loss under most peculiar circumstances. Imagine her standing at the refreshment table, while one of her guests intrudes an arm through the window behind her, unclasps and removes from her neck a string of pearls worth a fabulous sum of money. Naturally her first thought was to recover the pearls, and to her distracted mind the only way seemed to be to demand that no one should leave the house. Of course she now regrets her words, for no loss can excuse such treatment of guests. But I am sure you will forgive her, especially the ladies, who will appreciate her feelings. Now, in regard to the pearls I may state that I have undertaken to recover them. Fortunately I witnessed the theft, though from a distance, so that I could not prevent it. But I know who took the pearls, and who has them. Consequently it is unnecessary to cause anyone any further annoyance in the matter. To the thief, I will say that I understand the motive of the theft, and that I am in a position to promise that that motive can be consummated if the pearls are returned to me within three days. If they are not returned, it will be necessary to have the person arrested and imprisoned.'"

"A bold stroke, and ingenious too," exclaimed Mr. Barnes. "The thief, of course, could not know whether you saw the act or not, and if a person of high social position it would be too great a risk not to return the pearls."

"So I argued. Of course, had it been a man, he might have taken even that risk, believing that my threat was a 'bluff,' as we say in poker. But a woman—a woman would not take such a risk, especially as I promised that her purpose could still be fulfilled."

"Now it is my turn to be mystified. Did you not say that your sphinx maiden was absent? Who else could steal the pearls? What other woman, I mean?"

"Why, no other woman, of course. Therefore it followed that my little mysterious maiden must have been present, which merely means that as soon as she found that madame would insist upon having the pearls, she boldly plotted to recover them. Her first move was to rush off and change her costume. You see, I was the one she most feared. Others might know her face, but they would not know her reasons for committing such an act. I could do that but I could recognize her by her costume only. Thus I was sure that she was still in the house, though differently attired."

"How did your plan result?"

"Of course she brought me the pearls, though not until the third day. She delayed action as long as she dared. Then she came to me openly and confessed everything. It was really a pitiful tale. She was an orphan, living with an aged aunt. She met the young man, and at once they loved. After a time she began to suspect that he was not absolutely true to her, and she followed him to the first masquerade to spy upon him. She overheard enough that night to make her believe that the young man was making a dupe of her. Then she also heard the men plotting the robbery, and feared that he might be hurt. Seeing me she told me enough to prevent that. Then she went home, and brooded over her sorrow until she decided to go into a convent. Then came the second fête, and the temptation once more to watch her fickle swain. This time what she heard brought her happiness, for did he not give up the other woman for her? Did he not even yield up his greatest family treasure, the pearls?

"She decided to recover the pearls, and she had the courage to carry out her purpose. When compelled through fear of arrest to bring them to me, she was delighted to know that they would not be restored to Madame Damien. It was when I told her this, that she drew from her bosom the pink pearl which is now in the centre of the string, but which does not belong to the set as they came from the brow of the idol.

"'There is a story,' said she, 'that these pearls each represent the price of a maiden's honor; the price of withdrawing from the service of God's temple. So I will add this pearl to the string, for I had promised to devote myself to God's work, and now I am going to my lover. This pearl was worn by my mother, and it is said that her mother also wore it, and that her blood stained it the color that it is. Her stupid husband, my grandfather, doubted her wrongfully and stabbed her with a dagger, so that she died. I think the pearl is worthy of a place among the others.'

"I took the pink pearl, agreeing with her that it might better be with the others. Then, as she turned to go, I asked her:

"'Why did you choose the costume of the Sphinx for the ball?'

"Her reply astonished me, as it will you. She said:

"'Why, I did not represent the Sphinx. I was dressed as Isis.'

"A strange coincidence, was it not?"

# IX

## A PROMISSORY NOTE

Mr. Mitchel walked into the office of Mr. Barnes one afternoon as the clock struck two.

"Here I am, Mr. Barnes," said he. "Your note asked me to be here at two, sharp. If your clock is right, I have answered your summons to the second."

"You are punctuality itself, Mr. Mitchel. Sit down. I am in a good humor. I flatter myself that I have done a clever thing, and we are going to celebrate. See, there is a cold bottle, and a couple of glasses waiting your arrival."

"You have done something clever, you say? Some bright detective work, I suppose. And you did not honor me this time by consulting me?"

"Oh, well," said the detective, apologetically, "I should not be always bothering you with my affairs. It's business with me, and only amusement with you. When I have a matter of grave importance I like to have your assistance, of course. But this case, though interesting, very interesting, in fact, was really quite simple."

"And you have solved it?"

"Oh, yes; it is completed. Wound it up at noon to-day; ended happily, too. Let me fill your glass, and I'll tell you all about it."

"We will drink to your success. 'All's well that ends well,' you know, and this case you say is ended?"

"Oh, yes; the tale is complete down to the word 'finis.' Let me see, where shall I begin?"

"Why, at the beginning, of course. Where else?"

"Sounds like a reasonable suggestion, yet it is not always so easy to tell just where a story does begin. I often wonder how the romance writers get their stories started. Does a love story, for example, begin with the birth of the lovers, with their meeting, with their love-making, or with their marriage?"

"I am afraid that love stories too often end with the marriage. If yours is a love story, perhaps you may as well begin with the meeting of the lovers. We will take it for granted that they were born."

"So be it. I will transpose events slightly. Here is a document which was forwarded to me by mail, and evidently the sender expected me to receive it before the visit of a man who intended to consult me in a serious case. Oddly enough, the man called before the package reached me. Thus I had his story soonest; but perhaps it will be better for you to read this first, after which you will better comprehend the purpose of my client."

Mr. Mitchel took the type-written pages and read as follows:

"My dear Mr. Barnes:—

"Within a few hours after reading this statement you will receive a visit from a man who will introduce himself as William Odell, which is not his true name, a circumstance which, however, is of no consequence. He will ask you to interpose your reputed skill to save him from fate. I am ready to admit that you have great skill and experience, but it will be utterly useless for you to interfere in this matter, for, as I have said, the man is seeking to escape from a doom which is his fate. Who ever altered what was fated to be? We may philosophize a little and ask what it is that we mean, when we speak of 'fate'? My view is that fate, so called by men, is naught but the logical and necessary effect of a cause. Thus if the cause exists, the effect must follow. So it is with this man, whom we will call Odell. The cause exists, has existed for a number of years. The time for the effect is now approaching; he knows this; he knows that it is fate,— that he cannot escape. Yet, with the hope of a hopeless man, in his last extremity he will ask you to turn aside, or at least to defer, this fate. This you cannot do, and that you may understand the utter futility of wasting your time, which I presume is valuable, I send you this statement of the facts. Thus comprehending the incidents precedent to the present situation, you will appreciate the inevitable nature of the occurrence which this miserable man seeks with your aid to set aside."

"I thought you said this was a simple case, Mr. Barnes," said Mr. Mitchel, interrupting his reading.

"I found it so," replied Mr. Barnes, sipping his wine.

"The writer says that the 'occurrence' was 'inevitable,' yet am I to understand that you prevented it?"

"He thought it to be inevitable. I disagreed with him, and prevented it."

"I hope you have not been over-confident."

"There is no danger. Did I not tell you that the affair ended?"

"So you did. I forgot that. This paper is entertaining. I will read on."

The statement went on as follows:

"I was born and reared and spent all my life in Texas. In fact, you may consider me a cowboy, though it is long since I have thrown a lariat, and one would hardly count me a boy

*now. What a life do we lead down there on the Texas plains!
Miles and miles of country stretching in easy undulations
from the rising-place to the set of the sun. Day after day in
the saddle, till one imagines himself a part of the animal
which he bestrides. How often in play have I dropped a red
bandana, and then picked it from the grass as I galloped my
horse by at top speed!*

*"One day I was riding along, free from all worldly care,
happy, contented. My horse was going easily, though we had
several miles yet to cover. Glancing carelessly ahead, neither
seeking nor expecting adventure of any kind, I thought I
saw, a hundred yards or more ahead of me, the bright red
of a handkerchief in the grass. A bandana dropped by a
cowboy perhaps. With nothing better to do, I touched my
horse's flank, and with instant response his head was down
and we charged the spot. Leaning so low on one side that
I could have touched the ground easily with my hand, we
rapidly neared that bit of color, and I was almost upon it
before I realized that it was something more than a lost
handkerchief,—that it was really a bundle of some sort. Yet
in time I noted this, and therefore exerted enough strength
when I clutched it to lift it firmly from the ground, though
the weight of it astonished me. Swinging myself back upon
my horse, I brought him to a walk, that I might better
examine my prize. Imagine my feelings when I found that
the little bundle contained a thing of life—a baby girl!*

*"There is no need to extend this part of my tale. How
the child got there I never learned. Whether it was dropped
from a wagon travelling along the trail, or deposited there
purposely by one of those fiends who accept the pleasures
of life and shirk its responsibilities, I do not know. Indeed,
at the time I took but a passing interest in the affair. I had
picked up a baby on the plains. What of it? How could a
cowboy like myself be expected to evince any great interest in*

*a baby? My father was rich, and I had always been indulged in all things, though always held rigidly by what I was taught to consider the rules of honor. I had had a taste of the big world too, for I had been first at a military academy, and afterwards had graduated from Harvard. Then I had gone back to Texas, back to the life on horseback in the open air, the life that I loved best. So you can understand that women and babies had not yet come into my mind as necessary adjuncts to life.*

*"The child was given into the care of the very negro mammy who had practically reared me, my mother having died when I was yet a boy. Thus it was not until Juanita—I forget how she got the name, but so she was called—was twelve, that I began to feel some personal responsibility in relation to her future. My father meantime had died, and I was master of the old home, the ranch and all the stock. Thus there was no lack of money to carry out whatever plan might seem best. I took counsel with some women of our town, and the end of it was that Juanita was sent as far north as Atlanta to boarding-school. Here she remained until she was sixteen, but she never really enjoyed herself. A child of the plains almost literally, one might say, living through her earlier girlhood with little if any restraint, the duties of the school-room were irksome to her, and she longed to be back in Texas. This yearning grew upon her so that at length she began to make references to her feelings in her letters. I had missed her from about the place more than I should have imagined possible, and the strong inclination was to grant her wishes and bring her back; but I knew the value of education, and felt in duty bound to urge her continuance of her studies. When first she went, it had been arranged that she should remain in Atlanta studying for eight years, but finally I offered as a compromise that she might come home at the end of six, at which time she would*

*have been eighteen. You may guess my surprise when one morning on my return from a long ride after the cattle, I saw a horse dashing swiftly towards me, and when close enough, recognized Juanita on his back. Breathless she pulled up beside me, and before I could speak cried out:*

*"'Now don't say you are going to send me back. Don't say it! Don't! Don't! Don't! It would break my heart!'*

*"What could I do? There she was, exuberant in her happiness, all the wild energy of her animal spirits aroused by the exhilaration of that liberty for which she had so long yearned. Of course I thought a good deal, but I said nothing.*

*"'Watch me!' she exclaimed. 'I haven't forgotten how to ride. See!'*

*"Like a flash she was off towards a clump of bushes fifty yards away. I called after her, fearing that four years of school life would have left her less of a horsewoman than she imagined. But she only laughed, and when near the hedge raised her horse with the skill of an adept and cleared it by a foot.*

*"During the next two years the whole tenor of my life was changed. Juanita went with me everywhere. Like myself she lived in the saddle, and soon she could throw a lariat or round up a herd of cattle as well as almost any of my men.*

*"What wonder that I learned to love the girl? Philosophers tell us that two may meet, exchange glances, and love. Madness! That is admiration, magnetic attraction, passionate desire,—what you please,—it is not love. Love may spring from such beginning, but not in an instant, a day, an hour. Too many have been wrecked by that delusion, wedding while intoxicated with this momentary delirium, and awaking later to a realization of a dread future. For what can be worse misery than to be married and not mated? No, love thrives on what it feeds on. Daily companionship, hourly contact breeds a habit in a man's life,*

creates a need that can but be filled by the presence of the one who excites such heart longings. Thus we learn to love our horse or dog, and the possession of the animal satisfies us. So when we come to love a woman, to love her with that love which once born never dies, so, too, possession is the only salve, the only solution. After two years I realized this, and began to think of marrying my little one. 'Why not?' I asked myself. True, I was forty, while she was but eighteen. But I was young in heart, energy, and vitality. And who had a greater right to possess her than myself? None. Then a dreadful thought came to me. What if she did not love me in return? My heart turned cold, but I never dreamed of coercing her. I would tell her my wish, my hope, and as she should answer so should it be.

"This was my determination. You will admit that I was honorable. Having formed my conclusion I sought a favorable moment for its execution. At this you may wonder. Were we not together daily, riding side by side, often alone with God and Nature for hours together? True! But I dreaded a mistake. Should I speak when her heart was not ready, the answer might blight my life.

"So I waited day after day, no moment seeming more propitious than another. Yet when I did speak, it was all so simple, that I wondered at myself for my long anxiety. We had been riding together for three or four hours, when, reaching a shaded knoll in which I knew there was a cold spring where we might refresh ourselves and our horses, we stopped. As she jumped from her horse, Juanita stood a moment looking back and forth across the plains, and then, in full enjoyment of the scene, she exclaimed:

"'Isn't it all grand! I could live here forever!'

"My heart leaped, and my tongue moved unbidden:

"'With me?' I cried. 'With me, Juanita?'

"'Why, yes; with you, of course. With whom else?'

"She turned and gazed into my eyes frankly, wondering at my question, and my hand burned as with a fever as I took hers in mine, and almost whispered:

"'But with me, little one, as my own? As my very own? As my little wife, I mean?'

"A dainty blush beautified her cheek, but she did not turn away her eyes as she answered:

"'Why, yes. As your wife, of course. I have always thought you meant it should be. Always lately, I mean.'

"So she had understood before I had known myself. She had been simply waiting, while I had been worrying. I had but to reach forth my hand and grasp my happiness. Well, I had been an ass not to know, but at last the joy was mine.

"Be sure there was little further delay. The wedding was simple yet impressive. Cowboys came from miles around, and one and all they kissed the bride. We had a feast on the grass, the tables extending a quarter of a mile, and all were welcome. There were no cards of invitation; all within fifty miles were my neighbors, and all neighbors were expected at the cowboy's wedding. The ceremony was held out in the open air, and five hundred men stood with bared heads as the worthy father gave me my treasure and declared her mine before God and them.

"Thus Juanita came to be mine own. First given to me by that Providence who rules the Universe, when the unguided steps of my horse carried me to the tiny bundle lying on a boundless plain, and lastly given to me with her own consent by the worthy man who united us in the name of the Father of us all. Was she not mine then, and thenceforward forever? Could any man rightly take her from me? You shall hear.

"A year passed. A year of happiness such as poets prate of and ardent men and maids hope for, but rarely realize. Then the serpent entered my Eden. The tempter came, in the form of this man who tells you that his name is Odell, but who lies when he tells you so. He was from the North, and he had a fine form and a fair face. Fair, I mean, in the sense that it was attractive to women. He soon had the few young women of our neighborhood dangling after him, like captured fish on a blade of palmetto. I saw all this, and, seeing, had no suspicion that with the chance to choose from so many who were still unclaimed, he would seek to win my own dear one.

"I cannot dwell on this. Indeed, I never knew the details, only the finale. The blow came as unsuspected as might an earthquake in a land where tranquillity had reigned for centuries. I had been away all day, and for once my wife had not ridden with me. I had myself bidden her remain at home, because of the intense heat of an August sun. She had begged to go with me, perhaps fearing to be left alone. But I knew nothing, suspected nothing of the ache and terror in her heart. When I got back, it was already dark, and having been away from Juanita all day, I called for her at once. The empty echoes of my voice coming back as the only answer to my cry struck my heart with a chill, and a nameless, hideous dread seized me. Had anything happened? Was she ill, or dead? Dead it must be, I thought, or she would have answered. I wandered through the house; I searched the whole place; I sprang back upon my horse and rode from house to house throughout that whole awful night. I discovered nothing. No one could tell me aught. At daybreak I returned fagged out, with a vague hope that perhaps I had made some blunder and that she was still at home. At last, in the room where I kept my accounts and transacted business, I found a note upon my desk which explained the horrible truth. Here is a copy of it. Note the hideous braggadocio. It read:

"'I. O. U. One wife. (Signed) L—R—.'

"*That you may fully appreciate how this taunt stung, I must remind you that, as I have said, my father had taught me to follow most rigidly the rules of honor. In transactions involving even very great sums of money, it was not uncommon amongst us cattlemen to acknowledge an indebtedness in this primitive, informal way,—simply writing upon a slip of paper, perhaps torn from the edge of a newspaper, 'I. O. U.', giving the amount, and adding the signature. No dates were really necessary, though sometimes added, because the possession of the paper proved the debt, the cancellation by payment always leading to the destruction of the I. O. U.*

"*Thus this heartless young brute from the North had not only stolen from me my chief treasure, but he had left behind an acknowledgment of his debt in that form which was most binding among us.*

"*Does it cause you surprise to have me say that I carefully preserved that bit of paper, and swore to make him meet the obligation when the day of reckoning might come? This explains to you that cause, which at the outset I said brings with it a result which now is, and always has been, inevitable. Of course it is certain that had I been able to find my betrayer while my anger still raged, and my anguish yet at its most acute point, I would simply have shot the man on sight, recklessly, thoughtlessly. But I could not get trace of him, and so had time to think.*

"*Too late I learned that I had made one dreadful error. I have told you my views of love, how engendered and how nourished. My mistake was in thinking that such a love is the necessary rather than merely the possible result of constant companionship between congenial spirits. In my own heart the fire of true love burned only too brightly, but with Juanita, poor child, it was but the glow reflected from my own inward fires that warmed her heart. She was happy with me, sharing my life, and when I asked her to marry* me, mistook her calm friendship for what she had heard called love. Love she had never experienced. When later the younger man devoted himself to her, she was probably first merely intoxicated by an overpowering animal magnetism, which was nothing but passion. But even as I have admitted that this impulsive desire may drift into the truer, nobler quality of love, so, later, I found, must have been the case with my cherished one.

"A full year passed before I had the least idea of the whereabouts of the elopers. Then one day the mail brought me a brief, plaintive note from her. All she wrote was, 'Dear one, forgive me. Juanita.' The date showed that it had been written on the anniversary of our wedding, and from this I knew that the day had brought to her remorseful memories of me. But the envelope bore a postmark, and I knew at last that they were in a suburb of the great metropolis.

"I started for New York that very night, bent on vengeance. But one approaches a revengeful deed in a different spirit a year after the infliction of the wrong, and so by the time I reached my destination, my mind had attained a judicial attitude, and my purpose was tempered by the evident wisdom of investigating before acting. I had little difficulty in finding the nest to which my bird had flown, and a happy nest it appeared to be. It seems like yesterday, and the picture is distinct before my vision. I came cautiously towards the cottage, which was surrounded by a grassy lawn, and my heart came into my throat with a choking sensation as suddenly I saw her there, my little Juanita, lazily swinging in a hammock under a great elm, singing! Singing so merrily that I could not doubt that she was, for the moment at least, happy. So, then, she was happy—happy with him. The thought affected me in a twofold manner. I resented her happiness for myself, and gloried in it for her own sake. I did not venture to interrupt her life by intruding myself into it. I quietly prosecuted my inquiries, and learned that she was known as his wife, indeed that a regular marriage had taken place. Thus at least he gave her the apparent protection of his name. Moreover, I found that he was still kind to her, and that the two were counted a happy couple.

"Therefore I returned to Texas, and never again set eyes upon my dear one, in life. But before leaving I perfected arrangements whereby I might receive regular communications, and so be in the position to know how it fared with Juanita, and I am bound to admit that the reports were ever favorable. So far as I know, he always treated her with loving kindness. In exchange for this, he must count that he has been left undisturbed by me. On that score, then, we are quits. But the paper on which he wrote that infamous I. O. U. remained, and so long as it was in my possession it was an obligation still to be met.

"Five years elapsed, and then one day suddenly I was summoned by telegraph. Juanita was ill—was likely to die. I sped North as fast as the swiftest express train could travel, but I arrived three hours after her sweet spirit had flown. He did not recognize me as I mingled with the crowd in the house at the funeral, and so got a last glimpse of her face. But after the grave was filled, and the little mound was covered with flowers, the mound which held all that had stood between him and fate, I stepped forward and stood where his eyes must meet mine.

"At first he did not recognize me, but presently he knew me, and the abject terror that came into his face brought to me the first sensation of pleasure that I had experienced since that hour in which I had found my home deserted. I stepped back into the crowd, and I saw him look about eagerly, and pass his hand across his eyes, as though brushing aside some horrible vision. But he was soon to learn that it was no spectral fancy, but myself with whom he had to deal.

"*I waited till nightfall and then sought him at his house, and told him my purpose. I showed him that bit of paper on which he had scrawled the words 'I. O. U. One wife,' and I told him that in exacting a settlement we would change the letter 'w' to the letter 'l.' That for my wife, I would expect his life, in return. I gave him a respite of a few days, but this he will explain to you. I know this, for twice have I seen him approach your offices, and then alter his mind and depart without going in. But his fate is now so near that by to-morrow, at the latest, he will no longer have the courage to delay. He will go to you. He will lie to you. He will endeavor to obtain your aid. Fool! Of what avail? He cannot escape even if you undertake to assist him. But after reading the truth, as here written, will you?*"

Mr. Mitchel put down the last page of the statement, and, turning to Mr. Barnes, he said:

"And you say you have thwarted this man's purpose?"

"Yes; absolutely. Of course, that tale of his makes me sympathize with him, but the law does not grant a man the right to murder even when a wife is stolen. Certainly not after the lapse of five years."

"I should think that the author of that document would be a man who would carefully plan whatever scheme he might have decided upon, and if you have really thwarted him, then you have been very clever. Very clever, indeed. How was it?"

"To explain that," replied Mr. Barnes, "I must begin by telling you of the visit of this man who calls himself Odell. You will note that the Texan says that his adversary 'will explain,' etc. Thus he evidently intended his communication to reach me before the visit of my client. But it was otherwise. Mr. Odell, as we must call him, came here two days ago, whereas that communication did not reach me until yesterday morning."

"Did this man Odell tell you the same story as that sent to you by the Texan?"

"Essentially the same, yet differing materially in some of the details. He came into my office in a very nervous, excited frame of mind, and even after I had asked him to be seated and to state his business he seemed half inclined to go away. However, he finally concluded to confide his trouble to me, though he began the conversation in a singular manner.

"'I hardly know,' said he, 'whether you can help me or not. Your business is to detect crimes after they have been committed, is it not?'

"'It is,' said I.

"'I wonder,' said he, 'whether you could prevent a crime?'

"'That would depend much upon the circumstances and the nature of the crime.'

"'Let us say that a murder was contemplated. Do you think you might be able to prevent it?'

"'Do you know who is threatened? Who is the person to be murdered?'

"'Myself.'

"'Yourself? Tell me the circumstances which lead you to believe that such a danger threatens you.'

"'The circumstances are peculiar. I suppose I must tell you the whole miserable story. Well, so be it. Some years ago I went into one of the southern states, it matters not which, and there I met a young girl with whom I fell madly in love. There is nothing out of the common about the story except as regards her guardian. I suppose that is what he would be called. This man was quite a wealthy ranchman, and it seems that he had found the girl when an infant, on the open plains. He took her home, and raised her. Of course he grew fond of her, but the fool forgot that he was twenty years older than herself and fell in love with her. Consequently I knew that it would be useless to ask his consent to our marriage, so we eloped.'"

"That is a different version," interrupted Mr. Mitchel.

"Very different," said Mr. Barnes. "But when I heard it, it was the only version known to me. I asked him how long a time had passed since the elopement, and he replied:

"'Five years. I married the girl of course, and we have been living until recently up the Hudson. A month ago she died, and in grief I followed her body to the grave. The last sod had just been placed on the mound, when looking up I saw the man, the guardian, let us call him, standing glaring at me in a threatening manner. I was startled, and as a moment later he seemingly disappeared, I was inclined to believe that it had been merely a trick of the mind. This seemed not improbable, for if the man harbored any ill-will, why had he not sought me out before?'

"'Perhaps he did not know where to find you,' I suggested.

"'Yes, he did. I know that, because my wife told me that she wrote to him once. But it was not imagination, for that same night he came to my house, and coolly informed me that now that the girl was dead, there was nothing to delay longer his purpose to take my life.'

"'He told you this openly?'

"'He made the announcement as calmly as though he were talking of slaying one of his steers. I don't know why, for I am not a coward, but a terrible fear seized me. I seemed to realize that it would be useless for me to make any resistance; whether he chose to take my life at that moment or later, it seemed to me that I could and would make no effort to save myself. In fact, I imagine I felt like a man in a trance, or it might be in a dream-disturbed sleep wherein, while passing through dreadful experiences, and wishing that some one might arouse me, yet I myself was powerless to awaken.'

"'Perhaps the man had hypnotized you.'

"'Oh, no. I don't make any such nonsensical claim as that. I was simply terrified, that is all,—I who have never known fear before. Worse than all, I have not for an instant since been able to escape from my feeling of helpless terror. He talked to me in the quietest tone of voice. He told me that he had known of my whereabouts all the time, and that he had spared me just so long as the girl was happy; that so long as her happiness depended upon my living, just so long had he permitted me to live. Throughout the interview he spoke of my life as though it belonged to him; just as though, as I said before, I might have been one of his cattle. It was awful.'

"'Did he say when or how he would murder you?'

"'He did worse than that. He did the most diabolical thing that the mind of man could conceive. He explained to me that he considered me in his debt, and that the debt could only be cancelled with my life. And then he had the horrible audacity to ask me to give him a written acknowledgment to that effect.'"

"'How? I do not understand.'

"'He drew out a large sheet of paper on which were some written words, and handed me the paper to read. This is what I saw: "On or before the thirtieth day from this date I promise to pay my debt to the holder of this paper."'

"'How very extraordinary!'

"'Extraordinary! Nothing like this has ever occurred in all the world. The man asked me practically to give him a thirty-day note to be paid with my life. Worse than that, I gave it to him.'

"'You gave it to him! What do you mean?'

"'At his dictation I copied those words on a similar sheet that he furnished, and I signed the hellish document. Don't ask me why I did it. I don't know, unless in my terror and despair I thought at the moment only of getting rid of my visitor, and of gaining even the short respite that here seemed held out to me. At all events I wrote the thing, and he folded it carefully and put it in his pocket with a satanic smile. Then he rose to go, but further explained to me that as the note said "on or before" thirty days, he would feel at liberty to conclude the matter at his own pleasure. This doubled the horror of the situation. What he said next, however, seemed to offer a ray of hope, if hope might be sought under such circumstances. He told me that if I could by any means manage to live beyond the limitations of the note, he would return the paper to me to be burned, and in that case I might consider the matter terminated.'

"'Why, then, he did give you one chance of living.'

"'I have tried to make myself think so. But as I have thought it over, sometimes I imagine that there is merely an added dev-iltry in this,—that he held out this hope only to intensify my sufferings; for total despair might have led me to suicide, thus shortening the period of my mental agony. If this was his pur-pose, he succeeded only too well. A dozen times I have been on the verge of blowing my brains out to abbreviate the tor-ture, when the thought has come to me that as another day had passed finding me still alive, so might the remaining ones; that I might escape after all. So I have lived and entered another day of torment.'

"'But why have you allowed this affair to so prey upon your mind?'

"'Allowed it? How could I have escaped from it? You do not know the expedients of that fiend. I will tell you a few of the things that have made it impossible for me to forget. In the first place, every morning I have received a postal-card on which would appear some figures,—"30 minus 1 equals 29,"—"30 minus 2 equals 28,"—"30 minus 3 equals 27," and so on. Can you imagine my feelings this morning when the card was placed in my hand on which I found "30 minus 28 equals 2"?'

"'But why have you read these cards?'

"'Why? Why does the bird go to the snake that devours it? The cards have exerted a fascination for me. In my mail I would look first to see if one were there. Finding it, I would read it over and over, though of course I would know in advance the ghoul-ish calculation that would be there. But this is not all. On the third day I was about to smoke a cigar, when its peculiar shape attracted my attention. I looked at it a long time stupidly, and then broke it in half. Inside I found a slender metal tube, which later I discovered was filled with some horribly explosive preparation. I do not think that any other cigar of that nature has reached me. But, my suspicions once aroused, I began opening my cigars, to make sure, and in this manner, of course, they were rendered useless. Why, I have been suspicious even of cigars offered to me by some of my best friends. The more cordial the presentation, the more certain I have felt that the man might be in the plot against me. So I have been obliged to forego smoking, a great trial, as you may imagine, in such a condition of mind as I have been in, when a sedative would have been so acceptable.'

"'You might have used cigarettes,' suggested the detective.

"'Cigarettes? It seemed so at first. Of course not those ready-made, but I might make them for myself. I made one. Just one! I rolled it, using paper and tobacco that had been in my own room for over a month. When I applied a match the thing sizzled like a firecracker. Whether or not some powder had been dropped into my tobacco, I do not know. Undoubtedly I could have obtained fresh tobacco and fresh paper, and thus have enjoyed the longed-for smoke. But I tell you I have been unable to think these things out. I have been as feeble-minded as any imbecile. For a few days I obtained a little consolation out of liquor, but one night after taking a drink I thought I noticed a sediment in the bottom of the glass. I looked at it closer, and there it was. A whitish powder. Undoubtedly arsenic.'

"'Why not sugar?' said Mr. Barnes.

"'I don't know. That never occurred to me. Perhaps it was. At all events I have not had a drop of anything since, except water. No tea, no coffee, no liquor that might hide a poison. Only clear water, drawn from the hydrant with my own hands, into a cup that I carried about my person, and washed out before every draught. I was determined that he should not poison me except by poisoning the reservoir. This necessitated adopting a plan for eating that would be equally safe. So I have taken to eating at restaurants, a different one for every meal.'

"'You have allowed yourself to become morbid on this subject. I should not be surprised if this man really has no intention of committing this murder, but has taken this means of having revenge, by causing you a month of mental suffering.'

"'I hardly think that. He has made several efforts to kill me already.'

"'In what manner?'

"'Well, twice, in my own house, I was shot at from without. I heard the report of a pistol each time, and a ball passed close to me and entered the wall at my side. After the second attempt I decided to change my place of abode, and took a room at my club. The room had but one window, and that opened on the interior court. I was particular that it should not be exposed to the street. For several days nothing happened; then one night, just as I was putting out my gas, and consequently standing by the window, again I heard a pistol shot, and another bullet whistled past me, all too close. The odd thing was that though I had an immediate investigation made, it is certain that my enemy was not in the building.'

"'In that case, the shot must have come in accidentally. Some one opposite was probably handling his pistol and carelessly touched the trigger, causing the explosion. Naturally, when he found that you had nearly been shot, he chose not to make any explanations.'

"'However that may be, I thought it best to move again. This time I found a room in a hotel, where the only ventilation is from a skylight opening upon the roof. In there at least I have felt safe from intruding bullets. But I am disturbed by the regularity with which those postal-cards come to me. The address has always been changed as I have moved from one place to another.'

"'Evidently your man keeps an eye upon you.'

"'Very evidently, though I have never set eyes upon him since his visit on the night when he made me give him that diabolically conceived promissory note. Now that is the story. Can you do anything for me?'

"'Let me see; according to the calculation on the card that reached you this morning there are still two days of respite?'

"'Not of respite. There is no respite from my torture till the end comes, be that what it may. But there are two days remaining of the thirty.'

"That was the problem, Mr. Mitchel," said Mr. Barnes, "which I was called upon to solve. Bearing in mind that I had not yet received the other man's communication, you will, of course, concede that it was my duty to endeavor to save this man?"

"Undoubtedly. It was your duty to save the man under any circumstances. We should always prevent crime where we can. The question here was rather how you might be able to accomplish this."

"How would you have proceeded, had the case been in your care?"

"Oh, no, Mr. Barnes," said Mr. Mitchel, laughing. "You cannot be allowed to get my advice after the affair is over. I must come in as principal or spectator. In this instance I am merely a spectator."

"Very well. As you please. My plan, I think, was as ingenious as it was simple. It was evident to me either that we had to deal with a man who did not intend to kill his victim, in which case any course would save him; or else the affair might be serious. If the man really was plotting murder, the affair occupying so long a time was unquestionably premeditated and thoroughly well planned. Whatever the scheme, it was equally obvious that we could not hope to fathom it. The blow, if it should come, would be swift and sure. Consequently but one course lay before us."

"And that was?"

"To remove our man to such a place of safety that the blow, however well conceived, could not by any possibility reach him."

"Ah, well argued! And could you find such a place?"

"Yes. A private room in a safe-deposit vault."

"Not bad. Not half bad. And you did this?"

"Without delay. I explained my purpose to the officers of one of these institutions, and before another hour had passed I had Mr. Odell 'safely deposited,' where none could reach him except myself."

"Of course you supplied him with eatables?"

"Yes, indeed, and liquor and cigars beside. Poor fellow! How he must have enjoyed his cigars! When I visited him yesterday, on opening the door of his room he looked like a spectre in a fog. Now I must further remind you that I put Mr. Odell in this safety-vault before receiving the letter from the Texan, firmly believing at the time that we were taking unnecessary precautions. After reading the Texan's story I altered my mind, becoming convinced that any other course would have been fatal. Indeed so impressed was I with the determination of this man to have Mr. Odell's life, that though I had the intended victim absolutely safe, still I felt it my duty to make assurance doubly sure, by remaining at the vault myself throughout the rest of the final twenty-four hours, which terminated at noon to day."

"Then you released your prisoner?"

"I did, and a happier man than he you never saw. He stood out in the open air and took a long breath as eagerly as a drunkard drinks his tipple."

"And then what?"

"Why, then we separated. He said he would go to his hotel for a good sleep, for he had little rest in that vault."

"And that, you think, ends the case?"

A quizzical tone in Mr. Mitchel's voice attracted Mr. Barnes's keen sense of hearing, and, slightly disturbed, he said:

"Why, yes. What do you think?"

"I think I would like to go to that man's hotel, and I think we cannot get there too quickly."

"Why, what do you mean? Explain."

"I cannot explain. There is no time. Do not waste another minute, but let us go at once and call on your client."

Mystified, Mr. Barnes jumped up, and the two men hurried out of the building and up Broadway. They had only a few blocks to walk, and were soon in the elevator of the hotel ascending to the top floor where was that room whose only communication with the outer world was a skylight. Reaching the door, Mr. Barnes tried the knob, but the door was locked. He knocked first lightly and then more violently, but there was no response.

"It is useless, Mr. Barnes," said Mr. Mitchel. "We must break in the door, and I fear we may be too late."

"Too late?" said Mr. Barnes, wonderingly; but without losing more time throwing his weight against the door it yielded and flew in. The two men and the hall-boy entered, and pointing to the floor where lay the body of a man, Mr. Mitchel said:

"See! we are too late."

They lifted the man to the bed, and hastily summoned medical aid, but he was dead. While the hall-boy was gone to call the doctor, Mr. Barnes ruefully said:

"This is incomprehensible to me. After reading that Texan's letter, I was so assured that however vengeful he might be, still he was an honorable man, that I felt positive he would keep his word, and that this man would be safe at the expiration of the note."

"You were entirely right in your estimate of the Texan's character, Mr. Barnes. Your fatal error was in regard to the expiration of the note."

"Why, the thirty days expired at noon to-day."

"Very true. But you have overlooked the usual three days' grace!"

"The devil."

"Just so; the devil,—in this instance the devil being the Texan. Ordinarily the extra three days is an extension demanded by the maker of the note, but in this instance it has been utilized by the deviser of the scheme, who, knowing that his man would be on guard during the thirty days, misled him by a promise of safety thereafter. But he did more than that."

"What do you mean?"

"Why, how has he accomplished his purpose? How has he killed this man up here in a locked room, which has no window through which a bullet might be fired?"

"I do not know; that is another puzzle to be solved."

"I have already solved it. The promissory note is the vehicle of his vengeance,—the means by which the opportunity was obtained, and the means by which the end has been consummated. You will recall that Odell told you that the Texan promised that if he should live beyond the limitation of the note it would be returned so that he might burn it, and he might then consider the matter terminated. These were very suggestive words, and have wrought this man ruin. Evidently soon after he reached this hotel, feeling that at last he had escaped his threatened doom, an envelope was sent up to him, which contained the so-called promissory note. It being too dark in here to read, he lighted his gas. The reception of this paper caused him satisfaction because it seemed to show that his adversary was keeping faith. It had been suggested to him that he might 'burn' the note, and so 'terminate' the affair. Therefore he set fire to the paper, which evidently had been charged with an explosive substance. The explosion not only stunned if it did not kill the man, but it extinguished the gas, leaving the jet open, so that if not destroyed by the explosive he certainly must have been asphyxiated by the escaping gas. Here on the floor is a bit of the paper, and we can still see a few of the words which we know were contained in the promissory note. Then there is the gas turned on, while it is still daylight without. Am I right?"

"Unquestionably," said Mr. Barnes. "What a diabolical scheme from conception to the final act! But suppose that Mr. Odell had not burned that paper? Then the scheme must have failed."

"Not at all. You still overlook the three days of grace, of which but a few hours have yet expired."

# X

## A NOVEL FORGERY

Mr. Barnes was wondering whether he would soon have a case which would require special mental effort in its solution. "Something that will make me think," was the way he phrased it to himself. The same idea had occupied him for some time. Not that he had been idle, but his "cases" had all been of such a nature that with a little supervision it had been safe to entrust them entirely to his subordinates. Nothing had occurred to compel his personal investigation. On this morning, however, fate had something peculiarly attractive for him. His office boy announced a visitor, who, when shown into the detective's sanctum, introduced himself thus:

"I am Stephen West, cashier of the Fulton National Bank. Is this Mr. Barnes?"

"Yes, sir," replied the detective. "Is your business important?"

"It is very important to me," said Mr. West. "I am interested to the extent of forty thousand dollars."

"Forty thousand dollars! Forgery?" Receiving an assenting nod, Mr. Barnes arose and closed the door of the office after instructing the boy to prevent his being disturbed. Returning to his seat, he said: "Now then, Mr. West, tell me the story. All of it, as far as you know it. Omit no detail, however unimportant it may seem to you."

"Very good. My bank has been swindled out of forty thousand dollars in the most mysterious manner. We have received four checks, each for ten thousand dollars. These were signed with the name John Wood, one of our best customers. In making up his monthly balance these checks were sent to his house in the usual order of business. To-day Mr. Wood came to the bank, and declared them to be forgeries."

"Were these checks paid by you personally?"

"Oh, no. We received them through the Clearing-House. They had been deposited at the Harlem National Bank, and reached us in the routine way. They were taken on four different days."

"Who was the depositor at the Harlem Bank?"

"There is a mystery there. His name is Carl Grasse. Inquiry at the Harlem Bank shows that he has been a depositor for about a year. He had a seemingly flourishing business, a beer-garden and concert place. Recently he sold out and returned to his home in Germany. Before doing so he drew out his deposits and closed his account."

"How is it that you did not yourself detect the forgeries? I supposed you bank people were so expert nowadays that the cashing of a worthless check would be impossible."

"Here are the forged checks, and here is one cashed by us since the accounting, which is genuine. Compare them, and perhaps you will admit that anyone might have been deceived."

Mr. Barnes examined the checks very closely, using a lens to assist his eyes. Presently he laid them down without comment, and said:

"What do you wish me to do, Mr. West?"

"To me it seems like a hopeless task, but at least I should like to have the forger arrested. I will gladly pay five hundred dollars as a reward."

Mr. Barnes took up the checks again, examined them most carefully with the lens, and once more laid them down. He strummed on his desk a moment and then said suddenly:

"Mr. West, suppose that I not only arrest the guilty man, but recover the forty thousand dollars?"

"You don't mean to say—" began Mr. West, rather astonished.

"I said 'suppose,'" interrupted Mr. Barnes.

"Why, in that case," said Mr. West, "I would gladly give a thousand more."

"The terms suit me," said the detective. "I'll do my best. Leave these checks with me, and I'll report to you as promptly as possible. One moment," as Mr. West was about to depart; "I will make a memorandum of something you must do yourself." He wrote a few lines on a sheet of paper and handed it to Mr. West, saying, "Let me have those to-day, if possible."

One week later Mr. West received the following note:

"STEPHEN WEST, *Esq.:*—

*"Dear Sir—I have completed my investigation of your case. Please call at my office at four o'clock. If convenient, you may as well bring with you a check for fifteen hundred dollars, made payable to*

"JOHN BARNES."

"Great heavens!" ejaculated the cashier upon reading the above, "he tells me to bring fifteen hundred dollars. That means he has recovered the money. Thank God!" He dropped into his chair, overcome at the sudden release from the suspense of the previous week, and a few tears trickled down his cheek as he thought of his wife and little one who would not now be obliged to give up their pretty little home to make good his loss.

Promptly at four he was ushered into the presence of Mr. Barnes. Impatient to have his hopes confirmed, he exclaimed at once:

"Am I right? You have succeeded?"

"Most thoroughly," said the detective. "I have discovered the thief, and have him in prison. I also have his written confession."

"But the forty thousand dollars?"

"All safe and sound. Your bank does not lose a dollar—except the reward." Mr. Barnes added the last after a pause and with a twinkle of his eye.

"Oh, Mr. Barnes, that is a trifle compared to what I expected. But tell me, how was this trick played on us? Who did it?"

"Suppose I give you a detailed account of my work in solving the riddle? I am just in the humor for telling it, and besides you will be more appreciative."

"That is just what I should most desire."

"Very well," began Mr. Barnes. "We will go back to the moment when, after scrutinizing the checks, I asked what you would give for the recovery of the money. I asked that because a suspicion had entered my mind, and I knew that if it should prove to be correct, the arrest of the criminal and the recovery of the money would be simultaneous. I will not explain now why that should be a necessary sequence, as you will see that I was right. But I will tell you what made me entertain the suspicion. In the first place, as you know, of course, John Wood uses a private special check. The forgeries were upon blanks which had been stolen from his check-book. Thus the thief seemingly had access to it. Next, as is commonly done nowadays, the amount of the check was not only written, but also punched out, with the additional precaution of punching a dollar mark before and after the figures. It would seem therefore almost impossible that any alterations had been made after the check was originally drawn. Such things have been done, the holes being filled up with paper pulp, and new ones punched afterwards. But in this case nothing of the sort had been attempted, nor indeed was any such procedure necessary, for the checks were not raised from genuine ones, but had been declared by Wood to be forgeries outright. That is, he denied the signatures."

"Certainly. They were declared to be spurious."

"Exactly. Now that was all that I knew when you were here last except that the signatures seemed to be very similar. It was possible that they were tracings. The plain deduction from this was that the forger was some one in John Wood's establishment; some one who could have access to the check-book, to the punch, and also have a chance to copy the signature, if it was copied."

"All that is quite clear, but how to proceed?"

"I instructed you to send me a list of all the checks which had been paid out on John Wood's account, giving their dates, numbers, and amounts. I also asked you to procure for me from the Harlem National Bank a similar list of checks paid on order of Carl Grasse. These two lists you sent to me, and they have been very useful. As soon as you left me, and whilst awaiting your lists, I tried some experiments with the forged checks. First I argued that if the signatures were traced, having been made, as it were, from a model, it would follow necessarily that they would exactly coincide if superimposed the one upon the other. Now whilst a man from habit will write his name very similarly a thousand times, I doubt if in a million times he would, or could, exactly reproduce his signature. The test of placing one over the other and examining with transmitted light satisfied me that they were not tracings. I compared each check with each of the others, and with the genuine one which you also left with me. No two were exact counterparts of one another. Still this did not completely prove that they were not tracings, for an artistic criminal might have gone so far as to trace each check from a different model, thus avoiding identity whilst preserving similarity."

"Mr. Barnes," said Mr. West, admiringly, "you delight me with your care in reasoning out your point."

"Mr. West, in speculating upon circumstantial evidence the most thorough care must be used, if one would avoid arresting the innocent. Nothing, to my mind, is stronger proof against a criminal than a complete chain of circumstantial evidence, but again, nothing is so misleading if at any stage a mistake, an omission, or a misconstruction be allowed to occur. In this case, then, as I was starting out to prove what was merely a suspicion, I determined to be most careful, for indeed I dislike following up suspicion at any time. A suspicion is a prejudgment, and may prove a hindrance to correct reasoning. Not entirely satisfied, therefore, I took the next step. A tracing can be made in either of two ways: with a lead-pencil, or with a stylus of glass or agate. The former leaves a deposit of the lead, whilst the latter makes an indentation upon the paper. In the first case the forger will attempt to remove the lead with an erasing rubber, but will not succeed thoroughly, because some of it will be covered by the ink, and because of the danger of injuring the surface of the paper. In the latter instance, if he be a very thoughtful man, he might undertake to remove the indentation by rubbing the opposite side with the end of his knife or with an ivory paper-cutter. In either case a careful scrutiny with a strong glass would show the burnishing upon the reverse side. I could find nothing of the sort. Taking one of the checks I applied a solution to remove the ink. A thorough examination disclosed that there was no sign either of the graphite, or of the indentation from the stylus. In fact, I became satisfied that the signatures had not been traced."

"But what did that prove? They might have been imitations made by a clever penman."

"They might have been, but I doubted it; and since you ask, I will give my reasons. In the first place, the signatures were accepted at your bank not once, but four times. It would be a remarkably clever man to deceive experts so well. However, I did not abandon this possibility until further developments showed conclusively to my mind that it would be a waste of time to follow up that line of research. Had it been necessary to do so, I should have discovered who in the place had the opportunity to do the work, and by examining their past I should have received a hint as to which of these was most likely to be my man. For any man who could have the ability to commit such a clever forgery must have acquired it as a sequence of special skill and aptitude with his pen of which his friends would be cognizant. Once I looked up such a man, and found that as a boy he had forged his parents' names to excuses for absences from school. Later he turned to higher things. In this instance I was satisfied that the only person having the access to materials, the knowledge of the financial condition of the concern, and the ability to write the checks, was Mr. John Wood himself."

"John Wood!" exclaimed the cashier. "Impossible! Why, that would mean that—"

"Nothing is impossible, Mr. West. I know what you would say. That it involved his having an accomplice in this Carl Grasse? Well, that is what I suspected, and that is why I asked for an additional reward for the recovery of the funds. If I could prove that John Wood made the checks himself, they ceased to be forgeries in one sense, and the bank could rightfully charge the amounts against his account. But let me tell you why I abandoned your theory that an expert penman was at work. Observe that though you would have honored a check for forty thousand dollars drawn by John Wood, yet the forgeries were four in number. That showed that the man was not afraid of arousing your suspicion. The only man who could feel absolutely sure upon that point was John Wood. But there is another pretty point. These checks being spurious, and yet being numbered, could arouse your suspicion in two ways. If the numbers upon them greatly varied from those upon genuine checks coming in at the same time, the fraud would have been detected quickly. On the other hand, he could not give you correct numbers without being either in collusion with his bookkeeper or else duplicating the numbering of other checks. That the latter course was pursued, exempted the bookkeeper. All the numbers on the forged checks were duplicates of those on genuine ones."

"But, Mr. Barnes, that did not arouse our suspicion, because—"

"Just so," interrupted Mr. Barnes, "but let me tell you why, as the *why* is a very significant link in our chain. Your list of this man's checks helped me there. About a year ago Carl Grasse appeared upon the scene in Harlem, buying out a beer-garden, and starting an account in the Harlem National Bank. Now observe that prior to that time, from the first check sent to you by Wood, the strictest regularity as to numbering obtained. There is not a break or a skip anywhere. But in February, the month after Carl Grasse moved to Harlem, there is a duplication in Wood's checks. Two have the same numbering, but both are for trifling amounts, sixteen dollars in one instance and forty in the other. You possibly passed it over. Next month, I find two duplications, and from then on this apparent mistake happens no less than ten times."

"Mr. Barnes, the bookkeepers did notice this, and we spoke to Mr. Wood, but he said it was simply a clerical error of his own due to haste in business hours."

"Exactly, but he was paving the way for his big coup. He was disarming you of suspicion. This one fact satisfied me that I was on the right track, but your list gave me even better corroboration. On February 1st I find that Wood cashed a check payable to himself for ten thousand and fifty-nine dollars. On February 2d, Carl Grasse opened an account with the Harlem Bank, depositing ten thousand dollars, paying in the amount, in cash. This might seem but a coincidence, but by looking over the books of the beer-garden, which is still in existence, Grasse having sold it out, I find that on February 2d, Grasse paid his employees just fifty-nine dollars. The difference, you see, between Wood's draft and Grasse's deposit."

"It certainly seems to connect the two, when we remember that the final forgeries were checks signed by Wood in favor of Grasse."

"Precisely, but follow this a little further. For several months there is nothing to connect the two so far as their banking goes, but note that during this lapse Grasse does not draw a single check in favor of himself, nor does he deposit any checks from others. His transactions with his customers are strictly cash, and his checks are all to dealers, who supply him with his stock. None of these are for large amounts, and his balance does not exceed twelve thousand dollars at any time. On October 1st he deposited five thousand dollars in cash. On the day before that, Wood drew that amount out of your bank. On the 12th, this is repeated by both, and on the 14th, Grasse cashes a check for twelve thousand dollars, taking cash. This goes through successfully, and the Harlem Bank is made to see that Grasse commands large amounts and uses large amounts. This is repeated in varying amounts in November, and again in December, the bank by this time being quite ready to pay out money to Grasse. On January 2d, Wood has his check account balanced. On the 3d, Grasse deposits Wood's check for ten thousand dollars. This goes through the Clearing-House, and is accepted by your bank. The Harlem Bank is therefore satisfied of its authenticity. On the 5th, Grasse deposits check number two, and at the same time cashes a check for ten thousand dollars. The second spurious check goes through all right, and on the 10th and 15th, the transactions are repeated. On the 20th, Grasse explains to the Harlem Bank that he has sold his business, and is going home to Germany. He closes his account, taking out his money, and disappears from the scene. You are forty thousand dollars out by a clever swindle, with nothing to prove your suspicions save a few coincidences in the banking records of the two men."

"But assuredly, Mr. Barnes, enough evidence upon which to arrest Mr. Wood?"

"To arrest him, yes. But to convict him? That is another affair. Without conviction you do not recover your money. No, my work was by no means finished. I first sought to follow Grasse. I did not have far to go. At the Hamburg-American line I found him booked, but investigation showed that he never sailed. The ticket which he bought has never been taken up."

"Then the accomplice is still in this country?"

"No; the accomplice is not in this country," said Mr. Barnes, dryly. "Don't get ahead of the story. At this stage of the game I made some singular discoveries. I found, for example, that Carl Grasse slept over his saloon, but that he frequently would be absent all night. I also learned that when he did sleep there, he would leave about nine o'clock in the morning for that mysterious realm, 'downtown.' When he slept elsewhere, he usually reached the saloon at eight, and still went 'downtown' at nine. It was his general custom to get back about five in the afternoon. Extending my researches in the direction of John Wood, I learned that he was customarily at his office at ten o'clock, seldom leaving before four. Moreover, at his apartment the janitor told me that he frequently slept elsewhere, and that when he passed the night at that place, he would leave about seven in the morning. Do you follow me?"

"Do you mean that John Wood and Carl Grasse are one and the same person?"

"That idea entered my mind about this time. Up at the saloon I found some other small evidences that this was a probability. You see, a man may disguise his personal appearance, but it is difficult for him to change his habits with his clothing. For example, I found that Mr. Wood always uses Carter's writing fluid, and Mr. Grasse had the same predilection, as the empty bottles attest. Moreover, the bottles are of the same size in both places. Next I observe that both men used the same make of stub pens. Again note that though Carl Grasse is a German name and the man was keeping a beer saloon, he was never seen to drink beer himself. John Wood has the same antipathy to malt. But most singular is the fact that this man, who so carefully laid his plans, should have actually bought a check-punching stamp of the same make and style of figures as that used in the Wood establishment."

"Perhaps he did that so that he could make the spurious checks uptown instead of downtown, where he might be discovered."

"More than likely, but he should have taken it away with him. There is always some little detail of this kind that even the most skilful overlooks. He probably thought that the similarity of the instruments would never be detected, or made to count against him. It is nothing in itself, but as a link in a chain it mends a break. There was one fact, however, at wide variance with the theory of the identity of the two men. Wood is of ordinary build, with black hair and smooth-shaven face. Grasse is described as very stout, with red hair and whiskers. Of course, following the theory of impersonation, if Wood transformed himself into a stout man, totally different clothing would be needed for the two parts which he played. I found that Wood always dressed in the finest broadcloth, whilst Grasse wore conspicuous plaids. Supposing that he wore a red wig and false whiskers, I determined to find the man from whom he had procured them. I guessed that he would avoid any well-known place, and I began my hunt in the costumers' shops on Third Avenue. I went to several without obtaining any clue, when at last fortune favored me. I found a place where, upon their books, in last January was a record of 'red wig and whiskers' for the same customer. Moreover, they had furnished this person with a 'make-up' for a fat German, giving him the necessary 'pads,' as they are called, a suit of underwear wadded so as to increase the proportion of the body. Can you guess what I did next?"

"I think not."

"It was an inspiration. I ordered a similar outfit for myself, including the plaid suit. This morning they were delivered to me, and, dressed in them, I induced the costumer to go with me to Wood's place. As soon as I was shown into his presence, I began to talk in a most excited, angry tone. I said 'Mr. Wood, I come for satisfaction. I am Carl Grasse, the man you have been personating uptown. I am the man whose name you forged to the back of your own checks. And this is the costumer who sold you the disguise. Am I not right?' This last speech I addressed to the costumer, who, to my intense satisfaction, said, 'Yes, that is the gentleman; but I did not know he was going to impersonate anybody.'"

"What happened then?" asked the cashier.

"Well," said Mr. Barnes, "I had better luck than I had expected, though, in line with my hopes. You see, my sudden appearance before him, my words, and my rapid speech, all tended to confuse him. He suddenly heard himself accused of forging the name of 'Carl Grasse,' and for the moment thought only of defending himself from that charge. He was utterly taken back, and stammered out, 'I did not forge anybody's name. The checks had my own signature, and the endorsement—that was "Carl Grasse." There is no such person.' Then suddenly seeing that he was making a mistake and incriminating himself, he exclaimed, 'Who the devil are you?'

"'I am a detective,' I answered, quickly seizing his arms and putting on a pair of manacles, 'and I arrest you for swindling the Fulton Bank, whether your offense be forgery or not.' That settled him. He wilted and began to cry for mercy. He even offered me money to let him escape. I delivered him to the Central Office officials, and since then the Inspector has obtained a voluntary confession from him. Are you satisfied, Mr. West?"

"I am more than satisfied. I am amazed. Mr. Barnes, you are a genius."

"Not at all, Mr. West, I am a detective."

# XI
## A FROSTY MORNING*

"Thank heaven, you have come," exclaimed Mr. Van Rawlston, as Mr. Mitchel entered. "I have a thousand pounds on my mind, and—"

"Never heard of the disease," interrupted Mr. Mitchel. "If you consider mind and brain to be synonymous, the locality is popularly supposed to be inundated with water occasionally—but then, you mentioned a thousand pounds, and, a pound being a pint, we would have a thousand pints, or five hundred quarts, and—well, really, your head seems hardly large enough, so—"

"I am talking of money," ejaculated Mr. Van Rawlston, sharply; "English money. Pounds sterling."†

"The deuce you are! Money, eh? Money on the brain! Oh, I've heard of that. It is a very common disorder."

"Mitchel, I sent for you to help me. I am up to my ears in a mystery. I've been in this room nearly all day trying to solve it. I've had your friend Barnes working on it for several hours, yet we have made no progress. In despair I thought of you; of your

---

*This story first appeared in *The Black Cat* for August 1898.

†Although economic comparisons are always complex, in terms of wealth, £1,000 in 1895 is the equivalent of at least £115,000 in 2020, or US$150,000.

cool, keen, analytical brain, and I decided that you could discover the truth, if any man can. But if you are in a jesting humor, why—"

"A thousand pardons, old friend. That is one pardon for each of your pounds. But, there, forgive me, and I will be serious. I received your note late, because I did not reach home until dinner time. You asked me to call here as soon as possible, and here I am within half an hour of reading your message. Now, then, about this thousand pounds sterling. Where are they, or is it, as you are most accustomed to speaking. The plural or singular verb seems to be a matter of choice with large amounts."

"The money is in this room."

"In this room? You know that, and yet cannot find it?"

"Therein lies the mystery. I had it in my hands this morning, and within a few minutes it had vanished."

"Now, Mr. Van Rawlston, if you are presenting a problem for me to solve, I beg of you to be minutely accurate in your statements. You say 'had vanished.' That is manifestly an impossibility. I presume you mean 'seemed to have vanished.'"

"There was no seeming about it. It was a single bank-note, and I placed it on this table. Five minutes later it had disappeared."

"'Disappeared' is a better word, by long odds. It passed out of your sight, you mean. That I can believe. The question then arises, how was this disappearance managed. I say managed, which is an intimation of my belief that the note did not hide itself, but rather that it was hidden. From this postulate I deduce that two or more persons, besides yourself, were present at the time of said disappearance of said bank-note. Am I correct?"

"You are, but really I can't see how you have guessed that there was more than one person with me!"

"It could not be otherwise. Had there been but one person in this room with you, you would not think, you would know absolutely that he took the note. That you have a doubt as to the identity of the culprit, shows that you suspect one of two or more persons."

"Mitchel, I am delighted that I sent for you. You are exactly the man to recover this money."

"What about Barnes? I think you mentioned his name?"

"Yes. Naturally my first thought was to send for a detective, and I remembered him in connection with that ruby robbery of yours, which occurred at my house. He is now following a clue which he considers a good one, and will report during the evening. But perhaps I should relate the exact circumstances of this affair. The details are strikingly curious, I assure you."

"Now that I know that Barnes is on the scent, I may say that I am eager for the fray. Nothing would please me better than to succeed where he fails. Every time I outwit him, it is a feather in my cap, and another argument in favor of my theory that the professional detective is a much over-rated genius. Allow me to light a cigar, and make myself comfortable, in exchange for which privilege I will devote my undivided attention to your tale of woe."

Mr. Mitchel drew forth a handsome gold case, which bore his monogram in diamonds, and selected a choice Havana, which he puffed complacently as Mr. Van Rawlston proceeded.

"Some thirty years ago, or more," began Mr. Van Rawlston, "there came into my office a young Englishman, who introduced himself as Thomas Eggleston. The object of his visit was curious. He wished to borrow four thousand dollars upon collateral. Imagine my surprise when the security offered proved to be an English bank-note for one thousand pounds. It seemed odd that he should wish to borrow, when he could readily have exchanged his note for American currency, but he explained that for sentimental reasons he wished not to part with this note permanently. He desired to redeem it in the future, and keep it as a memento—the foundation of the fortune which he hoped to earn in this new land."

"A singular wish," interposed Mr. Mitchel.

"Singular indeed. So much so that my interest was keenly aroused. I agreed to advance the sum demanded without charge. Moreover, I put him in the way of some good speculations which paved his way to success at the outset. It was not long before his thousand-pound note was back in his possession. Since then we have been close friends, and I was not surprised, when he died a few days ago, to find that I had been named as executor of his estates. Now I must speak of three other persons. When Eggleston came to this country he brought with him a sister. A few years later she married a man named Hetheridge, a worthless scamp, who supposed he was marrying money, and who soon abandoned his wife when he learned that she was poor. I think he drank himself to death. Mrs. Hetheridge did not survive him very long, but she left a little girl, now grown to womanhood. Alice Hetheridge is one of the persons who was present when the bank-note disappeared. A second was Arthur Lumley, of whom I know little, except that he is in love with Alice, and that he was here to-day. Robert Eggleston was also present. He is the nephew of the deceased, and proved to be the heir to the bulk of the estate. He has only been in this country a few months, and has lived in this house during that time. Now I come to the events of to-day."

"Kindly be as explicit as possible," said Mr. Mitchel. "Omit no detail, however trifling."

"My friend died very unexpectedly," continued Mr. Van Rawlston. "On Saturday he was well, and on Monday dead. On Wednesday morning, the day of the funeral, his man of business brought me his client's will. I learned by it that I was chosen an executor, and I undertook to make its contents known to the family. I appointed this morning for that purpose, and when I came, I was surprised to find young Lumley present. Alice took me aside, and explained that she had invited him, and so I was silenced. I asked her to bring me a certain box described in the

will, which she did. It was locked, the key having been brought
to me with the will. I took from it a packet which contained a
bank-note for a thousand pounds; the same upon which I had
once loaned Eggleston money. There were also some govern-
ment bonds, and railroad securities. Having compared these
with the list attached to the will, I then read aloud the testament
of my dear friend. A part of this I will read to you, as possibly
shedding some light upon the situation."

"One moment," interposed Mr. Mitchel. "You said that the
packet taken from the box contained the bank-note as well as
the bonds and other securities. Are you sure that the note was
there?"

"Oh, yes. I found it first, and placed it on the table in front of
me, while I went through the other papers. When I looked for
it again, it had vanished. I say vanished, though you do not like
the word, because it seems incredible that one would dare to
steal in the presence of three others. But listen to an extract from
the will. After bequeathing all of his property to his nephew,
Eggleston inserted this paragraph:

"'To my dear niece I must explain why she is not named as my
heiress. My father married twice. By his first wife he had a son,
William, and by my own mother, my sister and myself. When
he died, my half-brother, William, was ten years my senior, and
had amassed a considerable fortune, whereas I found myself
penniless and dependent upon his bounty. He was not a generous man, but he presented me a bank-note for a thousand
pounds, and paid my passage to this country. My first impulse,
after my arrival, was to make my way as rapidly as I could, and
then to return to William the identical bank-note which he had
given me. For this reason I used it as collateral, and borrowed
money, instead of changing it for American currency. By the
time the note was again in my possession my brother had given
me another proof of his recognition of our consanguinity, and
I decided that it would be churlish to carry out my intention.

Recently William lost his entire fortune in unfortunate speculations, and the shock killed him. Before he died he gave his son Robert a letter to me, reminding me that all that I owned had been the fruit of his bounty, and claiming from me a share of my fortune for his son. I took Robert into my house, and I am bound to say that I have not learned to love him. This, however, may be a prejudice, due to the fact that he had come between me and my wish to make Alice my heiress. It may be in recognition of the possibility of this prejudice that I feel compelled to ease my conscience by bequeathing to William's son the fortune which grew out of William's bounty. The original bank-note, however, was a free gift to me, and I certainly may dispose of it as I please. I ask my niece Alice to accept it from me, as all that my conscience permits me to call my own.'"

"An interesting and curious statement," commented Mr. Mitchel. "Now tell me about the vanishment of the note."

"There is my difficulty. I have so little to tell. After reading the will, I laid it down, and reached out my hand, intending to give the bank-note to Alice, whereupon I discovered that it had disappeared."

"Tell me exactly where each person was seated."

"We were all at this table, which, you see, is small. I sat at this end, Alice at my right hand, young Eggleston at my left, and Lumley opposite to me."

"So that all three were easily within reach of the bank-note when you placed it upon the table? That complicates matters. Well, when you discovered that you could not find the note, who spoke first, and what comment was made?"

"I cannot be certain. I was stunned, and the others seemed as much surprised as I was. I remember that Eggleston asked Alice whether she had picked it up, adding, 'It is yours, you know.' But she made an indignant denial. Lumley said nothing, but sat looking at us as though seeking an explanation. Then I recall that Eggleston made a very practical suggestion."

"Ah, what was that?"

"He laughed as he did so, but what he said was reasonable enough. In substance it was, that if each person in the room were searched, and the note not found, it would thus be proven that it had merely been blown from the table by some draught, in which case a thorough search should find it."

"Was his suggestion acted upon?"

"You may be sure of that. I declined once to allow my guests to be searched when that fellow Thauret suggested it, at the time of the ruby robbery. And you will remember that the scoundrel himself had the jewel. That taught me a lesson. Therefore when Eggleston made his suggestion, I began with him. The search was thorough, I assure you, but I found nothing. I had as little success with Lumley, and I even examined my own pockets, with the vague hope that I might have inadvertently put the note in one of them. But all my looking was in vain."

"Might not one of these men have secreted the bank-note elsewhere, and then have possessed himself of it after your search?"

"I took care to prevent that. As soon as I had gone through Eggleston, I unceremoniously bundled him out of the room. I did the same with Lumley, and neither has been allowed in here since."

"What about the young lady?"

"It would be absurd to suspect her. The note was her property. Still she insisted upon my searching her, and I examined her pocket. Of course, I found nothing."

"Ah, you only examined her pocket. Well, under the circumstances, I suppose that was all you could do. Thus, having sent the three persons out of the room, you think that the-bank-note is still here. A natural deduction, only I wish that the woman might have been more thoroughly searched. I suppose you have looked about the room?"

"I sent for Mr. Barnes, and he and I made a most careful search."

"What view does he take of the case?"

Before Mr. Van Rawlston could reply there was a sharp ring at the door-bell, and a moment later Mr. Barnes himself was ushered in.

"Speak of the devil, and his imps appear," said Mr. Mitchel, jocularly. "Well, Mr. Imp of Satan, what luck? Has your patron assisted you? Have you had the devil's own luck, and solved this problem before I fairly got my wits upon it? You look flushed with victory."

"I did not know you were to be called in, Mr. Mitchel," replied Mr. Barnes, "and I am sorry if you shall be disappointed, but really, I think I can explain this affair. The truth is, it did not strike me as very complex."

"Hear that," exclaimed Mr. Mitchel. "Not complex! The sudden vanishing of a thousand-pound note, before the very eyes, and under the very noses, as it were, of four persons, not complex! The devil certainly has sharpened your wits; eh, Mr. Barnes?"

"Oh, I don't mind your chaffing. Let me explain why I considered this case simple. You will agree that the note was either mislaid or stolen?"

"Logical deduction number one," cried Mr. Mitchel, turning down a finger of the right hand.

"It was not mislaid, or we would have found it. Therefore it was stolen."

"A doubtful point, Mr. Barnes," said Mr. Mitchel, "but we will give you the benefit of the doubt, and call it logical deduction number two." He turned down another finger.

"If stolen the note was taken by one of three persons," pursued the detective.

"He leaves you out of it, Van Rawlston. Well, I suppose I must give you the benefit of the doubt this time. So there goes L. D. number three." He dropped another finger.

"Of these three, one actually owned the note, and another

had just heard of the inheritance of a large fortune. The third, therefore, comes under suspicion."

"Illogical deduction number one," said Mr. Mitchel, sharply, as he turned down a finger of the left hand.

"Why illogical?" asked the detective.

"First, people have been known to steal their own goods; second, rich men are often thieves. Mr. Lumley, being in love with the owner of the note, was as unlikely to steal it as she was herself."

"Suppose that he had stolen it before he heard that his sweetheart was to inherit it?"

"In that case, of course, he may have desired to return it, and yet not have had the opportunity."

"Such was probably the fact. That he stole the note I am reasonably certain."

"How did he get it out of this room?" asked Mr. Van Rawlston.

"He must have hidden it elsewhere than in his pockets," said Mr. Barnes. "You overlooked the fact, Mr. Van Rawlston, that you cannot thoroughly search a man in the presence of a lady."

"Good point," exclaimed Mr. Mitchel. "You have your wits about you to-day, Mr. Barnes. Now tell us what you have learned in corroboration of your theory."

"Lumley is in love with Miss Hetheridge. Up to a few hours ago, he was a clerk, upon a salary not sufficient to permit him to marry. Curiously enough, for one would hardly have thought him so foolish, when he left this house he went direct to his employer and resigned his position. Next, I traced him to a business agency, where he obtained an option to purchase a partnership in a good concern, agreeing to pay five thousand dollars for the same."

"Five thousand dollars! About one thousand pounds," said Mr. Mitchel, thoughtfully.

"The scoundrel!" cried Mr. Van Rawlston. "Undoubtedly he is the thief. I trust you have arrested him, Mr. Barnes?"

"No. He left the city by a train leaving the Grand Central an hour ago."

"Track him, Mr. Barnes. Track him to the end of the earth if necessary. Spare no money. I'll pay the expense." Mr. Van Rawlston was excited.

"I do not know his destination," said the detective, "but, fortunately, the train is a 'local,' and he cannot go far on it. I will do my best to catch up with him. But no time is to be lost."

As he hurried out, Mr. Mitchel shouted after him:

"Luck, and the devil go with you, Mr. Barnes." Then, turning to Mr. Van Rawlston, he continued: "After all, shrewd detective though he be, Mr. Barnes may be on the wrong scent. The note may still be in this house. I do not like to say in this room, after your thorough search. Still, if it could be managed, without the knowledge of Eggleston and Miss Hetheridge, I would like to remain here to-night."

"You wish to make a search yourself, eh? Very good. I will arrange it. By the way, I should tell you that there is to be an auction here to-morrow. Eggleston had arranged a sale of his library before his sudden death, and as the date was fixed and the catalogues sent to all possible buyers, we have thought best to allow the sale to proceed. This being the library, you will see the necessity for settling this mystery before to-morrow, if possible."

"A crowd coming here to-morrow? Excellent. Nothing could be better. Rest easy, Van Rawlston. If Barnes does not recover the bank-note, I will."

It was already nine o'clock in the evening, and Mr. Van Rawlston decided to go to his own home. Upon inquiry he learned that Eggleston was not in the house, and that Miss Hetheridge was in her room. He dismissed the servant, and locked Mr. Mitchel in the library. Next he went upstairs to Miss Hetheridge, told her that he had thought best to lock the library door, and bade her good night. Passing out to the street, he handed the door-key to Mr. Mitchel through the front window.

Left thus alone in a strange house, Mr. Mitchel dropped into an easy chair and began to analyze the situation. He did not light the gas, as that would have betrayed his presence, but the glowing grate fire shed light enough for him to see about him.

Mr. Eggleston had amassed a great collection of books, for the library was a long room occupying the whole of one side of the house, the parlors being on the opposite side of the hallway. Windows in front overlooked the street, and at the back opened upon a small yard. Just below these back windows extended a shed, the roof of an extension, which served as a laundry.

Mr. Mitchel went over in his mind the incidents which had been related to him, and two of his conclusions are worthy of note here:

"Barnes argues," thought he, "that Lumley may have taken the bank-note before he knew that it had been bequeathed to his sweetheart. But the same holds good with the girl herself, and might well explain her stealing what was really her own property. That is one point worth bearing in mind, but the best of all is my scheme for finding the note itself. Why should I trouble myself with a search which might occupy me all night, when by waiting I may see the thief take the note from its present hiding-place, always supposing that it is in this room? Decidedly, patience is a virtue in this instance, and I have only to wait."

A couple of hours later, Mr. Mitchel started up from a slight doze, and realized that he had been disturbed, though at first he could not tell by what.

Then he heard a sound which indicated that someone was fitting a key into the lock. Perhaps the thief was coming! This thought awakened him to his full faculties, and he quickly hid among the folds of some heavy draperies which served upon occasion to divide the room into two apartments. The door opened, and he heard the stealthy tread of soft footsteps, though at first the figure of the intruder was hidden from his view by the draperies which surrounded him. In a few moments his suspense was at an end. A young woman, of girlish figure, passed by him and went over to the fireplace. She was in a dainty night-robe, her long black hair hanging in rich profusion down her back. She leaned against the mantel, and gazed into the fire without moving, for some minutes, and then turning suddenly, crossed the room, going directly to one of the book-shelves. Here she paused, then took down several books which she placed upon a chair nearby. Her back was towards Mr. Mitchel, but he could see her reach into the recess with her arm, which was bared by the act, the loose sleeve of her gown falling aside. Then there was a clicking sound just perceptible to the ear, and Mr. Mitchel muttered to himself:

"A secret closet, with a spring catch."

In another moment, the girl was replacing the books, and, this done, she hurried from the library, locking the door after her. Mr. Mitchel emerged from his hiding-place, and, going to the shelf where the girl had been, removed the books and searched for the spring which would unlock the secret compartment. It was not easily found, but Mr. Mitchel was a patient and persistent man, and after nearly an hour discovered the way of removing a sliding panel, and took an envelope from the recess behind. Carrying this to the fireplace, he dropped to his knees, and withdrawing its contents, held in his hand a Bank of England note for one thousand pounds. He looked at it, smiled, and said in a low tone:

"And Mr. Barnes was so certain that he would catch the thief!" Then he smiled again, replaced the books on the shelf, decided that the large sofa might serve as a comfortable bed, and so went to sleep.

He was awakened early, by a sense of cold. Starting up, for a moment dazed by his unfamiliar surroundings, he gazed first at the gray ashes of the dead fire in the grate, and then looked towards the windows thickly covered with frost, and shivered.

Remembering where he was, he threw his arms about, and

walked up and down the long room to start his blood moving, and induce a little warmth. Presently he went to the back windows and looked at the beautiful frosting, which resembled long fern leaves. Suddenly he seemed unusually interested, and especially attracted to one of the panes. He examined this closely, and taking a note-book from his pocket made a rapid sketch of the pattern on the glass. Then he raised the sash, looked out upon the shed, and emitted a low whistle. Next he stepped out through the window, went down on his hands and knees upon the tinned roof, and looked closely at something which he saw there. Returning to the room, one would have said that his next act was the most curious of all. He again opened the secret panel, and replaced the envelope containing the bank-note. Then he went to the table where Mr. Van Rawlston claimed that the note had vanished, and he sat in the chair where Mr. Van Rawlston had been when he read the will.

Several hours later when Mr. Van Rawlston came in, Mr. Mitchel was sitting in the same chair looking through a Bible.

"Well," said Mr. Van Rawlston. "How did you pass the night? Did the thief pay you a visit?"

"I think so," replied Mr. Mitchel.

"Then you know who took the note?" asked Mr. Van Rawlston, eagerly.

"Perhaps; I do not like to jump to conclusions. This is a magnificent Bible, Mr. Van Rawlston. Is it in the sale to-day? If so, I think I will bid on it."

"Oh, yes; it is to be sold," replied Mr. Van Rawlston, testily. He thought Mr. Mitchel merely wished to change the subject, and at that moment he was more interested in bank-notes than in Bibles. He had no idea that Mr. Mitchel really coveted the Bible. But then he did not know that Mr. Mitchel collected books as well as gems. He was therefore much astonished, some hours later, when the auction was in progress, to find Mr. Mitchel not only bidding on the Bible, but bidding heavily.

At first the bidding was spiritless, and the price rose slowly until Mr. Mitchel made an offer of five hundred dollars. After a moment's hesitation young Eggleston bid fifty dollars more, and it was seen that the contest was now between him and Mr. Mitchel. Bidding fifty dollars at a time the price rose to nine hundred dollars, when Eggleston remarked:

"I bid nine-fifty," then turned to Mr. Mitchel and added, "This is a family relic, sir, and I hope you will not raise me again."

"This is an open sale, I believe," said Mr. Mitchel, bowing coldly. "I offer a thousand dollars."

"One thousand and fifty," added Eggleston, quickly.

At this moment Mr. Barnes entered the room, accompanied by a short, young man, and Mr. Mitchel's attention seemed attracted away from the Bible. The auctioneer noticing this, called him by name, and asked if he wished to bid again.

"One moment, please," said Mr. Mitchel. "May I look again at the volume?"

It was passed to him, and he appeared to scrutinize it closely, started slightly as though making a discovery, and handed it back, saying:

"I have made a mistake. I supposed that this was a genuine Soncino, but I find that it is only a reprint." Then he turned to Eggleston with a curious smile, and said, "You may have the family relic. I shall not bid against you."

The auction over, the crowd dispersed, and when all strangers had departed, Mr. Mitchel nodded meaningly to Mr. Barnes, and approached young Eggleston, who was tying up the Bible in paper. Touching him upon the arm, he said very quietly:

"Mr. Eggleston, I must ask the officer here to arrest you!"

Eggleston's hands quivered over the knot, and he seemed too agitated to speak. The detective realizing that Mr. Mitchel had solved the problem, quickly stepped closer to Eggleston.

"What does this mean?" asked Mr. Van Rawlston.

"Call Miss Hetheridge, and I will explain," said Mr. Mitchel.

"No, no! Not before her!" cried Eggleston, breaking down completely. "I confess! I loved Alice, and wished to make it impossible for her to marry Lumley. The note is here! Here, in the Bible. I stole it, and hid it there!" With nervous fingers he tore off the wrappings, and rapidly turning the pages searched for the note. "Heavens! It is not here!" He looked at Mr. Mitchel inquiringly.

"No; it is not there. You paid too much for that Bible. Mr. Van Rawlston, I prefer to have the lady called, if you please."

Mr. Van Rawlston left the room, and Mr. Mitchel addressed Mr. Barnes.

"By the way, Barnes, have you abandoned your theory?"

"I suppose I must now, though I had not up to a moment ago. I found Mr. Lumley, and accused him of the theft. He would offer no explanation, but willingly agreed to return with me."

"We seem to have arrived just in time," said Mr. Lumley, quietly.

"In the very nick of time, as you shall hear," said Mr. Mitchel. "Ah, here is Miss Hetheridge. Will you be seated, please, Miss Hetheridge." He bowed courteously as the young woman sat down, and then proceeded.

"I did not think that the bank-note had been removed from this room. Why? Because I argued that the theft and the hiding must have necessarily occupied but a moment; a chosen moment when the attention of all three others was attracted away from the table where it lay. The one chance was that Miss Hetheridge may have hidden it in the folds of her gown. The men's pockets seemed too inaccessible. I agreed with Mr. Barnes, that the lady would scarcely steal what was her own, though even that was possible if she did not know that it was to be hers. For a similar reason, I did not suspect Mr. Lumley, and thus by elimination there was but one person left upon whom to fasten suspicion. I supposed he would return here during the night to recover the bank-note, and I remained in this room to watch for him."

At this Miss Hetheridge made a movement of her lips as though about to speak, but no words escaped, and she shrank back in her chair.

"During the night," proceeded Mr. Mitchel, "Miss Hetheridge came into this room, and hid something. After she had left the room, relocking the door with a duplicate key, I found what she had hidden. It was a one thousand-pound note."

There was silence for a moment, then Miss Hetheridge cried out:

"I can explain!"

"That is why I sent for you," said Mr. Mitchel.

"The note was my own," said the girl, speaking rapidly, "but after the disappearance of the other, I was afraid to have it in my room lest it be found, and seem to inculpate me. I only received it a few days before my dear uncle died. He told me that his brother William had sent it as a present to my mother upon her marriage, but as he had doubted the good intentions of my father, he had kept the matter a secret. As both my parents died, he had held the note in trust for me. He did not invest it, because he thought that his own fortune would be an ample legacy to leave me. A short time before he died, I passed my twenty-first birthday, and he gave me the note. That is the whole truth."

"To which I can testify," interjected Mr. Lumley. "And I may now add that Miss Hetheridge had not only promised to be my wife, but she offered me the use of her money to buy the partnership, which to Mr. Barnes seemed such a suspicious act."

"I have only to explain then," continued Mr. Mitchel, "how it was that I decided that Miss Hetheridge was not the thief. This morning I found heavy frost on the window-panes. Upon one, however, I noticed a circular, transparent spot, where the pattern of the frosting had been obliterated. Instantly I comprehended what had occurred. The thief, the real thief, had come in the night, or rather in the morning, for I know almost the hour. He stood upon the shed outside, and melted the frost by breathing upon the pane, with his mouth close to the glass. Thus making a peep-hole, he must have seen me asleep on the sofa, and so knew that it would be useless for him to attempt an entrance. As the person who did this trick stood upon the shed, I had but to measure the distance from the shed to his peep-hole to be able to guess his height, which I estimated to be more than six feet. Next, there was some very interesting evidence in the frost on the tin roof. The marks made by the man's feet, or his heels rather, for the frost was so light that only the impressions of the nails in the heels would show. My own made complete little horseshoe-shaped marks composed of dots. But those of my predecessor were scarcely more than half a curve, which proved that he walks on the side of his foot, thus slightly lifting the opposite side from the ground, or roof, as it was in this instance. This much decided me that Miss Hetheridge was not the thief, and I returned her bank-note to the place where she had hidden it. Then I sat at the table where the will was read, and studied the situation. The easiest way to hide the note quickly seemed to be to slip it into the Bible which stood on the table. Therefore I was not surprised when I found the bank-note which I have here."

He drew forth the bank-note from his pocket and handed it to Mr. Van Rawlston, who asked:

"But why, then, did you try to buy the Bible?"

"I had no idea of doing so. You forget that I had not seen Mr. Lumley. He, too, might have been six feet high, and he, too, might have had the habit of walking on the side of his heel, as I quickly observed that Mr. Eggleston does. With only one of the men before me I decided to run up the price of the Bible, knowing that if he were guilty he would bid over me. Mr. Eggleston followed my lead, and I was almost sure of his guilt, when he made the remark that he was buying a family relic. It was a possible truth, and I was obliged to go on bidding, to see how anxious he was to possess the volume. Then, as I said a while ago, Mr.

Lumley arrived in the nick of time. One glance at his short stat-
ure, and I was ready to let the Bible go."

"You said you could almost tell the hour at which this man
peeped through the window," said Mr. Barnes.

"Ah, I see! You wish me to teach you tricks in your own trade,
eh? Well, frost forms on a window-pane when the thermometer
is near or below thirty-two. On the wall here I found a recording
thermometer, which discloses the fact that at three o'clock this
morning the temperature was as high as forty-five, while at four
it was below thirty. Frost began to form between those hours. At
five it was so cold, twenty degrees, that I awoke. Our man must
have come between half-past four and five. Had he come before
then, his peep-hole would have been fully covered again with
frost, whereas it was but thinly iced over, the mere freezing of
the water of the melted frost, there being no design, or pattern,
as there was over every other part of the window-pane. So I may
offer you a new version of an old saw, and say that, 'Frost shows
which way a thief goes.'"*

---

*There are hundreds of variant wordings, but the original early American proverb is along the
lines of "straw shows which way the wind blows." Some versions refer to "a feather" or "from
which point of the compass the wind comes," etc. The earliest recorded usage is in 1774, in a letter
from Joseph Galloway to William Franklin, the Governor of New Jersey, reproduced in *Letters of
Members of the Continental Congress*, Edmund C. Burnet, ed. (Washington: Carnegie Institute of
Washington, 1921), 4.

# XII

## A SHADOW OF PROOF

*(Letter from Mr. Barnes to Mr. Mitchel)*

"MY DEAR MR. MITCHEL:—

"I am leaving town in connection with a matter of considerable importance, and am thus compelled to abandon a little mystery unsolved. It is not a very serious case, yet it presents certain unique features which I fancy would make it attractive to you. I therefore take the liberty of relating to you the occurrence as it was told to me by the person who sought my aid, as well as such steps as have been taken by me towards its elucidation, I must confess, however, at the outset, that though I have learned some things, the knowledge thus gained appears to me to complicate the affair, rather than otherwise.

"Two days ago a district messenger boy brought me a summons, on scented paper. The writer was a woman, who explained that she wished to entrust to me the investigation of 'a great mystery involving the honesty of one or two of our society leaders.' I was urged to call without loss of time, and was at the Madison Avenue mansion within an hour.

"In response to my card, I was shown up to the lady's boudoir, where I found Mrs. Upton eager to unfold her story, which evidently to her mind was of paramount consequence. I accepted an invitation to be seated, and she began at once, assuming a low tone, which was almost a whisper, as though she imagined that when talking with a detective the utmost stealth and secrecy were essential.

"'Mr. Barnes,' she began, 'this affair is simply awful. I have been robbed, and the thief is a woman of my own social status. I am horrified to discover that one of my set could stoop so low as to steal. And then the thing itself was such a trifle. A diamond stud, worth two hundred dollars at the outside valuation.* What do you think of it?'

"Observe that she had told me little enough before asking for an opinion. She seemed to be a woman of mediocre mental grasp, though perhaps as bright as most of the butterflies that flit about the fashionable ballrooms. I decided to treat her as though she were really very shrewd, and by a little flattery I hoped perhaps to learn more than she might otherwise be willing to confide to a detective, a class of beings whom she too evidently looked upon as necessary evils. I answered her in about these words:

"'Why, Mrs. Upton,' said I, 'if you really know the thief, and if, as you say, she is a society woman and rich, it would seem to be possibly a case of kleptomania.'

"'Kleptomania?' she exclaimed. 'Kleptomania? Rubbish! That is the excuse all rich women give for what I call plain stealing. But your idea is not new to me. I believe in being perfectly just in these matters. I would not harm a flea, unless he had bitten me; but when he does bite me, I kill him. There are no halfway measures that will suit me. No, Mr. Barnes, there is to be no compromise in this case. I will not condone theft, even if the thief be respectable and rich. And as for

---

*More than $6,000 in 2020 US dollars.

kleptomania, as I've said before, I've looked that up. I find it is a sort of insanity. Now there is no insanity in this case. Quite the contrary, I assure you.'

"'You are very keen in your perceptions, Mrs. Upton,' I ventured. 'If we set aside the kleptomania idea, why, then, do you imagine a rich woman would steal a thing of such little value?'

"'Spite!' she snapped back without a moment's hesitation. 'Spite, Mr. Barnes. Let that be your cue. But I must tell you just how this happened. You see, I hold a somewhat influential position in the society of "The Daughters of the Revolution," and because I do have some influence, I am constantly bothered by people who could not become members rightfully, if their titles were closely scrutinized; so they undertake to gain their end through me. They grow suddenly attentive, effusive, gushing. I am their "dearest friend," they think me "so charming," "so beautiful," "so delightfully cosmopolitan and yet so exclusive." To hear them talk you would be persuaded that I belong to both Belgravia and Bohemia in the same moment. But I usually see through their wiles, and long before they broach the subject I say to myself, "My dear madame, you want one of our society badges to pin on your breast; that is what you are after." Then at last comes the note asking for a "confidential interview," and when I grant it a lot of documents are shown to me which are meant to uphold the candidate's claim to membership. But there is always the little flaw, the bar sinister as it were, which they hope to override through influence; through my influence, which I may state, they never get.'

"'Ah, then, this lady, whom you suspect of taking your stud, had hoped to join your society?'

"'I cannot answer that with a single word. I cannot say either yes or no. You see, there are two women.'

"'Oh, I thought you knew the thief?'

"'So I do. I know it is one of two women. If I knew exactly which, of course I should not need your help. But you have interrupted my story. Where was I?'

"She evidently thought me an ass.

"'Oh, yes,' she resumed. 'I was telling you how people bother me to get into our society. Well, a woman of that kind has been fairly running after me all winter. She is a Mrs. Merivale. She was born an Ogden, and some of the Ogden branch are fully entitled to membership. But, unfortunately for her, she traces back to the brother of the Revolutionary Ogden, and her ancestor, far from fighting for our independence, is said to have made quite a tidy fortune by observing a shrewd neutrality; sometimes crying for England and sometimes the reverse, according to the company present. Of course, that is not Mrs. Merivale's fault; it all happened too long ago for her to have had any influence. But, you see, she is not in the direct line, and we only recognize the direct line. Heavens! if we did not, who knows where we would end? No, collateral branches are out of it, so far as our society is concerned, and I told her so plainly this morning. Of course, you can see how she might be spiteful about it. It was a great disappointment to her.'

"'Then you think this Mrs. Merivale took your stud just to annoy you?'

"'Dear me; how stupid you are! Did I not tell you there were two women? The other is Mrs. Ogden Beaumont. You see she clings to the family name. She also was an Ogden, and in the line. She is a member, and she had considerable influence in our society at one time. But she lost it by just such schemes as she is trying to persuade me into. She manoeuvred till she had two or three of her friends elected, who have even less claim than her cousin, Mrs. Merivale. Finally, it got so that if she were to propose a name, the Membership Committee would be suspicious at once. Now she wants

Mrs. Merivale elected, and according to her little plan I was to be the cat's paw. The scheming of those two women to get into my good graces has been a source of amusement to me all winter, and the climax came this morning, when I told them both very frankly that I had seen through them from the start. Mrs. Merivale was horribly disappointed, but she behaved like a lady. I must admit that, though she said some bitter things, things she will be sorry for, I assure you. But Mrs. Beaumont just lost all control of her temper. She stormed and raged, and said vile things, all of which had as little effect on me as a pea-shooter would against the rock of Gibraltar. So the two women went off, and in less than five minutes I discovered that my diamond stud had gone with them.'

"'Gone with them? Of that you are sure?'

"'Of course I am sure. Do you suppose I would make such a charge without knowing that I am in the right? Come with me, and I will convince you.'

"'She led the way into a little anteroom next to her boudoir. It was not more than eight feet square, and not crowded with furniture. The floor of hardwood, covered by one large silk rug, afforded little opportunity to lose anything by dropping it. There were four chairs, a small reading-lounge, a revolving case filled with novels, a handsome piano-lamp, and a little tea-table with all requisites for making tea.

"'This is my little den where I retire when I am wearied by people and things,' continued Mrs. Upton. 'Here I am surrounded by my friends, the people that our best writers have created. I love my books, and I get as fond of the characters as though they were all living; more, I think, because I do not come into actual contact with them. I can admire the nice people, and the mean ones may be as mean as they like without affecting me. Well, I was lying here reading when these women were announced, and as I was too comfortable to get up and dress, I thought I would have them up and excuse my toilet on the plea of indisposition. "Indisposed" is always a useful word; indisposed to be bothered by the visitors, you know,—the nicest of all the white lies. So they came up here and sat around my lounge and began to bring their all-winter's scheme to a climax. After a while, when I saw that the time had arrived to disillusionize these women, I dismissed my headache and got up to have a frank talk with them. As I arose my diamond stud dropped from the collar of my waist* which I had opened, and I picked it up and placed it on that little tea-table. Then we had our little scene. It was as good as a play. I kept my temper, as a hostess always must, but my guests were not so self-possessed, and, as I have said, Mrs. Merivale said a few things, and Mrs. Beaumont a great many more, that would not sound pretty coming out of a phonograph. Then they left, and I walked to my window and saw them jump into their carriage, Mrs. Beaumont slamming the door herself with a bang that must have weakened the hinges. That is all, except that I immediately remembered my stud and came here for it. It was gone.'

"'I suppose, of course, you have searched this room, under the possibility of its having dropped to the floor?' I inquired.

"'Yes, indeed,' she answered. 'I had my own maid up, and superintended the search myself. But I took the precaution to see that nothing should be removed from the room. I had the door closed, and then we took up the rug carefully and shook it. Nothing fell from it, and the stud was not on the floor or elsewhere. You can see yourself that it cannot be a difficult matter to search this little room thoroughly. It has been done without success, but if you like you may search again. I assure you that nothing has been taken from the room. If one of those two women has not taken that stud, you may count me an idiot.'

---

*"Waist" here probably refers to a shirtwaist blouse or dress, rather than the customary meaning of the beltline, and so the "collar" probably refers to an open collar at the neck.

"'You have admitted that your maid was in this room, and that brings another possibility into the case,' I said.

"'You mean that Janet might have taken it? Not at all a possibility. In the first place she is devoted to me, as my people adopted her when she was but a child, and she has been personally in my service for more than ten years. No, Janet would not do such a thing, but even if she would, she could not have done so. I took precautions.'

"'What precautions?' I asked.

"'Why, she would need one hand to pick it up, and I not only kept both of her hands occupied, but I did not permit her to stoop to the floor.'

"'How could you keep her hands always occupied?' said I.

"'Why, most of the time she was handling the broom, and that requires two hands. It was only when she shook the rug and moved the sofa that her hands were otherwise occupied. I myself did the searching, and I am absolutely certain that Janet had not the least opportunity to pick up so much as a pin.'

"'And you think that one of your friends would do what you would not attribute to your maid?'

"'Assuredly. In the first place these women are not friends of mine; after to-day, I should rather say enemies. Moreover, I would trust Janet as I would few of my real friends. You see I have not tested all my friends, and I have tested Janet. She has had temptation enough and opportunity enough to rob me a thousand times over, were she so disposed. No, I tell you one of those two women has that diamond stud.'

"'Would you mind saying which one you are the more inclined to suspect?' I asked.

"'Why, that is a hard question. Sometimes I think one, and then again the other. Mrs. Beaumont showed so much venom that I can see more reason to suspect her if I decide from motive alone. It is really her scheme to get her cousin *into the society. It is she who feels most thwarted, because of her lost influence. On the other hand, I cannot remember seeing her within reach of the tea-table, while Mrs. Merivale was near it all the time. So Mrs. Merivale had the opportunity, while the incentive through temper was with Mrs. Beaumont.'*

"This was the little problem which I was asked to solve, and I think that you will comprehend my meaning when I say that it was intricate because of its very simplicity. Let me enumerate the facts so as to get a sort of bird's-eye view of the situation.

"First, we have two women present when the missing property is placed on a table accessible to at least one, and possibly to both. Second, a small room, with floor devoid of cracks, and covered by a rug easily moved and shaken. Third, only a few pieces of simple furniture in the room. Fourth, the visitors depart, and the property is missed. Fifth, a search without discovery, a third possible thief entering upon the scene.

"We have apparently but four solutions; either one of the three women took the stud, or else the alleged loser lies. I omit the possibility that the stud was merely mislaid or accidentally out of sight in the room; this, because I personally conducted a search, which was so systematic as to make it absolutely assured that the stud was not in the room when I looked for it.

"Of the four theories, then, I preferred first to consider that one which the mistress declared to be ridiculous. I insisted upon seeing and catechising the maid Janet, thereby deepening madame's doubts as to my ability. After talking with this girl for half an hour, I felt so convinced of her integrity that I mentally eliminated her from the case. Next in order we had the two visitors, one of whom, according to Mrs. Upton, had a motive while the other had the opportunity. The first postulate always is that the guilty person must have both opportunity and motive, unless indeed we are dealing with an insane person, when motive may be eliminated, though frequently the insane are actuated by quite intelligible motives. Thus we seemed obliged either to discover that Mrs. Beaumont had an opportunity to obtain possession of the stud, or else that Mrs. Merivale had a motive, except that the latter may have simply acted upon the opportunity without motive, in which case we would be dealing with the kleptomaniac. After due consideration I decided to call separately upon these two ladies, and went to Mrs. Merivale first.

"She courteously received me, and as soon as I met her I was pleasantly impressed by her personality. After five minutes' talk I was certain that if she took the stud, it was, after all, the act of a kleptomaniac, and that no petty motive of revenge would have tempted this high-born, beautiful gentlewoman to descend to theft. She asked me the object of my call, and looked at me so frankly that there was no chance for subterfuge. Consequently I openly declared the purpose of my visit.

"'Madame,' said I, 'I regret very much the embarrassing nature of my errand. But you visited Mrs. Upton this morning, I believe?'

"'I did, in company with my cousin, Mrs. Beaumont.'

"'Did you happen to notice that while you were there she placed a diamond stud on the tea-table?'

"'Yes; I remember the circumstance perfectly, because of the impression which it made upon me.'

"'Would you mind telling me what that impression was?'

"'Why, simply that it was very discourteous, or at least very untidy. When we were shown to her room, she was lying down, with the collar of her waist open. After a while she arose, the stud dropped to the floor, and she picked it up and *placed it on the little tea-table. I thought that it would have shown a greater sense of propriety if she had replaced it and fastened her collar.'*

"'Do you recall whether the stud was still on the table when you left?'

"'Why, no! How should I? I paid no further attention to it whatever.' Then as a new idea entered her mind, her eyes flashed, and the color rose in her cheeks as she said to me sharply:

"'You cannot mean that Mrs. Upton dares to intimate—'

"'She intimated nothing,' I hastened to interject. 'Immediately after your departure the stud was missed, and the most thorough search has failed to discover it. In these circumstances Mrs. Upton sought my aid, and I drew from her the details of her morning's experiences.'

"'I imagine you had little difficulty in drawing forth the details." She said this with a sneer, which made me understand how this woman could say unpleasant things without forgetting her dignity.

"'I assure you,' I hastened to add, 'Mrs. Upton knows nothing of my visit here. I have on my own responsibility called with the idea that if I could obtain an account of your visit from yourself, there might be some slight difference in the two stories which would show me how to proceed.'

"'I know no more than I have told you, and as I am far from being interested in Mrs. Upton's lost baubles, I must beg you to excuse me from further discussion of the subject.'

"I was dismissed. It was courteously done, but done nevertheless. I could do nothing but take leave. Still I made one venture,—

"'I must ask your pardon for intruding, but, as I have said, I thought you might be able to supply a missing detail. For example, do you recall whether Mrs. Upton's maid entered the room while you were there?'

"'I am sorry, Mr. Barnes,' said she in courteous but firm tones, 'but I must decline to pursue this conversation further.'

"That was all. I had seen one of the suspected persons, and learned nothing. Still an interview of this character is bound to leave an impression, and in this case the impression was very strongly in favor of Mrs. Merivale. Without irrefutable proof I could not believe that this dignified, frank woman had stolen the stud. For the time at least I also dismissed all theories of kleptomania.

"Thus my attention was directed toward the woman who had a motive, but was reported to have lacked the opportunity. I called at once upon Mrs. Beaumont.

"This lady is of quite a different mould from her cousin. Older by at least ten years, she is still handsome, her beauty being, however, physical in character only. She lacks the self-poise and dignity which renders Mrs. Merivale's beauty so much more attractive. Moreover, she is voluble, where the other is reserved, a trait which I welcomed as affording me more opportunity to gain some possible clue to truth.

"She came into her reception-room where I awaited her, evidently brimful of curiosity. I had sent in my card, and it seems she had heard of me in connection with that somewhat famous wager of yours.*

"'Mr. Barnes, the detective, I believe,' she said as she entered.

"'At your service, madame,' I replied. 'May I have a few minutes' conversation with you upon a trifling, yet quite puzzling matter?'

"'Why, certainly,' said she, 'but don't keep me in suspense.

---

*In Ottolengui's novel *An Artist in Crime* (New York: G. P. Putnam's Sons , 1892), after a discussion of Barnes's clever capture of a criminal named Pettingill, Mitchel bets Barnes $1,000 that "I can commit a crime which will be as much talked of as his, and that I will not be captured, or rather I should say convicted." Of course, Mitchel wins the bet. Note that in the Prefatory to this volume, Ottolengui states that the events recounted here occurred shortly after the events of *An Artist in Crime.*

*I am burning with curiosity to know why a detective should call on me.'*

"I thought that this woman might be caught by a sudden attack and made the venture.

"'A diamond stud was stolen from Mrs. Upton this morning, while you were there!' I said, watching her closely. She did not flinch, but seemed honestly not to comprehend the suggestiveness of my words.

"'I do not understand you,' said she.

"'It is not a serious matter, madame, but Mrs. Upton placed a diamond stud on her tea-table while you and Mrs. Merivale were with her, and missed it a moment after you had left. Therefore—'

"This was plain enough, and she grasped the truth at a flash. In an instant she gave me evidence of that temper against which I had been warned by Mrs. Upton.

"'You dare to insinuate that I took her miserable little stud? I wish my husband were at home; I would have you horsewhipped. No, I wouldn't either. It is not you who suspect me, it is that self-sufficient she-devil, Mrs. Upton. So she accuses me of being a thief, does she? Well, mark me well, Mr. Detective, I shall make her pay dearly for that insult. I have stood enough of that woman's impertinent superciliousness. This is going too far. If she has a shadow of proof against me, she can meet me in open court. Do you understand me? Go back and tell Mrs. Upton, with my compliments, that she must either prove that I stole her stud, or else I will sue her for libel. I'll let her see with whom she is fooling.'

"'Really, Mrs. Beaumont,' said I as soon as I found a chance to speak, 'you have rather gotten ahead of my intentions. I assure you that no accusation has been made against you.'

"'Indeed!' said she, scornfully uplifting her nose. 'And pray, then, why have you called? Certainly Mrs. Upton cannot imagine that I would be interested in the petty thieving that goes on in her house.'

"'The point is just this, madame,' said I. 'The stud was placed on a tea-table while you were present. Mrs. Merivale has told me that she remembers this distinctly. When you had left, the stud was missed, and the most thorough search has been made, not once but twice, without finding it. Indeed, there is no place in the room where it could have been lost. According to the story of Mrs. Upton, the affair, trifling as it is, is a really puzzling problem. But I ventured to hope that either Mrs. Merivale or yourself might remember some incident which might give me a clue; such, for example, as the entrance of one of the house servants.'

"'That is nothing but a smooth story invented by yourself,' said she, 'in order to pacify my righteous indignation. But you cannot deceive me. Mrs. Upton has told you that I stole her stud, and you have come here to endeavor to prove it.'

"'In justice to Mrs. Upton,' said I, 'I must state, on the contrary, that she very distinctly told me that you could have had no opportunity to take the stud, as you were not at any time near enough to the tea-table to touch it.'

"'If she told you that, it shows how little observation she has. I don't at all object to admitting that I had the thing in my hand.'

"'You had it in your hand!' I exclaimed, surprised.

"'Yes. It happened in this way, Mrs. Upton received us with her collar unbuttoned, in the most slovenly fashion. After a while she got up from the lounge, where she was feigning a headache because too lazy to arrange her toilet before receiving guests. It was then that the stud fell to the floor. She picked it up and placed it on the table. When we were leaving she led the way out of the room, Mrs. Merivale following, and I leaving the room last. As I passed, I *thoughtlessly picked up the stud and looked at it. I then put it back. I have a vague idea that it rolled off and fell to the floor, but I can't be sure.'*

"'That is singular,' said I; 'for if it fell to the floor it should have been found.'

"'Undoubtedly. Very likely it has been found; I should say, by one of the servants. You will never induce me to believe that Mrs. Upton took the trouble to search for that stud without help. She is too lazy by far.'

"I thought it best to keep discreetly silent, preferring not to mention the fact that the maid had been in the room. It being evident to my mind that this woman would adhere to this story, true or false, I deemed it prudent to at least appear to believe her.

"'I am much indebted to you, madame,' said I. 'You see that, after all, my visit has led me to the truth, for we know that the stud probably fell to the floor, and is therefore either still in the room, or else, as you suggest, one of the servants may have picked it up.'

"'All that is very well, Mr. Barnes,' said she; 'and you are very clever in shielding Mrs. Upton. But, as I said before, you do not deceive me. This matter is more serious than you imagine. That woman has worked systematically for two years to supplant me in our society, "The Daughters of the Revolution." Just now she fancies that she has triumphed over me; but in spite of that, she is jealous of my influence with the members, and would go to any extreme to injure me socially. She well knows that I did not take her stud, but she is quite willing to allow this suspicion to drift out to the world, knowing that it would be difficult to prove my innocence of a charge so vaguely circulated, and that there might be some who would turn aside from me because of this shadow. Now this I shall not permit. If she does not prove her charge, I shall certainly sue her for libel, and have the *whole matter cleared up in the open tribunal of the law. You may tell her this from me. There shall be no halfway measures. One thing more before you go. I must call my maid.'*

"She rang a bell, and a moment later her maid responded, and at her mistress's orders went upstairs and brought down a jewel-case of large size. This, Mrs. Beaumont opened, and taking out the contents strewed them on the table.

"'There, do you see these?' said she with pride in her voice. 'These are my jewels. Mrs. Upton perhaps is richer than I am, but I defy her to show such jewelry as I have. Some of these things are two hundred years old. Here is a necklace which one of my ancestors wore at the first inauguration of Washington. Here is another which my grandmother wore at the coronation of Queen Victoria. Here is an emerald ring, presented to my own mother by Napoleon. And you see what the others are. Nearly all have some history which adds to their intrinsic value. And with these in my possession, to think that that woman would accuse me of stealing a common little diamond stud! It makes my blood boil. But I have told you what course I shall pursue, and you may warn Mrs. Upton.'

"This ended the interview. I had gained some information at least, for I had learned that Mrs. Beaumont did have the opportunity to take the stud, but, on the other hand, the motive for such an act seemed less tenable. She certainly would not take it for its value, and in view of her own magnificent array of jewels, she would be less likely to imagine that she was giving Mrs. Upton any great annoyance by the petty theft. Then, too, her assertion that Mrs. Upton is systematically seeking to undermine her influence in their society connections, affords a possible reason for our last theory, that Mrs. Upton lied in declaring that the stud had been stolen. Thus the matter rests, as I have had no opportunity to have another interview with Mrs. Upton. If you call on her,*

*I am sure that you will be well received because of the fact that she knows all about your outwitting me in that wager matter. Trusting that you may care to give this little affair some of your time and attention, and with the belief that you will certainly unravel the tangle if you do, I am*

> "Very sincerely yours,
> "JACK BARNES."

*(Letter from Mr. Mitchel to Mr. Barnes)*

"MY DEAR BARNES:—

"I read your letter with considerable interest. As you very truly say, the case was intricate because of its simplicity. As you had followed up three theories with apparently the result that you were at least tentatively satisfied that neither held the key to the mystery, it seemed proper to take up the affair where you had left it, and to endeavor to learn whether or not Mrs. Upton had lied to you, and still had the stud in her own possession. For this and other reasons I decided to adopt your suggestion and call upon Mrs. Upton. I did so, and, as you surmised, was cordially received. She met me first in her parlor, and I at once stated to her the object of my visit.

"'Mrs. Upton,' said I, 'you are perhaps aware that I have a friendly regard for Mr. Barnes, the detective, ever since the affair of my little wager. I have received a letter from him this morning in which he states that an important criminal case compels him suddenly to leave the city; he has also given me a succinct statement of the few facts in relation to the loss of your stud, and has asked me to interest myself in the solution of this little mystery.'"

"'And you mean to do it?' she exclaimed impulsively. 'Why, how delightful! Of course you will find out all about it. To think that you, Mr. Mitchel, the man who outwitted Mr. Barnes, will take up my case! I am honored, I assure you.'

"I give you her exact words, though her flattery was somewhat embarrassing. In the course of the conversation she referred to you in terms which I repeat, though I do not at all share her poor estimate of your ability.

"'Of course,' said I, 'I am not a detective, yet I do take a trifling interest in these little problems. I find it mentally exhilarating to measure minds, as it were, with these wrong-doers. Thus far I have generally been successful, which, however, only proves my claim that those who stoop to crime are not really ever sound mentally, and consequently, either from too little or from too much care, some slight detail is overlooked, which, once comprehended by the investigator, leads unerringly to the criminal.'

"'Ah, how delightfully you talk!' said she. 'I am so glad you have taken this up, for, do you know, I rather thought Mr. Barnes a little dull, not to say stupid. Why, he actually suggested that my maid took the stud!'

"Here, I thought, was an opportune moment to follow the method which you employed with Mrs. Beaumont, and by a sudden, unexpected accusation, to endeavor to surprise the truth from her. I said:

"'Oh, Mr. Barnes has given up that idea now, and has almost adopted one even more startling. He thinks that perhaps you took the stud yourself.'

"I had expected from your estimate of this woman's character, which you recall was not very flattering to her mental calibre, that if indeed it were true that she had concocted this little scheme to injure a society rival, thus taken unawares she would feign great indignation. On the contrary, she *laughed so heartily, and spoke of your theory so lightly that I was practically convinced that again we were on the wrong scent. All she said by way of comment was:*

*"'Well, if that is the result of his investigation, he is a bigger fool than I took him to be. It is certain, therefore, that he will never discover the truth, and so I am doubly glad that he has gone out of town, and that you have consented to take his place.'*

*"'You must not so quickly condemn Mr. Barnes,' said I, feeling bound to defend you. 'He has really worked in this matter quite systematically, and this final theory has been reached by exclusion.'*

*"'I do not understand,' said she, puzzled.*

*"'Well, first he accepted your assurance that the maid Janet was not guilty because she had no opportunity. Then he called upon Mrs. Merivale, and from his interview with her judged that she too must be innocent, a view in which I must concur after reading his report of what passed. Then he called upon Mrs. Beaumont, and though she admitted, what you did not yourself observe, that she actually took the stud in her hand when leaving the room, yet it seems equally certain that she replaced it, as she says she did. Thus, if the stud is really not in the room, there apparently could be no other explanation than that you are misleading us.'*

*"'Us? Does that mean that you too held the view that I merely pretend that the stud was lost?'*

*"'My dear madame,' I replied: 'such an idea, of course, seems preposterous, but a detective cannot set aside any theory without thorough investigation. In an analysis of this character the personal equation must have a secondary place. In this affair it could not help us at all. Perhaps you will not understand my meaning. But do you not see that it is just as inconceivable that either of the other ladies should have stolen this stud of yours, as it is to believe that*

you merely pretend that it is lost? From the view-point of the impartial investigator there can be no choice between these propositions.'

"'I must say that you are not very flattering,' said she, troubled, as she realized that social position could not protect her from suspicion any more than it would the other women. 'Why, I have my enmities, of course, and I frankly admit that I do not love either Mrs. Merivale or Mrs. Beaumont, especially not the latter. Still, to concoct such a scandalous calumny against an innocent woman would be awful. I could not be so low as that.'

"'I believe you,' said I, and I did. 'But, on the other hand, would it not be equally low for these ladies, your social equals, to stoop to petty theft?'

"'I suppose you are right,' said she reluctantly; 'but how did the stud disappear? Don't you see that I had strong evidence against one of them? It was there when they were in the room, and gone when they had left. There must be some explanation of that. What can it be?'

"'Of course,' said I, 'there must be, and there is, an explanation. The most plausible seems to be the one suggested by Mrs. Beaumont, that it rolled from the table to the floor when she put it back. It seems incredible that two searches have failed to discover it, yet it is a small object, and may be lying now in some crevice which you all have overlooked.'

"'I think not,' said she, shaking her head dubiously. 'Suppose you come up and see for yourself. You won't find any crevices. Why, we have even run wires along the line where the seat and back of the lounge are joined. No, the stud is not in that room.'

"And now, friend Barnes, we come to the finale, for I may as well tell you at once that I have found the stud,—that, indeed, as soon as I looked into the room, I suspected that it was within those four walls, in a place where no one had *thought of looking, though, to mystify you a little more, I may say that it may not have been in the room when you made your search.*

"*I enclose with this a sciagraph, that is to say, a picture taken with the X-ray. You will observe that the skeleton of a small animal is discernible surrounded by a faint outline which suggests the form of a dog. If you understand something of anatomy, look where the stomach of the dog should be, and you will notice a dark spot. This is the shadow of the missing stud, which, as Mrs. Beaumont suggested, must have dropped to the floor. There it evidently attracted the attention of Mrs. Upton's pet dog, Fidele, who took it into his mouth, with the result, shown in the sciagraph. You will ask how I guessed this at once? In the first place I had perfect confidence in the thoroughness of your search, so when I saw the dog in the room, lying on a silk pillow, two pertinent facts were prominent at once. First, the dog may not have been in the room when you examined the place, and consequently you could not have counted him in as a possible place of search. Secondly, he might easily have been present when the two ladies called, and this was probable since his mistress was lying down and the dog's sleeping-pillow was near the head of the lounge. If you noted this, you may not have comprehended its use; perhaps you took it for one which had slipped from the lounge. At all events, I do not consider that you have been at all at fault. I had better luck than you, that is all.*

"*Very sincerely yours,*
"ROBERT LEROY MITCHEL.

"*P. S.—I do not myself believe in luck. I must also state that Mrs. Upton has sent letters of apology to the other ladies. The dog, Fidele, is to undergo an operation to-morrow. One* of our most skilful surgeons has agreed to regain the stud and preserve the life of the pet. A laparotomy, I believe they call it.—R. L. M."

## THE END

# READING GROUP GUIDE

1. Which story was your favorite? Your least favorite? Why?

2. A few of the stories read almost as jokes—for example, "The Missing Link" and "A Shadow of Proof." Do you think that Ottolengui intended them seriously? Was Ottolengui making serious points about evolution and scientific technology?

3. Which character did you find to be more appealing to you—Barnes or Mitchel? Why? Their styles of "detecting" are very different—do you think that one is better at his job than the other? Do you think that Ottolengui is suggesting that the ideal detective has some of each one's characteristics?

4. Do you think that Mitchel is a realistic, believable character? Why or why not?

5. Why do you think the stories of Sherlock Holmes are more popular than Ottolengui's stories?

6.    Some writers of this period—the "Sherlock Holmes hiatus"—tried to create detective characters that were similar to Holmes himself. Do you think Ottolengui had this in mind?

7.    What makes a good mystery short story in your opinion? Is it important that there be a criminal who is caught and punished?

# FURTHER READING

**BY RODRIGUES OTTOLENGUI**

NOVELS AND SHORT STORY COLLECTIONS

*Conya: A Romance of the Buddhas.* (1890, serialized in an
   unknown Charlotte, NC, newspaper)
*An Artist in Crime.* New York: G. P. Putnam's Sons, 1892.
   Featuring Jack Barnes and Robert Leroy Mitchel.
*A Conflict of Evidence.* New York: G. P. Putnam's Sons, 1893.
   Another Barnes and Mitchel case.
*A Modern Wizard.* New York: G. P. Putnam's Sons, 1894.
   Another Barnes and Mitchel case.
*The Crime of the Century.* New York: G. P. Putnam's Sons,
   1896. The final full-length Barnes and Mitchel case.
*Before the Fact.* Eugenia, ON: Battered Silicon Dispatch Box,
   2012. First book publication of six stories about Barnes
   and Mitchel that were originally published in *Ainslee's
   Magazine* in 1901.

## NONFICTION

*Methods of Filling Teeth: An Exposition of Practical Methods.*
Philadelphia: S. S. White Dental Manufacturing, 1892.
*Table Talks on Dentistry.* Brooklyn: Dental Items of Interest
Publishing, 1928.

## SIMILAR DETECTIVE FICTION OF THE PERIOD

Cadett, Herbert. *The Adventures of a Journalist.* London:
Sands, 1900.
Davis, Richard Harding. *In the Fog.* New York: R. H. Russell,
1901.
Meade, L. T., and Clifford Halifax. *Stories from the Diary of a
Doctor.* London: George Newnes, 1894.
Morrison, Arthur. *Martin Hewitt, Investigator.* London:
Ward & Lock, 1894.
Sims, George R. *Dorcas Dene, Detective.* London: F. V.
White, 1897.

## CRITICAL STUDIES

Buard, Jean-Luc. *Rodrigues Ottolengui: Artiste ès crimes.*
New York: La Bibliothèque internationale Rodrigues
Ottolengui, 2018. In French.
Panek, LeRoy Lad. *The Origins of the American Detective
Story.* Jefferson, NC: McFarland, 2006.

# ABOUT THE AUTHOR

Benjamin Adolph Rodrigues Ottolengui ("Rod" to his family and friends) was born in 1861 in Charlotte, South Carolina, to a Sephardic Jewish family, the son of Daniel Ottolengui, a playwright and newspaper man, and Helen Rosalie Rodrigues Ottolengui, an author. Ottolengui attended the College of Charleston, but in 1877, at the age of sixteen, he moved to New York City, where he took up an apprenticeship with a dentist. In 1885, he received a Master of Dental Surgery degree and began a career that would last until 1933, bringing him professional accolades and deep involvement in developing fields of dentistry. He specialized in orthodontia and root canal therapy and became an important force behind the fledgling American Society (later, Association) of Orthodontia. His 1891 text *Methods of Filling Teeth* was the standard work on the subject for many years. Ottolengui was one of the first to use dental radiography, pressure anesthesia, and cast gold inlays. He was a fiery speaker and advocate for the policing of dental practice and often spoke out against charlatans, quacks, and other illegal practitioners in New York City. He was also an amateur taxidermist, a photographer, and an entomologist of some note, specializing in the *Plusia* moth. Ottolengui was a charter member of the New York Entomological Society, and his collection of moths is an important part of the American Museum of Natural History.

In the 1890s, as he was establishing himself, he apparently had time on his hands, for Ottolengui turned to writing fiction. Though his first novel was a romantic adventure, *Corya: A Romance of the Buddhas* (serialized in a Charlotte newspaper), he soon turned to crime fiction. Ottolengui invented a pair of detectives, "Inspector" Jack Barnes, a professional detective with his own agency, and Robert Leroy Mitchel, a wealthy amateur, friend, and occasional rival of Barnes. While Ottolengui certainly knew the work of Arthur Conan Doyle and the success of the Sherlock Holmes tales, Barnes was no Watson and Mitchel no Holmes. Each was wholly original, and each had his own skills and abilities of deduction. Four novels of their adventures followed swiftly, the first published in 1893. These were well received, and newspaper advertisements touted him as "the American Conan Doyle." In 1895, following in Conan Doyle's footsteps, he tried his hand at short stories, quickly selling four in 1895 and another in 1898. He rounded these out into a collection, *Final Proof*, published in 1898. Ottolengui's work was apparently popular, reprinted several times and translated into various foreign languages. In 1901, however, after writing six more stories of Barnes and Mitchel, Ottolengui retired from the writing of fiction. Today, Ottolengui has no entry in any of the three major encyclopedias of crime and mystery fiction,* though *Final Proof* is cataloged in Jacques Barzun and Wendell Hertig Taylor's *A Catalogue of Crime* and is very favorably described in Ellery Queen's vital checklist of detective short stories collection, *Queen's Quorum.*

---

*Encyclopedia of Mystery and Detection* (Steinbrunner & Penzler), *Encyclopedia Mysteriosa* (DeAndrea), and *Oxford Companion to Crime & Mystery Writing* (Herbert) all lack entries for Ottolengui, although Herbert at least mentions two of the stories in this volume in entries on "Forensic Pathologist" and "Murderless Mystery."

# CASE PENDING

Another murder, another unanswered question. And
Detective Mendoza hates to leave things undone.

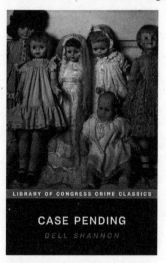

Hers was the kind of casual homicide that occurred every week in a city
like Los Angeles in the sixties. Beaten, robbed, and left in an abandoned
lot, Elena Ramirez's death was like many others…in fact, nearly identical to a murder that happened six months earlier—a case that Detective
Luis Mendoza was never able to solve.

The detective isn't a fan of puzzles but knows one when he sees it.
He puts two and two together—these vicious murders must have been
committed by the same deranged individual—and leads the charge into
a case that is astounding in its complexity.

**"Shannon's attempt to portray racial prejudice and the effects of
poverty in LA was noteworthy for its time. A worthy reissue."**

—*Booklist*

For more books from the Library of Congress, visit:
**sourcebooks.com**